KEYSONG

D.J. McPhee

KANNON

Published by Kannon, an imprint of Timeless Awareness Publications
Bellingen, New South Wales, Australia

First published in 2017
New Edition 2026

National Library of Australia Cataloguing-in-Publication entry:

McPhee, D.J. 1968–
Keysong/D.J. McPhee.
9780994242563 (pbk.)
Fantasy--Fiction
Speculative fiction--Young adult fiction.
A823.4

Cover design by D.J. McPhee

)

Printed in the United States
ISBN: 9780994242563

To Martin Galafassi

CONTENTS

ACKNOWLEDGMENTS

Huge thanks to all those who made it possible for *The Druid Prince* duology to make it to print, particularly Lorae Harbottle-Purs (copyeditor), Kerrie Le Lievre, Shayla Olsen and Jessica Stewart. I would also like to acknowledge the following people who have read and made editorial comments on parts of earlier versions of *Keysong*: Martin Galafassi, Sharon Dunne, Linda McConkey, Ondine Weate, Georgia Carter Mathers, Dionne Lister, Victoria Norton, Lauren Wynder and Selena Hanet-Hutchins.

AUTHOR'S NOTE

Some books are like portals that drag us (willingly) into other worlds. We are more susceptible to this when we are young. The first book portal I crossed was J.R.R Tolkien's *The Hobbit*, which transported me at the age of eight to Middle Earth, right into the parlour of one Bilbo Baggins. Once there, I didn't want to come home. Mostly because the idea of second-breakfast appealed to me greatly, but also because I found that world so rich and engaging.

The world of my everyday existence was pale and uninteresting compared to Bilbo's world, though inarguably safer. My world had no Gandalf or Lady Galadriel, only soapie stars and dull politicians. On the upside, my everyday world had no orcs or mountain trolls to threaten me in the dark hours of the night. Still, I would have willingly forgone the safety of my run-of-the-mill existence for a little danger if it meant I could tramp in the Misty Mountains or visit the enchanted woods of Lothlórien.

My love for the world that Tolkien created was total and unquestioning. That changed one autumn morning when I was eighteen. I remember it vividly. It was a cool morning, the kind of morning perfect for reading in a patch of sunlight by a window. I'd settled myself by just such a window after breakfast to finish re-reading *The Lord of the Rings*. I hadn't picked up those books for many years and had thrown myself into the re-reading with some excitement. When I finished *The Return of the King* later that day I was left with an uneasy feeling.

By that point I had noticed the strong environmental messages of Tolkien's work. As a budding environmentalist myself I found that element of the books gratifying. But now, on this re-reading, I could not help but notice a few things that unsettled me. All the good characters, the heroes and heroines, were white people, some of them were even described that way – the White Lady Galadriel for example. Worse, all of the bad or evil characters were often described in language associated with non-white people. The only exception to this was, of course, Saruman, but his presence in the novels does not lessen the sense that the books present white people as good and black people as bad. Also, none of the main characters are female. Out of a cast of hundreds, the female characters are all secondary or incidental to the story. The single exception is Galadriel, but even she could not be described as a main character, appearing in only a handful of scenes.

This unease with a world I loved so much percolated over the years and deepened when I noticed the same things in a lot of other fantasy fiction. With the release of the first *Lord of the Rings* film in 2001, a film that made visual the concerns I'd had with the language of the books, my unease transformed into a desire to "write back" to Tolkien, to create a fantasy world in which women and girls were central and people of colour were represented fairly. It took me another handful of years to get started on the actual writing. The result of that "writing back" to Tolkien is *The Druid Prince*, a traditional fantasy duology that includes all the things we expect of the genre (elves, dragons, magic) but that features all different types of people.

The Druid Prince is not much of a departure from Tolkienesque fantasy. It isn't meant to be. It's not about creating something completely new. It's about celebrating Tolkien-inspired fantasy whilst making it more inclusive and appealing to young adult readers. It's "writing back" rather than simply writing. As one reviewer said: 'Reading *Waycaller* is like visiting a world you're familiar with and love but meeting a whole lot of interesting, fascinating and likeable new people.'

I do hope that each reader finds a character or two to love *The Druid Prince*, but mostly I hope they see themselves positively reflected in it.

PART 1: THE DARK HOST

EVEN OTHERLINGS SHOULD NOT SIMPLY VANISH

Songarielle, citadel of the mountain elves

"That's ... that's ... No, that's an entirely indecent proposition." Dorothea Butters' head was spinning. She had just survived an attack by a Dark Sending that fell the sovereign of the elves himself. Now she was standing, somewhat shakily she had to admit, in that dratted courtyard at the heart of the Druid Chambers where the dark deed had happened, cornered by Kashashem and Alva. "You say I have potential for, for ... You say *what* now?" She sputtered so much a small bomb of spittle launched from her lips and landed on Lady Kashashem's hand, where it glistened like dew on a black river stone just for a moment before the druidess wiped it away.

"You have potential to be a druid," Kashashem repeated, wiping her hand once more with the handkerchief Alva had handed her. "Possibly a very good druid, if you apply yourself."

Dorothea's face turned a deep pomegranate red and burned hot. She'd never felt such a fiery irritation, not in her whole life. "Apply myself? *Apply* myself! Look here, you pointy-eared lunatic—"

Alva gasped. "Miss Butters!"

"I'd no sooner apply myself to a deep bowel purge than to the blasphemous hogwash you lot call druidry—"

"Dorothea!" It was Alva's turn for her face to burn red.

"Still your sacrilegious tongue, Alva!" Dorothea puffed herself out to her full, formidable girth. "I see what's happened now – that Aelf Ethelwulf, *supposed* friend, has lured me here to this accursed nest of elves and druids to be *seduced*, yes, *seduced*, into the indecent arts of your godless kind.

3

Well, I declare I shall not be seduced, I shall not!" Another bomb of spittle shot from her lips and hit Alva square in the eye. Alva half-gagged and wiped the spittle away with an ill-look on her face.

"Dorothea Butters of Bright!" Kashashem's voice was stern and threatening. "You are behaving like one of the village idiots Bright is famous for—"

Miss Butters hissed. "How dare you impugn my—"

"Enough," Kashashem warned, standing tall over Dorothea, "you will listen to what I have to say and for once you will not interrupt."

Dorothea stilled; on the outside seemingly obedient, but her eyes and the redness of her face betrayed the anger inside.

"You have a gift for magic, Dorothea of Bright. Most probably you inherited this gift from your grandmother, Belladonna, who herself inherited it from her own grandmother who was half-elvish."

Dorothea's face went from red to white to grey in mere seconds. She staggered to a bench and sat down. "Those dratted rumours are true then," she muttered, almost to herself. "My beloved grandmammy was part elvish." She thought a moment, her face contorting with increasing distress. "That makes me one-thirty-second parts elvish." She let out an involuntary moan of despair.

"That's not all that much," Alva said in a comforting tone.

"It's more than any decent Brightling should have, and enough to taint me with blasphemous magic." She moaned again, feeling as though she'd been poisoned by something fetid and fatal.

Kashashem stepped close to Dorothea, throwing her in shadow. "Miss Butters, I mean no offence but you are too much like the rest of your kind – bigoted, narrow-minded, terrified of anything different and wilfully ignorant of the wider world. You simply must open your mind. If you don't, you will end up like the rest of your kind, mired in superstition and hate."

Dorothea looked into Kashashem's face, blinking in shock, then turned to Alva. "If that's her not wanting to offend, I'd hate to hear what she'd say if she really wanted to hurt my feelings."

Alva smiled. "We're not saying you have a gift for magic to insult you, Dorothea. From our perspective your gift is a good thing, perhaps a great thing. To us, discovering magic in others is a source of joy."

"It is up to you," Kashashem added, "if you choose to train as a druid or not. We shan't force you into anything." The head of the Druid Order paused. "But you must make a decision soon. Events are such that we must not dally. The time for indecision passed when that Dark Sending crawled down these walls." She gestured to the roofline above the courtyard.

"Decision? Soon? What? No, I can't, I need—"

"You may have a little time to consider it," Kashashem said. "Tell Alva your decision when you come to it and she will inform me." She glanced toward the corridor where the fallen elvish king had been carried just moments before. "Right now I must go to King Dhudhannan's side. His life, and the fate of all Elvinidd, hangs in the balance." Kashashem nodded to Alva and left the courtyard. Dorothea watched her go without a thought in her mind. She was too shocked to think. Alva sat beside her on the bench.

"We can discuss your gift and what it means some more, if you like."

Alva's gentle tone and proximity to Dorothea alarmed her for some reason. She leapt up from the bench and hurried to the door. "I can't, Alva, I ... I just can't. I must go, I must be sure that my Jack and little Harrie are safe. I ... I simply must go."

Dorothea wended her way through the labyrinth of the Druid Chambers with as much speed as she could muster. She exited the main door, trotted down the front stairs and had crossed half the great square before she stopped to take a breath. In front of her loomed the temple of Amallayne. Tall, beehive-shaped and made of grey stones, Dorothea thought it looked like a giant grave marker. Though she'd told Alva she wanted to check on Jack and Harrie, and in truth she did, now that the prospect of entering a temple dedicated to one of the tricksy Faeden was at hand she had reservations. Who would have thought that Miss Dorothea Butters, best cook in Bright and among the fattest halflings in all the dells, would ever lower herself to enter a heathen temple, especially one so dark and damp-looking. Mere weeks ago such a thing would have been unthinkable, but since Jack and Harrie crossed her threshold she'd done many things she couldn't have imagined before. Many of them unpleasant things, like being chased across Anwynn by goblins and vile Fellwood elves. Even so, some things had not been so bad. She had enjoyed her time with Jack and Harrie, strange otherlings though they were. If she were honest with herself—and she did pride herself on her forthrightness and honesty—she had to admit her heart had taken to those two, disturbingly thin younglings.

She took a deep breath, deciding that she must put her decency at risk and enter the dratted temple of Amallayne. Anything for Jack and Harrie, Eugene bless them. She took only a few steps toward the temple when she stopped at the sound of a commotion nearby. In the avenue leading into the great square, the one lined with ever-flowering Alder trees, a crowd of elves had gathered. They were staring up at the ancient trees and many of these elves were clearly shaken. Dorothea watched them closely for a moment, her powerful halfling eyesight allowing her to see that the leaves on the sacred Alder trees were yellowing and falling to the ground.

As if an ill omen, dark clouds rapidly gathered on the horizon, like roiling ink, and blocked out the sunlight. Dorothea's gut tightened with a sense of dread. Elves all along the length of the avenue gasped and shouted with disbelief and fear. Soon many of them were fleeing. One woman's terrified voice rang clearly on the air: "They wither, the Alders wither." These words were taken up by others until finally an alarmed elvish man just feet from Dorothea shrieked in shocked dismay: "Lord Dhudhannan is dead!"

Those words were still echoing around the square when loud sizzling thunder cracks boomed over the citadel. Everywhere people screamed and ran, their feet pounding on the cobblestones like drums of doom. Dorothea dashed toward the temple. As she mounted the stairs explosions rocked the city. A blue streak of lightning flashed out of the sky and slammed into the temple itself.

"No! Jack! Harrie!" Dorothea hurled herself up the stairs and into the temple. Everywhere pilgrims were taking cover. Another flash of lightning struck a huge golden door at the far end of the temple. The door was blown off its hinges and rang like an evil bell. Bells summon the Pale Mother, Dorothea thought to herself with terror. She dashed across the fore-chamber of the temple and reached the golden doors to the inner sanctum. Before the ruby statue of Amallayne were Jack and Harriett, but they weren't alone. A dark-skinned girl was with them. The girl seized Jack by the hair and bent down to take hold of Harriett with her other hand. Harriett was limp and pale. Dorothea's heart sank. Jack struggled to break free but the girl was stronger. A swirling ruby flame erupted and engulfed all three of them. Dorothea screamed. The girl transformed in the flames, she shimmered with power. She was clearly Faeden. The Faeden's black hair danced on-end in the air as if blown by an invisible wind. Her skin shimmered and sizzled, emitting dark electricity from every pore. Then she, Jack and Harrie vanished. Dorothea screamed again, scrabbling over the ruined golden door in a vain hope to follow after them. That's when she heard a slight moan. She turned and saw Aelf unconscious on the floor, crushed beneath one of the doors. She rushed over to him, calling out, "Help, please help, my friend Aelf is dreadfully injured." She knelt beside Aelf and took his hand, her mind racing. Where had that Faeden taken her younglings? What would she do to them? Would she ever see them again? In that moment she knew without words that she would take up Kashashem's offer to train as a druid. Indecent or not, she would do anything to find Jack and Harrie, and fight any foul Faeden who dared to hurt them.

RILL

Songarielle, citadel of the mountain elves

Ellisenn kept pace behind Master Wadget, not an easy task as the Oakling moved fast, especially for such a small being. Wadget scarpered along with such speed that sparks flew when his claws struck the cobblestones. The sound of boot soles on the street behind him assured Ellisenn that Daniselle was keeping up. Without warning Wadget turned into a narrow lane. When Ellisenn followed, the turn was so tight that his shoulder scraped the wall of the storehouse on the corner. He winced when he heard his jacket snag on the stonework and tear. The jacket had been a gift from his mother on his coming of age, less than a week ago.

So much had happened in that week, the most momentous being the assassination of King Dhudhannan, struck down by a dark Sending. Ellisenn had watched in despair when the king was moved from the Druid Chambers to the royal apartments, fatally wounded, the aloof Anarra Settonett at his side, holding his paling hand in her own. Now the Bright King was gone. Dhudhannan, Lord of the Elves for eight thousand years, lost to them forever in an attack lasting just moments. And why? Answering that question was what brought Ellisenn to this narrow laneway in the merchants' district of Songarielle, accompanying Wadget as the druid master hunted the sorcerer behind the assassination.

Wadget skidded to a stop, bringing Ellisenn and Daniselle to a halt behind him. "Somewhere 'ere," Wadget whispered, facing the dead end of the alley and holding up a small green hand to motion for silence. "I sense somethin' wicked has come this way." He peered at the wall in front of them, the back of another storehouse, his eyes tracking up the stonework toward the roof.

In the sky beyond the storehouse a thin plume of

fragrant white smoke coiled up to mingle with a few high clouds. The smoke from the offering fire at the House of Amallayne. Ellisenn had often watched that thin coil of smoke rise into the sky above Songarielle, twisting on the mountain air like a ribbon caught on a light wind. The human pilgrims who came to visit Amallayne's temple looked out for that white plume when they crossed over the last high pass onto the plateau. The sight of it filled them with joy and spurred them on for the final leg of their long journey to Songarielle. It was also the first thing the dragon-riders saw on approaching the mountains, a beacon that led them straight to the elvish citadel. The Waycaller, Jack, would be in Amallayne's temple now. Perhaps he'd added to that ribbon of scented smoke by burning an offering of flowers as he called on Amallayne for aid in their struggle against Serza and the followers of the Pale Mother, a struggle even more dire now that King Dhudhannan was dead.

Jack's face filled Ellisenn's mind – those deep blue eyes that seemed to reflect everything that was vulnerable in the world. Ellisenn's thoughts over the last days often turned to those eyes, to Jack's fair face as Ellisenn had carried him in his arms and put him to bed in Daniselle's house. So much worry troubled that face, but still it seemed the face of someone strong beyond their knowing, of someone good and steadfast. A shiver coursed down Ellisenn's spine. He shook his head to clear it, but still those eyes burned in his mind. Sometime soon he was going to have to face what was happening—

A sizzling green ball of light streaked through the air and struck the ground by Ellisenn's feet, nearly knocking him over. The tingling sensation coursing through him quickly turned to a shudder of horror. A hooded figure was scrambling down the stone wall of the storehouse ahead of them like a four-limbed spider. The figure leapt to the ground effortlessly, lurched into a standing position and rapidly covered the ground between them. Daniselle drew her sword. Wadget hissed, brandishing his wand and discharging a sudden flash of light that brought the figure to a stop less than a few yards away, motionless as if caught in an invisible web.

"A halflin'!" Wadget cried, saying out loud what Ellisenn was thinking – who or whatever this was looked about the same size and shape as Dorothea Butters. The figure writhed, struggling for release. Wadget jerked his wand once more. With another flash of light the figure was lifted into the air, still motionless but with arms spread wide to make a bizarre cross. "That'll keep her still," he grumbled.

Ellisenn didn't ask how Wadget knew the sorcerer was female but wasn't surprised that he did. Oaklings discerned things more or less invisible to others.

"Not such easy targets when we know yer there, are we, me halflin' friend?" Wadget smirked at the suspended sorceress. Though the motionless halfling didn't respond, Ellisenn felt pure hate emanating from her, hate directed at them. "Speak!" Wadget commanded, slashing his wand towards her face, releasing her tongue. "How did yeh come to be here, an' why did yeh attack Lord Dhudhannan?"

"I have nothing to say to you, upstart Oakling!" The voice was similar to Miss Butters', resonant despite the small size of its owner, but also unlike it. It had a hateful iciness instead of Dorothea's overflowing warmth. Shrieking like a beast from hell and suddenly writhing and wriggling again, having somehow managed to throw off some of Wadget's magical restraints, the sorceress raised her hand and threw another ball of energy straight at the druid master. Wadget flicked his wand and deflected the ball of energy, his eyes narrowing intently as he watched the halfling sorceress writhe and struggle for release. He jerked his wand once more and the sorceress was still again, her arms pinned to her sides now.

"This one's been touched by somethin' very dark," Wadget whispered, almost to himself. "An' that touch has left her much changed, more powerful than I would've thought possible. Even the worst of the Dread ain't so powerful."

"Touched by what?" Daniselle asked quietly from behind them, her voice full of apprehension.

"Well, that we must find out. I can't risk lettin' her loose enough ter speak again," Wadget said, "but maybe there's a way we can *see* why she's here an' why she killed Dhudhannan." He motioned Ellisenn and Daniselle closer. "What I'm goin' ter do is a tricky bit o' magic. This sorceress is strong, she's sure ter resist, so I'll need yer help, Ellisenn. It's a risky thing ter do, 'cause it'll leave us vulnerable ter attack. Daniselle, yeh must stand guard. If anythin' or anyone enters this alley, lop their head off first an' ask questions later."

"Happy to, Oak Lord," Daniselle said, smiling, actually pleased by the prospect of a beheading. Ellisenn rolled his eyes. He would never understand mountain elves.

"Now, come here, Ellisenn, an' take me hand." Ellisenn did as he was told. He was surprised at how warm and strong Wadget's little clawed hands were. He'd expected them to be cold and soft but they were quite hard and callused. Clearly Wadget did more with his hands than wave a wand around. "Just relax yer mind, Ellisenn. I'm goin' ter draw on yer power, all yeh need do is keep yer mind open ter me, an' stay on yer feet no matter what happens."

Ellisenn nodded and relaxed his mind as best he could. He felt the Oakling's mind reach into his, like a claw wriggling into a tight space. It was an unsettling and uncomfortable sensation. There was a sharp stab and then it was as if a flare had lit in his mind. A stream of pure energy surged from deep inside him and rushed along the nerve endings in his spine and arm to Master Wadget's hand. Ellisenn's knees buckled a little. He had to concentrate to stay steady. Wadget grunted with the effort but took hold of Ellisenn's power and pointed his wand directly at the sorceress, muttering an incantation. Ellisenn didn't hear the incantation clearly, he was too busy trying not to crumple under the strain of so much power coursing through him, but he could tell that it was ancient and complex. As soon as

Wadget had uttered the words there was a brilliant flash of light and the alley went totally, impenetrably black and silent, all sound and light consumed by the sudden darkness. All Ellisenn could perceive was Wadget's hard little hand in his, and that stream of warm energy buzzing through him. Everything else was consumed in shadow. The alley was gone, Daniselle was gone, the storehouse in front of them was gone. The sorceress was hidden in shadow as well. He jumped and nearly dropped Wadget's hand when a strange shimmer appeared in the air ahead of him. Slowly the shimmer took the shape of the sorceress, but not the form of her solid body: a ghost-like form, a translucent spectre made of energy.

The spectre of the sorceress hung in the black for a moment, shining dimly, before glowing brighter and brighter. Soon it cast a luminous light that filled the space in front of them. The light swirled with vapours and those vapours formed into shapes.

Ellisenn had only experienced something like this once before, when he'd been taught how to use a memory stone, but this was different. The scene before him was not solid like those in a memory vision but translucent and ghostly. Ellisenn guessed that these glimmering shapes were not memories but thoughts, thoughts given shape and movement. It was as if the sorceress' mind was a candle and the glimmering shapes in front of them were the shadows it cast.

As Ellisenn watched, the shapes moving around the suspended sorceress came into focus, showing a hooded figure moving through a dark passageway. The figure's shape gave its identity away as the same halfling sorceress now trapped by Wadget's magic. The passageway was lined with deep niches. These were filled with bones and skulls bearing the high cheek structure of elves. The passageway looked to be part of a burial ground. The sorceress' voice echoed in the dark, saying just three words: *The Lost Necropolis*. Wadget hissed, and Ellisenn knew why. The Lost Necropolis, the most ancient elvish burial ground, its whereabouts forgotten millennia ago, was the rumoured home of the earwisps, the Tiqq. The mere mention of that place filled Ellisenn with dread. The sorceress shuffled through the passageway and came to a large lead door, which bore a seal with a warning in elvish: *Enter not this place lest the doom of all dooms descend upon you!* The halfling sorceress ignored the warning, raised her hand and cast a pulse of energy to crack open the door. As it split open, a flash of bright purple light burst into the corridor, knocking the sorceress to the ground. The passageway shook with a violent tremor and filled with dust, debris and something else, something very strange: thin creeping tendrils of purple mist. Another, brighter flash of purple caused Ellisenn to flinch and close his eyes as the halfling's voice rang out: "The Gift! The Gift is mine!"

Ellisenn opened his eyes to see that the scene had changed. Now the sorceress was standing at the great circle of Bright, the portal to the otherworld, a Vellenor assassin just vanishing in a flash of blue light at the centre of the standing stones. The sorceress, chuckling to herself, walked back toward a village, its twinkling lights visible off beyond a small hill. "The Pale Mother will love me above all others for this! When the Waycaller and her children are dead, the Queen of Doom will be free and will rule over us all once more!"

The images shimmered and changed again and showed the sorceress on her knees, wailing, pounding the sodden ground with her chubby fists. All around her were huge, ancient trees covered in greenly-glowing moss and lichen. Ellisenn recognised the place instantly as Fellwood Forest. "Why?" the halfling wailed. "Why has the Gift abandoned me?"

"Because you are unworthy, ain't you," sneered a voice from up in the trees. Ellisenn looked up to see a female Oakling, very old and decrepit, sitting in one of the lower branches, gleefully swinging her clawed feet to-and-fro. "Mog is much worthier, isn't she? Oh, yes. Much worthier. She didn't fail the Pale Mother, oh no, Mog didn't fail to kill the Waycaller. The Secret Gift wants to whisper to me now, 'cause I is much more powerful than you, oh yes. The Gift likes power, loves it. That's why it left you. You isn't great enough for it. An' now I gots it caught in this here trap, hasn't I." She tapped a lead jar sitting beside her in a nook of the bough. "Oh yes, I gots it safe in here for when Morrigan wants it used next. I dares not use it, oh no, Thullu's power is not to my tastes. Morrigan's power tastes best, oh yes, very tasty is the Pale Mother's green power. But it won't be *you* she asks to use it, oh no, it'll be one of her Dreads. I hope it's not that Hect, baldy bat-ears she is! Oh no, best the Pale Mother trusts me to keep the Gift and never use it, oh yes, that's what'd be best."

The halfling wailed even louder, throwing herself onto the soggy ground. If she weren't so clearly evil, Ellisenn might have felt sorry for her. He watched her pound the ground, thinking about what Princess Sarritt of Fellwood had told him, that Prince Serza had taken Thullu's Gift from Mog. That must have been some time after this pathetic scene. A wave seemed to roll through the images then and Ellisenn guessed this indicated the passage of years. When the vapours reformed into clear shapes again Ellisenn gasped.

The halfling sorceress, still hooded and cloaked, stood in a grassy dell buffeted by a strong wind. At the centre of the dell a small lake sat dark and heavy, an island with a standing stone in its centre. Surrounding the halfling were three skinwearers, all in the process of changing from beast to man, their snouts shrinking, their paws and claws contracting, their fur changing to skin. Bundled on the ground nearby were the skinwearers' victims, the ones they'd bitten in order to take human shape. They were all dead. To Ellisenn they looked like ordinary traders, men from the land of Harshan. Once the skinwearers had completed their transformation, panting, they bowed to the halfling sorceress. Her black cloak rippled on the wind as if filled with snakes. She looked up to a hollow, glimmering moon hanging silently overhead and spoke: "The night elves we seek, Anarra Settonett and the other, will halt soon to take cover and sleep for the day. You will find them on the edge of the Empty Plains at the foothills of the Craggy Mountains. Take care not to give them any warning. Bring them to me, here, and the Pale Mother will reward you most richly."

The skinwearers nodded and without a word jogged into the night, towards the snowy peaks of the mountains visible beyond the dell. Ellisenn barely had time to wonder why the sorceress had ordered the kidnap of Anarra before the scene shimmered and changed.

Now the halfling sorceress, her body rigid, her eyes rolling back into her head, sat in a wing-back chair in a dimly lit room. She muttered a stream of incantations that Ellisenn recognised as the spell that casts a dark Sending. An oil lamp hanging in an otherwise cold grate flickered, providing the only light, but even that dimmed as the Sending rose out of the halfling's body like a vast shadow and streaked out through an open window. "Quickly," the halfling moaned, "the bog nags have failed, catch the children in the open before they reach the safety of Butters Nob. Kill them! If you cannot kill them both, then just kill the girl. You must kill the girl!"

The images stuttered and changed. Two scenes unfolded in quick succession. First, the sorceress hidden in the shade of a stand of trees, watching Harriett gather wildflowers in a field by a stream, with Aelf, Miss Butters and Jack nearby. The halfling moved toward Harriett but stopped when Jack walked over to join his sister. The hissing voice of the sorceress echoed in the tree-shade, a hiss of pure hate and frustration. In the second scene the sorceress, concealed this time in the shadow of a building in one of Songarielle's cobbled lanes, watched as Harriett, Jack and Miss Butters were led towards the Songarielle Senate and the Druid Chambers by Daniselle. "Should I do it now?" the sorceress wondered to herself. "Should I attack the girl with so many elves ready to come to her aid? No, I will wait. There will be another chance." As she receded into the shadows she noticed that Jack was watching her and hissed once more.

When the images reformed next they showed the halfling squatting in a dark alleyway. "This is my chance," she whispered to herself. "Serza approaches! I sense him using Thullu's Gift to weaken the wards over Songarielle as he comes." She conjured another Sending, this one hurtling up over the rooftops of Songarielle towards the Druid Chambers. Her head drooped so that her chin touched her chest. Her tongue lolled out of her mouth and the whites of her eyeballs gleamed in the dark. "Kill the king," she moaned. "Kill the king and then the otherworld girl, then kill them all!"

The images faded and the alley was black again. Only the ghostly form of the sorceress remained, still bound tight and suspended in the air before them. Wadget's voice rang out of the silence: "Why, sorceress? Why have yeh done these terrible things? Show me!"

The spectre of the sorceress shone brightly again, casting that luminous light swirling with vapours that quickly formed into shapes. A vast chamber solidified around them. Above them a domed ceiling took shape, held up by a circle of elaborately carved columns. In the centre of the chamber a circular dais of marble rose, easily six feet high, surmounted by a huge, green granite sarcophagus. The lid of the coffin was carved with the features of an elvish queen, her long hair chiselled into the stone as if cascading down the sides of the sarcophagus. A flight of marble stairs leading up onto the dais was flanked by two life-sized statues of Sovereign Guards, their helms shaped into dragon heads. At the top of the stairs sat a throne made of bones, the curved backrest crowned with a row of skulls. It was clear to Ellisenn that this ugly thing was not meant to be there but had been added later. It soon became clear by whom.

Out of the swirling vapours, a very handsome young man took shape on the throne – olive-skinned and almond-eyed with black hair tied in a top-knot. On the floor of the chamber before him appeared an awful scene: hundreds of dead things, wolves and bears and people, all milling about, their sightless eyes turned to the man on the throne. Swirling in the air of the chamber were threads of purple mist, some of which took shape as tiny, pointy-eared beings no bigger than one of Ellisenn's hands, all of them female with cat-like green eyes and red hair. Earwisps! This was the fabled hive in The Lost Necropolis, the hive of the Tiqq Empress herself.

Among the dead things and earwisps were living people, mostly human but some elves, all staring up at the throne in rapture, clearly possessed. At the base of the dais stood the halfling sorceress, still hooded, but her head bowed. Her cold voice echoed in the chamber like ice cracking.

"I come at the Pale Mother's bidding," she said.

"This I know." The young man sneered, which turned his beauty to ugliness. "Do not think to tell *me* of the Screaming Queen's will."

The halfling bowed her head, somewhat stiffly, as though she hated to do it. "What is your command, Mighty Rill? The Pale Mother places me at your bidding."

"This I know as well," the man said, smiling now. "The Empress of the Tiqq has use for you." The man clutched at his left ear, where a stream of purple wisp was pouring out. The wisp took shape on his shoulder. The Tiqq now perched there looked like all the others—shaggy red hair, cat-like eyes—except, unlike the others, she wore a crown made of the wing bones of a tiny bird, a wren or swallow. Everyone in the chamber dropped to their knees, dead things as well as live ones.

"You are privileged to see me in this form," the Tiqq Empress said, straightening her black robes.

"Yes, Empress Rill." The halfling's voice was muted, her head still bowed. "What would you have me do?"

"First, I would have you keep your tongue and listen."

"Yes, Empress."

"It may surprise you, halfling, that I have grown weary of graveyards and tombs." The empress gestured around the burial chamber. "I wish to rule from a great palace, a palace in a high place above ground, a palace full of living things. I wish for beautiful hosts for all of my subjects, powerful hosts worthy of the Tiqq. Long have I despaired that my wish would never come to pass, until a vision came to me, a vision of the Screaming Queen. Sad she said she was, that she had not embraced us long ago, that when she turned us away in those beginning days we went to Thullu to be our Lord and Master. A change of heart, that's how she put it. Her heart has changed, and that change has opened her heart to the Tiqq. Some of my people think that to abandon Lord Thullu for the Screaming Queen is sacrilege, but they are wrong. Thullu is aloof and silent. He has not shown himself here for ten thousand years! Why should we stay true to him when he treats us so? The Screaming Queen is our natural mother. And we will have her released from her prison so that we may worship her and glory in her protection."

"Yes, Empress Rill," the halfling agreed, surprise clear in her voice.

"The Screaming Queen has promised us dominion over the elves. Every last one of them will become hosts for my people. They shall rue the day they ever named us monsters! But that shall not pass if the Pale Mother remains trapped in Uffern. And so we come to our task for you."

"Whatever the Pale Mother and the Empress of the Tiqq desire, I will do."

"Yes, you will." The empress sneered, glaring at the halfling with those cruel green eyes. "Our task for you is not an easy one; it requires great trickery. When the Waycaller and his dratted sister are finally killed, the prophesy will die as well. Then the Screaming Queen will be free, but the Pale Mother will still need time to regain her powers. The curse Amallayne and Danuss placed on Morrigan's voice still lies heavily on her. The druids and the elves know this, they will attack her as soon as Darkgate opens. We cannot allow that. We must stop them from attacking in full force."

"How, Empress Rill?"

"We have discovered that there are still a handful of the Ehmaarim, the night elves, alive. With the Dreads' aid we have been hunting them down and killing them. We will not kill them all however, some we will leave alive. One in particular, a girl by the name of Anarra Settonett. You, halfling, will kidnap this girl, so that one of my Tiqq can possess her. She is very young and will be easy to control. Then you will place her on the elvish throne."

"But Dhudhannan is on the elvish throne—"

"Which is why you must kill him! The throne goes to the ruler, the Thane, of each high house in turn. By elvish law, it must be the Thane of the Ehmaarim who takes the throne next. With Dhudhannan dead, the throne must go to the only surviving member of the high house of Ehmaara, the girl who will be in the control of one of my earwisps, this Anarra. I will send hollow-wolves to help you achieve this."

"Yes, Empress, I will do as you ask. But what of Prince Serza of Fellwood? He has the Secret Gift and with it he plans to conquer all of Anwynn and usurp the Pale Mother."

"He is of no consequence! He is no match for Morrigan once she is free!" Empress Rill's face transformed into a mask of rage. "All of that is *your* doing! *You* stole Thullu's Gift! *You* took it to that deranged Oakling, Mog! It is because of *you* our greatest treasure is now in Serza's hands! This is why we asked Morrigan that it be *you* sent to us for this task! You will pay for your theft by losing that which is most dear to you!"

"And what is that?" The halfling's voice was still defiant, though it trembled a little with fear.

"Your free will."

A streak of purple wisp shot from among the crowd behind the halfling sorceress and entered her left ear at such speed that she was knocked over. Empress Rill laughed and returned to wisp form. The wisp re-entered the ear of her handsome young host. It was his voice that rang out in the chamber next:

"You now belong to the Tiqq, halfling, and will grow ever more powerful as the Tiqq possessing you thrives on your thoughts and feelings and joins her powers to yours. Go and perform your duties for us and the Screaming Queen. We cannot fail now!"

The sorceress staggered to her feet and headed out of the chamber. The images shimmered, fading, then were completely blown away as a huge explosion rocked the alleyway and threw Wadget, Ellisenn and Daniselle to the ground.

Ellisenn shook his head, dazed, and saw that Daniselle was just sitting up, dazed as well. Wadget scrambled to his feet, looking around. The halfling sorceress was gone. Wadget's restraining spell must have broken when he was knocked down. A sizzling sound above heralded another explosion, this time streets away. Black smoke billowed into the sky. Ellisenn looked up to see a streak of blue lightning arc over Songarielle and strike nearby. The ground shook with the impact. The sound of horns and drums filled the air. *Serza approaches!* the halfling had said. *I sense him using the Secret Gift to weaken the wards over Songarielle as he comes.* The meaning of those words was now clear.

"The citadel's under attack," Wadget shouted. "We'll have ter let the halflin' go fer now! Ter the walls!"

Ellisenn raced towards the dragon-coops with Daniselle, his mind still reeling with what Wadget had forced the halfling sorceress to reveal. The sorceress had killed King Dhudhannan to place Anarra on the elvish throne. But the kidnapping attempt on Anarra had failed. Anarra Settonett was not a pawn of Empress Rill. And Anarra Settonett had indeed been crowned the new Elvish Sovereign. Just moments after the death of the Bright King, the Bright Queen was anointed. Queen Anarra would lead the elves in the fight against Morrigan, and now, surely, against Empress Rill.

Ellisenn wished he was more confident that they would win that fight, that Elvinidd would be spared another great war, and that the children of Morrigan would fail in their quest to kill Jack and Harriett. He wondered for a moment why the sorceress' hate and murderous intent had been focussed more on Harriett than on Jack — Jack was the

Waycaller after all – but that was not something the sorceress had revealed. Nor had she given away her identity.

Ellisenn entered Jossa's coop behind Daniselle mere moments later. The silver dragon was already stamping with anticipation to join the defence of the citadel. Ellisenn couldn't help but think of the last time he'd seen the dragon. That night, when he had carried the Waycaller in his arms. Jack's dark blue eyes filled his mind again. His spine tingled. Yes, he was going to have to admit what was happening to him. As soon as the battle was over.

TOMB

Tomb of the Ancient Oracles, Southern Pix

They were in a very dark and cold place, a circular space with a vaulted ceiling made of old stonework. Jack sat up and looked around. Harriett was lying beside him, the slow and rhythmic rise of her chest showing that she was breathing. As Jack's eyes adjusted to the darkness he made out a series of large stone crates, arranged around the perimeter of the chamber. The crates radiated from the centre of the room like the points on a clock face. As his eyesight improved he discerned an oval doorway and a dark flight of stairs descending into the vault from far above. They were underground.

Jack looked harder at the circle of crates. No, not crates: coffins, stone coffins. They were in a mausoleum or tomb of some kind. Each sarcophagus had the relief of a hooded and cloaked female figure on its lid. Then he remembered Laynie. Where was she? *What* was she? He jumped to his feet and cast his eyes around, searching for the dark-skinned girl who, for all Jack knew, was some kind of witch. He spotted her sitting on the floor nearby, her back against a coffin, one of her knees nonchalantly raised as if she were leaning against something as ordinary as the trunk of a tree.

"Where are we?" Jack demanded.

"This is the Tomb of the Old Oracles of Senn, on the edge of Fellwood forest, that was once in the Kingdom of Pix." Her demeanour was cold and unfriendly.

"We're in the Kingdom of Pix? Why have you brought us here?"

"You asked for my help. Don't you remember?"

Jack thought back to when he'd called out Laynie's name in the temple. He'd asked her to help save Harriett and Aelf, not to bring them here.

"I didn't ask to be brought here," he said.

"Humans, you are all so alike." Laynie sneered. "You think you know what you want and when you get it you don't want it."

"I don't know what you're talking about! Now tell me why you've brought us here, and you can tell me who and *what* you really are while you're at it!"

"Can you not tell, little human child? Am I not the very likeness of my effigy at Songarielle?"

Jack searched his mind to try and understand Laynie's strange comment. The only statue in Songarielle he'd seen was of a goddess, her arms outstretched, her hair flowing upwards in the air as if on a wind.

"Amallayne?" he stammered. He laughed, then broke off. "No, you can't be." His mind struggled to comprehend what she was suggesting.

"There is nothing *I* cannot be, little boy," Laynie, or rather Amallayne, said, smirking in a way that reminded Jack powerfully of Hob. "You sought my aid and I am giving it, even though you defiled my gift to you, the blessing of my own power that courses through your veins, by *returning* the girl child."

"Returning?" Jack's voice caught in his throat. "What do you mean?"

"Your little sister was at the very gateway of death; no human ever returns from there. It is forbidden for a human to use magic to deny death."

"I'm glad I did it if Harrie would've died if I hadn't. I don't care if it's forbidden. Forbidden by who, anyway? By the likes of you and Hob?"

"It is forbidden by Lord Thullu, who is the father of life and of death, the bringer of darkness and of light. Lord Thullu's will cannot be refused. Even we Faeden do not dare deny death. You risk damning yourself by doing this thing. Lord Thullu will not abide it."

"Oh well, I'll just add Thullu to the list of Faeden who want us dead, no biggie really." His heart thudded despite his attempt at bravado. With every hour he spent in Anwynn, he made more enemies, each one more powerful and terrifying than the last.

"Have a little faith, Jack. Perhaps it was her time to die; perhaps her death was destined, was something meant to be." She sighed and stretched out her legs.

"*Meant to be?* Are you nuts? And have faith in what? In the likes of *you?* No thanks. You weren't there when we needed you! So I did all I could to save her!"

"And save her you did," Amallayne continued, "but by denying death, you have changed the basic nature of your sister's life-force. This, Lord Thullu has prohibited for your kind."

"What do you mean?" A rising anxiety twisted his gut. Had what he'd done harmed Harriett somehow?

"Just as the elves are ageless and immortal, humans are fatal. They are meant to live only briefly and then die. This is how it was at the beginning, at the making of the universe by the will of Lord Thullu. The fatal nature of humans is part of the balance of things, the balance between the Bright Powers and the Dark Ones, as is the agelessness of the elves. By bringing your sister back from the portal of death you risk changing her fatal nature. That can only lead to abomination. Would your sister have chosen such a thing if she knew where it might lead, what she might become?"

"Become?"

"What is something that is not dead but not alive if not a monster?"

That hit Jack in the gut. "I didn't know," he sputtered.

"There is much you do not know. It is the nature of being fatal."

"All I wanted was to save her." He wiped away tears as they formed in his eyes. What had he done? Had he made Harriett into some kind of monster? Not dead but not alive?

"Stop feeling sorry for yourself," Amallayne said. "It may be that she is unchanged, that you have not brought doom down on her. And lucky it was that I stopped you from doing the same to the druid."

"Aelf? Will … will he die?"

"Aelf Ethelwulf will recover. It was simply not his time to die."

"What about Songarielle?" Jack asked, remembering the army of trolls, goblins and Dark Elves and suddenly desperate for news of the city's fate.

"Songarielle is weakened but not destroyed. Do not worry, the elves and the druids will prevail this time. Serza is a very powerful sorcerer, especially now that he wields Thullu's Gift, but when we left the temple he instantly detected your departure and turned to pursue you. Without its master, the dark army will be vanquished, but the dark prince cares nought about that. Preventing you from falling into Morrigan's hands is an obsession for him now. He is driven mad by his desire to remove every possible way that Morrigan might escape."

Jack instantly looked toward the shadowy stairwell, fearing that Serza might be just about to come down the stairs.

"Do not worry," Amallayne reassured him, "I am far more powerful than he, and besides, I've sent him on a bit of a wild goose chase. I let him think that you opened a Way to the far north of the Empty Lands. He will not find us here, so far to the south."

Jack felt his stomach unclench, but not completely. His anxiety was still close to panic level. "Is there anything you can do to help Harrie, if she is changed? If anything bad has happened to her because of what I did?"

Amallayne said nothing. She just stared at him, weighing him up.

"I'm sorry I did it, okay—"

"You should be," she said flatly.

Jack stood in the dark tomb, feeling utter hopelessness. He had made everything worse, rather than better. The story of his life to date.

"Do not despair," Amallayne said, her voice a little softer

than before. "It may be that your sister is unaffected." Amallayne looked intently at Harriett, who lay quite still on the floor. "I detect no difference in her, not yet at least. She seems to remain human. Besides, there is another reason for hope. All is not lost – the Waycaller is alive and has not fallen into our enemies' hands. You might still counter Serza, and thwart Morrigan's plans for escape."

"How?" Jack asked.

"First, awaken your sister for she must hear this also."

Jack went over to Harriett and shook her gently while whispering her name. She stirred almost immediately and, after a brief moment, her eyes slowly blinked open. Jack gasped. Harriett's eyes had changed; where before they were the deep colour of a sapphire, just like his own, now they were a blue so pale they were almost white. Harriett closed her eyes again and took a deep breath, struggling to wake. Jack looked over to Amallayne, certain he had harmed Harriett, that he had turned her into a monster. Amallayne's eyes were wide, fixed on Harriett. A moment later she had rearranged her face to give the same impression of disinterest that so reminded Jack of Hob, but too late. Jack had seen the shock on her face.

"Her eyes, does this mean ..." He couldn't bring himself to finish the sentence.

"That she is a monster? No, not necessarily. It is a superficial change. She may yet be the same irritating child she always was." She was affecting a disinterested voice but Jack could hear the uncertainty underneath.

Harriett's eyelids opened in response to their voices. She looked around with eyes the colour of frosted glass. Jack doubted he would ever get used to those eyes. She didn't look like Harriett anymore. She took in the vaulted ceiling and the dark space, registering that they were no longer in the temple of Amallayne.

"Jack?" she mumbled, not quite alert yet.

"It's okay, Harrie," Jack said in as comforting a voice as he could muster. "You're going to be alright."

Harriett propped herself up on her arms and looked into his face, her features showing fatigue but also relief and trust. It made Jack sick to think that she trusted him so much, when he may have changed her in a way that they would all regret, that might bring Thullu's wrath down on her. She smiled at him and surveyed the gloomy vault they were in, her relief replaced by confusion.

"Where are we?" she muttered.

"We're in the Tomb of the Old Oracles of Senn," Jack explained. "Amallayne brought us here. Don't worry, we're safe."

Harriett gasped, now totally confused. "Amallayne?" She sat up and looked around, taking in the stone sarcophagi and the stairs leading upwards. She saw Laynie resting against one of the coffins.

"You ... what are you doing here?" she asked.

"That's Amallayne, Harrie," Jack explained. "She brought us here."

"Amallayne? But ... how?"

"Jack beseeched. I came," Amallayne said. "It is not difficult to understand, even for one such as you." She stood, her dark skin seeming to draw in the shadows from all around the tomb, making the vault lighter, warmer. "Now we must talk, about the doom that descends on all of Anwynn, which I have worked hard for aeons to prevent."

THE KEY

"Do we have to talk here?" Harriett asked, looking around at the gloomy tomb.

"Here is as good a place as any." Amallayne brushed dust away from the top of the nearest coffin and leant against it, as if to say that a tomb was a perfectly normal place to meet.

"Why did you bring us here?" Jack asked, irritated by Amallayne's typical Faeden disregard for human feelings and wanting a clear answer.

"I would think that were obvious. You asked me to help you overcome your enemies. That is what I am doing."

"By bringing us to a tomb?" Jack asked.

"This is a sacred place to the Pixish. Among all the human peoples, the Pixish are most loyal to me. But that is not why I have brought you here. This place sits on the border with Fellwood Forest, and into Fellwood you must go."

"Why?" Jack and Harriett asked together, both thinking of Mog.

"When I made Morrigan's domain a prison and sealed her inside, I created Darkgate, a barrier powerful enough to restrain her. This, I am sure, the druids have told you. What you do not know, what I have kept secret from all, even the druids, is that I also created a key that controls Darkgate. Without the key, no magic or sorcery, not even the power of the Faeden, can cause Darkgate to open. In other words, there are only two ways to open the gate – by using the key, or by extinguishing the line of otherworld Waycallers. While you are alive, Jack, and without the key, Darkgate remains closed and Morrigan remains imprisoned."

"Where is this key?" Harriett asked, sizing up Amallayne as though the Faeden might suddenly pull it out of a pocket.

"That is the problem. While I was ... elsewhere – the key was taken by goblins from its hiding place in the deepest part of the Great North Wood. The goblins know not its real power or worth but simply took it for the sake of the taking. They are born villains and thieves. The goblins carried it to their fortress at Pitmouth, at the head of the caves above the gateway to Uffern—"

"The key is right there, where Morrigan is?" Jack's voice sounded appalled, matching the sick feeling in his stomach. He didn't bother to ask what she meant by 'elsewhere', surmising it was the mysterious realm the Faeden occupied when they weren't in the human world, where they were so overwhelmed with bliss they were unaware of anything else.

"Yes. If the goblins discover what it is, they will loose Morrigan. Worse still, Serza has learnt of the key and wishes to destroy it, thinking that destroying the key will ensure Morrigan's continued imprisonment. He is mistaken. Destroying the key will do the opposite. If the key is destroyed, Darkgate will open. None of us, not even Serza, wants that."

Harriett raised her hand to interrupt. Jack blinked at her – only Harriett had the gumption to shush a goddess. "Wait, how did Serza find out about the key? And why does he think destroying it means Morrigan can't ever escape?"

Amallayne hesitated before answering, clearly weighing up if she should tell them everything. "I cannot say for certain how Serza learned of the key, but the Faeden you know as Hob has visited the dark prince more than once of late. Serza's mind is not fully open to me, but open enough for me to discover that."

Jack was appalled. "Hob? Hob told Serza about the key? And lied about what would happen if it was destroyed?" He glared at Harriett, daring her to defend Hob this time.

Harriett bristled. "Maybe Hob went to Serza to—"

"To what, Harrie? To what? Hob has no good reason to buddy up to Serza. I knew it all along. He's evil and now we have proof."

Harriett's brow wrinkled as she desperately tried to think of an excuse for Hob having met with Serza. It was obvious she couldn't come up with anything when her eyes fell to the floor and she fell silent.

"So, what are *we* supposed to do about this?" Jack asked, desperately. "I mean, aren't you a goddess? Can't you just fix it? The Druid Council seemed to think you could."

"I could simply destroy Serza, smite Pitmouth so that it became a funeral pyre for all the goblins of the world and take back the key to ensure Darkgate remains sealed forever. It is well within my powers to do so. But I won't."

"Why?" Jack demanded. "Why won't you help us? You could have saved Harrie yourself, you could have stopped Serza attacking Songarielle, but you didn't! Why won't you help?"

"The druids and the elves think they are very wise, and very good, but they do not really understand we Faeden. I cannot break my covenant with Lord Thullu."

"What's that?" Harriett asked.

"A single, simple magical law that we Faeden cannot break. All Faeden must abide by the Will and the Word of Lord Thullu. We cannot act against Thullu's will, not even if we wanted to. Nor can we interfere with his children, the Tiqq."

"I don't understand," Jack said. "How is the covenant preventing you from helping us?"

"The Prince of Fellwood may be under the protection of Lord Thullu. He wields the Secret Gift, perhaps with the Lord of Chaos' blessing. I cannot harm nor hinder him. I cannot stop him from seeking the key."

"What?" Jack gasped again. "But he could be acting alone, couldn't he, without Thullu's blessing?"

"Perhaps," Amallayne said quietly. "When it comes to Lord Thullu or the Secret Gift, I am blind, I cannot tell. It is possible that Serza is acting alone. It is also possible that there is a reason why the dark prince has turned on Morrigan. Perhaps he has a new god now. Perhaps he has dedicated himself to the Lord of Chaos."

"That's really bad, isn't it?" Harriett asked.

"Lord Thullu is much more powerful than any of the Faeden. If Serza is under his protection, we will not prevail against him." Amallayne sounded resigned more than alarmed, unlike Jack whose heart was trying to pound its way out of his chest.

"Great," Harriett said, her voice as gloomy as their surroundings. "That's just great."

"Why don't you and the other Faeden just ask Thullu to remove his protection from Serza, I mean, if he even has it?" Jack asked.

"Lord Thullu is the First of the First. He is as much a mystery to us as he is to you. I have never spoken with him, though all Faeden sense his presence at all times. We do not ask the Lord of Chaos for anything. He gave us existence. It would be wrong to ask for even a small thing more."

"Fantastic," Jack huffed. "If you won't help, we might as well just climb into one of these coffins and be done with it."

"No need for that just yet," Amallayne said. "There is a loophole."

"I don't like the sound of that," Harriett said.

"If you were to choose, of your own free will, to go to Pitmouth and retrieve the key, then it would not fall into Serza's hands. I would not have interfered, and Darkgate would stay closed."

"But, Serza will still be after us. He'll still be trying to conquer all of Anwynn." Despite himself Jack hoped Amallayne would offer a solution to that problem, despite her lack of assistance so far.

"Yes, he will," Amallayne said. "I cannot advise you on how to defeat the Prince of Fellwood, but I will say this: the power of the key combined with the power of the Waycaller is exceeded by nothing else, bar one of the Faeden and Thullu himself. It may be that such power is a match for the Secret Gift."

"What do you mean?" Jack asked, feeling hopeful for the first time since they'd arrived in the tomb.

"I cannot explain. I must be careful of the covenant. I

may have said too much already."

"But you haven't said anything!" Harriett's voice echoed in the dark chamber. "You've just dropped a really weak hint!"

Amallayne chose not to respond to that. "Now," she continued in a quelling voice, "I must be clear. I have told you about the key to assist you to deter Morrigan, who is an outcast, not so that you might hinder Serza. I also must be clear that I cannot offer much more assistance, for that would risk breaking my covenant with Lord Thullu. Though, if you do choose to journey to Pitmouth, you may sorely need assistance."

"So, basically," Harriett said, "you're not going to help at all."

"But I have helped you, by telling you how you might thwart Morrigan and about the power of the key."

"But," Jack began, "we have to go to Pitmouth on our own, which, correct me if I'm wrong, is like a fortress crawling with nasties, and try to find and take this key off the goblins and then somehow figure out how to use it to stop Serza, all by ourselves?"

"That is about right, yes." Amallayne smirked.

"Can't we take someone with us?" Harriett asked. "Like Aelf or Wadget or somebody?"

"Aelf will take some time to recover. Wadget and the rest of the Order are busy dealing with Serza's little incursion into Elvinnid."

"Little incursion!" Jack snarled. "There were thousands of goblins and Dark Elves and trolls! That was hardly a little incursion!"

"That was just a fraction of the dark host at Serza's command. Even if the druids and the elves of Songarielle kill every last one of them that would not put even the slightest dent in Serza's army, and that was just the forces of Fellwood. There are also the Dreads of Bonemound and the goblins of Pitmouth who are yet to throw in their lot."

"I'm starting to think we might be outnumbered,"

Harriett moaned.

"Not only that but running out of time as well. Serza has tried direct assault to take you twice now and failed. He is not a fool. Soon, he will change tactics," Amallayne explained.

"To what?" Jack asked nervously.

"His mind is not clear to me because of the power of Thullu's Gift, but I suspect he will soon decide that if he cannot take you, then no-one shall. I am sure that his new tactic will be to eliminate any chance of Morrigan's disciples getting to you before he does by—"

"Killing them all," Harriett muttered.

"Yes. With all threat to you removed, Serza will then turn to Pitmouth to destroy the key. The dark prince thinks if he destroys the key he will not need the Waycaller, that Morrigan will be trapped forever and he will become lord over all the dark beings in her place."

"So, we have to get this key before Serza can get to Pitmouth?" Jack asked.

"Yes. If you go, and that is entirely your decision, you must not wait, you must go immediately. It will be hard enough getting into Pitmouth now, try doing it while it is under siege by Serza's armies."

Amallayne said this all too smugly as far as Jack was concerned. He looked at his little sister, whose face, though still pale from her ordeal, showed more courage than he felt.

"The dark prince has amassed his troops on the border of the Empty Lands, making a show of waging war on Elvinnid and Pix, but I sense that his true objective is Pitmouth. His move on Elvinnid is merely a feint to deceive Hect, the Dread witch of Bonemound, his greatest rival and enemy. If I'm right about his desire to eliminate any chance of Morrigan's disciples getting to you before he does, his armies will turn south-east toward Bonemound before Hect can mount a force able to block him. Once he overcomes the Dread temple, he will take Pitmouth and destroy the key. Without the aid of the Dreads, the goblins will quickly submit to Serza's authority. They respect the authority of violence more than anything else. Once Serza has lordship over Fellwood, Pitmouth and all the Swampmere, he will turn on the human kingdoms and the dominion of the elves. That would mean a second Doom War. Every corner of Anwynn would burn."

Jack shivered as an image of Serza's army marauding through the Halfling Dells rose in his mind. He couldn't allow that to happen. Harriett seemed to be thinking the same thing.

"So, so what kind of key are we looking for?" she asked in a thin voice.

"It does not look like any kind of key. The key is not actually a key." Amallayne looked pleased with herself, which made Jack uneasy. Any time a Faeden looked pleased about something, that was the time to worry.

"Oh, let me guess," Harriett said. "Is it a ring? Or a crystal shard? It's always a ring or a crystal shard."

"No, it is not a ring nor a crystal shard. Morrigan's power was in her voice so I used a like-power to create the key. The key is a song."

"A song?" Harriett said. "That's kind of original."

"Thanks." Amallayne smiled, pleased with herself again.

"So, is this song written down or what?" Jack asked, wondering how he was going to be able to recognise this song when he found it.

"The Keysong is contained within an … instrument, shall we say."

"What kind of instrument is it?" Jack asked.

"It is an instrument of unique make. No such instruments exist in your world. But you do not need to know what it looks like, as it will make itself known to you. It will respond to that within you that came from me, the power of the Waycaller. It will be drawn to you. It is for that reason that no-one else could succeed at this task."

"So, what do I do if I find it?" Jack asked.

"*When* you find it, take it to the halfling village of Bright. Nowhere else is so far from Pitmouth. It will be safe there."

"There you go, Jack," Harriett said, regaining some of her old energy. "You've been saying you wanted a proper quest."

"No, I haven't! You're the one that's been going on about quests! I just want to get us home!"

"We can't go home until we get the key away from Serza and make sure Morrigan stays locked up," Harriett said, as if explaining it to a brain-damaged monkey.

"I know!" Jack snarled. He paused to think, though why he did so he didn't know because there was nothing for him to think about. He had no choice. If he didn't attempt to find the key to Darkgate then Serza would destroy it, accidentally releasing Morrigan, who would then surely go after them, to end the line of human Waycallers and break open the Veil between the realms for good. "Alright," he huffed, "I'll do it. But only if you take Harriett somewhere safe until I get back."

"I'm afraid I cannot," Amallayne said.

"Why?" Jack demanded, reaching breaking point.

"Because if you are killed before you find the Keysong then the power of the Waycaller will arise in Harriett. If she is not there to complete the task then we will fail. No-one else but the Waycaller can retrieve the Keysong."

"You're going to send a nine year old child into a goblin fortress! What kind of goddess are you?" Jack shouted.

"I am not sending Harriett anywhere. It is her choice and hers alone. But there is no point you going without her. The odds of one of you perishing are very high. It is simply logical that you both go."

"You're a monster," Jack said, glaring at the Faeden. "Miss Butters was right about the lot of you."

"Monster I may be, but there are worse monsters on your trail, and the fate of the Two Realms rests in your hands. Will you go? Will you prevent Darkgate from being opened? Will you go into the midst of darkness to protect Anwynn, and your own world?"

Jack and Harriett looked at each other. Harriett just

shrugged, as if to say 'I'll go if you go'. Jack got a very bad feeling that if they went on this quest one or the other of them wouldn't come back. But what choice did he have? If they didn't go they would both perish, and a whole lot of others as well. And he would never be free to search for their mother if the threat of Morrigan was forever hanging over their head. "Alright," he sighed. "Alright, we'll go."

Amallayne stepped towards them, her eyes widening in surprise. She said nothing, but her wide eyes spoke volumes. The challenges Jack and Harriett faced were likely beyond them, and if they failed all of Anwynn would be lost to one monster or the other, Morrigan or Serza. Nevertheless, they were prepared to try, to fight. Her head dropped a little, as if some sadness had suddenly overcome her.

"I didn't expect you to take on this challenge," she whispered, "though I hoped you would." She looked up at them and Jack saw tears in her eyes. "It gladdens me that you have made this choice. But I am also sad that it has to be so. Much danger will you face, and little assistance will you have."

"We'll be alright," Harriett said. "We've been okay so far."

"It has been such a long time since such valour has been shown in the world, and by two so young." Amallayne looked around the tomb, as if remembering a distant past. "Once there was much valour in the world. I had many friends then. Now, my friends dwindle in number, and only a few of the Pix remain truly loyal. Those that lie here," she said, gesturing to the stone coffins, "were my most faithful friends, along with the old Kings of Pix." She looked into Jack's eyes, revealing to him her sadness over this loss. "There has not been an Oracle for millennia, and the Kingdom of Pix is a shadow of its former glory. Pix is no longer a beacon of peace, just another realm where intrigue and commerce reign."

For long minutes Amallayne was silent, reviewing her memories. She looked over each of the coffins of the Oracles in turn, stopping at one in particular and caressing the face of the stone relief, that of a young, sturdy-looking woman, hooded and cloaked like all the others. "This was the last of the Oracles, murdered by Morrigan herself." The goddess Amallayne sighed, a terrible sound that echoed sadly in the chamber. "I loved her greatly. It was her loss that finally prompted me to act against the Pale Mother."

There was another long pause in which Jack felt a little uncomfortable, as if he and Harriett were watching the very private moments of someone's grief. "Perhaps," Amallayne said suddenly out of the silence, "perhaps there is some aid I can give that will not contravene the covenant."

She grabbed hold of the stone lid of the sarcophagus and, even though it must have weighed close to a ton, heaved it aside as if it were paper. She placed it against the wall and looked into the coffin. "Hello, my old friend," she said to the mummified corpse lying inside. The mummy was that of a woman, wearing a white dress-coat beneath a royal blue hooded cloak. "Do not disturb your slumber. I merely have need of the gift I once bequeathed you."

Amallayne rummaged around in the coffin and pulled out a dusty object. In the dark Jack wasn't able to make out what it was. "This," she said, "is an ancient tool of the Oracle of Senn. It enhanced the Oracle's visions of the Three Times and enabled her to share those visions with others. I created it myself and gave it to the first Oracle. After that it was handed down from one Oracle to another, until the last Oracle, my dear friend, perished in the Doom War." She hesitated a moment and then, to both Jack and Harriett's surprise, walked over to Harriett and handed it to her. "Here," she said, "it is yours now."

"But, but what am I supposed to do with it?" Harriett stammered, looking at the small thing in her hands. It looked like an ordinary bangle made of twists of copper, only not a complete circle but rather a u-shape, a kind of wrist torc.

"The Oracles of old, unlike the Seers who only see into the future, could see all three times: past, present, and future," Amallayne explained as she replaced the lid to the sarcophagus. "This will help you to do that, to avoid danger on your journey."

"What's so great about seeing the past? I mean, it's already happened," Jack said.

"To see the past clearly is a very powerful thing. Would you not give anything to know the truth about what happened to your mother, to your father? Seeing the future is not always a gift. The future is full of uncertainty. Seeing the past brings certainty, and with it wisdom. It was the ability to see into the past, more than anything, that made the Oracles of Senn so revered."

"But, how can I use it? I'm not an Oracle." Harriett held it loosely in her hand, as if the metal were hot and might burn her fingers.

"It will obey you because I have given it to you," Amallayne explained. "Ask questions while wearing it and it will provide an answer. There is a bit of a knack to it – time is tricky – but I'm sure you will master it."

"But—" Harriett's complaint was stopped short by the sound of footsteps. They all turned toward the dark flight of stairs descending into the vault and saw that accompanying the sound of footfall was the flicker of firelight. Someone was descending into the tomb carrying a torch. Jack motioned for Harriett to hide the torc. She slipped the bracelet in her pocket as the light penetrated deeper into the crypt.

"I must go," Amallayne whispered.

"Who is it?" Jack asked, his heart thumping again.

"He is a Pixish pilgrim, no danger to you," the Faeden assured them. "I must go. My involvement in this must remain a secret. Remember, no-one must know your true purpose. Make your way to Pitmouth, through Fellwood Forest. Find the key and carry it to the circle at Bright. Do that and all will be well."

"Wait," Jack said, "I have more questions—"

"Find the answers with the torc."

Before Jack or Harriett could protest any further,

Amallayne's eyes changed to swirling black whirlpools. Her hair danced on end and her skin emitted dark electricity from every pore. In seconds the goddess was enfolded in a pillar of fire that sounded like a million voices, uttering that same strange incantation. She vanished, leaving them alone in the tomb, blinking and dazed.

They turned to face the stairs, Jack's mind racing to figure out what to do given they did not know who would emerge or how they were going to explain what they were doing there.

DENN

Jack and Harriett dashed behind one of the stone coffins just as a tall, dark-haired man entered the tomb. His unruly black hair hung at his shoulders, only partially obscuring what, even in the darkness of the crypt, were clearly deep blue eyes. His skin was pale and his face, square-jawed and strong-looking, was adorned with dark stubble. Dressed in a fitted black jacket and trousers, he also wore a long hooded cloak. At his waist was sheathed a sword, the hilt of which shimmered with the light of the flaming torch he carried in his hand.

The torchbearer walked into the midst of the tomb, his boot heels striking firmly on the stone floor, setting off echoes that rebounded throughout the small space. Jack's first impression was of someone who shouldn't be messed with. A handsome man of about thirty, he walked with a determined attitude. His muscled bulk showed that he was both strong and agile.

Jack and Harriett watched as the man proceeded to the coffin from which Amallayne had only recently removed the copper torc. He knelt down on one knee and bowed his head forward, his dark hair falling to obscure his face. In a reverent though clear voice he spoke, as if to the body of the woman inside the stone tomb.

"Mistress of the Three Times, heed my plea. I go now to the goblin nest at Pitmouth. Guide me on my journey. I seek to avenge my brother, murdered by goblin fiends. Steady my will and sharpen my sword. And when my life is spent, though my body may lie in goblin lands, carry my spirit to the blissful abode of the Bright Ones." His voice echoed his gait, determined and strong but with a touch of sorrow. He stayed there for the longest time, kneeling before the tomb of the last Oracle of Senn, evidently praying.

Jack couldn't help but think that the man's appearance in the tomb at the same time as them couldn't be a coincidence.

It was beyond good luck that an armed, clearly competent warrior turned up just when they needed someone to guide them into Fellwood and was on his way to their own destination, Pitmouth. If the man's presence wasn't a coincidence, then who might have sent him? Not Amallayne, for she didn't want anyone to know she'd been there. Not the druids, for they couldn't have had time to send someone to meet them in the tomb, in the Kingdom of Pix, so far away from Songarielle. Who then? With a stab of fear he thought of Morrigan, or Serza. Could either of them have sent the man here to trap or kill them? As Jack continued his internal deliberations, the man sighed and stood to his full height, readying himself to leave.

"It is rude," the man began, as if to the air around him, "to spy on a man at prayer. But I will forgive you, if you come out from your hiding place and introduce yourselves."

Jack and Harriett looked at each other in surprise. What should they do? Clearly the man knew they were there, so what was the point of hiding any longer? They both stood up from behind the sarcophagus and nervously walked out into the centre of the vault. Jack wondered if these would be the last steps they took. Would this stranger end their quest in this dark and creepy vault by running them through with his sword? When he and Harriett reached the man they looked up into his blue eyes, which took them in and assessed them in a quick moment.

"You are not Pixish," the man said, apparently not intending to run them through, "though your hair and eyes make you seem so. Your attire and your bearing betray you. You carry none of the marks of the four kingdoms. Where are you from?"

As usual it was Harriett who spoke first. "Well, we're from Scotland, originally," she said, a little sheepishly.

Jack glared at her, his lips silently forming the word 'blabbermouth'.

"I have not heard of it. It is not in the four kingdoms, or in the Dominion of Elves, though I know nought of the

Halfling Dells beyond the Craggy Mountains. Is that where you're from?"

"Do we look like halflings to you?" Harriett said, echoing Hob's long ago annoyance at the effrontery of being mistaken for a halfling.

"You are overly tall and yet not overly fed," the man said, "so I must assume that you are not of that kind."

"We're human, like you," Jack said, "only we grew up somewhere else."

"Seems to me you have yet to complete the growing." The man smiled. "But where did you begin growing, where is this Scotland?"

"We're not allowed to say," Jack answered, before Harriett could blurt that they were from the otherworld.

"By whose command?" the man asked.

"Wadget's," Jack lied.

"Wadget? Of the Druid Council? What cause have two younglings to be associating with members of the Druid Council?"

"We're ... we're not allowed to tell anyone," Jack said, ignoring an annoyed look from Harriett. "We're on a mission and we can't talk about it."

"Dark times they are indeed if the Druid Council is relying on little younglings." The man scratched at the stubble on his chin.

"I'm seventeen," Jack asserted, sick of being called little.

"My apologies, I did not mean to offend. My name is Denn. May I have your names, or are they secret as well?"

"I'm Harriett and this is my brother Jack."

"Pleased to meet you, Harriett and Jack. Now, I have tarried too long underground. I do not enjoy sunless places. Will you accompany me above or does your mission require you to stay here in the tomb?"

"Sure, we can come with you," Harriett said, without even looking to Jack for direction.

"We were already finished here," Jack added, in a 'take charge' kind of voice, not wanting to look like he was being

43

led around by a little girl.

The stairs from the vault to the tomb entrance at ground level went on for ages – Jack figured the crypt must be at least six stories underground. When they finally mounted the last step they entered another circular chamber almost exactly the same as the one housing the sarcophagi below. They were instantly dazzled by bright sunlight streaming in from a small, oval-shaped door. Denn extinguished the torch, put it in a brace by the stairwell and led them outside.

As Jack walked out into the sunshine its warmth instantly lifted his spirits. It was afternoon now and though the sun was low in the sky it was still throwing a golden light that heated his skin and bestowed a sense of security. He looked around, taking in the beautiful scene before him. They were in the midst of a wide and shallow valley of golden grass which moved in waves, like a golden lake stirred by an afternoon breeze. The sea of gold was broken up here and there by a gnarled tree with dark bark and olive-green leaves. All the way to the horizon rolled low hill after low hill, a series of shallow valleys that appeared to go on forever. Jack turned at a gasp from Harriett. She was looking back at the structure they'd just exited.

"It's like a big stone beehive!"

Jack thought Harriett was quite right. The Tomb of the Old Oracles of Senn was a beehive-shaped structure built out of flat, grey stones.

"Now I know that something is amiss here," Denn said quietly. "Why did you not notice the tomb's shape as you entered?"

"Umm … we were just in such a hurry to get inside," Harriett lied.

"That does not explain why you do not recognise the shape. Have you not seen other buildings like this?"

"No," Harriett said. "How many beehive-shaped buildings could there be?"

"In Pix there are many. Most Pixish buildings take this shape."

"Really?" Harriett asked.

"Do you take me for a deceiver?" Denn asked indignantly, his blue eyes sparking in the sun.

"No, she doesn't," Jack said. "It's just an expression of surprise."

"If you had travelled only a little in Pix you would know that all our buildings are fashioned this way. This makes me think you have never been in Pix before." Denn thought on this briefly before he continued. "The only way for you to be in this place, without seeing any other Pixish buildings, is if you came out of Fellwood."

He drew his sword and brandished it in their direction. "Which of the foul ones is your master? Is it the dark prince or the Witch of Bonemound? Or is it Krungle, the goblin king? Answer me!" As he shouted, his black hair fell over his face to form a mask of menace. "Are you in league with the goblins, the Dread sorcerers or the Vellenor? Tell me now!"

"None of them," Jack said. "You have to believe us. We're not in league with anyone. We're trying to stop Morrigan from taking over the world!" As the words left Jack's mouth he immediately regretted it. He had just told this complete stranger about their quest.

"Now who's a blabbermouth?" Harriett sniped.

"Well if you haven't noticed he has a sword and its pointed right at me! I'd like to see you do better under the circumstances!"

"So typical, Jack, not everything's about you. I'm here too you know and he's also pointing the sword at me! Aren't you, Denn?"

Denn opened his mouth to respond but Harriett cut him off.

"And I didn't crack like a scaredy cat and tell him about Morrigan, you did."

"You can't talk! You told him our names!"

"Big deal," Harriett said defiantly.

"Big deal? Big deal! You're such a little pain, Harriett! You're always opening your mouth and saying whatever comes into your head!"

"And you're always blaming me for everything!"

"If you two don't stop squabbling," Denn shouted, "I'll run you both through!"

They shut their mouths. Harriett crossed her arms over her chest in anger and Jack glared at the ground. Denn re-sheathed his sword and stepped toward them. "Clearly," he started, "there is more to you both than meets the eye. But if Morrigan is involved, I can't believe that the Druid Council would send you on this quest alone. I have never seen two younglings so unfit for such a task. Now, tell the truth, what are you two doing here?"

Perhaps because of the strength and steadfastness that Denn projected, Jack decided to trust him, despite Amallayne's warning. He told Denn everything: about the skinwearer attacking them in Cairnbawn, their crossing into Anwynn, their journey to Oakholme, the confrontation with Serza, their encounter with Mog, their dragon-flight to Songarielle and then Serza's surprise attack on the elvish citadel. Then Jack told Denn that he was a Waycaller and that Morrigan wanted to kill him and Harriett so that she could escape. Finally, Jack described to Denn how Amallayne had magically carried them from Songarielle and given them a quest to ensure that Morrigan remained imprisoned. He left out some things. He didn't mention the Keysong, or Ting. He did describe how Amallayne had asked them to go to Pitmouth before she vanished from the vault as Denn came down the stairs. At each mention of Amallayne's name, Denn's eyes widened and he touched his thumb to his lips, apparently a Pixish sign of deep veneration.

"I was right. There is much, much more to you than meets the eyes," Denn said smiling. "In Pix we grow up being told stories of Amallayne's victory over Morrigan, the making of the Veil and the Waycallers. There are no mortals alive today but yourselves whom Amallayne has graced with her presence. I am honoured to meet you. But I can't allow you to go into Fellwood alone."

"But, Amallayne said we have to go alone," Harriett started.

"Amallayne, the Great Goddess, is beyond our understanding, but one thing I am certain of: she would not wish to send two children into Pitmouth without aid. I believe the grace of the Bright Ones has brought me to this place at this time so that I might offer you assistance, and offer it I do. My life is yours, such as it is. Besides, my journey takes me to Pitmouth also. We might as well journey together."

"You're going to Pitmouth to avenge your brother?" Jack asked.

"I am. The goblins of Pitmouth slew my younger brother at the onset of winter last. He was my only remaining family. The goblins killed my mother and father when I was but a child. Our home is only a few hours ride from here. The goblins sleep in their burrows in Fellwood Forest by day and make regular sport of attacking our compound by night. Then they carry whatever spoil they steal from us to their king at Pitmouth."

"I'm sorry about your brother," Harriett said, patting Denn on the forearm.

"Thank you, little one," Denn said, running his fingers through his dark hair, his voice a little less firm than before. "It is my goal to kill Krungle, the goblin king, who has harried these borderlands far too long."

Harriett listened, absentmindedly patting along Denn's arm to his bicep. "Ooh, your muscles are really big," she said suddenly. "Much bigger than Jack's. Jack's arms are like chicken wings."

"Harrie!" Jack yelled. "Do you mind!"

"Well they are!" she asserted. "No matter how much he pumps his dumbbells," she explained to Denn, "they just don't get any bigger."

"I do not know what dumbbells are nor how they are pumped," Denn said. "I dare say I am glad for it. I suspect I would not approve of their use. Now, back to more important matters: will you accept me as your guide and protector? I will lead you to Pitmouth and back again and give my life if necessary to ensure your safe journey home."

"Wow!" Harriett exclaimed. "You Pixish people have a real gift for the dramatic!"

After Jack and Harriett accepted Denn's offer of assistance, he led them over to the shade of a gnarled tree where, much to their surprise, a big, startlingly blue horse contentedly grazed.

"That horse is blue!" Harriett squealed.

"His name is Cobalt," Denn said, "and he is blue at that."

"How did he become blue?" Jack asked.

"It was Cobalt's misfortune to be born white. The colour white is a bad omen in Pix, because of Morrigan, the White Demoness. Cobalt is deeply ashamed of his white coat and is therefore particularly fond of a blue truffle that grows at the base of these trees."

"I don't get it," Jack said.

"The truffles Cobalt eats have permanently dyed his coat blue."

"Do all the white horses in Pix turn themselves blue?" Harriett asked.

"No. Most horses do not care what colour they are. Pixish horsemen, on the other hand, care a great deal. We do not breed from a white horse and so their kind is rare. On the odd occasion that a white foal is born it is normal for the owner to dye its coat to some other colour. Red, being the colour of Amallayne, is the most common. As far as I know, Cobalt is the only blue horse in Pix or anywhere else for that matter."

"He's cool," Harriett said, going over to pat the horse on the nose.

"I disagree," Denn said. "He is hot-blooded by nature and the colour blue is not much better than white for a horse."

"Why?" Jack asked.

"The blue horse is one of the symbols of Thullu." Denn didn't need to say any more. Jack and Harriett knew only too well why a symbol of Thullu was unwelcome in Pix, the heartland of Amallayne's followers.

"But that's not Cobalt's fault," Harriett said. "You shouldn't hold it against him."

"You may be right," Denn said. "But some might ask why a white horse, especially an intelligent one, chose to turn the next worst colour, rather than a nice acceptable red. It smacks of attention seeking."

"Cover your ears, Cobalt," Harriett said, stretching up and covering the horse's ears for him. "Don't listen to him. I think you look lovely." Cobalt whickered approvingly and passed a defiant glance toward his master.

"The day wanes," Denn continued brusquely. "It isn't safe to travel by night. We shall sleep in the tomb and cross into Fellwood tomorrow."

"Will we be safe in the tomb?" Jack asked. "From goblins, I mean?"

"We will invoke the hearth ward, by lighting a fire," Denn explained. "That will keep all fell beings out. And as the building is stone with solid foundations it will be impervious to the goblins' main weapon, fire. This is why all Pixish buildings are made this way. We live with fiends at our back and have had to adapt."

"I'm sorry but, how did the goblins kill your brother?" Harriett asked. "Wasn't he safe inside at night?"

"The goblins dug under the wall of our barn and managed to set a fire inside. It was just before dawn. My brother and I went out to protect the animals. He was killed in the fray."

"Was Cobalt in the barn?" Harriett asked.

"Yes," Denn answered, "he was the main reason we went out into the night. He is a fine horse, despite his brazen colour." At that Cobalt clopped over to Denn and nuzzled into the crook of his owner's arm. Denn patted Cobalt's big head and the horse twitched his ears and whinnied. The two were clearly more than horse and rider. They were friends.

As the sun moved lower in the sky, Denn led Cobalt, Jack and Harriett into the entrance chamber of the Oracle's tomb. He unbridled Cobalt and removed his saddle bags, leaving the horse to wander around the chamber, grazing on mounds of grass that Jack and Harriett had gathered for him. Denn took a small brazier out of one of the saddle bags and placed it in the centre of the room. He carefully stacked small kindling and bunches of dried grass in the bottom of the grate and then pulled out a small bag and tipped its contents into the brazier as well. Jack leant in to look and saw that the brazier was now filled with coal. Denn lit the kindling with sparks from a flint. The burning twigs and dry grass filled the tomb with a woody scent.

"Will any fire invoke the hearth ward?" Jack asked.

"No," Denn explained, "there must be some kind of man-made covering overhead and a grate of some kind as well. An open campfire is not enough. The cave-fires of the trolls do not invoke the ward either. Though the caves have ceilings, they are natural. Besides, trolls do not use grates, just a ring of skulls."

"Gruesome," Harriett said as she came over to join them. The paleness of her eyes almost shone in the dark. Jack turned away rather than look at them.

"Very gruesome," Denn agreed. "In the wild, a lean-to of branches and leaves with this little brazier has sufficed."

"What about a tent?" Harriett asked. "Would a tent work?"

"Yes, so long as the brazier is beneath a roof, even if only a hessian sack stretched over some sticks, it will work."

Once the coals were fully alight Denn closed and bolted the iron doors to the tomb and they settled down on beds of dried grass, which were occasionally depleted by a grazing Cobalt. As the darkness deepened, Denn shared between them his rations of cheese and hard bread. As they ate, Jack's eyes wandered to Denn's swords. There were four of them, all housed in a kind of leather quiver, only for blades rather than arrows. One sword in particular caught Jack's attention. It was a fine weapon, made from some kind of black metal, thinner than Jack would expect of a sword and quite long. Its hilt was intricately decorated, designed to mimic the shape of a stylised tree, with the handle forming the trunk and sidebars curving downwards like the weeping bows of an iron willow. In the centre of the blade, running from the hilt toward the tip deep in the quiver, were three rows of strange patterns. As Jack gazed at the patterns, the firelight seemed to make them move and he realised it was writing.

"I doubt you have seen a sword of this kind before," Denn said, noticing that Jack's attention had been on the one blade for a long while.

"No, but until recently I haven't seen many swords really, just a few in museums and stuff."

"But once we got here, to Anwynn, we've seen lots and lots of swords," Harriett interrupted. "Too many, really. Most of them have been in the hands of goblins."

"Ah, but a goblin sword is a short and unrefined thing," Denn said. "This blade is elegant. It was made a very long time ago, at the time of the Old Kings of Pix."

"You mean, before the Doom War?" Jack asked.

"Yes. It is an heirloom passed down in my family. Family legend tells that this sword was wielded at the Battle of Bright."

"Really? By one of your relatives?" Jack asked, impressed. The Battle of Bright was thousands of years ago. That meant the sword was really old.

"Yes, though which ancestor wielded it is long forgotten. It is not of Pixish origin; the swordsmiths who have examined it are sure of that, at least. It is likely of elvish make."

"Is that elvish, the writing on the blade?" Jack asked.

"Likely, though I know no elves who could translate it for me."

"It's cool," Jack said, his eyes tracing the shape of the blade.

"Wield it and it becomes warm soon enough, especially when it drips with the blood of a recently felled goblin."

"No, I meant ... never mind. It's very nice," Jack mumbled.

"Nice? Nice is not the word for it, lad. Sharp, brutal, deadly: those are the right words for it. Go on, take it up, feel the weight of it in your hand."

"Are you serious?" Jack stammered.

"I wouldn't let him touch it if I were you," Harriett warned. "He can't even pick up a razor without cutting himself. Not that he even *needs* to shave; he just does it to show off—"

"Harrie!"

"Shut up?" she said, smirking.

"Yes, please shut up."

"Go on, lad," Denn pressed. "Take it in your hand."

Jack stood and went over to where the sword quiver was propped against Cobalt's saddle. When he took hold of the hilt he was shocked at how heavy it was. As he drew the blade out of the quiver and lifted it up, he could feel the weight of it tugging on his muscles, from his forearm all the way up to his shoulders. Wielding this thing would take some serious strength, especially in a fight. With both hands he raised it so that it was horizontal to his body. His arms trembled with the strain of it but he ignored that and attempted a jab at the air in front of him. Gravity took control and the weighty sword tipped toward the ground so that he almost dropped it. Harriett stifled a snicker.

"You have never wielded a blade before?" Denn asked, though Jack's performance had already confirmed that fact.

"No," Jack said, placing the sword gently back against the saddle bags.

"How do you expect to survive in Fellwood forest, let alone the black fortress of Pitmouth, unarmed and with no fighting skill whatsoever?" Denn's shock at the complete lack of forethought on their part showed equally in his voice and on his face.

"I … I don't know," Jack answered, defeated.

After a pause, Denn said, "Not to worry, lad, we have a long journey ahead of us. I will see to it that you learn how to wield a sword. If you're not completely useless, by the time we reach Pitmouth you should be able to defend yourself."

"Oh, Denn," Harriett said with a grin, "you're going to be very disappointed."

After that Denn took up guard position by the doorway. While he watched the door, Jack and Harriett whispered to each other about what had happened to them so far and their next move, into Fellwood Forest. The clip-clopping of Cobalt's hooves around the chamber covered their voices whilst adding a strange but comforting music to the darkness.

"I don't feel so frightened having Denn and Cobalt with us," Harriett whispered.

"I feel the same. But still, we need to have a plan."

"Isn't the plan to go to Pitmouth and get the Keysong?" Harriett asked.

"Yes, but I mean we need a plan for eventualities."

"For what?" Harriett asked, a little too loudly.

"For whatever unpredictable stuff might happen," Jack hissed. "Like, what will we do if we run into goblins?"

"Ask Denn to kill them?" Harriett's face was serious.

"Well yes, but what will *we* do? I hate the idea of depending on Denn, or anyone else, like we're helpless and out of control. We need to look after ourselves."

"Okay, so what will we do?"

"We have to use what we have and what we know."

"But we don't have anything and we don't know nothing."

"Don't know *anything*," Jack corrected.

"That's what I said."

"No, Harrie … oh never mind. What I mean is we have learnt some things, like about the hearth ward, and we have the torc from Amallayne—"

"And the seeing stone," Harriett added.

"And we know that the pentagram wards off Dark Elves

and goblins. We've learnt all kinds of stuff. And the torc can supposedly answer our questions. That's a pretty good start I'd say!"

"Don't forget about Mum's old book, *The Word of Thullu*. It's got to have stuff in it that can help us."

"I forgot about the book! All in all, I think we shouldn't be too worried. Denn will handle all the nasty stuff, you know, the warrior stuff, and we can help out by using our magical objects and what we've learned."

"That sounds like a good plan," Harriett yawned, her eyelids looking heavy. "It's just a shame you can't open a Way to Pitmouth. That'd be a lot easier."

"It would," Jack whispered, "but nothing in Anwynn seems easy and I'd rather not tip off Serza to where we are He senses it when I open a Way."

Harriett didn't respond, just nodded, sighed and fell into a deep sleep. Jack lay awake for a long while, thinking, going over in his head all the things they'd learnt since crossing the Veil, and pondering how he and Harriett might use the objects they'd acquired in case of emergencies. He wished he could plumb his mother's book for more information but the tomb was just too dark. He eased it out of Harriett's jacket anyway and flicked through the pages, comforted by the fact that their mother had left them something useful. Though he couldn't see clearly, he thought the book was opening on the same page over and over, just as it had in Mog's house. He couldn't make out what the page was about but could tell it was the first page of a chapter with a heading. Part of the heading was the word 'Power' but that was all he could read. The book would have to wait till morning.

After a while his mind turned to the earwisp, Ting. He wondered why she was being so quiet. A brief hope flared: maybe she'd been dislodged from his ear when Amallayne transported them from Songarielle to the tomb! Jack hoped that was the case. He would give anything not to be possessed anymore. As he lay there, making plans for how he might protect Harriett and himself in case of a sudden goblin attack, and feeling very relieved that Denn had promised to teach him how to fight with a sword, he slowly slipped into sleep.

❧ ❧

When Jack woke the next morning he had a sore, crick neck. He soon discovered why when he looked up and saw Cobalt eating the very last of his grass pillow. The sight of a huge blue horse eating your pillow first thing in the morning was certainly not a pleasant one.

"Oi! Cobalt, get away from my pillow!" The horse whinnied and playfully trotted away, as if eating someone's pillow and giving them a crick neck was a great game. Jack rubbed his eyes and lifted himself up on his elbows to look around. The brazier was still aglow with red coals and the door to the tomb was still closed. Denn, accompanied by Harriett, looked like he was just about to unbolt the door. "What time is it?" Jack asked.

"Just after dawn," Denn answered. "The sun is high enough now to make it safe for us to venture out."

"Did anything happen during the night?" Jack asked, amazed at how deeply he'd slept on the grass bed.

"Nothing. It was a strangely uneventful evening."

"Why strangely uneventful?" Harriett asked as Denn slid the heavy bolt aside.

"In this part of the world a night without goblins is unusual."

"Maybe they're on holidays," Harriett mused.

"Or perhaps they have other tasks at hand, which worries me," Denn said.

"Why?" Jack asked.

"Goblins are creatures of habit. When they change their habits even a little it means they've found something more wicked to entertain them."

Denn swung open the tomb doors. The gentle light of early morning poured into the chamber, bringing with it a cool, fresh breeze filled with the scent of grass. Jack joined Denn and Harriett at the doorway and looked out. The sky was the brilliant magenta of dawn, peppered with darker ruby clouds. The rolling plains of Pix glimmered with early morning dew, and the crisp light of the rising sun cast long shadows behind gnarled trees and caused the dew to shimmer at the crest of the low hills, making them appear to be golden waves with peaks of pink.

"So beautiful," Harriett sighed.

"This is a golden land," Denn said, "once the treasure of Pix, now abandoned, empty. All the millennia of trouble and violence at the hands of goblins and Vellenor have not dimmed its beauty at all. But Morrigan never ventured this far south. She struck directly north from Vellenhive to Amaltor. That is why the Empty Lands, once as beautiful as this, are now a wasteland. Morrigan's feet have despoiled the soil and her voice poisoned the very air."

"Vellenhive? We've never heard of that before," Jack said.

"It is the name given to the hidden palace of the Dark Prince of Fellwood. Thousands of Vellenor, and their goblin servants, dwell there. It is rumoured to be like a vast ant nest, carved into black stone, deep among the Banewood trees in the darkest part of Fellwood Forest."

"Banewood?" Jack asked.

"A wicked tree," Denn explained. "They grow overly large on blood fed them by the Dark Elves."

"What?" Jack gasped as Harriett, frightened, took his hand.

"The Vellenor of Fellwood have long watered the Banewood with blood to grow them ever larger. They are monstrous plants indeed. Some say the oldest ones have minds of their own."

"And we're going in there?" Harriett asked, swallowing nervously.

"We must. To reach Pitmouth, Fellwood has to be crossed," Denn said resignedly.

"Is it very far?" Harriett moaned.

"It is many days travel," Denn explained, "and our route will take us through the very heart of Fellwood and along the edge of Swampmere."

"Swampmere is where Bonemound is, isn't it?" Jack asked.

"Yes, Swampmere is a vast marsh. In the centre of the marsh is an island on which Bonemound sits, the home of Hect and her followers, the Dread."

"Why is it called Bonemound?" Harriett asked, swallowing hard once more.

"Because it is a mound made of bones," Denn said, "built up over thousands of years to form the island on which the temple of the Dread sorcerers was built. The Dread are fewer in number these days, but there are still enough of them to make me want to steer clear of Bonemound, not the least because it is the high temple of all dark sorcerers."

"So, Pitmouth, it's in the Swampmere, near the Spinepeaks? We saw a map," Jack explained in response to a questioning expression from Denn.

"Yes, the goblins nest in the caves above Morrigan's tomb, which is deep under the Spinepeak Mountains. Pitmouth is ruled by Krungle, the goblin king, who is ally to both Bonemound and Fellwood. But he is a coward and is more servant to the Vellenor than equal. Soon he will be a dead coward."

Jack and Harriett stared up at Denn. The look of steely determination on his chiselled face made them feel glad they were not goblins. In fact his face was so determined they had no doubt that King Krungle's days were numbered. Denn looked down at them and smiled.

"Enough talk of dark things," he said, forcing a smile. "It is a beautiful morning and we are not in Fellwood yet. Let's eat some breakfast and prepare for our journey."

After a breakfast of dried bread and cheese, Denn repacked his saddle bags and cleaned up the ash left by the brazier. Jack and Harriett sat on a small slope nearby, close to

Cobalt who was grazing happily beneath the morning sun, his blue coat an almost perfect match for the sky above. Jack flipped through the pages of his mother's old book, looking for information that might be useful in their journey through Fellwood. Once again, the book kept opening on one passage:

> The greatest of the Waycallers do not rely on the magic of stones to open the Way. They become the Way. In so becoming, the Waycaller gains the Three Exalted Powers that are beyond ordinary sorcery and magic. The Three Powers are the Power of Coming and Going, the Power of Seeing by Touch and the Power of Breaking the Cord. The least of the powers is the Power of Coming and Going, of movement, the First Power. The First Power is the ability to travel from place to place at will, and to magically move objects with the mind.
>
> To such a one only the Way Between the Two Realms must be undertaken through stone circles, and only through the Great Waypoints, the circles of Bright in Anwynn and Cairnbawn in the otherworld that form the bridge between the worlds. The Waycaller who has become the Way can use the First Power to banish their enemies to the vast pits of Uffern, where the Pale Mother serves her eternal sentence locked behind Darkgate.

If Jack could just work out what this passage meant, he thought they might actually stand a chance of completing their quest alive. But how could he *become* the Way? What did that even mean? He'd also really like to know how to use his power to banish his enemies to the pit of Uffern. That would be a really handy trick, especially as they were about to go into Fellwood and encounter who knows what. He read the passage over and over, but the words remained just as impenetrable and vague. He flicked through the book looking for more about the 'Three Exalted Powers'. How might he use them to keep Harriett and himself alive? He couldn't find anything by just scanning. He would have to read the book from cover to cover.

Harriett had grown bored watching Jack read and sat fondling the copper torc given to her by Amallayne. She slipped it on and off, judging how well it fit. Jack watched her slide it on and off a dozen times before she decided it looked best on her left hand. She raised her arm to look at the bracelet in the sun.

"I wonder how this thing works," she mused aloud, jangling the bangle in Jack's face. Jack took hold of her wrist to take a better look at the torc. Maybe it had writing on it, some kind of instructions?

As soon as Jack's fingers touched the torc, his vision filled with sparkling silver light. The grass sparkled, the trees shimmered. It was as if every atom of the world around him had become particles of glitter. Harriett gasped. The look on her face told him that she was experiencing the same thing. The glittering silver light obscured everything in sight— Cobalt, the Tomb of the Old Oracles of Senn and even the sky and the rolling plains—leaving just Jack and Harriett in a glittering halo. The light pulsed and grew even brighter, turning almost white. This whiter light took hold of him and Harriett and dragged them into itself. Jack resisted, not knowing what might happen if he allowed himself to be drawn away by the light, but he wasn't strong enough. The harder he resisted the harder the light dragged on him. A second later, he couldn't resist anymore and felt himself and Harriett being pulled rapidly away, as if his body had become light and was racing through a glittering, light-filled universe.

When Jack's vision returned he was no longer sitting on the small rise by the Oracle's tomb. He was in a huge circular dome made of flat grey stones. He was still holding onto Harriett's wrist. The ceiling above them was lost in shadow. Small oval windows set high in the curved walls let in late afternoon sunshine, which streamed in to strike the flagstone floor. The chamber was empty of furnishings, bar a single, very simple wooden bench at one end, directly opposite a closed door at the other, also oval.

"At least we know we're still in Pix," Harriett said, gesturing around them. She was right. The building's style was clearly Pixish.

"The question is not where you are, my girl, but *when* you are," a female voice said from a dark shadow beyond the simple wooden bench.

Jack and Harriett stared into the shadow. A cloaked figure walked out into the dim light, skin glowing, emitting a silver halo. Harriett raised her own hand and saw that her skin was also glowing silver.

"This is not your true body," the figure, a woman by the voice, explained in response to Harriett's fascination with her glowing hand. "These bodies were created by the torc to facilitate the visions. They are simply projections." The woman's voice was kind and gentle. She was wearing a white dress-coat beneath a blue hooded cloak. Her eyes were in the shadow of her drawn hood. Even so, something about her instantly allayed Jack's anxiety about being transported to some strange place.

"Are you ... are you an Oracle?" Harriett asked, her icy eyes wide with awe.

"You judge well, little girl. But I do, after all, wear the garb of the Oracle and this building is the Oracular Hall in Pixett, where the Pixish come to seek my guidance." The woman took a few steps toward the wooden bench and sat, patting the space beside her for Harriett to join her there. Harriett tentatively walked across the flagstones and, pausing for just a moment to ensure it was okay, sat down. Jack followed her over but remained standing. He felt that he shouldn't be there, that this was something only Harriett was meant to see.

"So, where ... I mean, *when*, am I?" Harriett asked the woman.

"You are out of your own time. You have travelled here by use of the torc." The woman indicated the torc on Harriett's hand and then raised her arm to show Harriett the very same torc on her own wrist.

"But, how can it be on your wrist and on mine at the same time?" Harriett asked.

"The torc has carried you, and me, into the timeless in-between."

"The timeless in-between?" Harriett echoed.

"Yes. The normal rules of the universe do not apply here, thus the torc can be on your wrist and mine."

"Why did it bring you here?" Harriett asked.

"Because I am the only person able to answer your question."

"About how the torc works?"

"Yes. I alone hold that knowledge."

"So, how does it work then?"

"It is very simple really, once you get the hang of it. But there are some rules. The torc can show you things from the past, the present and the future. It can also bring you here, to the timeless in-between, where you may converse with the Oracles who, at other times, wore the bracelet. The torc only responds to its rightful owner, that person who was granted the torc by Amallayne. It can be used to foresee dangers ahead, to understand the current state of things and to better know the past. However, the torc will not allow itself to be used to gain riches or power. Do you understand?"

"Yes, I think so," Harriett answered.

Jack could see that Harriett felt an instant trust for this woman. He felt much the same. Something in the woman's bearing communicated kindness and care. She also seemed very familiar. "But, say I want to know a safe way somewhere, like through Fellwood Forest. What should I do?"

"To see something, you simply ask the torc to show you. Just say 'Show me the path through Fellwood Forest as it is now and will be' and the torc will show you. You will then be able to plot a safe course."

"That *is* quite easy," Harriett said, relieved.

"Yes, but be wary of overuse. Going backwards and forwards in time can lead to confusion. It is important to always keep clearly in your mind what is past, what is now and what is yet to be. Confusing the three times can lead to disaster. Also, do not speak much of what you see in the future, for others may act on what you tell them, thus changing the future and rendering your vision useless." Jack could see Harriett's mind working as she took this in, and then remembered what Amallayne had told them about the bracelet.

"Amallayne said something about the Oracles using the torc to show others their visions," he said quietly. "Is that why I'm here?"

"Yes, Jack. You were holding the torc when it carried Harriett here. Whoever is touching the torc will see the vision," the Oracle explained.

"Oh, that's cool," Harriett said, looking into the woman's face, searching under the hood for her eyes. "I feel like I know you," she said. The oracle didn't respond, remaining still beneath her blue hood.

The thought of his parents, and the warm familiarity emanating from this hooded woman, caused Jack to ask another question, even though he barely dared to hope that the Oracle would be able to answer it.

"Do you ... do you know where our mother is?" As he asked, he was overwhelmed by a rush of sadness and found tears welling in his eyes. He wiped them away and looked down to see that Harriett was wiping tears away from her eyes as well.

"Our Dad," Harriett said. "Our dad was killed, but we don't really know what happened to him. And our mother, she disappeared when I was just a baby. I only have Jack now, and I love him but ... but—"

"But you wish you still had your parents?" the woman whispered. Harriett nodded, reaching out and taking Jack's hand, clearly unable to speak any further on the subject. "I cannot tell you much – as an Oracle I am bound not to endanger the future by speaking of it. I can only guide by hints, by clues."

"Clues? Like in a crossword puzzle?" Harriett sniffled through the words.

"Something like that. Child, do not despair. Your mother's destiny is not yet decided. She lives and you may be reunited yet."

A smile spontaneously bloomed on Harriett's face. Jack felt that smile mirrored on his own lips.

"That is not to say she is not in danger," the Oracle added in response to Harriett's and Jack's evident relief. "Much is still to pass before I can tell you more, but know this: if you follow your heart, and never lose hope no matter what difficulties arise, you and your mother may one day be reunited. That said, much must unfold before that reunion can take place."

"*May* be reunited? Does that mean it isn't for sure?" Harriett asked.

"Nothing is certain, torc-bearer, but I do not think it is your destiny to be an orphan."

Jack's heart filled with a warm sensation. He thought this sensation must be hope. As he mulled over what the Oracle said, he noticed that the flagstone floor had started to glimmer silver. He looked up and saw that the walls of the beehive-shaped hall were also permeated by the glittering light. "What's happening?"

"Harriett's question is answered," the Oracle said. "You will now return to your time."

"But ... but I want to ask a lot more ... and how do you know our names?" Harriett stuttered.

Before the Oracle could answer, the silver light began pulling Jack and Harriett away. The last thing Jack saw was the Oracle lowering her hood, revealing eyes of the palest, snowy blue. Harriett gasped; she'd seen it too. Then their bodies were light again and they were racing through a glittering universe.

When the silver light subsided he and Harriett were exactly where they'd been before, sitting together on a low rise beneath an early morning sun. It felt distinctly like they had not moved at all. Harriett took off the torc and looked around in surprise.

"Jack," she whispered, "was that real? Because if it wasn't, I think Denn must have fed us some of Cobalt's blue mushrooms for breakfast." She sniggered and Jack joined her.

"No, it was definitely real."

"How long were we gone?"

"I don't think any time passed," Jack said, perplexed.

"Is that possible? To go somewhere else, I mean *sometime* else, and no time pass?"

"One thing I've learned about Anwynn: anything is possible."

"Jack, she said that one day we might see Mum again! Isn't that great?"

"Yeah, if it's true. How could she know that though?" Jack wanted to believe it as much as Harriett, and she was so desperate not to be an orphan that she would believe anything. He had to remain objective though, stay cautious. It wouldn't help either of them to cling to a desperate hope. "Weren't all the Oracles from a long time ago, like thousands of years?"

"Yes, they were. I don't know how she knew. Maybe she looked into the future and saw it—"

"Harriett, I know you want to believe that we'll see Mum again, and I want to believe that too, but we can't dwell on that now. It'll just upset us." He took a deep breath. "We have to go to Pitmouth and—"

"Find the Keysong."

"Yes. We can't afford to be distracted by anything else. We've got to have our wits about us. It's not like at home. If we get distracted here things could get really scary."

"What kind of scary?"

"*Dead* scary," Jack said seriously. "We could die, Harrie."

"Alright, I'll try and focus. But I'm not giving up hope. I know we'll see Mum again." As she said this she must've seen in Jack's eyes that he still couldn't let himself believe it fully. "Poor Jack," she said, "always so gloomy."

"I hope we see Mum again, Harrie, I really do. But hope doesn't make things real."

"Maybe in our world that's true, Jack, but not here in Anwynn. Here hope does make things real."

"Magic makes things real. Magic and hope are not the same thing."

"That's how much you know, Jack. Hope and magic *are* the same thing." Harriett had that look on her face that told him he would never change her mind.

"I can see by the freaky glint in your eyes that you're not going to listen to me, so just go ahead and believe what you want. Just don't make me listen to you prattle on about it."

"Speaking of freaky eyes, did you see the Oracle's eyes? They were weird: really pale blue, nearly white."

Jack realised then that Harriett didn't know that her eyes had changed colour. How could she? There were no mirrors in the tomb and he hadn't told her. Worse still, she didn't know that she had been close to death and that Jack had used magic to save her, potentially altering her very nature. What should he do? Should he tell her and risk scaring her half to death? She would find out soon enough. Eventually someone would mention her eyes and then she would know that Jack had kept it from her. He decided to tell her about the eyes at least. The possibility that she was changed on a deeper level he would keep secret until he had no choice but to tell her. He might never have to say anything, Amallayne had said that Harriett might not be changed after all. A dark thought flashed in his mind. He saw Harriett lying at his feet, the bloody sword in his hands. Was that scene the result of his using magic to return Harriett from the brink of death? Had he made her into some kind of monster? Would she become something so terrible that one day he would be forced to kill her, to kill his own sister? He shuddered and cast that thought from his mind. No, Harriett was just Harriett. It was only her eyes that had changed, nothing more. He banished any doubt that she was anything other than ordinary, hyperactive Harriett from his mind and turned to tell her about her eyes.

"Harrie, her eyes were exactly like yours."

"Don't be silly, Jack. My eyes are the same colour as yours."

"Not anymore."

"What are you talking about?"

"Back in Amallayne's temple, there was an explosion, and you were hurt pretty bad."

"I know, I've still got the lump to prove it." She rubbed at a place at the base of her skull, ruffling her already messy black hair.

"When you were unconscious, I was pretty worried you were ... that you were hurt really bad, so I called on the Way to save you—"

"Can you do that? Use the Way to heal people?"

"Apparently. Anyway, I called on the Way to heal you and when you woke up, well, your eyes had changed colour."

"Seriously?"

"Seriously. They're very pale blue, almost white."

"Like ... like the Oracle's?"

"Yes, exactly the same."

"But, how could we have the same eyes?"

"I don't know, but her eyes were just like yours, and sort of familiar. Really familiar actually."

"I thought she was familiar too. I was sure I knew her, but how could I?"

Jack stopped himself from telling her what had just arisen in his mind – that the reason for the oracle having eyes like Harriett's was because she was their mother, that she had gone through an ordeal similar to Harriett's and been changed by it. Jack dared not hope such a thing might be true, let alone speak it out loud. There was too much to discount it. Their mother was not an Oracle and would not be as old as that woman was. Nevertheless, Jack couldn't dislodge the feeling that the Oracle was not a stranger.

"Are you two ready to go?" Denn shouted from beside the tomb where he had caught and begun to re-saddle Cobalt.

"Yes," Jack and Harriett shouted back in unison. They

rose and dusted their clothes of grass and twigs. As Jack headed down to Denn, Harriett grabbed his hand to stop him.

"It can't be a bad thing that she had the same colour eyes as me," she said a little shakily. "I mean, she was good, wasn't she? One of the good guys?"

"Yes, I think she was." For a moment Jack contemplated telling her the whole truth.

"She told us how to use the torc to find a safe way through Fellwood," Harriett continued, "that's got to mean she's good."

"Yeah, that's right," Jack said, his spirits lifting a little. He wanted to say something to Harriett to reassure her but before he found the right words Denn distracted him.

"Are you two planning to come down from that hill any time before dusk?" he called.

"Sorry," Jack and Harriett called back before jogging down the hill to join him.

"We need to set out for Fellwood before we lose anymore daylight," Denn explained as they gathered around Cobalt. "Believe me, you do not want your first glimpse of that foul wood to be in the dark of night."

INTO FELLWOOD FOREST

They rode through the undulating grassland of southern Pix, all three mounted on Cobalt's sturdy blue back. Although Jack found riding on Cobalt's back much less challenging than riding a dragon, especially one soaring high in a night sky, it was nevertheless uncomfortable, especially for three. Jack was seated in front of Denn, wedged between the horseman and the saddle horn, which poked him in the stomach whenever Cobalt lurched down a hill. After the first hour Jack found that the rolling hills had totally lost their appeal. He'd developed a strong irritation for everything to do with the place, having been forced to sit in this uncomfortable position because of a Pixish custom.

"No Pixish horseman allows another man, or lad over a certain age, to ride behind him in the saddle," Denn had explained. "It is not proper for two males of age to share a saddle at all, but as you are *horseless* we have no choice." Denn had made the word 'horseless' sound like an accusation, as if being horseless meant that Jack was somehow unmanly. "You will sit forward in the saddle, and the girl-child in the rear. That way I will keep my dignity."

Riding in front of Denn, like a girl, made Jack flush red. He didn't say anything though, far too proud to admit his discomfort, but squirmed in the saddle and winced whenever the horn went a little too close to his groin.

"What are you doing, boy," Denn growled, "trying to unseat the lot of us?"

"No, just avoiding getting gored to death by this stupid saddle horn!"

Harriett snorted from behind Denn, which made Jack fume. By the time they topped another small golden hill and saw ahead of them a vast, green expanse of forest, Jack was convinced he would never walk properly again.

"There it is." Denn sighed. "Fellwood Forest, the most

loathsome forest in all the world."

"How big is it?" Harriett asked from behind Denn, sounding awed. The forest stretched all the way to the horizon in every direction.

"Immense," Denn replied. "Bigger than any of the four kingdoms, bigger even than the Dominion of Elves. To cross it from end to end would take many months. Thankfully we need only cross a portion of it to reach Pitmouth."

Denn urged Cobalt down the rise. Jack winced as the downward movement sent the saddle horn probing into his upper thigh. When they reached the edge of the forest a narrow gap in the wall of trees came into view, marked on either side by man-sized standing stones.

The stones bore carved versions of curved swords arranged to form a kind of three-legged swastika. Jack thought it looked like a mark of warning for all those who dared to enter Fellwood uninvited. Beyond the stones, a narrow path led into the green darkness, more like a tunnel than a path. Cobalt, wary of the menacing overhang of the trees, stamped his hooves, hesitating at the tree line.

"We shall pause here a while," Denn said. "There are often goblins and Dark Elves abroad, just within the forest. We will listen and watch to be sure it is safe to enter."

Denn dismounted and then helped Harriett down. Jack slid down by himself, his legs stiff and tingling. Denn squatted down before the gap into the forest, peering into the gloom, and stayed that way for some time, still as a stone.

Harriett soon grew restless, as Jack knew she would, and led him away from Denn for a whispered conversation.

"Do you think now we're literally on the verge of entering the forest, we should test out the torc, you know, to see if we can find a safe way through?"

"Yeah, I suppose that makes sense."

Harriett reached into her pocket, pulled out the torc and slipped it on. She held her hand out to Jack, who took hold of her wrist.

"Do you remember what the Oracle said about how to

use the torc to show us a safe path?" she whispered.

"Yes, she said to just ask."

"Show me the path through Fellwood Forest as it is now and will be."

Jack was surprised that Harriett had remembered the words perfectly. Almost immediately the world around them turned to particles of glitter emanating a powerful silver light. The silver light took hold of them and drew them into it. Next thing, the glowing silver forms of himself and Harriett were flying through the trees, as if glowing birds, soaring along above the path through the forest. But he was not seeing the forest and the path as a solid thing, but rather as if he were seeing two visions of the forest superimposed one onto the other. He realised that he must be seeing the present and the future at once.

They flew through the forest for what must've been hours and saw not a sign or a hint of goblin, Vellenor or anything else. They continued forward until, a couple of hours of flying later, they reached a juncture of pathways, a crude crossroads in the middle of a very dark section of the forest. In the centre of the crossroads was a stone marker bearing strange carvings. Jack and Harriett were drawn towards the marker, descended to the ground and landed before it. The marker had two symbols on it: one indicating the path to the right, the other the path directly ahead. The symbol indicating the path directly ahead looked to Jack like three human thigh bones with two of the bones crossed diagonally over a third vertical one to form a kind of six-armed cross. As Harriett stepped closer to investigate the stone, a party of at least a hundred goblins emerged from the glowing light to the left, led by two vicious-looking Vellenor warriors, their scimitar-shaped swords hanging at their sides. The elves were not completely solid and it was clear that Jack and Harriett were invisible to them. This led Jack to believe that the elves existed in the future.

For some reason, both Jack and Harriett's attention was drawn back in the direction from whence they came. They both looked over their shoulders. Just yards back and approaching the crossroads, completely unaware of the dark beings coming from the other direction, were ghostly versions of Denn, Jack and Harriett astride Cobalt. They were also not completely solid, also of the future. Jack knew instantly that the two parties would come upon each other at the crossroads and that there were far too many goblins for Denn to handle alone. He began to panic. Harriett spoke then, startling him.

"Show me what will happen if we hide before the crossroads and wait for the goblins to pass." Again, Jack was surprised at how perfectly Harriett had phrased the question. As soon as she said this the vision shimmered and Jack watched as the ghostly versions of himself, Denn, and Harriett dismounted and left the path, leading a reluctant Cobalt by the reins. They hid among the trees, just back from the crossroads. The goblins emerged into the juncture only seconds later and continued on to the right, completely unaware that Denn and the others were hiding nearby. After a sufficient wait the ghostly trio emerged from their hiding place and continued cautiously on their way. Jack and Harriett also resumed flying forward in the direction indicated by the symbol of the cross of three bones.

Another hour later they came to a particularly large and rotten-looking tree that forced the path to curve around it. As with the road marker, the tree demanded their attention. Its limbs looked like the twisted arms of a giant and its roots like creeping tentacles. Was this a Banewood? As they moved closer to the tree a black fog formed all around them and Jack's vision dimmed. He felt a sense of menace. Lurking amongst the dark fog he thought he could see the stealthy movements of a small, hooded figure, but couldn't see clearly who it was. Feeling uneasy, he urged Harriett to move away from the tree. Almost immediately, the fog cleared and the sense of menace passed. Perhaps this was how one experienced a Banewood tree when in a vision? What had Denn said, that the Banewoods were rumoured to have minds of their own?

Jack felt them being drawn on again and was soon flying along the path once more, Harriett's silver form beside him. Again, they flew through the forest for about an hour and saw not another sign or hint of goblin or Vellenor. Then they emerged from the forest onto a path that skirted the edge of an enormous marshland. Standing on this path, looking out over the marshland, were the ghostlike figures of Denn, Harriett and himself. They had made it through! Despite goblins and Vellenor and the strange black fog, they had made it through!

All of a sudden everything in Jack's vision froze and, just like in the Oracular Hall, all seemingly solid things started to glimmer silver. The very bark and leaves of the giant trees were permeated by the glittering light. The pools of murky water in the swamp were sparkling as if quicksilver. Harriett's question had been answered. They had been shown a safe path through Fellwood Forest. Then the silver light pulled them away.

Jack found himself exactly where he'd been when Harriett had slipped on the torc, standing apart from Denn, holding his sister's hand with a finger on her bracelet. Harriett took the torc from her wrist and returned it to her pocket. She looked up into his eyes, her pale blue ones full of wonder.

"The Oracle said we shouldn't speak much about the vision," she said, sounding much more mature than her normal self.

"Okay. That was a great idea, Harrie. If we're careful not to mess up the future by talking about it, we'll get through Fellwood safely."

Harriett smiled, her pale eyes shining, clearly pleased with herself.

"Come," Denn said from the edge of the forest. "I have listened long enough. There are no goblins or Dark Elves nearby, at least for now. Into Fellwood we go."

They remounted Cobalt and, at Denn's urging, the blue

stallion carried them into the gloom of Fellwood Forest. As they passed the stone warning markers, and Jack readjusted to the rolling movement of Cobalt's gait, he realised something: in the vision of the future, Cobalt had not been there at the edge of the marshland. A sharp stab of surprise struck at his heart. Was something going to happen to Cobalt? Would the blue horse not make it through the forest? In another few steps of Cobalt's long legs, his worry was replaced with the more pressing worries of the present as the darkness enveloped him and his attention was drawn to the forest around him.

The path was well worn, probably trod for millennia by Vellenor and goblins alike, its surface compacted and firm. The tangle of interlocked boughs and gnarled and twisted tree trunks formed a kind of tunnel through which the path weaved. The canopy overhead was so dense that practically no light penetrated. Not a sound, neither a bird nor the rustle of a breeze, could be heard. Hanging from every twig and branch were long tendrils of grey moss that emitted a faint green glow.

"Haghair," Denn said, nodding at the long tendrils of moss. It was instantly obvious to Jack how it got its name; it looked like the long, tangled locks of an old witch.

Fellwood Forest was a dark, silent place. Its immense age, colossal vastness and dense silence weighed down on the party as if they were shouldering the canopy above on their very own backs. It was also cold, devoid as it was of sunlight.

"How do the Vellenor live in here?" Jack asked. "It's miserable."

"The Vellenor wallow in misery. They are a morose breed. They love the dark and the cold," Denn said quietly.

"But they're elves, so they can go out in the sunlight, can't they?" Jack asked. "I mean, they're not like goblins that die in the daylight?"

"The Vellenor can go out in daylight, though they rarely do. Their eyes are adjusted to gloom and so they do not fare well in the bright of day."

As they pressed further into the forest, the path bending slightly to the left and downwards, it grew even darker and more silent. What little light that had fallen on the path from the gap in the trees where they entered had vanished. Now there was no light at all, bar that emanating from the luminous haghair. The only sound was the slow clod of Cobalt's hooves on the compacted earth and the hushed rhythms of their own breathing. They rode in silence for long moments, each of their hearts feeling the burden of such an unhappy place.

"It's really depressing in here," Harriett whispered, stating what they were all feeling. Jack didn't answer. The gloom of Fellwood made him ill-disposed to talk.

They did not stop for lunch. Denn simply pulled some dry bread out of his saddle bag and they chewed on it astride Cobalt as they continued on their way through the forest. Denn thought, and Jack agreed with him, that the quicker they got through Fellwood the better. As it was, it would be days before they saw sunlight again. They rode through the afternoon until it was so dark that they could barely make out the shapes of the trees around them.

"We best make camp here," Denn said, "before it is so dark that we can't see well enough even to light a fire."

They dismounted and left the path, Jack moving very awkwardly, his thighs so bruised and sore that he'd become bow-legged, like an aged cowboy. Jack spotted Denn and Harriett watching him waddling about, smirking at each other, and braced himself for the inevitable jibes.

"Are your pants too tight, lad? Or are you just walking that way for amusement?" Denn said, chuckling.

"Go to hell," Jack replied. "Your obsession with dignity has disfigured me! I'll never father children!"

Harriett and Denn laughed out loud, their voices echoing among the dense knot of trees, cutting through the gloom.

"Perhaps," Denn said, chortling, "but I think that was always in doubt. If I were you I wouldn't be blaming the saddle. I'd be looking to your hair and its adverse effect on the lasses. Even a lad as well-formed and good looking as you won't win a lass with that bird's nest."

"Shut up," Jack spat as he hobbled ahead, leaving them to laugh behind his back.

Just a few yards off the path they found a small space in-between two large trees where there was just enough room for them to gather. Denn tied Cobalt to one of the trees and set about building a lean-to.

He gathered branches, vines and huge clumps of the glowing haghair and, directing Jack and Harriett to help him, fastened poles between the trees using the vine as rope to form the square framework of a rudimentary roof. Using other branches, Denn made a cross-hatch ceiling on top of which he piled the moss and other leafy branches. Before long they were beneath what, though not exactly solid, was definitely a shelter. It was a bit rough and ready for Jack's liking, but it was high and wide enough to encompass the whole of the small clearing.

Denn moved Cobalt into the centre of the lean-to and tied his reins to a strong branch that formed part of the ceiling. On either side of Cobalt, Denn, Jack and Harriett piled more haghair to create makeshift beds. Denn took the brazier out of his saddle bag and prepared the fire. It was a tense moment as Denn struck the flint, trying to get a pile of moss to catch light. When it did so, Jack breathed a sigh of relief. Denn added coals to the brazier and soon the shelter was bathed in light and the slight warmth that the fire emitted.

"There, now we are protected by the hearth ward," Denn said, casually scratching his stubbly chin, "but we should remain vigilant. The fire may attract the denizens of the forest. If any come we will still need to defend the shelter. If they manage to burn it down, then we're done for."

After another very unsatisfying dinner of dry bread and old cheese, Jack and Denn took turns sleeping and keeping watch. During Jack's first watch, which started around midnight, he sat staring beyond the fire at the wall of blackness that was Fellwood Forest. The brazier provided enough light to illuminate the shelter but beyond that Jack could barely make out the trunk of the nearest tree. It seemed to him that Fellwood swallowed all light and sound, like some huge, many limbed monster.

He huddled close to the brazier, trying to keep warm by the meagre heat of its fire, his stomach grumbling with hunger. He thought back over the many and varied dishes of food that Miss Butters had provided. He wished that she was with them now, both because she'd proven herself reliable in an emergency and also because she could cook up a storm. What he wouldn't do for one of Miss Butters' amazing cheese dumplings right now.

Thinking about Miss Butters caused him to remember what Daniselle had said about halflings being tough, and Miss Butters being tougher than most. He wondered what she'd meant by that. With unease he recalled that Wadget and Aelf were manipulating Miss Butters for unknown reasons. He realised that if Wadget and Aelf were manipulating her, then the Order of Druids must be behind it.

Was this why Kashashem, the Head of the Order of Druids, had wanted to speak with Miss Butters after their meeting in the Druid Chambers? Jack felt a slight sadness rise. Perhaps he would never know what the Order wanted of Miss Butters. Perhaps he would never see the halfling again. Who knew what was going to befall any of them? None of them might survive. Amallayne had said the odds of one of them perishing were high.

Jack dwelt on these thoughts and stared out into the blackness of the forest. For all he knew, the cause of their demise could be lurking out there right now, watching them, waiting for an opportunity to pounce.

He nervously stoked the coals and got them burning a little brighter, hoping to ward off whatever evil might be hiding in the shadows among the trees. He checked each direction for any hint of movement. There was nothing, just a wall of still, silent darkness. Then something grabbed hold of his shoulder. He spun around, fists raised, ready to fight whatever had grabbed him.

WHISPERS IN THE DARK

"Harriett! You nearly scared me half to death!" Jack dropped his fists, puffing with relief.

"I'm sorry, but I need to pee," Harriett said in a whisper, her pale blue eyes anxious. "I need to pee real bad. I've been holding it in for ages and I just can't hold it in any longer."

"Why were you holding it in?" Jack asked, bewildered. In answer to his question Harriett motioned to the wall of darkness surrounding them.

"I didn't want to go out there," she said, jigging from one foot to another, her face full of discomfort.

"Well, just go in here, over there at the edge of the shelter."

"Are you mad, Jack? What if Denn wakes up? I'm not peeing in front of anybody, not him and not you either."

"Harrie, this is no time to be prudish."

"I'm not being prudish! I just really need to pee. Can't you take me, Jack? Just a little way out."

"No way, I'm not leaving the shelter and neither are you."

"But Jack, I'm going to wet my pants! Please?" Harriett's jiggling from foot to foot intensified and so Jack, against all better judgement, got up and led her to the edge of the shelter.

"Keep your eyes and ears peeled," he warned. "At the first hint of trouble we're racing back here full pelt."

"Okay," Harriett said.

"I mean it, Harrie, any sense at all that there's something out there and we run straight back here and wake up Denn."

"Okay, okay, can we just go now?"

Perhaps it was just in his mind but the minute they stepped out from under the shelter, and away from the protection of the hearth ward, Jack felt a sense of doom descend. They crossed out into the darkness and walked slowly toward the shadowed hulk of the nearest tree. Jack looked back to the shelter with its small fire and slumbering Denn, just a few feet distant, but seemingly a world away.

"Okay, this is far enough. Go behind this tree," Jack said. Harriett didn't need to be told twice. She hurried behind the tree and was enveloped in darkness. Jack couldn't see her but could hear her rustling around. "Hurry up, Harriett," he said, looking about. "I don't like being out here one bit." She didn't answer. Jack waited and listened. The rustling had stopped. There was just silence. "Harriett?" Jack called softly. "Harriett!"

"I'm kind of busy," her little voice answered from close-by. Jack tingled with relief.

"Just talk to me so I know you're okay," Jack said.

"Okay," she said before slipping into silence again. Jack waited a moment but still she hadn't said anything more.

"Harriett?"

"What?"

"I told you to talk so I know you're alright!"

"It's very hard to do two things at once, Jack!"

"Well just hurry up," Jack said, casting his eyes back to the safety of the shelter. The longer they spent in the darkness the more tense he felt.

As he stood there waiting he heard something very alarming. Another small voice, but not that of his sister. *Jack,* the voice said in his ear, *go back to the fire, the forest isn't safe.*

"Oh no," Jack moaned, more because Ting's voice had returned than because of the warning she'd given him.

"What's the matter?" Harriett asked from the darkness. At the same time, Ting hissed in his ear: *Something comes! Quickly, back to the fire.*

"Harriett, we've got to get back!" There was a rustling and Harriett appeared at his side. Together they rushed back to the safety of the hearth fire. As soon as they crossed under the lip of the shelter they felt the sense of safety embrace them. Peering back out into the darkness, they couldn't see anything but somewhere off in the gloom they heard a muffled sound, as if something were shuffling through fallen leaves on the muddy ground.

"What is it, Jack?" Harriett asked.

"I don't know," Jack answered, thinking of the hooded figure that he'd first seen on the journey to Wadget's house, and then again in the dark lane in Songarielle. As he stared into the shadows, trying to make anything out, Ting whispered in his ear again. *It does not come closer. Perhaps some forest thing on its own business. We are safe here.*

"Can you see anything, Jack?" Harriett asked.

"No, I think we're okay. It was nothing. Go back to bed."

"Okay," Harriett said. "Oh, and thanks for taking me to, umm, you know."

"That's okay. But next time go during the day."

Harriett nodded in acquiescence and lay back down on her bed of haghair. Jack sat by the brazier and waited for her to fall asleep, his heart pounding. Once Harriett's breathing was slow and even, he whispered in the direction of his left ear.

"I thought you were gone."

Oh no, not me, Ting answered smugly. *I'm not going anywhere.*

"Great," Jack said, feeling the anxiety of being possessed all over again.

Not to worry, Jack, Ting giggled. *It's not so bad being an earwisp's host, you'll see.*

"I'd rather not see. Look, wouldn't you be happier with some other host? I mean, I'm a bit dull really."

Oh no, Jack, I love having you as my host! Besides, how can I help you if I leave?

"Help me? Help me what?"

Help you overcome Morrigan, of course, Ting said rather bluntly.

"So you meant what you said at Songarielle? You weren't lying to me?"

No, Jack, I wasn't lying. I care about you and want to help you.

"Well then, show yourself," Jack said. "I'm not in the

habit of talking to people I've never seen."

We don't usually show ourselves to people, Ting said anxiously. *It is frowned upon.*

"Well, if you want to help me then we have to meet each other properly." Jack waited as Ting apparently deliberated whether or not to exit Jack's ear and show herself in her true form. A few minutes passed and then she answered.

Alright, but you have to promise, Jack, you have to promise not to think I'm horrible.

"Okay," Jack said, stealing himself to see something rather awful come out of his ear.

A slight ringing started in Jack's left ear, followed by a curious itchiness around his eardrum. A second later a thin, purple wisp of mist drifted out from his ear and gathered before him by the brazier. As Jack watched, it solidified into the shape of a tiny person. Jack found himself looking into the green eyes of a very small being, no bigger than his hand.

Ting looked like a tiny elf. She was thin, pointy eared, with shaggy, red hair and almond-shaped eyes. She was wearing black tights, a fitted black shirt and pointy black shoes. She looked up at Jack with a coy smile on her lips but a sheepish look in her eyes.

"See, I'm horrible, aren't I?" she asked self-consciously. Her voice had about it a strange quality, as if it was accompanied by the ringing of tiny glass bells.

"No, you're not horrible." Jack said, relieved that this was in fact true. Ting wasn't horrible at all.

"Truthfully?" Ting asked. "You truthfully think me not horrible?"

"I think you're perfectly fine looking," Jack said, unsure what an appropriate response would be.

"What of these tights?" Ting asked, turning to one side to better show her miniscule leggings. "Do they make me look hideous?"

"Ah, no, they don't," Jack said, a little alarmed at the direction their first face-to-face meeting was taking.

"I think they do," Ting sighed, "but it is nice of you to

say that they don't. Even if you do think that nasty she-elf Anarra is prettier than me."

"What does it matter if I do think she's prettier?" Jack asked.

"So you admit it!" Ting shrieked, making Jack instantly regret what he'd said. "You admit you think Anarra is prettier than me!" She dropped down onto her bottom, pulled her knees up to her chest and rocked to-and-fro in an almighty sulk. "I knew it! I knew you liked her more than me!" Jack was totally perplexed. He felt he had been unwittingly drawn into an ambush. He had no idea what this had to do with anything.

"Look," he said cautiously, "I'm not saying I *do* think Anarra is prettier, I'm just asking why it matters—"

"Typical!" Ting sighed. "All hosts are the same in the end! I suppose I couldn't expect you to understand."

"Understand what?" Jack demanded, flabbergasted.

"My feelings, of course!" Ting broke into tiny sobs.

"*Your* feelings!" Jack said, appalled. "Who possessed who?"

"Oh, I just knew you were going to bring *that* up!" Ting broke down into fully-blown weeping. It sounded like the chiming of dozens of miniscule bells. Jack felt instantly guilty, though he was not sure why.

"Look, Ting, let's just start over. Let's try and be friends," he suggested hopefully.

"Truthfully?" Ting asked between sobs. "You truly want to be my friend?"

"Sure, why not?" Jack tentatively agreed, thinking of perhaps a hundred reasons why he shouldn't be friends with an earwisp, particularly an earwisp permanently on the verge of hysteria. Besides, he needed all the friends he could get. After Ting dried her tears, Jack asked her why she wanted to help him and got a rather vague answer.

"If Morrigan is loosed we will all suffer."

"Fair enough," he said. "But, when did you get into my ear?" he asked. "And how did you cross the Veil?"

"I first came into your ear at the moment before the dimming of the sun in your world."

"The eclipse?"

"Yes. As for how I came to be in your world, there are some things I can't tell."

"Did you cross with the skinwearer?" Jack asked.

"No," Ting said firmly. "That thing crossed alone."

"Why can't you tell me?" Jack asked. "You took up residence in my head after all. You kind of owe me."

"Earwisps have many secrets that we can't share. We have many enemies."

"Okay, but can you at least tell me *why* you've moved into my ear?"

"I had to guide you here, to Anwynn. I didn't know the skinwearer would be there. Once I realised it was pursuing you, I had to act quickly to get you to open the Way Between."

"But why did you want us to come here?"

"I was acting on behalf of a friend, a dear friend who wanted to meet you, eventually."

"Your friend?" Jack asked, intrigued. "Who is that?"

"I cannot tell you that." Ting turned her green eyes away, unable to look Jack in the face. "I'm sorry, but that must stay a secret – much depends on it remaining so."

"Let me get this straight: you inhabited my head and brought us to Anwynn all on behalf of your friend, but won't tell me who that is?" He stared at her, amazed.

"Yes," Ting said, digging into the soft ground with the toe of her pointy shoe. "Once you meet my friend, you will understand why it is so important to keep this secret. Until then, you mustn't tell anyone about it," Ting begged. "If anyone finds out about this, we will all be in very grave danger."

"More danger than being hunted by Morrigan and Prince Serza?"

"Oh yes, much, much more danger than that."

"But—"

"Please, trust me, Jack. I would never do anything to hurt you or Harriett, nor would my dear friend. What I just told you must stay secret."

"Okay, I won't tell anyone," Jack said, with some trepidation. He found that he did trust Ting, but surely the Druid Order should know that a being who can possess and control others, and raise an army of the dead, had schemed to bring Jack and Harriett to Anwynn to meet this mysterious 'friend'. He decided to hold off for now, but if Ting did anything to damage his trust he would tell the druids everything.

"Thank you, Jack, you are truly a good boy," Ting said sweetly.

"I want to ask you something, and I want you to answer me truthfully."

"Of course, Jack, I would never lie to you."

"When we left the circle of Bright, I heard your voice echoing mine and Harriett's—"

"We grant thee the power to lead us beyond this circle," Ting recited knowingly.

"Yes, so you had to say that to pass out of the circle at Bright. How come Hob didn't know you were there when he led us out of the circle, and how come Amallayne didn't know you were in my ear when she took us to the Tomb of the Old Oracles of Senn, and for that matter how come you weren't stopped by the pentagram on the door at the Druid Chambers?"

"Ah, Jack, you have come to the reason why we are so despised. Earwisps have a magic that is very powerful. We are an ancient breed, nearly as old as the Faeden. Over all the time of our existence we have refined our skill at camouflage, deception and domination. No being is immune to our power, for our power comes directly from Lord Thullu, who is our Lord and Father. We are invulnerable to practically all sorcery and enchantment, except when we are in our fleshly form. Even then, only the power of the greatest sorcerers or druids is a match for us. As for the Star of Seren, that has no power over earwisps, or over the Faeden, for both of us existed before the morning star was born."

"The morning star?" Jack asked.

"Yes, in your world it is called the morning star. The elves call it Seren, the prophet star. The druids call it Phosphoros, the light bringer. It has many names. Its light protects against the Dark Ones and is death to goblins and trolls."

"So, your, ah, people, existed before even the stars?"

"Oh yes, we existed for a long time when there were no planets and no stars, there was just space and us drifting through eternity as wisp. Lord Thullu was there, in the void, and so were the Faeden. Then Lord Thullu created the planets and stars, Seren the first among them, followed by all kinds of life: the Oaklings first, then the elves and all the others. Then we earwisps learnt to take hosts, and bodily form."

"You mean, you were there when Thullu created the universe?" Jack asked, astounded.

"No, the universe was here already, as a void, but we were there when Lord Thullu filled it up with stuff."

"Stuff? Like planets and stars and life as we know it?"

"Yes, stuff like that."

"Wow, for little things you've really been places—"

"Just because we are little does not mean we are inconsequential," Ting spat. "No other being has the favour of Lord Thullu the way we do. No other being, not even the Faeden, has been allowed dominion over the dead. That power Lord Thullu allows only us. We have powers that even the Faeden do not have!"

"The Faeden must loathe the fact that you have powers they don't."

"Oh yes, that is why they hate us. It was they who first turned human-kind and elves against us. Long ago, when the race of elves was still young, the Faeden, jealous of the power Lord Thullu granted us, waged a mighty war on us, a terrible war, terrible."

"Who won that war?" Jack asked, thinking he knew the answer.

"The Faeden did," Ting sighed. "We were forever banished to the places of the dead. Where once we lived in harmony with our hosts, now we have to deceive and dominate them, or animate corpses and live on the sour memories of those no longer living."

"You ... you can do that? You can feed on the memories of the dead?" Jack swallowed hard, starting to see the true power of earwisps.

"Yes, but it does not nourish us – we become weak. That is what the Faeden want of course, to keep us weak to punish us for showing them that they are not all-powerful. We have become little better than fiends, starving and desperate, feeding on the dead and the weak. So few of us are able to rise above our situation. So few of us are good anymore."

"So, before this war, who were your hosts? The ones you lived with in harmony?"

"The elves were our first and most adored hosts. Together the Tiqq and the elves discovered many, many secrets. They loved us once."

"And now the elves hate you more than any other thing."

"Yes, thanks to the Faeden, the elves hate us. Love so often sours into hate," she finished enigmatically.

Jack took this information in and then remembered his and Harriett's first moments in Anwynn, when they'd met Hob.

"Hob, he sensed your presence, didn't he? Though he didn't know what you were. And yet Amallayne didn't sense you at all."

"No Faeden has ever detected my presence before. There is more to that silly Hob than meets the eye. He is very dangerous. But, in the end he didn't find me, did he? I tricked the Tricksy One!" Ting giggled.

"Well, I'll say one thing. I'm glad you're on my side," Jack smiled.

"I'm glad you believe me now," Ting said. "I'm not like other earwisps. I would never hurt you."

"I do believe you, though after everything I've heard about Thullu I probably shouldn't. Your people worship him, don't they?"

"Yes, most of the Tiqq revere Lord Thullu above all others, some though are turning to Morrigan. More and more of them as she grows stronger."

"Everyone is afraid of Thullu, even the Faeden. Is it just because he's powerful or because he's, you know, evil?"

"The Lord of Chaos is beyond mere good and evil. He is neither and both."

Jack didn't find that answer very satisfying. He scratched his head, looking out into the dark forest, thinking. "Okay, but, should I be worried that he's helping Serza? Should I be scared that we're facing a fight with Thullu as well?"

"The Lord of Chaos has not appeared to the Tiqq for many thousands of years. We no longer know his will." Though Ting's answer was vague, her tone was anxious.

"It sounds like you think I *should* be scared Thullu is helping Serza."

"If Lord Thullu is protecting and assisting Prince Serza, then even I, a Tiqq, a child of Lord Thullu, would be *terrified*."

The sound of Denn rolling over on his mossy bed, stirring to take the next watch, interrupted them.

"Jack," Ting whispered, "Denn cannot know I am here. The Pixish hate earwisps as much as elves do. I must hide in your ear—"

"Can't you hide somewhere else, like in my pocket?"

"I can't remain in this form. I am vulnerable this way and my powers weakened. Please, Jack, I promise I'll be good."

"Alright, but respect my privacy. No looking in parts of my brain where you don't belong."

"Yes, Jack," Ting whispered as Denn began to rouse. "No peeking, I promise." Ting's body dissolved into purple mist and drifted up and into Jack's ear. This time Jack didn't feel a thing. He wished he had. It was a bit disturbing that he could be possessed and not feel any different at all.

By the time Denn woke and took over the watch, no hint of Ting remained. Jack went to his bed of haghair and lay down, ruminating over all the things Ting had said, in particular the fact that Thullu may well be helping Serza. It also worried Jack that Hob was the only Faeden to have ever detected Ting's presence. Jack had never liked Hob. The way he looked down his nose at 'lesser breeds' made Jack feel that he couldn't be trusted. The very idea that Hob was able to detect Ting when the Great Goddess Amallayne herself couldn't made him feel very uneasy.

When these thoughts threatened to drive away his sleep he turned his mind to Anarra. Thinking of her deep blue eyes was like a talisman of calm, but then another worry rose. Why had King Dhudhannan wanted to see Anarra after the attack on the Druid Chambers? It must have been very important for the king to have asked for her in that moment, when he was dying. His stomach tightened. He had a bad feeling that whatever it was would keep him and Anarra from seeing each other. Soon these thoughts gave way to the empty thoughts of exhaustion and, while listening to the impenetrable silence of Fellwood Forest, he fell into a troubled sleep.

BOBCAT

Over the next few days the small party's routine was depressingly unvaried. Each morning they rose at dawn, ate an increasingly meagre breakfast, dismantled their shelter, repacked Cobalt's saddle bags and continued along the well-worn and ancient path through Fellwood Forest. On most mornings, Denn gave Jack lessons in sword fighting. Jack found the lessons challenging but fun. Denn had loaned Jack one of his swords for the purpose; the elegant sword with the tree-shaped hilt, made of black metal. Slowly Jack got used to the weight of the sword in his hands. Following Denn's detailed instructions about how to thrust, how to parry, how to block, he began to feel that one day he might be able to hold his own in a real fight.

The lessons with Denn were a needed distraction from the forest around them, and the uncertain fate ahead of them. Even Harriett took advantage of the distraction, watching Denn and Jack practice and providing a running commentary. On the third day, at the end of a particularly vigorous swordcraft lesson, Denn said, "You are proving not to be wholly useless, lad. You might make a swordsman yet." Jack flushed with pride. He hadn't felt so good about himself since ... well, he'd never felt that proud of himself before. Denn patted him on the back and they packed up camp and resumed their journey.

The character of the forest was as unvaried as their routine – the same tangle of interlocked boughs and gnarled and twisted tree trunks forming an ever narrower tunnel through which the path crept. The deeper into the forest they went, the more robust the haghair that grew on the ancient trees became. Thick, darkly glowing moss soon festooned every single twig and branch. Long tendrils of the glowing stuff hung down from above like an eerie curtain of hair that creepily brushed against the tops of their heads.

The canopy overhead did change however. It became even denser so that less and less light and sound penetrated. At the end of each day Jack thought the forest couldn't possibly get any darker or gloomier but each following day he found that it could and did. He discovered new meanings for the words dark, cold and black. It became increasingly difficult to tell the difference between night and day. If it weren't for Denn's uncanny sense of time they would have been completely turned around as to whether it was morning, noon or midnight. The misery of Fellwood weighed more and more heavily on them all. Even Cobalt felt it. The blue stallion's withers sagged as if he was carrying not just the trio on his back but the whole weight of the darkness as well.

Their routine at night was just as monotonous. Each night they built the shelter, lit the fire to invoke the hearth ward and then Denn and Jack took turns keeping watch. Each night Jack slept fitfully, his dreams filled with a sense of foreboding and doom. The deeper into the forest they went, the more disturbing his dreams became, so that by the night of the fourth day he had a fully blown nightmare.

The nightmare began with the image of a large, beaten copper door, not polished and shining like the golden door at the temple of Amallayne, but a lacklustre, grimy door with a shabby green patina due to age and lack of care. The door was inside a deep cave, damp and very dark. Beyond it Jack sensed a great malevolence. He knew then that the door was Darkgate and that Morrigan was beyond.

In the dream he passed through the door and was confronted by Morrigan's terrifying face: pale-skinned, green-eyed, mouth scarred and burned. She emanated a cold, dreadful menace. She opened her mouth, as if in a scream of fury, but nothing came out, bar that sickening vibration that made Jack feel nauseous and terrified, as if he was going to die.

In the midst of the fear, Jack realised he had experienced this dream many times before but had found it so terrifying that on waking he'd suppressed all memory of it. He also knew that the influence of Fellwood, and their proximity to Pitmouth where Morrigan's prison lay, meant that not only would he have more and more of these dreams but he would not have the benefit of forgetting them afterwards. As Morrigan silently shrieked in his face, he struggled to escape the dream. When he finally woke he sat bolt upright, resisting the urge to vomit.

He sat still, waiting out the nausea, wiping his eyes. He could hardly tell the dawn had come. The brazier was aglow with red coals, throwing the only light. Denn and Harriett sat by the fire nibbling dispiritedly on yet more dry bread. "What time is it?" Jack asked.

"Just after dawn," Denn answered. "Not that you can tell in this foul place."

"Are you okay, Jack?" Harriett asked. "You look a bit peaky."

"Yeah, I'm okay. Didn't sleep well."

"My dreams have been filled with fell fiends," Denn said. "It is the influence of the wood."

Jack nodded in recognition and dragged himself over to the brazier to take the clump of bread offered by Harriett. After breakfast they continued with their now monotonous routine – dismantling the shelter and repacking Cobalt's saddle bags. About an hour later they remounted Cobalt and continued along the dark path, the gloom and glumness of the forest silencing them again.

A full day of riding later the sombre trio came around a bend in the path to a sight that gave Jack a jolt. Up ahead of them was a crossroads. In the centre of the crossroads, just as in the vision Jack and Harriett had shared, sat the stone marker with its strange carvings. Until now Jack hadn't quite believed that the torc had worked, and certainly hadn't realised how accurate the visions were. His appreciation of the power of the torc quickly turned to apprehension when he remembered that a party of a hundred goblins, led by two vicious Vellenor warriors, was about to emerge from the path to the left. They were only yards back from the crossroads. If Jack didn't act now they'd be seen. He panicked and thumped Cobalt with his feet.

"Off the path!" he hissed. "We have to get off the path!" Before Denn realised what was happening, Harriett slid out of the saddle and grabbed hold of his arm. "Quickly," she said, "goblins!"

"What? I don't see any—"

"There's no time! Off the path! Quickly!" Harriett hissed, grabbing hold of Cobalt's reins and trying to drag him off the path.

"Harriett, have you gone mad?" Denn demanded a little too loudly for comfort. Jack slid off the horse and joined Harriett in pulling on the reins.

"Quiet!" Jack said. "We have to get off the path!" At almost precisely the same moment Ting's voice rang in his ears. *Jack! I sense many goblins!* Jack didn't need any further encouragement. He used all of his strength to forcibly steer Cobalt toward the undergrowth at the side of the path. Denn dismounted, affronted that someone would dare take control of his own horse.

"Wait just a minute, lad," he began, but he didn't have time to finish his sentence. Harriett grabbed him by the hand, hissed "goblins!" once more and dragged him off the path.

The three only managed to get a few feet off the path and hide behind a clump of interlocked trees when the goblins emerged into the crossroads. Denn spotted them and ducked down, whispering to Cobalt to be silent. Jack and Harriett were pressed up against the rough bark of one of the trees, well out of sight. Afraid to even breathe, the three listened to the plodding sound of feet as the goblins moved through the crossroads and continued on to the right. Just as in the torc vision, the goblins were completely unaware that Denn and the others were hiding nearby. After a sufficient wait, Denn turned to Jack and Harriett.

"How did you know?" he whispered.

"I have my ways." Harriett smiled mysteriously, thoroughly enjoying the attention. They waited a little longer, just to be sure that the goblins were out of earshot, and then emerged from their hiding place and continued cautiously along the path. When they reached the crossroads the path to the right was empty, bending out of sight fifty yards ahead. Harriett hopped in place, clearly exhilarated and proud of herself. She had managed to be a real help rather than a hindrance.

"Where do you think the goblins were going?" Jack asked.

"That path leads directly to Bonemound," answered Denn. He bent and scrubbed the stone marker with his hand, dislodging centuries of grime and lichen, to reveal a horrible emblem: four skeleton hands arranged wrist to wrist to make a kind of terrible flower. "This mark is Bonemound's sign."

"So long as they aren't going the same way as us," said Harriett, "I don't care where they're headed."

"I wish I shared your sentiment," Denn began, "but those were Vellenor leading Fellwood goblins. A party of Fellwood beasts that size has no business going to Bonemound carrying arms. Perhaps this is why the path has been so quiet. The Dark Ones of Fellwood are occupied elsewhere."

"Amallayne said that Serza's army would turn on Bonemound," Jack said, a little disappointed that Amallayne's prescience was proving accurate.

"If that be true," Denn thought aloud, "then our path to Pitmouth may be easier than we could have hoped. If all the Dark Ones are at war at Bonemound, we will be able to journey to Pitmouth unhindered."

"Until," Jack said, "Serza turns on Pitmouth as well."

Denn looked at Jack and took this in, his eyes widening with alarm.

"We must not dawdle then," he said, "we must pick up the pace."

They continued onwards, the close call with the goblins giving Jack a rush of adrenalin that pushed the gloom of Fellwood out of his mind. Denn and Harriett were similarly energised. By the time they stopped to set up camp, they were all joking with each other, something they hadn't done for days. Even the dry bread they had for dinner didn't bring them down but instead was a source of amusement.

"At least we don't have to share it with those goblins," Denn joked about the bread. "Though, perhaps our stomachs would fare better if we did."

Not even the thought that Serza's massive army might be coming up the road behind them could dampen their spirits. Jack went to sleep that night with a sense that they were going to be okay, that Fellwood Forest would not get the better of them.

As if Fellwood had sensed Jack's newfound resistance to its gloom, the forest answered with all its oppressive might. The following morning Jack woke to a miserable, drizzly wet and cold day, as dark as night but worse for the mud and the biting chill. They packed up and got under way in silence. Soon Jack's hair was plastered to his scalp like a black helm. When he looked back to check on Harriett he found she looked much the same, her long eyelashes heavy with globs of water that clouded her eyes. Of all of them, Denn fared worst. His clothes were made for the plains of Pix, not the damp, bitterly cold forest. His charcoal hair hung wetly around his face, dripping onto his broad shoulders. After just a couple of hours riding he was soaked to the bone and trembling with the cold. He didn't complain however, just pushed on.

By late afternoon they'd all had enough and were ready to make camp, even though it was some hours before dusk. Even Cobalt was shivering from the cold now. Denn told Jack to keep his eyes peeled for a dry place to build a shelter, though he didn't hold much hope of finding one. Shortly afterwards Cobalt halted, apparently hesitant to go any further. Jack peered through the haze of drizzle. Ahead of them a particularly large and rotten-looking tree forced the path to curve around it.

"Banewood," Denn muttered.

The Banewood tree was so large it completely overshadowed all the other trees nearby. Its deformed roots spread out in every direction, like monstrous tentacles that crumpled the surface of the path. On the trunk of the tree, painted in ash, were strange markings: creepy looking circles and lines.

"Witchmarks," Denn whispered, almost to himself, staring with alarm at the strange drawings. As the mounted trio gazed apprehensively at the marks, a black fog emanated out of the ground around the Banewood's roots and crept toward them. Cobalt whinnied in fear and stepped backwards. Jack's hair stood on end. Once again he wished he wasn't at the front of the horse. Denn leaned forward, peering into the fog, his chest pressing against Jack's back.

"Something foul is afoot," Denn whispered.

Mere seconds later Jack spotted a small hooded figure lurking amongst the dark fog, in the shadows at the base of the Banewood.

"There!" he said, his voice catching in his throat. Could it be the same hooded figure that had been following them ever since they left Miss Butters' cottage in Bright? It had been hiding in the trees when they stopped to rest on the way to see Wadget. It had been lurking at the edge of the glade at Oakholme, before Serza attacked. It had even been in the shadows of a laneway in Songarielle. Now that lurking figure was blocking their path.

"What is it?" Harriett asked.

"I don't know," Denn answered, "but I don't intend to sit and wait for it to introduce itself." Denn dismounted and took a few steps forward. He raised his hand and, like Ellisenn had in the battle at Songarielle, formed a sign in the air in front of him. Instead of a pentagram, a Star of Seren, this was a circle, glowing dimly red. The sign of Amallayne. Jack and Harriett glanced at each other in surprise. Denn knew magic! The appearance of the red circle brought an instant sense of relief to Jack. It wasn't as large or bright as Ellisenn's clearly more powerful pentagram but even this small glimmering circle caused the fog to stop in its tracks. The limbs of the Banewood creaked as they bent away from the circle's light. "The fog is the evil will of the Banewood," Denn said, "summoned by the witchmarks, but what lurks within it I do not know."

The silence of Fellwood was shattered by a mad cackle from the hooded figure. Whatever it was lifted its own hand in response to Denn and, making a series of jerky movements, urged the fog, the mind of the Banewood, forward. The fog formed thin, worm-like tendrils that reached out to the red circle and took hold of it before dragging it down to the ground where it dissolved with a muffled pop. In response, Denn drew his sword and held it above his head. He uttered an incantation of some kind and the sword ignited with red flame. Denn drew a circle on the ground with his flaming sword, encircling Cobalt, Jack and Harriett still in the saddle, leaving them all encased in a pen of crimson fire.

"This dark one is stronger in magic than I. I can but hope the circle keeps it out," Denn declared.

The hooded figure moved forward abreast with the dark fog that crept toward them. Multitudes of worm-like tendrils of the fog curled upwards and caressed the hooded shape, making the small, black figure look like some kind of awful octopus. Each of the twisting tentacles emitted a high-pitched keening. The sound reminded Jack of the begging cries of baby birds, or the sound animals made when frightened. Only this sound was unnatural and awful. *I have sensed this evil thing before*, Ting whispered in Jack's ear. *I sensed it in the forest when you and your sister had left the protection of the hearth ward*. Whatever it was, Jack thought, it was determined and clever; it had tracked them across Anwynn, always catching up with them.

As the small figure reached the edge of the circle of flame it stopped. The tendrils of fog curled around the flames, completely surrounding them, and pressed inwards. It was as if the fog was squeezing the life out of the circle of fire. The flames began to dim and the circle slowly receded toward them, pressing Denn against Cobalt's side in an ever shrinking space. Cobalt whinnied with fear and Jack took hold of the reins in case he tried to bolt. Denn pointed his sword at the figure and, shouting another incantation, sent forth a burst of flame.

The flame broke on the figure like waves on a rock, having little, if any, effect. It cackled madly again and, outstretching its arms in an arcing movement, caused the volume of fog to grow until it encased them in a balloon of darkness. They couldn't see much beyond the circle, nor could they see the limbs of the trees overhead. It was as if they were inside a prison of smoke. The circle of fire dimmed even further and the fog pressed down on them from above, all the while the awful keening growing louder and louder.

"Finally you will die, little girl," the figure said in a twisted, female voice as it pointed a small, chubby finger directly at Harriett, her voice trailing into a mad cackle.

Out of nowhere a sizzling green ball of light streaked through the fog and struck the hooded figure squarely in the head, knocking her over. In an instant the fog recoiled, shrinking and receding back into the ground, like ink absorbed by a muddy sponge. The flame circle sputtered and returned to its full brightness, illuminating that the figure's hood had fallen aside. Jack, feeling a familiar and overwhelming loathing, gasped. It had to be Hephaestia Hatter, the halfling woman from Bright. She was the only other person who incited that exact feeling of loathing he remembered so well from when Hephaestia Hatter had visited Butters Nob. She shrieked in the direction the green orb had come from and staggered back to her feet. With one last menacing glance at Harriett, she stumbled into the forest, disappearing amongst the trees. Jack's heart pounded in his ears. He had been right all along, the sorceress wasn't after him, the Waycaller, but after Harriett.

With the sorceress' retreat Denn's face brightened with a broad smile. The smile quickly turned to a look of horror when he discovered who'd overpowered the halfling sorceress. Bounding toward them through the uppermost limbs of the trees was a huge, lion-sized spotted bobcat. Clearly an unnatural beast, its grimy fur stood up on end. Its weepy eyes glowed with menace and its mouth was packed with row after row of jagged teeth. The cat leapt from tree to tree effortlessly, rapidly covering the distance between it and the stunned trio. When it came within a few yards of them the bobcat transformed into a small, green-skinned being with claw-like hands and feet and long pointy ears. Mog!

After transforming into her true form, Mog didn't miss a step. She rushed forward, swinging one-armed from branch to branch like some demented ape, a look of pure wickedness on her face. She fired another green orb at the circle of flame. It instantly went out. She fired again and a ball of green energy hurtled toward Harriett, striking a tree branch above her and exploding, blowing Harriett from the saddle to land in the mud at the edge of the path.

"Harrie!" Jack dismounted and raced to his sister.

Denn took a fighting posture before the advancing Mog. Uttering incantations as quickly as his tongue could form them, he used his sword to send blast after blast of flame at the wicked Oakling. Trees exploded into flame all around her, but Mog evaded every one of Denn's attacks. She flicked her wand in his direction and he only just managed to dodge out of the way as a green orb struck a tree behind him. The tree exploded into a cloud of ash.

Cobalt turned and bolted in fear back down the path. With a mad and evil shriek, Mog fired at Cobalt and struck him in the side. Cobalt neighed in agonising pain and crashed to the ground.

"No!" Denn shouted as he leapt forward to stab at Mog as she dropped from a tree directly above him. Mog kicked out with her clawed feet and struck Denn in the face, tearing open his forehead and knocking him to the ground. Blood poured into Denn's eyes, blinding him. He tried to rise to his knees, uttering a strange call for help: "My Lord, My Lord help us!" His eyes rolled into the back of his head and he fell aside, losing consciousness.

Mog loped to where Jack was trying to rouse Harriett, who had not moved and didn't seem to be breathing. The Oakling grabbed Jack by the hair, pointing her wand at his throat.

"The prize is mine!" she shrieked. "Oh, the Pale Mother will love me now that I have the thing she wants!"

"Let me go!" Jack shouted. He swung and punched Mog square in the face. Mog shook her head, pointed her wand at him and with the smallest of flicks bound his wrists and ankles in tight rope.

"If you did not belong to the Pale Mother I would eats you alive!" she hissed, before drawing a short black blade and tracing it over his forehead to create a deep cut. Jack nearly passed out from the pain, which radiated out from the wound in burning waves. "Ah, he feels it burn," Mog gloated as Jack cried out in agony. "Don't fret little boy, my blade may be dipped in troll venom but it will not kill you straight away, oh no, you will burns and suffers a long time yet." She cackled, watching the blood ooze from the cut with glee. "Such trickly blood. My queen would not deny me a little taste, oh no, she wouldn't." Mog bent forward and lapped at the blood spilling over his brow. Her tongue felt like slimy sandpaper. "Oh, very nice, yes, very nice, salty, just a dash of trollsy poison, yes. Once the Pale Mother is done with him me thinks I will get him for dinner, oh yes—"

"I'm afraid you will have to wait for that meal," a drawling voice said.

Mog wheeled around to face the speaker and, on seeing him, howled with disgust.

"You!" Mog spat. Jack looked up through a veil of his own blood and pain and saw a youthful man, all dressed in blue velvet. Ting hissed in his ear: Hob!

Mog waved her wand frantically at the Faeden, sending

volley after volley of sizzling green bombs squarely at him. When they hit him they were simply absorbed with no effect whatsoever, like so many green puffs of smoke.

"You dare to defy the Pale Mother!" Mog shrieked.

"I'm afraid so," said Hob, as if completely disinterested in the conversation. "Oh, and by-the-by, as you are a denizen of an outcast and have attempted to kill those under my own protection I feel more than justified in doing *this*." Hob nonchalantly waved his hand in Mog's direction. Mog hissed defiantly and threw up a shield wall, steeling herself for what was coming. She turned to dust and crumpled into nothing.

Instantaneously, Jack's bindings turned to dust as well. He hauled himself up, unable to speak, barely able to breathe. With a mere flick of his wrist Hob had destroyed a living being, causing her to turn to dust. Jack's throat constricted. He trusted Hob less than ever now. He rushed to Harriett, dropping on his knees beside her. She still wasn't moving.

"Hob," he called, "please, help Harriett."

Hob meandered over and looked down at Harriett.

"She is merely unconscious, which I must say is the best way I've encountered her."

Jack jumped to his feet, his hands automatically curled into fists.

"Careful, little boy," Hob said with that infuriating smirk of his, his blue eyes alight with menace, "or I shall send you the way of Mog." Jack's fists clenched tighter, turning his knuckles a hot white. Hob flicked his hand in Jack's direction. Jack flinched, then felt the wound on his forehead vanishing. He glared at Hob, knelt back down beside Harriett and, cradling her in his arms, patted her on the face and resumed his attempt to rouse her.

"Harrie? Harrie, are you okay?" Harriett's eyelids fluttered and opened. She looked up into Jack's eyes and smiled lightly.

"I must have been knocked clear out," she said.

"You sure were." Jack sighed with relief. "I thought you were a goner."

Harriett sat up and saw Hob, who had wandered over to the unconscious Denn. Her face broke into a wide smile and she scrambled to her feet.

"Harriett, you shouldn't trust him," Jack began, but Harriett had already trotted over to Hob.

"Hi!" she said.

"Hello, little girl," Hob replied, noticing the now pale blue of her eyes. He stared at her a moment, surprised, then resumed an attitude of complete disinterest.

Jack joined them and watched as Hob healed Denn's wounds. Jack was surprised to see the careful attention Hob showed Denn. It was not at all the kind of off-hand attention he showed everyone else. With the touch of a finger to Denn's brow, Hob brought him around. When Denn's eyes opened, he saw Hob leaning over him and swiftly scrambled onto his knees, bowing his head and stuttering.

"My Lord! I … I never thought you would bless me so."

"It is nothing," Hob said, his voice free of its usual sarcasm. "Your heart called out to me and I came. Besides, Mog was a filthy old thing. Her existence irritated me."

"You saved my life! My Lord, how can I ever repay you?"

"What use is payment to a Faeden? Whole worlds spring from my fingers. It is enough that you show me reverence, unlike some others." He glanced at Jack, that sarcastic tone back in his voice.

"They are but children, my Lord, and they know not who you are," Denn said in Jack's defence.

"Sure we know who he is," chirped Harriett. "He's Hob."

"Hob?" Denn queried.

"It is what I am called by the halflings, and by some others," Hob explained. Denn practically convulsed with surprise.

"You … you bless us with your secret name!" he stuttered. "My Lord, your kindness is vast!"

"Speak no more of it," Hob commanded. At that Denn

went silent, taking Hob's command not to speak very seriously.

"Where've you been, Hob?" Harriett injected into the silence that followed.

"Here and there, abiding in pleasure."

"Cool," Harriett said, clearly unsure what Hob meant.

"But enough of that," Hob continued, looking down the path to where Cobalt lay still and cold. "There is another who needs aid." Hob stood and walked toward Cobalt, followed by Jack, Harriett and a very timid Denn. When they reached Cobalt it was clear that the horse was dead. Harriett burst into tears. Denn looked away, unable to stand the sight of his friend in that state. Hob knelt down and placed his hand on Cobalt's cheek. He stayed there, motionless for a moment, and then smiled. "He has not passed into the realm of the dead. He lingers at the gate, looking back. He loves you very much, Denn."

"What?" Jack said. "Do you mean he's still alive?"

"No," Hob said. "He is dead, but not irrevocably dead."

"What does that mean?" Harriett asked.

"It means that for all intents and purposes he is dead but not beyond the power of the Faeden. I can summon him to our own realm and from there restore him to his body."

A tingle of unease spread over Jack. Hadn't Ting said that the Faeden had no power over the dead? Hadn't Amallayne said it was forbidden to return the dead to life? Ting's voice in his ear echoed his thoughts. *No, he cannot, he dare not!*

"You mean, you can save him?" Denn asked the Faeden, his voice full of hope.

"I can and I will," Hob said. "It is brave for a Pixish horse to be blue, and such a beautiful blue." Jack noticed that Cobalt's hide was almost the same hue as Hob's velvet costume, a strange coincidence. Hob stood and, with another carefree wave of his hand, Cobalt's body dissolved into light, leaving the saddle and harness to drop into the mud like a kind of weird carcass. "I must go," Hob explained, "before the horse enters the gate." He looked into Denn's eyes and, as he also dissolved into light, said, "I shall return your steed to you when the time is right. In the meantime, stay safe, friend Denn, keep yourself well."

"Friend," Denn stammered in shock, "My Lord called me friend!"

"Why do you call Hob your Lord?" Jack asked suspiciously, seeing Denn in a new light. "He's just a Faeden."

"Just a Faeden!" Denn exclaimed appalled. "Do you not know who that was?"

"Sure, we told you," Harriett said. "That was Hob."

Denn looked at the two, clearly weighing up if he should tell them something, but then his face changed to a kind of worried, cautious smile.

"Listen," he said, "it is probably best that you don't tell anyone that I ... I mean, that I called out to ... to Hob. They might not understand. The Pix are meant to be committed to Amallayne and Amallayne alone. Besides, I called out as I was losing consciousness, it was an ... aberration."

"Hob's an aberration alright," Jack said, wondering what it was that Denn was keeping from them, and why he was so intent on hiding his association with Hob.

"We don't have to tell anybody," Harriett said, smiling. "Hob has helped us before. It doesn't matter to us."

"Also," Denn said seriously, "do not forget that he saved your lives from Mog and has promised to resurrect Cobalt. For these reasons alone you should show him at least a modicum of respect."

"Oh, I *love* Hob," Harriett declared. "I don't care what Jack says."

"What aren't you telling us, Denn?" Jack asked. "Who's Hob to you anyway?"

"He is one of the Faeden," Denn said cagily. "One who has long stood against Morrigan."

"Is that all?" Jack pressed.

"That is all."

Jack weighed this up but decided not to press Denn any further. The Pixish horseman was clearly uncomfortable at being interrogated on the matter. Harriett, however, felt no such reluctance.

"You should have told us you were a druid," she said.

"I am not a druid," Denn explained. "As a Pixish horseman I received a small amount of training in magic, but as you saw I am no match for a fully-fledged sorcerer."

"Do all horsemen learn to use magic?" Harriett continued, wheedling.

"No, only those of high rank. I was, once, a captain of the Pixish Horselords." Denn's voice was quiet, modest. "On my brother's death I gave up my post."

"So, what other druid stuff can you do?" Harriett pressed.

"No more questions," Denn said. "We must continue on our way. We need to find a place to shelter, for do not forget that the halfling witch is still out there somewhere, though I doubt she will recover from Mog's attack any time soon. Nevertheless, the comfort of the hearth ward will be welcome this night."

Jack and Harriett followed Denn without another word. Jack was exhausted, his fatigue made all the worse by a nagging worry. Hephaestia Hatter was pursuing Harriett. Wadget had said that Harriett would be mistaken for the Waycaller because she was a girl. Surely by now all Morrigan's minions knew that it was Jack who held the power? But still Hephaestia was after his sister. Why? He looked up to see that Denn and Harriett had walked ahead and were beginning to disappear into the gloom of the forest. He started after them, his worry growing with every step.

SIEGE OF BONEMOUND

The next morning Jack rose at dawn, as usual, to find Harriett already awake, keeping Denn company for the last moments of his watch. As Jack trudged over to them he noticed that Harriett had some kind of smear on her forehead. When he joined them by the brazier he saw that it was the distinct form of a pentagram, drawn in the centre of her brow with something black and smudgy.

"What on earth is that on your forehead, Harrie?"

"It's the Seren Star. I'm not taking any chances after what happened yesterday with Mog and that crazy witch."

"I don't think you're supposed to draw it on yourself, Harrie," Jack said, yawning. "Besides, you look like a lunatic."

"I don't care how it looks, Jack," she said earnestly. "So long as it stops that witch who's after us from blowing me into little pieces! Besides, I don't think it looks that bad. I drew it with soot from the fire."

"And you just sat there and let her do it?" he asked Denn.

"If I know anything, lad," Denn began, "it is that no precaution is too great when it comes to the Dark Ones. I say let her draw stars all over her body if she wishes. It certainly can't hurt."

Jack shrugged resignedly and sat down to eat another meagre breakfast. After he'd eaten, Denn gave Jack his swordplay lesson. For the first time, Jack felt he was handling the black sword well. Denn somehow sensed this and so intensified the lesson, pummelling Jack with heavy sword blows, which Jack parried and blocked. The sword went exactly where he intended it to go. It was as if the blade had become an extension of his arm. His newfound comfort with the weapon meant that their lesson went longer than usual. When Denn inevitably overpowered Jack, disarming him with a sudden and lightning fast parry, they were both sweating.

Jack's body ached with strain.

"Well done, Jack." Denn smiled. "You are well-suited to the sword."

Jack blushed, for though Denn's words were not exactly exuberant praise they were spoken in an unmistakably warm tone that made Denn's affection for Jack clear. When Jack went to return the black sword, Denn waved him away, handing him the scabbard instead and smiling. Jack didn't understand. He looked at Denn perplexed. "That sword belongs to you now," Denn explained. "The sword came alive in your hands. It is the custom in Pix that when a man masters a sword then ownership of that sword passes to him."

"You're ... you're giving the sword to me?" Jack stammered disbelievingly.

"If it is not such a poor gift that you would refuse it," Denn said sheepishly.

"Poor gift? Oh no, I love it!" Jack beamed.

"It is yours then." Denn smiled, then awkwardly thumped Jack on the shoulder and strode away. Jack looked at his new black sword and positively glowed with pride.

"Still can't shave without cutting yourself though, can you, Jack?" Harriett said. Jack ignored her, refusing to let her snipe burst his bubble. He had earned his very own sword! He couldn't believe it!

As Denn dismantled their shelter and prepared for the resumption of their journey, he allowed Jack and Harriett to rest a little in front of the fading coals of the fire. The respite was appreciated by both of them. Harriett was nursing bruised ribs from Mog's attack. She found it difficult to raise her arms much above waist level. Jack felt like he had been run over by a herd of stampeding horses, in a good way. Each of Denn's blows had reverberated down his spine with bone-shaking, jaw-crunching force. His head throbbed from exertion at swordplay and from not having slept properly. As he rubbed his head, he remembered the latest nightmare he'd had of Morrigan. As usual she'd been lurking behind the grimy copper door. As he remembered it the full horror of it returned. For a brief second he contemplated drawing a Seren Star on his own forehead. He quickly ruled that out. He just rubbed his forehead more vigorously, right on the spot where Mog had cut him. The cut was gone but it felt comforting to rub the spot anyway. It kept the memory of the pain Mog had caused him at bay.

"Why do you keep rubbing your head?" Harriett asked.

"I don't know, it doesn't hurt or anything but I kind of expect the gash to still be there," he answered, still rubbing his brow.

"What gash?" Harriett asked, having been unconscious for the whole of Mog's attack.

"Mog cut my forehead open; it was pretty deep and the blade was tipped with troll venom that really burned."

"What happened to the gash?" Harriett interrupted, her eyes narrowing.

"Hob fixed it – he waved his dainty fingers and it vanished."

"See, Hob's not that bad," Harriett said.

"Yeah, he is. Don't let him fool you. Don't forget he told Serza about the Keysong. Besides, you were unconscious when Amallayne told me this, but it is forbidden to tamper with death. Not even the Faeden can bring back the dead. Amallayne said Thullu himself forbids it. Hob must know that, but he says he's going to bring back Cobalt—"

"Seriously, Jack? You're suspicious of Hob because he promised to save Cobalt?"

"You don't understand. There's more to it."

"Then explain it to me."

He looked into her pale eyes, evidence that she was the result of the kind of tampering with death that Thullu had forbidden. Was it time to tell her about that? She would be terrified by the idea that some sinister change might one day overcome her, but at least she wouldn't be in the dark. Looking into those icy eyes he wished there'd been some other way to save her, but there hadn't been. He'd had no choice. He had broken Thullu's taboo. He and Hob had that in common. That thought made him shudder, but not as much as the thought that Harriett was the one who would pay for his breach of Faeden law.

A flash of inspiration came to him then. Ting, as one of the Tiqq, had power over death, granted to her people by Thullu himself. If anyone knew a way to prevent Harriett paying for his mistake it was her. Just then Denn finished taking down the shelter and walked over to douse the fire. Jack decided that as soon as Denn fell asleep that night, he was going to tell Harriett the truth and introduce her to his new friend.

After Denn finished dismantling the camp they set out on foot. Though Fellwood had not changed—it was still the same dark tangle of gnarled and deformed tree trunks—it was all the gloomier for Cobalt's absence. While riding on Cobalt's back, Jack felt they were somehow apart from the gloom around them. On foot it was a totally different story. The trees towered over them, making Jack feel small and powerless. The only good thing was that now the haghair festooning the trees didn't hang low enough to brush against the top of his head.

By dusk they were all weary from a long day at a swift march. Jack and Harriett were more than ready to make camp when Denn looked for a place to build a shelter and invoke the hearth ward. The Pixish swordsman built another lean-to between another set of large trees and started the fire in his trusty brazier, which he was now toting in Cobalt's saddle bags over his shoulder. Denn took the first watch, allowing Jack to drop onto his bed of haghair and fall instantly asleep. When Denn woke him some hours later he felt better but still not altogether refreshed. He staggered to the fireside as Denn stretched out on his haghair bed and closed his eyes. Jack waited for Denn to fall asleep and then crept over to Harriett and shook her gently. She opened her eyes immediately and sat bolt upright. With the smudged pentagram on her forehead she looked a little deranged.

"What's wrong?" she said, her voice alarmed.

"Nothing, I just want you to meet someone, a friend of mine." Harriett looked around and saw only Denn asleep nearby.

"Jack," Harriett whispered, sighing and wiping her eyes, "you're too old for invisible friends."

"She's not invisible," Jack said, leading his sister to the small fire. "She's an earwisp."

"An earwisp! Are you nuts, Jack? Why would you be friends with an earwisp?"

"She's not a bad earwisp, she's a good earwisp." Jack turned to his left ear and whispered. "Okay, Ting, it's alright, you can come out. I want you to meet Harriett." Jack smiled at Harriett and waited. Nothing happened. Harriett looked at him like he was a foolish toddler.

"It's okay, Jack," she soothed, "I won't tell anybody you've got an imaginary friend."

"I am not imaginary!" a tiny female voice asserted as a plume of purple mist exited Jack's ear and took form by the fireside. "I am just as real as you are!"

"Oh Jack, it's so cute!"

"It?" Ting was scandalised. "*It!*"

"Harrie didn't mean anything by that," Jack said swiftly, hoping to avert one of Ting's teary outbursts.

"It! How dare she call me *it!*" Ting was practically shrieking now. Jack worried that the noise would wake Denn.

"Ting," Jack said, "please, be quiet."

"I didn't mean to be rude," Harriett said, dropping onto her bottom beside Ting, "I was just surprised, that's all. I've never seen a pretty little sprite like you before."

"Pretty? Do you think I'm pretty?" Ting asked, her tone much more even.

"Oh yes," Harriett said sincerely, "I think you're lovely."

"Really?" Ting urged.

"Really," Harriett answered.

"I like your sister, Jack," Ting said, suddenly smiling. "At least she knows how to be nice to a sprite, even if she does have a dirty forehead."

Jack decided not to say anything to this, sensing that it may be part of another ambush to make him feel bad for something.

"Anyway," he started, "we need your help, Ting. When Serza attacked Songarielle and Harrie was hurt, I used magic to save her."

"I know, Jack, I was there. You shouldn't have done that, only the Tiqq have dominion over the dead."

"Wait, what?" Harriett stuttered. "I was *dead*?"

"Nearly completely dead, yes," Ting answered. "If you had gone much further, you could not have been brought back."

Harriett looked to Jack, her eyes round with shock.

"I'm sorry I didn't tell you. I didn't want to scare you."

"Oh, well, that worked, didn't it, Jack?"

"Did it?" Ting asked.

"No! I'm terrified!"

"It's okay, Harrie," Jack said. "You're okay now."

"Wait, is that why my eyes changed colour?"

"Yes." Jack watched as his sister's nearly white eyes filled with tears. Her mouth drooped open, her bottom lip trembling. Jack chose to press on and ask Ting for help. "Amallayne said that something might have changed in Harriett because of what I did, that, that she might—"

"Might what?" Harriett's watery eyes were as round as saucers now.

"You need not worry," Ting said firmly, "neither of you. A dark change only occurs if it is a dark power that brings the person back from the gate of death. Your power is not dark, Jack, so nothing dark can come of it, even though you went against Lord Thullu's will. Amallayne does not know all that we Tiqq know about these things. Death is *our* domain." Ting sounded rather smug.

"So, Harriett hasn't changed?"

"Oh yes, she has, and that change is why my dear friend asked me to bring you both to Anwynn, for my friend foresaw it."

Jack and Harriett both stared at the little sprite.

"What kind of change is it?" Harriett asked, her voice shaking.

"Nothing terrible," Ting answered, "but I cannot tell you more than that. My friend will explain it to you when you meet."

"When will that be?" Jack asked.

"Not now," Ting said mysteriously, "later."

"Well," Jack said, "you haven't been much help at all."

Ting looked a little abashed but didn't respond to his jibe.

"Ting," Harriett said, "please, can't you tell me anything more?"

The sprites face softened at the worry in Harriett's eyes.

"I must keep many things secret, or much will be lost. I *can* tell you that I am here to help you both, that you are not alone. There are many who seek to protect you, and not just the druids. My friend has done much to protect you both and works tirelessly to undermine the forces pitched against you. It is true that much darkness moves toward you, threatening to consume you, but know this: much good gathers around you as well, not the least the good that is within you both. Know this also: no power in Anwynn matches love and trust. The love you have for each other will protect you, as will the trust you place in your friends."

The next day they travelled at much the same pace as the day before, not stopping for lunch but gnawing on some very stale bread as they pushed ever forward along the path through Fellwood. As they walked Jack pondered the conversation of the night before. In particular the news that a mysterious figure, Ting's 'friend', had not only sent the little sprite to help them but was working to protect them. That news had lifted his spirits more than he thought possible. Jack also thought about Hephaestia Hatter and the fact that she was still out there somewhere, possibly sneaking up behind them right now, or waiting ahead behind one of the ancient trees with their twisted boughs draped with haghair.

Jack searched the path ahead for any sign of the sorceress. He nearly ran into Denn when the horseman stopped suddenly in front of him. He gestured for Jack and Harriett to stop and be quiet. They obeyed. Denn peered forward, craning his head, listening to something just out of earshot.

"Do you hear that?" he asked.

"Hear what?" Jack asked back. Before Denn answered Jack heard it himself, a sound that, though not unusual anywhere else, was so strange in the silence of Fellwood that it made his heart thump. It was the distant caw of a bird.

They quickened their pace. The path began to slope gently downwards and bend slightly to the right. As they came around the bend Harriett gasped. Ahead of them, like the opening to a long tunnel, was a gap in the trees bathed in a halo of sunlight. The bird cawed again, this time closer and more clearly. All three of them broke into a spontaneous run, dashing for the sunlight ahead. When they reached the halo of light, emerging from the forest onto a dusty road, they paused to take in the view. The road ran to the left and right of them, an enormous marshland directly ahead.

"Swampmere," Denn proclaimed. "We've made it through."

Jack and Harriett whooped with glee. Even though the huge, marshy swamp was not a pretty sight, it was nevertheless beneath a full, shining sun. Jack stood in the sunlight soaking up its warmth. It felt delicious and comforting and exhilarating all at the same time. Despite facing Hephaestia Hatter and Mog, and evading goblins and Vellenor, they'd made it safely through Fellwood!

The bird cawed again, directly above them. They all looked up to see it circling overhead, an ordinary raven. Jack had never been happier to see a bird in his life. Harriett laughed out loud, bending to pick up a stone and launching it at the wall of trees behind them.

"Take that, you dumb old forest!" she taunted. "We're safe and there's nothing you can do about it!"

Denn and Jack laughed as Harriett picked up another stone and launched that at the forest as well. The raven cawed once more, veering to the south-west. Jack followed it with his eyes, and started in alarm, causing Denn to follow his gaze. Far to the south-west, rising from a distant spot on the swampy horizon, were massive plumes of black smoke. The smoke billowed upwards from the ground and spread across the sky to form what looked like immense storm clouds. At first Jack thought it was a volcano, but as he watched he saw the slight but unmistakeable flash of blue lightning within the pillars of smoke.

"Oh no," he muttered, certain that the blue lightning meant that Serza was the cause of the massive ash cloud.

Harriett abandoned her stone throwing to see what Jack and Denn were looking at. "What is that?" she asked.

"Bonemound lies in that direction," Denn said. "The Dark Prince looses war on the Dread. Let us hope they wipe each other out."

If Serza is victorious he will advance along this road and endanger our journey to Pitmouth, Ting said in Jack's ear.

"How far is it to Bonemound from here?" Jack asked.

"Two days," Denn answered.

"And how far from here to Pitmouth?"

"About the same. What are you thinking, Jack?"

"I'm thinking that if Serza has already defeated Bonemound he might overtake us before we reach Pitmouth."

"There is no way of knowing what has occurred at Bonemound," Denn said soberly. "We will have to take our chances."

"I know a way we can find out," Harriett said. "The torc!"

After explaining the torc Amallayne had given Harriett to

Denn, which led to another round of reverent lip touching, Harriett took it out of her pocket and held it out to him and her brother. "It's only big enough for one of you to hold on to as well," she said.

"Someone must remain to watch over the others while they undertake the vision," Denn said, "and that best be me."

Jack took hold of one side of the wrist torc and waited. Harriett smiled in an unconcerned way and looked to the south-west.

"Show us what's happening now at Bonemound," she said.

Instantly Jack's vision was filled with that sparkling silver light. Every grain of soil and every drop of water in the swamp turned to glittering particles like minute balls of quicksilver. As the silver glitter obscured all in his sight, a powerful force took hold of him and Harriett and pulled them toward it.

With a jolt, Jack found himself hurtling through the sky, the marshlands of Swampmere rushing beneath him far below. He was hanging upright, the speed causing him to pivot unsteadily this way and that. He looked to his side and saw Harriett, aglow with silver light, zooming along beside him like a human bullet, her arms stretched before her to better facilitate her flight. In the air, without the hindrance of gravity, Harriett wasn't gangly or uncoordinated at all, but sleek and graceful. If it weren't for the dirty pentagram on her brow she would've looked quite angelic.

Jack copied Harriett and stretched his hands out in front of him. He found that flying in this position stabilised him and stopped him pivoting about. It also helped to allay the disorientation caused by moving so fast and so high up, with nothing between him and the ground but empty air.

As they hurtled in the direction of the billowing pillars of smoke, Jack got a sense of the vastness of Swampmere. As far as he could see there was nothing but bog and mud and tufts of reedy grass. The bog was broken here and there by small islands on which stunted, evil-looking trees grew. The trees looked half-starved of nourishment, their roots dipped into the mud like long barky fingers digging in the fetid marsh for something on which to feed. Mean-looking hawks circled over these scraggly little islands, on the hunt for whatever meagre form of life managed to survive there. Other birds were flocking south, gangs of ravens and vultures, presumably on their way to feed on battle carrion at Bonemound. They passed over these birds, and soon saw an astonishing sight.

Pillars of smoke loomed ahead of them, much vaster than they'd looked from a distance. They threw a shadowy gloom over everything. As Jack and Harriett moved closer the terrible sound of war reached their ears. The cries of goblins, the roar of trolls and the whump and crash of catapults and other machines of destruction. On the ground below them, partially obscured by swirling drifts of smoke and ash, legions of dark figures swarmed across the marshland. Goblins, trolls and Dark Elves, all bearing the scimitar swastika emblem of Fellwood on their armoured breast plates. *The army of Serza!* Ting hissed in Jack's ear. The army radiated outwards from the vast pillar of smoke in row after row, waves of fully armed monsters hell-bent on one thing – the destruction of Bonemound.

"There must be thousands of them!" Jack said in awe.

"Hundreds of thousands," Harriett shouted back.

Their pace slowed as they flew over the outer flanks of the dark army. Soon they could see the Dread temple of Bonemound, ablaze with smoke and flame. The temple looked to Jack like a squat windowless ziggurat of many levels, made of dark mud perched atop a mound-like island in the middle of the swamp. A forbidding looking place, the temple of Bonemound's tiers were decorated with rows of various kinds of skulls: elvish, human, troll and goblin. It had only one entrance that Jack could see: a huge armoured door, emblazoned with the revolting Bonemound emblem – four skeleton hands arranged wrist to wrist to make a flower.

Smoke and flame poured from holes in the ziggurat's

walls, the black smoke spiralling upwards to the sky from every quarter. Huge wooden catapults of varying sizes were lined up directly in front the temple, hurling flaming balls of sulphur at the walls, which exploded on impact, sending ash, dust, bricks and shattered skulls high into the air.

Jack and Harriett came to a halt directly above one of these catapults, manned by goblins under the direction of a whip-wielding Vellenor warrior. The catapult fired another round at the temple that landed squarely on the uppermost tier, exploding a portion of the walls and collapsing the ceiling. Inside the ziggurat, goblins and Dread sorcerers lay dead and mangled. Those not dead or wounded scampered to the cover of darkness that the remaining walls provided. The wounded goblins unable to reach the shadows screamed in pain as they began to sizzle and burn under the light of the sun. Thanks to Thullu's Gift, Serza's army was immune to daylight, which gave them an extreme advantage.

Three spinning balls of green light emerged from the shadows of the damaged ziggurat and hit the catapult below Jack and Harriett. It exploded with a deafening boom, killing the Vellenor overseer and sending goblins hurtling through the sky. One goblin, his arms and legs flailing like some bizarre bird, hurtled directly between Jack and Harriett, squealing the whole way. He slowed and started to fall, squealing right up until he hit the ground with a sickening crunch. *There are still Dread sorcerers alive inside*, Ting said, as another volley of green orbs flew out of the ziggurat in every direction to explode into catapults, advancing goblins and detachments of Vellenor. The army was so huge that this hardly made a dent on their numbers.

"Oh Jack, look!" Harriett said, pointing to the left of her at an appalling sight.

A wedge of thousands of dirty white creatures, eight foot tall and sporting big, bear-like claws on their hands and feet and long, needle-sharp teeth, rushed toward the ziggurat. The creatures pounded on the huge armoured doors and scaled the mud walls, using their claws to grapple with the mud bricks and scramble upwards. Harriett had never seen trolls before. Jack remembered how he felt when he first saw them. He'd thought they looked one third gorilla, one third bear and one third wolf. Harriett's face transformed into a mask of horror as the trolls, howling monstrously, reached the lowest tier of the temple and swarmed around it looking for a way inside.

Six Dread sorcerers emerged from the mud walls of the ziggurat itself, as if having walked straight through them. Jack lurched backwards, startled. The sorcerers were all very much like Hect; pale, bald, dressed in long coats of leather. They extended their hands toward the trolls in a series of grasping, claw-like movements, magically lacerating and tearing at the trolls' skin. The wounded trolls howled and retreated, blood staining their white fur. As the trolls fled, the Dread emitted flashes of green light from their hands that hit the furry creatures with a flash of flame. Burning, howling in agony, the remaining trolls launched themselves off the ziggurat to fall to their deaths below.

More and more trolls mounted the ziggurat and attacked the Dreads so that, no matter how powerful the sorcerers were, soon one, then a second, then a third sorcerer fell beneath the crush of savage, gnashing beasts. The remaining three Dreads escaped back through the mud walls, leaving the trolls to furiously pound and dig at the walls where they disappeared.

It wasn't long before the trolls at the base of the ziggurat bashed down the temple door and rushed inside, followed by huge numbers of goblins. Terrible screams, roars and growls emanated from the ziggurat as Serza's trolls and goblins fell on those inside. Green explosions from inside showed that the forces of Bonemound were offering some resistance. Soon even these explosions ceased and there was just the howl of trolls and the screech of goblins. For just a few passing seconds there was a silence that, after the deafening roar of the battle, chilled Jack to the bone.

The silence was broken by an outbreak of flashes of

green light from the uppermost, most damaged level of the ziggurat. Trolls howled, goblins screamed and then there was silence again. More flashes of green light preceded the sound of trolls and goblins in terror and pain. A pack of trolls emerged from the temple door, many of them wounded and clearly dazed, followed by equally wounded and dazed goblins, all fleeing the ziggurat. The silence descended again. After long moments there was an outbreak of laughter coming from a terrible female voice inside the temple. A rapid series of green orbs burst out of the temple to decimate hundreds of goblins and Vellenor at a time.

The besieging army fired up all of its catapults at once, aiming the sulphurous bombs at the uppermost tier of the temple. The thunderous rain of explosions, crashing walls and blasts of fire was deafening. Jack and Harriett covered their ears. After what seemed like an eternity of this, the barrage stopped. Along with the army below them, Jack and Harriett peered through the smoke and flame to see the damage.

The entire upper level of the ziggurat was exposed to the elements, every wall now a pile of rubble. Not an inch of the ceiling remained. Amid the decimation, smoke and flame, Jack made out a strange shape, a sphere of energy resembling grey glass. The sphere contained a solitary Dread, the Witch of Bonemound, Hect. Jack recognised her from his visions. Through the grey sphere Jack could make out her pale skin and bald head, her white-less eyes the colour of burgundy. Her ears were pointier than most Dark Elves and had a bat-like quality to them. She wore an ankle-length black frock-coat that reminded Jack of an undertaker's garb. She hissed at Serza's army and Jack noticed with a jolt of fear that her teeth had been sharpened to spikes and capped with copper points. They looked like nails. Harriett saw this as well and gasped.

From within the sphere came that eerie laughter again, a brittle cackle full of evil. The Vellenor soldiers at the front of the ziggurat stretched arrows into their curved bows and fired a volley. The arrows burst into dust on impact with the grey orb, which shimmered almost as if it was made of water. With the failure of their arrows, the Fellwood forces catapulted sulphur bombs at the grey sphere. On impact the sulphur bombs turned to clouds of ash. Hect cackled derisively, firing more green orbs to obliterate hundreds of her enemies from within the safety of the sphere.

"Enough," a sickening, nausea-inducing voice shouted, making Jack's head spin. A few yards directly behind Jack and Harriett, the Dark Prince, Serza, hovered in the sky. His pale lips were twisted into a sneer. "You weary me, hag. Surrender yourself or die with the rest of your kind."

"You are nothing," Hect screamed, "just a usurper and a *fool!*" Hect's terrible voice echoed across the marsh. As the echoes travelled they transformed into a high pitched, blood-curdling squeal. *Cover your ears!* Ting shouted. *It is the cry of the banshee!* Jack relayed the message to Harriett. The witch's high-pitched squeal caused goblins, trolls and Vellenor alike to shield their ears as well. For many, shielding their ears was not enough. Goblins, trolls and Vellenor dropped dead in their thousands, black blood seeping from their ears, eyes, noses and mouths. But not Serza. The Dark Prince simply clicked his fingers and the voice stopped. He made a clutching motion with his hand, directed at Hect in her solitary sphere. The sphere vanished with a pop.

Serza glared at the now defenceless Dread sorceress, a strange blue light emanating from his gaze. It was as if his eyes were openings behind which a blue sun burned, shining directly on Hect. She gasped and staggered.

"You dare!" she squealed. "You dare use the Secret Gift against me!"

"No power is beyond me now," Serza sneered. His eyes widened and that blue light, now intensified into a narrow beam, bore into Hect, who stumbled back and nearly fell. She shrieked and summoned a shield of green light to protect herself from the sun and Serza's assault, but to no avail. The light coming from Serza's eyes slowly but evenly burned through her shield spell, which soon failed. Hect mumbled a stream of incantations, becoming increasingly desperate. Jack knew that if not for those incantations Hect would already be dead. Her skin blistered and her clothes smoked. With a flash, her coat erupted into flame. She shrieked and threw it off, shooting one last volley of green energy at Serza. He deflected it with the merest flick of his hand. The Witch of Bonemound let out a blood-curdling howl and leapt into the air, transforming herself into a streak of black smoke, which rocketed upwards and away to the east. Serza fired a bolt of lightning after her but narrowly missed. He shouted in rage and took out his frustration on his own troops. With a jerk of his hand, the earth shook and split open. Hundreds of Fellwood goblins fell into the pit, squealing.

As the last squeal of the falling goblins subsided, Jack looked to Harriett, who was staring at Serza in horror. The Dark Prince had been victorious over Bonemound. Jack couldn't believe it. Serza cast his eyes over the battlefield, a definite expression of triumph replacing the rage. As the Dark Prince's pink eyes passed over Jack and Harriett they flickered and stopped. He stared directly at them, as if straining to see something just beyond his vision.

"He can't see us, can he?" Jack asked quietly.

"He shouldn't be able to," Harriett said, her voice unsure. They couldn't do anything other than watch as Serza stared in their direction. Just seconds later their question was answered for them. A flash of recognition crossed Serza's face and he sneered.

"Waycaller," Serza spat. "I no longer need you! I have destroyed Bonemound! Now I will bury the Hag Queen Morrigan in her tomb!"

Apart from scaring the hell out of him, Serza's words told Jack something very important. Amallayne was right. Not only had Serza turned on Bonemound, just as she'd predicted, but his next move was also clear. He would turn toward Pitmouth in an attempt to destroy the Keysong, thinking that by doing so Morrigan would be entombed forever. But the Prince of Fellwood was wrong about that. Destroying the Keysong would release Morrigan, and then they would all suffer.

The Dark Prince of Fellwood stretched out a long finger and sent a thin bolt of blue lightning sizzling in their direction. Jack and Harriett dodged it just as their vision turned to sparkling silver and the light took hold of them. They were carried away in a blur of silver luminescence. In an instant they returned to the spot where an anxious Denn awaited their coming out of the vision.

"Jack," Harriett said, her voice shaking and her body trembling, "can you believe Serza did *all that* to Bonemound just because of you?"

"Not *because of* me; to stop Morrigan getting free so that he doesn't need me."

"Yeah, but still—"

"Don't, Harrie, please. If I think all that happened because of me ..." Jack felt physically ill.

"All what happened?" Denn asked.

Denn looked like he'd been punched when he learnt that Bonemound, the temple of the Dread sorcerers, long an object of fear for his people, had been reduced to rubble and all of its inhabitants killed, bar one.

"Long have my people hoped for the destruction of Bonemound. Now that its total devastation has finally come, I fear that I cannot enjoy it. We may all be doomed. How can we stand against one such as Serza?" Denn's voice was filled with anxiety.

"I don't know," Jack said. "All I know is that we have to get moving. Serza isn't far behind and he knows we're here. He'll put everything he's got into getting to Pitmouth as fast as he can."

"We best go then," Denn said. He tightened the straps to the saddle bags over his shoulder and started in the direction of the fortress of the goblin king. Jack and Harriett fell into step behind him, still dazed and shaken by what they'd seen.

The bog stretched out before them, broken here and there by small islands where those stunted trees or tufts of yellow grass grew. Another pack of ravens passed overhead, moving south to feast on the dead at Bonemound. Even though Swampmere was a harsh place, Jack couldn't help but be glad to be out in the sun and not under the heavy shade of Fellwood. It was good to feel warmth on his skin again. He smirked to himself. If he was going to die at Pitmouth, at least he would die with a tan.

PART 2: A DREAD SONG

SOVEREIGN

Anarra shifted her weight in the stone seat, placing her hands on the hard armrests a moment before moving them to her lap, then returning them to the armrests again. Made of snow white flecked with crystal, the throne of Elvinidd was beautiful but not comfortable. Though it glittered with the light streaming in through the high windows, it remained cold. Half-remembered facts came to her now, as if to distract her from her discomfort. The throne was one of four: the green granite throne of Tessarelle, the blue jasper throne of Merielle, the black granite throne of Ehmaara and this one, the marble throne of Songarielle. In the dim past the four elvish domains of mountain, wood, sea and night had been separate, each with its own ruler, each with its own throne. For thousands of years now the four realms had been united under the crown of the High Sovereign of Elvinidd, the winged crown that now sat uncomfortably on her own head.

Anarra found it ironic that such thinly beaten gold should seem so burdensome. As soon as it was placed on her brow she'd felt as if the weight of it was crushing her. She knew it was just her imagination but couldn't help adjusting the crown every few minutes. Had its previous wearers, the last ten Sovereigns, found it so ill-fitting? Perhaps not. She couldn't imagine Dhudhannan fiddling with it the way she was. The Bright King had worn it longest of all the sovereigns. He'd worn it in battle during the Doom War and was still wearing it when he died. She'd flinched away when the Thanes of the High Houses had removed it from Dhudhannan's lifeless body and tried to crown her with it. She'd still been holding the king's hand, which even then remained warm. It took Pelliah Tessar, Ellisenn's mother and the kindly Thane of the woodland elves, to calm her and convince her to put it on.

"The Bright King named you his heir before he passed,"

Pelliah had said gently. "You heard him utter the words yourself. It is ancient tradition. I'm sorry, but you have no choice in the matter. You must take the crown."

Anarra had allowed it to be placed on her head then. Instantly the weight of it, the responsibility it carried, had begun to change her. She had to let go of the idea of herself as Anarra the wanderer, the loner, the fighter. The person she had been all her life had to be put aside now. She had to somehow become worthy of the title of High Sovereign of all Elvinidd. She had to make her father and her people proud, even if it meant an eternity of service and never another solitary walk in the high hills where she'd once loved to roam.

She caught the scent of smoke. Though the fires were all out now, some quarters of Songarielle still smouldered. She'd seethed when the guards had stopped her from joining the defence of the citadel. When she tried to break out through a window they'd even threatened to take her sword away. The sword her father gave her to celebrate her coming of age just a year ago! She'd had to promise to stay seated on the throne until the danger passed, like a good girl, before they agreed to let her keep it. Her body had thrummed with shock and anger as Serza's attack raged outside. With every explosion she clutched the armrests more tightly, until her fingers turned white and ached. She couldn't relax until word came that Prince Serza had broken off the assault. Soon after that, news came that Aelf was badly injured and Jack and Harriett were missing. The relief she'd felt at Serza's departure vanished instantly. Did the dark prince have Jack and Harriett?

She adjusted the winged crown again, doing so furtively so that the guards who lined the walls of the throne room wouldn't notice. Two dozen of the Sovereign Guard were spaced evenly around the room, with another four on each of the two entrances. The Sovereign Guard weren't taking any chances on her safety, not after what happened to King Dhudhannan and the attack on the citadel. Three druids— Alva and two burly, white-cloaked men—stood to the right of the throne. They were under strict orders from Kashashem to prevent any magical attack. Alva still appeared shaken by her ordeal with the dark Sending, but the two tough-looking men were spoiling for a fight. Their hard eyes constantly scanned the room, lingering on the windows and doors, and their hands were slightly raised, ready to cast a spell at any moment.

Normal protocol dictated that the Sovereign of Elvinidd have a druid protector when travelling, but not for one to be positioned in the throne room itself, let alone three, and not one of them an elf. Protocol also dictated that a single troop of Sovereign Guards, not two, be assigned as the sovereign's personal escort. She'd known all this, about royal protocol, since she was a little girl. Her father had taught her everything he knew, and he'd known everything there was to know. As Thane of the High House of the Ehmaarim it had been part of his upbringing. Her breath snagged on the thought of her father. Her hand flew to her chest. For a moment she couldn't breathe. She closed her eyes, picturing him laughing. Her breath returned to her. The Waycaller, Jack Gordon, had awakened that memory for her. It had comforted her as she held King Dhudhannan's hand as he faded and slipped into eternal night. It had comforted her even more as the Thanes of the High Houses of the elvish domains gathered to anoint a new sovereign. The memory of her father was the only thing that kept her steady once the crown of Elvinidd was set on her head and she was led to the throne. It was the only thing that stopped her knees buckling as she mounted the royal dais as Pelliah Tessar called out: "Hail, Anarra Settonett, Thane of the House of Sett, and High Sovereign of all Elvinidd."

Anarra couldn't have taken the seat without that memory, without Jack's gift to her. She couldn't have stayed on it, raging inside, unable to fight to defend Songarielle. If she'd known that moment with Jack in Wadget's house would mean so much to her later, she would have thanked him more fully. She was certain, though, that Jack hadn't done it for thanks or reward. She hoped he did it because he'd decided it was the right thing to do, after careful consideration. In truth he'd probably just followed an impulse, and while there was nothing wrong with acting on impulse, it just wasn't very elvish. That was the problem with Jack. He wasn't elvish. Anarra strived to be more elvish than even the most ancient of her people. As a half-elf, she'd always felt she had something to prove.

Her feelings for Jack, although confusing, were undeniable. He had done an amazing thing by reminding her how much her father loved her. There was also an obvious attraction between them. Jack was very fair to look at, she couldn't deny that. He also had a dependable yet slightly roguish personality. None of that mattered though. She was a Settonett, the last high-born member of her race. She couldn't entertain an attraction to a human, even if he was the Waycaller. Despite this, Jack's face and smile often intruded on her thoughts. She tried to tell herself it was merely because of the extraordinary gift he'd given her. Who could put such a thing out of their mind easily? Still, she had to admit she dwelt on his smile and the way he looked in those snugly-fitting otherworld trousers just as much as on the kind thing he'd done. She blinked. Had she just thought that? A smirk curled her lips and died almost immediately. No-one knew where Jack was or even if he was alive.

The door to the throne room swung open. Kashashem strode in. A ripple of awe moved among the guards lining the walls. The druidess ignored it and paced to the throne. Miss Butters entered behind her, trotting to keep up and wearing an irritated look on her face. At least Anarra thought it was an irritated look. Miss Butters always appeared bothered about some thing or other.

"Your Majesty," Kashashem said, bowing her head. "The Sovereign Guard and the Druid Order together have secured the city."

"Thank you, Lady Kashashem, that is good news."

"That is the limit of the good news, I'm afraid—"

"You can say that again," Miss Butters grumbled from

Kashashem's side.

Kashashem glanced at her but didn't respond, addressing herself to Anarra instead. "Easily a third of the city lies in ruins, with many, many dead. The temple of Amallayne is destroyed, though the effigy is miraculously undamaged."

"Is there any word yet of the Waycaller and his sister?" Anarra hoped the question sounded like one asked by a queen concerned about larger issues, such as the danger to Elvinidd posed by their enemies getting hold of the Waycaller, not one asked by a teenage girl with a crush on a scruffy-haired otherworld boy.

"Don't waste your breath, girlie," Miss Butters spat. "They don't know where my younglings are. Probably ate up by trolls! My poor Jack and little Harriett!"

"Dorothea, calm yourself," Kashashem said coldly, "and you will address Queen Anarra as 'Your Majesty' or I will transform you into a swamp critter that slithers and oozes."

Miss Butters' face blew up and reddened, like an expanding balloon. Anarra intervened before the halfling could start blustering.

"Do not be too harsh on her, Lady Kashashem. Miss Butters did not mean to be rude, did you, Dorothea?" Miss Butters looked like she was about to say that she had fully intended to be rude so Anarra ploughed on. "She is just worried about Jack and Harriett; surely you understand that, Great Lady?"

"I do understand. We are all worried about Jack and Harriett, but that does not mean we can behave like trolls in a mud bath."

"Trolls ... mud bath ... *me*?" Miss Butters' eyes hardened with fury. Anarra steeled herself for the worst but they were all interrupted by Alva.

"Lady Kashashem, how fares Aelf? We heard he was injured, badly, but not if ..." She couldn't bring herself to ask if Aelf Ethelwulf would survive his wounds.

"Aelf's injuries are grievous," Kashashem said. "If he lives, he will not fully recover soon, perhaps not for many weeks or even months."

Alva stifled a sob with her hand. Miss Butters' face went from red to pale grey in an instant, her anger dissipating at the dire news of her friend's condition. Even the gruff druids accompanying Alva couldn't hide their distress. Their spell-ready hands fell to their sides and their eyes dropped to the floor.

The door to the throne room opened again. In came Wadget, leading Ellisenn and Daniselle. Anarra was pleased to see them safe. Though they bore the scorch marks and torn clothing of those recently in battle, they appeared unharmed. Only Ellisenn showed any sign of injury, in the form of a slight limp. The woodland elf's eyes scanned the room. Looking for what? Or who? Anarra thought she could guess. Wadget came straight up to the dais of the throne, eyeing the crown on Anarra's head with clear amusement.

"Well," he said, "I reckon yeh weren't expectin' ter have that ridiculous thing plonked on yer head when yeh decided ter come ter Songarielle."

"No, Oak Lord, I was not. Nor was I expecting to be held prisoner in this room while my friends battled the forces of Fellwood."

"Prisoner, yeh say," Wadget said, his ears waggling.

"The Captain of the Sovereign Guard and I thought it best our new queen stay here, where it is safe," Kashashem explained to Wadget, casting an amused glance at Anarra. "She has tried to escape once already, through the window."

"I am not a child," Anarra said. "I know how to use a sword."

"O' course yeh do," Wadget said, "but it's a queen we need now, not a swordfighter."

There it was. The responsibility of the throne had already changed what people expected of her, the way they looked at her. Already she was required to act differently to how she had acted all her life. She was to be a diplomat, not a brawler. She'd known that would happen, and she wasn't shrinking from it, but were they not going to give her any time to adjust?

"Your Majesty," Daniselle said, bowing her head reverently, "I of all present know what it feels to hear the call of the sword. Be patient. I am sure that in time you will be free to wield your sword in battle again. Until that day comes, I gladly offer myself as a sparring partner."

Wadget rolled his eyes but Anarra smiled in thanks. At least one of those around her understood what she was going through.

"Swords!" Miss Butters screeched, making everyone jump. "Who cares about swords? What about my younglings? What's being done to find my Jack and my Harriett?"

"What is this?" Ellisenn said, his voice cracking. "Has something happened to Jack?" He looked around the room, his eyes hard with anxiety, until they fell on Anarra. "Apologies, Your Majesty," he added, realising he'd spoken out of turn.

"Do not apologise, Ellisenn Tessar, for we are all anxious about the Waycaller's fate, me no less than anyone here." She hoped that sounded queenly while also delivering her true message. If anyone had a right to be anxious about Jack's fate, it was her.

"Let us not forget that there is a little girl missing as well," Kashashem said shrewdly, looking from Ellisenn to Anarra and back again.

"I, at least, haven't forgotten about Harrie!" Miss Butters cried, her amber eyes glaring at Anarra. "Poor, thin little thing. What's being done to find her?"

"I've done nothin', as I've just found out about it," Wadget said, looking to Kashashem.

"We only learned a short time ago. Aelf was found in the ruins of the temple, badly wounded, but Jack and Harriett were not there. I ordered a search of the citadel. They are not anywhere inside the walls."

"That is ill news," Wadget said, sitting on the floor and scratching his foot. "I'm sad ter hear it. What we learned from the sorceress who killed Dhudhannan is no better."

Anarra waited for Wadget to continue, but he was more interested in scratching between his toes. When it became obvious that Kashashem and the others were prepared to wait for the Oakling to finish with his feet no matter how long it took, she decided to press him herself. "What did you learn, Oak Lord?'

"That a plot was hatched ter kill yer father, kidnap yeh, kill Dhudhannan an' place yeh on that throne yer sittin' on."

"*What?*" Anarra's throat constricted and her mouth went instantly dry.

"Yes, Empress Rill o' the Tiqq is behind it, an' that makes me reckon that Thullu is involved after all. The Tiqq are Thullu's favoured children. The sorceress who carried out the plot was a halfling, a halfling in the thrall o' the Pale Mother. She felt Serza weakenin' the wards around Songarielle afore he made his assault an' took advantage o' it ter attack Dhudhannan."

"Impossible!" Miss Butters said. "No halfling would ever do such heretical and vile things!" She stamped her foot on the marble floor to emphasise her point.

"It is not impossible," Daniselle said. "We saw the evidence with our own eyes. This halfling sorceress has been following Jack and Harriett since they arrived in Anwynn. She sent a herd of bog nags after them, she cast a Sending that visited your home, she cast the Sending that attacked the Druid Chambers and … and… "

"Assassinated our Lord and Protector, Dhudhannan," Ellisenn finished when Daniselle couldn't. "It is true, Miss Butters, I also saw the sorceress with my own eyes. She is a halfling and she is in the service of the Pale Mother, there is no doubt."

"Well then, bring her here to me," Miss Butters hissed. She puffed out her chest, nearly doubling her girth. "Let me at the witch. I'll teach her not to be a heretic and stalker of younglings."

"I wish we could," Wadget said. "She escaped when Serza attacked. Besides, she's ear-whipped an' would be more than a match fer yeh."

Anarra raised a hand to stop Miss Butters disputing whether or not she could handle an ear-whipped sorceress. Her mouth was still dry with the shock that the earwisps had plotted to place her on the throne. She swallowed so that she could speak. She had questions she wanted answered straight away.

"Why did they do this?"

"With an ear-whipped elf on the throne o' Elvinidd, who could stand against Morrigan once the Waycaller was dead and Darkgate opened?"

"But I'm not ear-whipped, am I?"

"No, I don't reckon yeh are, yet."

"How can we know for sure?" Miss Butters asked, glancing at Anarra. From the moment of their meeting in the dells, the halfling had been suspicious of Anarra. She now clearly felt that her instant mistrust had been justified.

"There's no way to know," Kashashem said. "We just have to trust the queen when she says she isn't ear-whipped."

"There is a way," Wadget said. "An ol' incantation that reveals the presence o' the Tiqq."

"We cannot use that." Kashashem's voice was firm and final.

"Why not?" asked Anarra.

"Because apart from revealing the earwisp," Kashashem explained, "it kills the person possessed by it. Sometimes the incantation even kills the person if there isn't an earwisp at all."

"Oh well, small price to pay," Miss Butters said. "Let's have it then, what's this incantation?"

"Dorothea!" Kashashem sounded truly shocked.

"No, Miss Butters is right," Anarra said, barely believing she was saying it. "My life *is* a small price to pay if it means protecting the throne of Elvinidd and ensuring that Morrigan does not rise to power again."

Miss Butters stared at Anarra, blinking. "Perhaps, I've read you wrong, Miss Majesty."

"You can't be serious," Alva said. "If you allow that incantation to be used you are likely to die whether or not you are possessed. Do you understand that?"

"I understand perfectly well. Lady Kashashem, I command you to use the incantation."

"Anarra!" Kashashem's yellow eyes glistened. She stepped back, shaking her head.

"You will call me 'Your Majesty' and you will obey the command of your queen."

"No, I beg you, Your Majesty, do not make me do this."

"Lord Wadget, I command you to do it." Anarra's voice broke a little. If one of them didn't do it soon she feared she'd lose her nerve.

"Yeh can't command me, little queen. I'm not a subject o' Elvinidd. But, alright, I'll do it." Before Kashashem could stop him, Wadget whirled his wand over his head and muttered a series of strange words. The sound of thunder cracked in the room. A sudden hot wind swirled around the throne. Anarra's skin felt as if it burned. She broke out into a sweat and slumped in her chair, fighting to stay conscious. She heard Kashashem and Alva gasp. Someone said 'no' and then the sound of thunder whipped through the room again. The heat lifted and the cool air from the windows was like ice on her skin, a feeling so blissful she nearly cried out with relief. She couldn't cry out though, she was too weak even to sit up straight in the throne. Hands were on her then; rough, warm hands with claws. Wadget. She opened her eyes to see his large, brown ones staring back at her.

"Yer alive then, are yeh?" he said. "An' not ear-whipped, yeh'll be pleased ter know."

Other hands were on her then, smoothing the hair out of her eyes, wiping the sweat from her brow. "Back away from her," the owner of those hands said, "and let the poor girlie breathe." Miss Butters, her voice worried and warm with affection. That was interesting. In just moments the dynamic of their relationship had changed. All she'd had to do was nearly die. She smiled, or at least tried to, and with Miss

Butters' help pulled herself back into a sitting positon.

"The question of whether or not I'm possessed seems to be resolved." Her voice sounded frail even to her. Wadget chuckled. Kashashem stared at her, appalled. Ellisenn stared at her as well, but the look on his face was neither shock nor dismay. It looked to Anarra like a mixture of respect and wariness. That was interesting too. "If this halfling sorceress failed to have me ear-whipped, why did she kill Lord Dhudhannan?"

It took a moment for everyone to accept that Anarra was continuing as if she hadn't just nearly lost her life. When they did, it was Wadget who spoke.

"Maybe she thinks an inexperienced young queen is less a threat than a king who sat the throne fer millennia an' lived through the Doom Wars. Or maybe she killed him just 'cause she could. She seemed right deranged ter me."

"Or perhaps," Kashashem added, "she has not abandoned her plan to ear-whip the queen and will continue to try."

"That's possible," Wadget agreed. "We can't know. Yer queen will need ter be closely guarded 'til all this is settled."

Anarra didn't like the sound of that. She pulled herself straighter in the throne, starting to feel normal again. She'd been picturing her father, the image Jack had given her restoring her hope and much of her strength.

"Does this halfling sorceress have Jack and Harriett?" she asked.

"No," Wadget said. "She fled the citadel alone, o' that I'm certain."

"Does the dark prince have them then?" Daniselle asked, her hand involuntarily going to her sword.

"No, he does not," a voice drawled from the shadows in the corner of the throne room. A frenzy of movement followed. The guards roared and rushed to encircle the dais and Anarra, their swords drawn and pointed in the direction of the shadows. In the rush Miss Butters was jostled up onto the dais beside the new queen. Wadget whirled around, drawing his wand and casting a shield of energy between them and the figure emerging from the shadows. Daniselle drew her sword and Ellisenn his bow. They stood either side of Wadget. Kashashem, Alva and the other druids formed a line between Wadget and the guard-encircled throne, their hands all raised at the ready. Miss Butters balled up her fists and took up a position right in front of Anarra, the last line of defence, as if she alone would fend off any attacker.

"Impressive," the voice said, as its owner stepped out into the light. "You must feel so proud, Bright Queen, to have so many ready to lay down their lives for you."

"'Hob!" Wadget growled, pointing his wand at the beautiful, velvet-clad Faeden standing before them. "What are yeh doin' 'ere?"

"I come with news for the little queen," the Faeden said, stifling a bored yawn. His lips formed an unconvincing smile that did not reach his cold blue eyes. His long black hair hung loose over his shoulders, shining darkly.

"News about what?" Wadget asked.

"I will tell you, my little green friend, but first, let me make something clear." He flicked his hand towards the crowd protecting Anarra and in a blur of movement the guards were tossed aside as Wadget's shield spell popped. The guard's weapons vanished as their bodies were pinned motionless against the walls. Miss Butters flew backwards and struck the throne, falling to the floor unconscious. Daniselle was thrown to the ground. Wadget, Kashashem and all the druids staggered back, breathing hard and unable to speak. Daniselle lurched to her feet and backed off. Ellisenn, panting as though he'd been punched in the stomach, glared at Hob but did not move aside. Hob looked the woodland elf over and rolled his eyes.

"There's always one," he said, as if to himself, before speaking directly to Anarra. "I hope it is clear to you now, Bright Queen, that whatever power you wield, whatever forces you command, they are nothing compared to the smallest flick of my wrist."

"Your point is well made, Faeden." Anarra's heart pounded but she gave no impression of the fear coursing through her veins. "You said that you had news? Please, tell us what you came to tell us."

"Using the royal 'we' already, Anarra? How conventional of you." He sighed, strolled over to a window and looked out. The sun sparkled on his pale skin. He spoke as if to the sunlight itself. "The Prince of Fellwood does not have the Waycaller, nor does he have Jack's irritating little sister. They were carried to safety soon after Serza launched his attack on this wretched place."

"Carried to safety? By you?" Anarra guessed the answer before it came. Hob was not the type to help without there being something in it for him.

"Oh no, not by me. As I'm sure Wadget would tell you, I rarely involve myself in the affairs of lesser beings."

"Who then?" Anarra asked.

"It was Amallayne, the Great Goddess herself, who spirited them away."

A hush fell over the room. Even the guards pinned against the wall stopped struggling to break free.

"Where are they?"

"That I cannot say. All you need to know is that they are alive, unharmed and have not been captured by Serza or any of Morrigan's underlings."

"Why are yeh tellin' us this?" Wadget wheezed, struggling to form the words.

Hob waved his hand and the throne room became unnaturally still. The occasional sound of birds in the courtyard outside stopped. Even the sunlight coming in the window stilled. The sounds of the guards wriggling for release, of Wadget and the druids panting, vanished. No one moved. It took a second for Anarra to realise that not only were they not moving, they were not breathing at all.

"What have you done?" Her voice sounded higher and more frightened than she'd ever heard it sound before.

"I have frozen time. Listen to me, Anarra Settonett, this

is for your ears only. The prophecy races toward fulfilment. If you wish it to succeed, for the Bright powers to triumph over the Dark, you must act. You must invoke the ancient treaty and unfurl the ancient banner. Unite the five domains of the elves as one force as it once was long ago. Bring together the elves of the mountain, wood, sea, night *and* the elves of the dark. If you do not do this, all is lost. The prophecy will fail and your precious Elvinidd will be destroyed."

"The treaty is broken. You know this. It was broken thousands of years ago when the Vellenor betrayed the Bright Child and submitted to Morrigan. They are our enemies now. They will never join us under the same banner again."

"You must find a way, Bright Queen. Elvinidd's destruction is certain if you do not."

"Why are you helping me?"

"What I will tell you must never be repeated. If you do, I will burn you in an instant and then incinerate your entire race. I will scorch every last inch of Elvinidd until not a single blade of grass remains. I will cause all the water in Anwynn to turn to blood and all that is green to wither and die. That is just the beginning of the terror I will visit on the world if you speak one word of this to anyone."

Anarra dared not speak, she simply nodded.

"I need a favour."

"*What*?"

"Let me explain. Of all the Faeden I am the only one who never sought the reverence of lesser breeds. Amallayne wallows in the love of the Pix, even Morrigan is adored by her dark children. Since the beginning of time I have been alone, unloved by humans or elves and perfectly happy about it. That is until a little while ago, perhaps a thousand years, when one family of humans learnt of me and started to make offerings to me. Just little things, offered in a makeshift shrine in their modest home. Nothing I could ever want or need of course, flowers and tea and that sort of thing, but I found it all rather touching. As time passed they have lived and died and I grew rather attached to them. Now there is just one of them left. A good and solid man. I want him to survive, to be free and flourish, to seed a great family who will all love me."

"You are Faeden, can't you make it so that he survives?"

"Yes, I can make it so that he *survives*, but *flourish*, no, that is trickier."

"Evidently, if after a thousand years the family has all but died off."

"I am not used to assisting humans," Hob said, his blue eyes flashing. "I do regret not intervening sooner. This is why it is so important to me, especially now. My human will not flourish in a world ruled over by Morrigan, or even that piffling Serza. So they must be stopped. The only way for that to happen is for the elves to unite as one again. To flourish, my human also needs to feel content, to feel satisfied deep within himself. Humans seem to need contentment as a cow needs grass. As Faeden, I know what it is his heart truly yearns for, what will make him content. He needs love. Even the Faeden cannot force someone to love another. Love is funny like that."

"Wait, what are you asking of me?"

"Oh, don't flatter yourself. I have another maiden in mind for him. The maiden is elvish, and as such is under your dominion. When the time comes, you will command her to marry my human, and convince her to love him."

"I cannot guarantee that."

"You will do it, or Jack will die. The Waycaller faces many dangers now. If you grant me this favour, I will assist him. If I do not help him, he will surely perish and Morrigan will be loosed. Unite the elves and give my human a loving bride, or Jack will die and Anwynn will be destroyed."

"You would let that happen over this one person?"

"Yes, I will let the world burn if you do not help my human to find love and flourish."

"Alright, I will do my best. Who is this maiden, and what is the name of the man?"

"Oh, I'm not going to tell you that just yet, you might

blab and spoil things."

"I will not speak of it. You threatened to destroy Anwynn if I did."

"If you're going to be a good queen you need to learn to distinguish the difference between a real threat and a bluff."

"You ... you were bluffing?" she stammered.

"What would happen to my human if I destroyed Anwynn?"

"He would die."

"Yes, so clearly I'm not going to do that. But don't speak of it anyway, otherwise our deal is off and Jack *will* die. Oh, and do not forget to invoke the treaty, that is important. More important than you will ever understand."

A flash of blue light blinded her. Voices rang out in the room. The guards raced to her side, their armour clattering. By the time she could see again everyone was milling around her.

"Hob?" she asked, dazed.

"Gone," said Wadget. "Did he say anythin' else ter yeh?"

"No, just what you heard, that Jack and Harriett are alive and unharmed," Anarra lied.

"Tricksy devil," Miss Butters cursed, rubbing a growing lump on her forehead. "I never did like him."

"Lady Kashashem," Anarra said, swallowing hard. "Can you do something for me?"

"Yes, my queen, anything."

"I need to address the senate. Can you arrange that?"

"Yes, I can. I will have the senate gathered by nightfall." Her voice sounded curious and her eyes were questioning.

"Good. And about my security: I think just one druid protector is enough."

"Only if that one is Wadget." The druidess frowned, clearly wondering what all this was about.

"No, I want Ellisenn. If he's willing, that is."

Ellisenn hesitated, his eyebrows arching in surprise, but nodded his assent. Kashashem looked unconvinced. Anarra didn't want to have to explain why she wanted Ellisenn close by. She wasn't exactly sure herself. To her relief, Wadget intervened.

"The lad is gifted," Wadget said, "an' competent. Give the queen the protector she wants, or the guards'll be draggin' her back in the windows again."

"That's settled then," Anarra said, standing and heading toward her apartments before Kashashem could mount a protest. Ellisenn hesitated, but after a nod from Kashashem followed her. Anarra smiled. It had not been an easy first day on the throne and would not be an easy night facing the senate, but at least she'd had her first small victory.

Anarra waited outside the pavilion that housed the Songarielle senate. On the roof of the tallest building in the very centre of the senate complex, the pavilion overlooked the whole of Songarielle and the plateau where it sat. Unlike the rest of the senate buildings, with their mazes of corridors, chambers and courtyards, this place was open and light-filled. The senate pavilion's golden roof gleamed with the setting sun. Anarra looked out to the snowy peaks of the mountains, stained red, orange and pink by the falling light. Ellisenn stood a few feet away, standing guard. A trio of mountain elves, beautiful and elegantly-dressed older women, strolled by. They looked back over their shoulders at Ellisenn, lust evident in their eyes. Their lust was not misplaced. Ellisenn was more handsome than any man Anarra had ever seen. Even so, she somehow found Jack much more appealing. Perhaps Hob was right. Love was mysterious. But did she *love* Jack? There was an attraction, yes, but was that enough to be called love? She chided herself for this distraction from her purpose and returned to the speech she was rehearsing in her mind.

Her first address to the Elvinidd senate needed to achieve a lot of things, one of them practically impossible, the invocation of the ancient treaty between all the elves, Bright and Dark. The first part of her speech declared war on the Tiqq. That in itself would send a shiver of fear through the senate. She would then demand that the four human kingdoms join with them to face this threat. Demand, not ask. That would ruffle the feathers of the human ambassadors she'd asked Kashashem to invite to the senate meeting. In her very next breath she would declare war on the goblins of Pitmouth and on the trolls. Finally, she would declare war on Prince Serza; although only on the prince himself, not on the whole of the Vellenor. She'd thought it important to make that distinction. It would mean that, if Serza were deposed or killed, some of the Vellenor might be persuaded to honour the treaty. The vague reason she'd requested Ellisenn as a protector had now coalesced into a plan. She looked over to him and decided this was as good a time as any to set that plan in motion.

"Ellisenn, can I ask you something?"

"Certainly, Your Majesty."

"Do you remember, when you were a child, travelling through the foothills of the Craggy Mountains, in the far north?"

"My family often made that journey. It is the safest route between Tessarelle and Merielle. As Thane, my mother often travelled to see King Dhudhannan."

"Do you remember, once, when you were just a small boy, sensing someone hiding in the crags?"

"Yes. That was you and your father."

"How long have you known?"

"Only since just now, when you asked. I sensed two elves, I could tell one was young and one older. When you asked me about it just now I deduced it must have been you and your father."

"My father was impressed by your skill. He said you were special. I, however, was not happy at having been spotted."

"My ears are big, even for a woodland elf – it was no great feat."

"You are too modest. We heard your mother call your

name. I remembered it always and knew that it was you when we met in the Druid Chambers."

"I always wondered why you were hiding."

"We Ehmaarim withdrew from the world after the Doom War. We were always solitary, but the trauma of the war made us shy of others, even other elves."

Ellisenn looked into her eyes. She sensed he wanted to say something but whatever it was would have to wait. She needed to press ahead with her plan.

"It is rumoured that the girls of Tessarelle cannot get enough of you. The same appears to be true here in Songarielle. Are you popular in other places as well?"

"Which places do you mean?"

"Dark places."

"Are you referring to my friendship with Sarritt, Princess of Fellwood?"

"So it's true?"

"It is true that we are friends. It is true that she loves me. It is true that I care for her very much. It is not true that I recklessly bedded her, as the tongue-wags of Songarielle would have it."

"But she shared many secret things with you. Kashashem told me about your recent visit to Vellenhive."

He nodded, his lips drawn tight. She hoped she wasn't losing him, that he would still answer her next, more shocking question.

"How *much* does she love you? Is she twined to you?" Anarra felt uneasy asking the question. The twining, the experience of falling into lifelong, irrevocable love, was a very private thing among elves.

"No, I do not think so."

"Will she do anything for you, if you ask?"

"What is it you want of the Princess of Fellwood?"

"I want her to overthrow her brother."

Ellisenn hissed and took a step back, looking Anarra up and down as if he'd never seen her before.

"What are you looking at?" she asked.

"A little girl dressed up in royal clothes."

He continued to stare at her. She wilted a little under his gaze. It was a terrible thing she wanted Princess Sarritt to do, to betray her own brother, family ties are inviolate among elves, but it was the only way she could think of to ensure the success of the prophecy and protect Elvinidd and all of Anwynn. And save Jack.

"If Sarritt ruled in Fellwood, much would be different," she said, sounding more defensive than she would've liked.

"The thing you ask is monstrous, and far too dangerous. Sarritt would likely be killed." Ellisenn's voice was blunt and cold.

"Serza is the monster. With Sarritt on the throne of Fellwood, and with the Vellenor returned to the protection of the Bright Child, we could negotiate a peace. Serza will never agree to peace. He wants us all as slaves, or dead."

"I would ask no friend of mine to do such a thing. I will certainly not ask Sarritt who is my dearest friend of all."

"Jack will die," she said, feeling desperate. "I cannot tell you how I know this, but it is true. Jack will die if we don't somehow convince Sarritt to take the throne and agree to a peace."

Ellisenn stared at her, his eyes troubled. She could see his resolve wavering. So, she was right about Ellisenn's true feelings. She took a breath and continued.

"You are twined to him. You are in love with Jack, aren't you?"

Ellisenn stepped back, his handsome face paling before her eyes. He took a deep breath, then nodded. A couple of tears spilled down his cheeks.

She took a step closer to him. "I'm so sorry." It seemed a strange thing to say on learning that someone was in love, but she knew that Jack did not and would never return Ellisenn's feelings. She could see that Ellisenn knew that too. To be twined to someone, irrevocably in love, for all the ages an elf could live, and know that the person you loved would never love you back. She shuddered at the awful thought of it.

Ellisenn's heart must be breaking.

"Is this why you asked me to be your protector?" he asked. "To torment me?"

"No, Ellisenn, never. I suspected you were twined to him, and I, well, I have feelings for Jack too. I thought, perhaps, that you and I could be friends. It was later that I had the idea about Sarritt."

"Do you love him?" Ellisenn's voice had an accusing tone to it. She knew why. Just as she'd known that Ellisenn loved Jack, Ellisenn knew that her feelings for the Waycaller were not so clear.

"I care for him, I like him. There is an attraction between us."

"An *attraction* between you?" He said the word 'attraction' as though it were something trivial, meaningless. "Is that all?"

"On my side, yes. I think Jack's feelings for me are stronger."

"Yes, his feelings for you are much stronger, I think. Mine for him are unendurable. What a hopeless trio we are."

"Our feelings do not matter, Ellisenn. We must abandon and betray our feelings if it saves Jack and prevents the Dark Ones conquering all of Anwynn. We must go to war and be crueller to our enemies than we can stomach or forgive."

He stared at her, his eyes narrowing. She was getting quite tired of it.

"What are you looking at now?"

"A queen," he said. "*My* queen, beautiful and fierce to behold."

SEEING STONE

Squeezed between Fellwood Forest on one side and the stagnant pools of Swampmere on the other, the road to Pitmouth snaked into the distance ahead of them. The trio of Jack, Harriett and Denn unconsciously followed a path in the middle of the road, keeping both forest and swamp at an arm's length. The bog stretched out to the horizon, buzzards and the odd scrawny-looking raven the only visible life. Jack had wondered about the prey these birds survived on, but quickly stopped thinking about it when it occurred to him that perhaps their main sources of food were the carcasses of unlucky travellers.

"Denn," Harriett said, watching a trio of buzzards circling an island ahead, "tell me about the witch of Bonemound again – about how she was able to fly."

Jack groaned. Not this again. Since they'd travelled via the wrist torc and witnessed the destruction of Bonemound, Harriett had obsessed over Hect, in particular the gruesome way the witch had acquired the ability to transform into smoke and fly.

"I do not understand you, Miss Harriett. It is almost as if you seek me to scare you, as if you liked to be frightened."

"She does," Jack said. "Lots of otherworlders enjoy being scared. It's a thing."

"A thing?" Denn's eyebrow arched. "It is an unnatural thing."

"Oh, come on, Denn, tell me again. I like a scary story and that Hect is *really* scary. She had metal fangs and awful bloody eyes."

"You otherworlders are all turned about. It is not right to find the Witch of Bonemound titillating. She is a blood-drinker."

"Yeah, the blood-drinker thing," Harriett said, "tell me about that again."

"Much of Hect's power comes from consuming the blood of others. It is an ancient kind of sorcery that few dare use. Only the worst of the Dread were foul enough to do it. It destroys the mind and transforms the body into that of a monster – a shadowflyer."

"And shadowflyers can turn into smoke?" Harriett's eyes popped a little, her voice full of excitement and awe.

"Aye. A shadowflyer can transform into smoke and travel through the sky. Once a Dread becomes a shadowflyer, they cannot survive the sun except in the form of smoke. In the day, they travel as dark streaks of smoke. They can move through solid walls as if there is nothing there. They must drink blood under the light of a black moon to retain their power. On moonless nights, they fly unseen through the black sky to seek their prey."

"That's terrifying!" Harriett moaned, thrilled.

"Harrie," Jack said, "you are a sick twist."

"Heed your brother, Miss Harriett," Denn said firmly. "I am not over-familiar with otherworlders but even I know that you should not court trouble with fiends such as Hect."

"Just hearing stories about her isn't going to hurt," Harriett said. "I mean, we'll probably never see her again."

"Aye, perhaps so, but if you ask me, it is the *probably* that should dictate your actions. If there is even the remotest chance that you will face Hect again, I would never utter her name."

"Okay, okay, I'll try not to ask about her again."

Jack wasn't convinced, and apparently neither was Denn.

"Don't merely try, Miss Harriett, trying is not sufficient. Just don't ask about her again."

"Fine." She sulked. "I'll be a good girl and only think about un-scary things like flowers and pretty pink dresses."

"That would be for the best," Denn said.

Harriett stomped along, fuming, kicking stones into the shallow pools of the swamp by the roadside. She tired of that after about ten minutes and caught up with Denn and took his hand. "Don't be mad at me, Denn. I'll try not to think about shadowflyers again. It's just that they're *deliciously* scary."

"Miss Harriett," Denn said, "I do believe you are a lost cause."

The three continued along the road in silence, Jack pondering the strange predilections of nine year old girls. They walked at a swift pace for the rest of the day, hoping to put as much distance between them and Serza's immense army as they could. That night they camped up against the edge of Fellwood, under another of Denn's makeshift shelters. Denn insisted they stay alert. Serza's host was likely to march day and night and could catch up with them at any time. Jack and Denn had a fitful night, taking turns keeping watch in-between short periods of sleep.

Just before dawn the next morning, Jack was sitting up on the last watch of the night when Harriett woke. Yawning and stretching, she stumbled over to her brother and sat down beside him at the fire.

"Penny for your thoughts," she said, putting her index finger into the ash beneath the brazier and swirling it around. Once she'd collected a large gob of soot she used it to redraw the Seren Star on her forehead.

"Well, for one thing, I'm thinking I'd *kill* for a sarsaparilla. Apart from that, I'm thinking we might not make it through this, Harrie. We'll reach Pitmouth today. Even if we do get inside, what are the odds we'll find the instrument that holds the Keysong *and* manage to get out alive with it?"

"I don't know," Harriett said. "But what choice do we have?"

"None. We don't have any choice. That's what I like least about it."

"We'll be alright, Jack. We have been so far." She smiled.

"We're still alive mainly because of luck."

"Not just luck, Jack. We've also had a lot of help from our friends."

"Yes, but when we go into Pitmouth it'll just be us and Denn. I don't know if that's going to be enough."

"What about Ting? Could she help?"

"Maybe," Jack said. "There's one way she might be able to help, but it's not pleasant."

"Well, we have to ask her, Jack."

"I will. She's asleep at the moment – at least, I mean she's been quiet a while now."

"When she wakes up we have to ask her to help us. She's the only one who can."

"That's another thing that worries me. Ting's not exactly cool-headed. She's kind of out of control, actually."

"Jack, you're so unemotional you'd think a brick was hysterical. I mean, I'm pretty sure you even think I'm a bit full-on."

"A bit?" he said, rolling his eyes.

Harriett smiled and leant into him. He put his arm over her shoulder and hugged her. It was the first time in days he'd shown her any real affection. He felt bad about that. She must have been thinking the same thing because she sighed heavily. Jack's thoughts turned to how they might survive the dangers of Pitmouth. As he pondered it, he kept coming back to the powers he was meant to have as Waycaller, the three powers mentioned in his mother's old book.

"I wish I knew what that passage in the book meant, about *becoming* the Way. If I could figure that out maybe we'd have a chance."

"You'll work it out, Jack. You just need to stop stressing about it. I bet if you just relax it'll come to you like that." She snapped her fingers.

"Relax? You really are mental, Harrie. We're being pursued by an army of Dark Elves and monsters led by the most powerful dark sorcerer ever and, just for good measure, a halfling witch is after us. *And* we have to find some instrument, when we have no idea what it looks like, and somehow take it back to Bright. How am I supposed to relax with all that going on?"

"I don't know. All I know is that you're never at your best when you're stressed out. You *have* to relax, Jack. The whole of Anwynn is, like, depending on you."

"Way to help me relax, Harrie."

"Sorry. Actually, I'm not sorry. You really can be a bit dim, Jack."

"I beg your pardon?"

"In case you haven't noticed, Jack, every dark being around is after you—"

"Isn't that what I just said, Harrie? I'm more than aware of that."

"Well, ask yourself why? Why are Serza and Morrigan's followers and even Morrigan herself after you?"

"I don't know—"

"You *do* know, Jack. We *all* know. It's because you're the Waycaller."

"So?"

"So," she said as if speaking to someone who's recently been hit in the head, hard, "that means that as Waycaller you must be pretty powerful."

"All I can do is pop around, from circle to circle—"

"No, that's not true. You showed Anarra a memory, I know, she told me. You can heal – you healed me, Jack. You saved me from dying. That's a *lot* of power. Stop acting like you're all defenceless."

"I'm not acting all defenceless, I'm just … just—"

"In denial. In denial that you are the Waycaller, that you have a responsibility to Anwynn, that you have power."

"But I don't, Harrie, I don't know what these three powers even mean let alone how to use them, or even if I *can* use them! What if I'm no good as a Waycaller?"

"Jack, do you remember what Wadget and Aelf said about Thullu's Gift?"

"Yeah, but what's that got to do with this?"

"They said that with Thullu's Gift Serza could do almost anything, was almost as powerful as a Faeden."

"So?"

"So, Amallayne said that with the power of the Keysong you might be able to overcome Serza."

"What are you getting at?"

"You must be pretty powerful yourself, Jack, if you have a chance of defeating Serza while he has the Secret Gift. There must be a lot more to being a Waycaller than just 'popping from circle to circle'. Surely that's obvious?"

Jack stared at her. Was she right? Harriett stoked the fire with a stick and left Jack to his thoughts. He pulled out his mother's book. He caressed the title on the cover a moment, *The Word of Thullu*, and then flicked through its pages, looking for more on how to use his powers to get them through their next challenge. For the first time, he thought they might have a chance. Harriett had shifted something inside him, changed his doubt into a glimmer of hope. As the pages ruffled, the sound made him think of falling leaves. That reminded him of the miniature tree in the temple of Amallayne, how its tiny leaves had fallen before Serza attacked.

"Harriett," he said all of a sudden, turning to look directly into his sister's eyes. "If we don't come out of Pitmouth with the Keysong, all hell will break loose. If Serza destroys the key, Morrigan will be loose before anyone back in Songarielle knows what's happening. Even if Serza doesn't find the key, once he's defeated the goblins he'll turn on the elves and Pix."

"I know. But we can't warn them. Amallayne told us not to tell anyone about our quest."

"We told Denn and that's worked out okay," Jack said. "I suppose there's no point talking about it. We couldn't warn anyone even if we wanted to."

"Of course we can, silly. Have you forgotten about the seeing stone?"

"The seeing stone? Of course! We can use the stone to tell Aelf what's happening! We could contact him now and say that if we don't get back in touch in a day then he'll know that all hell is about to break loose. You're a genius, Harrie!"

"Well yes, that is obvious, but what will Amallayne do if she finds out we said something?"

"We can't be worried about that, Harrie. We have to give

the druids a warning. Besides, Amallayne is more concerned about not defying Thullu than about our friends. We have to help them, Harrie."

"Okay," Harriett said, withdrawing the small opalescent seeing stone from her jacket pocket. "But don't tell them too much, just in case. We can just say we're on an important quest and if we're successful we'll get back in touch in a day."

"Okay. So, do you know how to get it to work?"

"Sure," Harriett said confidently. "You just rub the surface, like this, and think of the person you want to speak to." Harriett rubbed the seeing stone, her eyes closed, apparently thinking of Aelf. They peered into the stone's surface, but it remained unchanged. Harriett rubbed the seeing stone again. "It might work better if I picture Aelf in my mind rather than just thinking his name." She closed her eyes tighter. Jack continued peering into the seeing stone and soon its surface shimmered and changed. The next moment he was looking into a light-filled room. A sheer blue curtain at a tall window billowed in a breeze.

"I know this room," Jack exclaimed. "This is the bedroom I slept in at Daniselle's house! There's a big mirror on the wall. I bet that's what we're looking through." They both peered deeper into the seeing stone, trying to see around the edges of the mirror into the room. They could just discern a large bed, with a figure lying on its side as if asleep. Whoever it was had shoulder length grey hair and a thin build. Jack was the first to recognise it was Aelf Ethelwulf.

"Aelf?" Jack called. "Aelf?" The druid didn't respond. "Do you think he's asleep, Harrie?"

"Maybe not," she said. "Maybe he's still hurt from the attack on Songarielle."

"Aelf?" Jack resumed. "Aelf, are you alright?"

Still Aelf did not move.

"Is he in a coma?" Harriett whispered.

They waited a moment before calling out quietly one last time. The druid didn't move so much as an eyelid. Just as they were about to give up, Jack heard the sound of approaching footsteps. As the footsteps grew nearer, a face loomed into view: the face of a beautiful mountain elf with large almond-shaped eyes.

"Daniselle!" Harriett shrieked. "Daniselle, we're so glad to see you!"

"And I you, younglings," Daniselle said, as if it was perfectly ordinary to communicate with two human children through a mirror in her spare bedroom.

"Daniselle," Jack started, "we wanted to get a message to the druids through Aelf. Is Aelf alright?"

"Aelf Ethelwulf is not yet healed," Daniselle said gravely, "though we hope he will soon be so. Kashashem herself ministered to his injuries."

"And Wadget?" Harriett asked. "How is Wadget?"

"Master Wadget is well, but busy. We are preparing to take war to the Vellenor army amassed on the border with Pix."

"They're not there anymore," Jack interrupted. "They've turned on Bonemound and destroyed it."

"Bonemound destroyed?" Daniselle queried with one markedly raised eyebrow. "How could such a thing be so?"

"Serza," Jack said. "Bonemound was no match for him."

"Bonemound existed before the Doom War," Daniselle said almost to herself. "Its destruction will surely change the world, although for good or ill I cannot say."

"We need you to get a message to the druids," Harriett said. "We're on a mission to Pitmouth—"

"Pitmouth is no place for children," Daniselle interrupted.

"Lucky I am not a child then. We have no choice but to go," Jack said. "We've already got through Fellwood and are less than a day away from Pitmouth."

"You passed through Fellwood unscathed?" Daniselle asked, sounding impressed.

"Yes, and if we're successful on our mission we'll get back in touch in one day. We'll use the seeing stone to connect with the mirror in your spare room by thinking of

Aelf again. If we don't get in touch, it means we've failed and the druids will have to prepare for trouble – maybe Morrigan-sized trouble."

"I will take your message to the council," she assured them before asking, "Are you completely alone?" Her face showed visible concern for the first time.

"We have someone with us," Harriett said. "He's a Pixish horseman."

Jack was glad Harriett hadn't mentioned Ting.

"I am thankful for that," Daniselle said. "The Pixish horsemen are both skilled and brave. But one horseman in the face of the Dark Ones at Serza's command *and* the goblins of Pitmouth comforts me little. Best you had a thousand horsemen."

"He's worth a thousand," Harriett said. "His muscles are huge."

"You are a strange child," Daniselle stated.

"You got that right," Jack smiled. "But I wouldn't want her any other way."

"Who's a strange child?" said a very familiar voice. The top of a small brown-haired head approached the mirror. "Who is it?" asked the voice again, bobbing up and down as if standing on tippy-toes to see into the mirror. "Ruddy elves, everything's too high to be decent!"

"Miss Butters!" Jack and Harriett cried in unison.

"Younglings? Younglings! Let me have a look at you!" The head disappeared and they heard the sound of a chair being dragged across the wooden floor. A moment later, Miss Butters had climbed up on the chair bringing her round face and warm amber eyes into view. "There you are, you foolish younglings! We had no idea where you'd got to. How dare you disappear without a trace, without a word to me! And without packing a single provision! I should be very angry, I should, but I am too relived to see you to remain vexed. What are you doing in this mirror?"

"We needed to get a message to the druids," Jack said, surprised at how happy he was to see Miss Butters safe and sound.

"Oh well, you've come to the right place," Miss Butters said. "Daniselle's house is practically crawling with druids. I even have to bunk with Alva! Can you believe it? Me, Dorothea Butters, in close quarters with a Pixish druidess."

"I'm sure it isn't all that bad," Jack said.

"I suppose it isn't at that. That Alva's rather decent. They reckon she's a Seeress. Ha! Seeress my bottom! Eugene spare me!" She chuckled. "Good heavens, what have you got on your face, Harriett? It looks unsanitary."

"It's a Seren Star," Harriett explained, "and it's not unsanitary."

"Looks unsanitary to me, and blasphemous to boot," Miss Butters sniped.

"Anyway," Jack said, heading off one of Miss Butters' diatribes about hygiene and religion, her two favourite subjects after food. "I'm glad you're all okay. The last time we saw any of you was just before Serza attacked."

"Yes, we're fine, but there were many who weren't so lucky. The streets were *littered* with dead," Miss Butters exclaimed. "Littered! Poor Aelf has barely opened his eyes more than twice since they brought him back here. Then there's my own little difficulty, but that doesn't deserve mentioning."

"No, go on, we want to know how you are as well," Jack encouraged.

"Confounded and perplexed is what I am, dears," she began, "for I've been told by Kashashem that I have the makings of a druidess! Can you believe it? They want *me* to join the order and get trained up in magic!"

"You're joking?" Jack gaped, then closed his mouth. So this was why Aelf and Wadget had been manipulating Miss Butters. They wanted her to go to Songarielle to see Kashashem and join the Order.

"No joke, my dear," Miss Butters continued. "I wish it were a joke! Though it wouldn't have been a very funny one if it were! No, it seems that's why Aelf came to the dells and befriended me in the first place. I should have known then. What use has a druid for a friend like me? Turned out he was sent by the council to assess my potential. I will have a strong word with him when he awakes, let me tell you! Needless to say, dears, I so impressed Aelf with my botanical knowledge, and my skills with rabbit husbandry and home brewing, that he spoke to Kashashem herself and recommended me very highly."

"That's so cool," Harriett said, smiling.

"Yes, cool," Miss Butters echoed. "They told me I can start my training whenever I like. Of course, I thought it was absolute blasphemy at first, but now that I've had time to think about it, I've decided I'm going to take them up on their offer."

"Really?" Jack said, surprised.

"Yes. With Morrigans and Serzas running wild all over the ruddy place I've got to do my bit. What kind of halfling would I be if I did nothing? Besides, I prayed to Eugene and felt a distinct divine message, a deep stirring, that it was the right thing to do. Either that or the elvish food I've been forced to eat has upset my stomach. Anyway, I've agreed to join the order and am awaiting my instructions!"

"That's wonderful!" Harriett beamed.

"Yeah, well done, Miss Butters," added Jack.

"It's sweet of you to support me, dears, but enough of me. How are you? You both look unforgivably *thin*! Have you eaten anything at all?"

"Not much actually – a bit of old cheese and some dry bread," Jack answered. Miss Butters immediately burst into tears.

"Oh, you poor little things! You must come back right away and I'll see that you're never hungry again!"

"For once," Harriett chuckled, "that doesn't sound too bad. I can't wait to sit down with you in your back garden in Bright and have a big meal."

The mention of Bright reminded Jack of Hephaestia Hatter. He had almost forgotten that he needed to tell the druids about her. He mentally kicked himself – how could he have nearly forgotten that!

"Miss Butters, Daniselle," he exclaimed, "I've just remembered, you have to tell the druids that Hephaestia Hatter is a sorceress. She's been following us since Bright, and she attacked us in Fellwood Forest."

Miss Butters' eyes bulged and she hissed.

"Hephaestia Hatter! We knew there was a halfling who'd gone over to Morrigan and now we know who it is. Oh, I've never liked Hephaestia. She was *thin* as a child, you know. I should've known she'd turn evil then. If I ever get my hands on her, why I'll … I'll tear her into teeny-weeny pieces, that's what!"

"Master Wadget discovered that this halfling sorceress was behind the Sending that killed the Bright King," Daniselle said. "It is good to know her name. When we encounter her again, I will join Miss Butters in rending the vile creature's body into pieces!"

Jack gaped at Daniselle. Hephaestia Hatter had killed Dhudhannan! His stomach roiled, remembering the writhing tentacles of the dark Sending. Hephaestia Hatter was after Harriett. How could he protect his sister against that? *Well*, he thought to himself, summoning some of the hope Harriett had ignited in him earlier, *I'm just going to have to. I have to protect Harriett and so I will.*

"We'd better go now," Jack said. "We've got a lot of distance to cover today."

"Bye, dears, keep well and we'll see you soon!" Miss Butters waved at them through the mirror with both chubby hands.

"Safe journey, safe return," Daniselle said. It sounded like a blessing.

"Thank you," Jack said, afraid he might never see Daniselle's or Miss Butters' faces again. "And thanks for saving us from goblins in the Empty Lands, Daniselle, and for letting us stay in your homes, both of you."

"My door is open to you at all times," Daniselle

answered.

"As is mine," Miss Butters echoed.

"Bye," Harriett said sadly. "We'll talk to you in a day!"

The seeing stone faded to blue opalescence once more.

SPINEPEAKS

As the sun threw its first golden rays over the swamp, they roused Denn, pulled down their shelter and set off, barely rested at all. They fell into a similar pace as the day before, which Harriett found hard going. Her shorter legs meant that she was moving at close to a run. The terrain was much the same as it had been since they left Fellwood Forest. Swampmere stretched as far as the eye could see, a monotonous bog populated with nasty-looking buzzards whose hungry black eyes watched them as they passed by.

Around midday, with the sun directly overhead, the landscape changed. The marsh here was less boggy and more like a series of interconnected ponds, full of reeds and evil-looking black water lilies. They stopped and ate some more bread and cheese. They were almost through the last of it. Pretty soon they'd have to do a Miss Butters and start eating grass. Harriett chewed her lunch while holding her sides against a stitch, swallowing in-between panting for air. She was finding the pace gruelling, though to her credit she hadn't complained. She'd seen the full fury of what was marching up the road behind them. After their paltry breather for lunch, they resumed their rapid march. As the afternoon waned, Jack spotted in the distance ahead the black shapes of a range of mountains, jagged and rocky like a row of crumbling towers.

"Spinepeaks," Denn said soberly. "So named because they have the look of a dragon's ridged spine."

The road began to slope gently upwards. The trees of Fellwood to their left began to thin out so that soon the forest became scrappy open woodland. As the sun dipped low in the sky they reached a squat ridge, rocky and covered with boulders and tufts of dead grass. Beyond the ridge rose the steep slopes of the jagged black mountains, the Spinepeaks.

Though this part of the road to Pitmouth was less picturesque than anything they'd seen so far, the trio kept reminding each other that at least it wasn't the shadowy path through Fellwood. As far as Jack was concerned, the only good thing about the dusty road was that it was out from under the menacing canopy of the trees. He was also glad it was dry. Alongside the road the wet fen of Swampmere gurgled and Jack was grateful they didn't have to wade through it. The black and greasy swamp waters were much deeper here, trapped up against the low ridge ahead of them. The reeds at the banks had black trunks topped by crimson seed heads, making them look like bloody spears. The fen threw off a very bad smell, a mix of rotten eggs and three day old road kill.

"That stench is most odious," Denn moaned late that afternoon. He pressed his nostrils closed with his thumb and forefinger.

"I've smelt worse," Harriett said. "Jack's socks for one."

"Oh, very funny, Harrie," Jack said, his nose crinkling with the offensive smell. "My socks don't smell anything like that. It smells like old man fart!"

"Yeah, like I said, just like your socks."

"You should be ashamed of yourselves," Denn chided, "mocking elders and talking about … private functions."

"Private functions?" Harriett chuckled. "It's not like we're talking about a tea party."

Harriett's chuckle was cut short by the distant trumpeting of a horn. They all stopped and looked around. The horn sounded again, somewhere behind them. Though Jack couldn't see anything coming up from the rear, the proximity of the horn made his skin erupt in goose-pimples. The horn sounded a third time, now accompanied by the far-off sound of beating drums.

"That is a troll war horn," Denn said, "and those are the goblin-skin drums of the Vellenor."

"Serza's army," Jack moaned.

"Aye, and by the sound of it they are less than a day's

march behind us."

"How far is it to Pitmouth?" Harriett asked, looking worriedly down the road.

"It is close," he said. "I think it is not far beyond that rise." He indicated the small boulder-strewn ridge in front of them.

Without another word the three broke into a jog. After just a few yards, Denn swept Harriett into his arms and increased the pace. An hour or so later, they summited the small ridge, barely able to catch their breath. A triangular valley lay before them. The ridge they were standing on formed the triangle's base and closed the valley to the swamp and forest just below. A jagged v-shaped range, jutting out from the Spinepeaks, formed the other two walls to the valley. At the head of the triangle, at the juncture of the cave-pitted cliffs of the ranges, was a huge, disorderly fortress: Pitmouth. The ramshackle huddle of black brick buildings clung to the side of the mountain, seemingly about to collapse to the valley floor below. In the centre of the huddle of buildings stood a tall square tower about six stories high, mounted by dozens of long flagpoles. The flagpoles all flew the standard of Pitmouth, a black triangular banner with the cross of three bones. Jack scanned the cliff face, noting that many of the caves surrounding the buildings were bricked up. Others were sealed with iron doors. The whole mountainside was criss-crossed with paths and tunnels that connected the caves and the black fortress. Rickety-looking bridges spanned the chasms that separated the black edifice at the centre of Pitmouth and the caves on either side. It all looked eerily deserted. As if hearing Jack's thoughts, Denn said, "The goblins do not normally wake till sundown. Their hearing is poor. They may still slumber unaware of their approaching doom."

"Don't they have guards?" Jack asked.

"Yes," Denn said, "but they are likely asleep as well. Goblins are lazy. We should take cover anyway. Standing here atop the ridge, silhouetted against the sky, makes us easy to spot from the battlements." He led them to cover behind some large boulders. The troll horns of Serza's army sounded again. They looked down to the marshland behind them. In the extreme distance, Jack could just make out what looked like a ribbon of black, stretched across the horizon, a ribbon that was moving steadily forwards.

"They're not exactly trying for a surprise attack, are they?" Jack said.

"They have no need for surprise," Denn explained. "Pitmouth's defences are weak. If not for the mountainside, a few trolls with war hammers could breach them. Serza's forces will make quick work of it, especially as the goblin king, Krungle, is a coward. He is likely to surrender before any fighting takes place."

"We've got to get inside before that happens," Jack said. "If Serza finds the keysong before us then we're all done for, both in Anwynn and our world. Besides, I don't want to be sneaking around in there once it's crawling with trolls and Dark Elves."

Denn took this in. He scratched his chin, thinking. He gazed toward the black fortress a while then looked back over the ridge to the ribbon of Serza's army on the horizon. He seemed for a moment to be caught in some inner turmoil. With a sigh, he came to a decision.

"Serza's presence here changes things. It is clear now that I will not be able to avenge my brother. I cannot confront Krungle *and* protect you on your quest. It is one or the other, and as your quest concerns the future of the whole world, I must put it first."

"Don't worry," Harriett said, "I'm sure your brother wouldn't mind."

"Thank you, Miss Harriett, I am sure of that also. Besides, revenge is not a noble quest. To save Anwynn from destruction, whether at the hand of the White Demoness or the Dark Prince Serza, now that is a noble endeavour." He thought another moment. "I have long felt, ever since that day in the Oracle's tomb, that meeting you both was a sign –

a sign telling me to abandon revenge and instead aid you. I am at peace with that now." The resounding of dozens of troll war horns broke Denn's ruminations. He peered in the direction of the approaching army.

"The Dark Ones move at an unnatural pace," he said, still staring into the distance. "They are well at home in the marshland. They will be upon us before night falls. I fear we will not find much shelter in this valley. We must go along the ridge and try to reach Pitmouth by skirting the base of the range."

Without another word, Denn led them along the ridge, taking cover behind boulders as often as possible. As the shadows lengthened and threw the triangular valley into darkness, they reached the base of the southernmost range. With haste they descended from the ridge to the valley floor and headed for the fortress at the head of the valley. They kept to the shadow of the range wall, hiding behind boulders and scree at the foot of the cliff wherever possible. The closer they got to their goal, the more anxious Jack grew. The lack of movement or noise within Pitmouth unnerved him. The sudden silence of the drums and troll horns of Serza's army deepened his anxiety. What was Serza up to? Why hadn't there been any kind of activity in Pitmouth? No sound of goblins arming themselves and preparing for battle, nothing. They continued following the cliff line up the valley, getting nearer and nearer the juncture of the ranges and the black fortress.

Sunset came as they scrambled over a particularly large pile of scree in the full shadow of the cliffs. On the other side of it they came out from behind a large boulder to find themselves face to face with four goblins. The goblins were guarding the entrance to a small cave and they were armed with gruesome long pikes. Harriett screamed and dashed aside as one of them lunged at her. The other three goblins launched themselves at Jack and Denn, screeching at the top of their lungs.

With lightning-quick speed Denn leapt into the fray. He

took on two of the goblins at once, slicing off the tips of their pikes with deft moves before stabbing one and then the other straight through their hearts. The two goblins dropped like lead weights. One of the two remaining goblins, a huge grizzly beast wearing a helm with a single dragon horn, jumped forward and nearly skewered Jack, who only just blocked the goblin's thrust with his black sword, after struggling to pull the blade from its sheath. The shrieking goblin kicked out and Jack parried and thrust with his blade, unceremoniously stabbing the goblin in the thigh. The goblin roared, tossed his pike at Jack and drew a filthy-looking broadsword. Jack dodged the pike and faced the goblin as it bore down on him. At the last moment he was shoved out of the way by Denn, who swung his sword at the goblin, cutting deep into its shoulder. Jack stumbled over a stone and fell to the ground, knocking his head hard. Denn took his eyes off the helmeted beast for a second, checking to make sure that Jack wasn't badly injured. In that moment the goblin thrust his broadsword straight through Denn's side. Denn roared with pain but still managed to swing his own sword and behead his attacker. Denn pulled the broadsword out of his body. Bleeding profusely, he turned on the last surviving goblin that was still bearing down on Harriett. Harriett was screaming at the top of her lungs but was otherwise paralysed with fear since her mad dash had trapped her against the cliff face.

In a split second, despite the throbbing pain in his head, Jack knew that Denn wouldn't get between the goblin and Harriett in time. If he didn't do something he was going to lose his sister – again. A rush of adrenaline killed the pain in his head enough for him to move. He staggered to his feet. His mind was empty of thought, his entire being filled with just one impulse – to save Harriett. He pointed a finger at the goblin and shouted: "Get away from her!" With a loud crack, a flash of silver light engulfed the goblin and blinded them all. When it cleared and their eyes readjusted to the shadows again, the goblin was nowhere to be found. Jack and Harriett stared at each other in amazement.

You have sent the foul one to the realm of monsters! Ting shrieked gleefully. *Well done, Jack!*

"Have you become the Way, Jack?" Harriett asked, still hoarse from her recent screaming.

"I ... I don't know," Jack said. "At least, I don't feel any different."

The sound of Denn groaning and falling to the ground grabbed their attention. They rushed to his side. The wounded horseman was lying beside the body of the beheaded goblin, a gush of blood staining the ground around him.

"Is that Denn's blood?" Harriett asked apprehensively.

"A bit of both, I think," Jack answered, looking at Denn's side. The blade had gone straight through from front to back.

"It is but a flesh wound," Denn groaned reassuringly. "The goblin has taken a slice of fat from my waist roll is all—"

"Waist roll? You're pure muscle and that sword has gone straight through!" Jack took off his jacket and wrapped it tightly around Denn's middle, stemming the blood flow. He whispered to Harriett, "It looks bad. I don't know what else to do other than try to stop the bleeding."

"I will be fine," Denn said. "We must continue."

"You can't walk like that," Harriett said. "You'll just make the bleeding worse."

"You can't go on alone," Denn grunted, lifting himself to his feet. He swayed on the spot, his face pale from loss of blood. Jack and Harriett exchanged concerned glances, not knowing how to prevent Denn from pushing on despite such a severe injury. Jack knew that if it wasn't a mortal wound now, it would be after crossing the rest of the valley floor to reach Pitmouth. Ting's voice in Jack's ear shared his concern. *Silly proud Pix! He is too badly hurt to go on! He must rest here until we return!* There was a brief pause and then a wicked giggle. *I have an idea. Look into his eyes, Jack.*

"What?" Jack said, causing Denn and Harriett to look at him as if he were crazy.

Just look into his eyes! I will do the rest.

Jack went over to where Denn was swaying on the spot and, feeling a bit of a fool, looked into the horseman's eyes.

Denn returned Jack's gaze. "What are you doing, lad?" Jack gave no answer, just stared into Denn's eyes. Denn's unsteady stance made it difficult for Jack to keep eye contact. He took Denn by the shoulders to steady him. Denn looked at Jack's hands on his shoulder and then back into his eyes.

"Are you going to kiss me, lad?" he groaned, his blue eyes worried.

"What? No, I am not!"

"Well, if you're thinking about it I'd rather you didn't. I knew I shouldn't have shared a saddle with you."

"I'm not going to kiss you! Just hold still." Jack intensified his gaze into Denn's eyes and heard Ting muttering some kind of incantation. Jack's vision shimmered and changed. It was as if he was looking through a strange lens. Everything had turned to shades of purple. Denn's face, looming before him, looked alien. His skull glowed a dark purple, shining through skin and flesh like a lamp.

"What's happening?" Jack said.

"I was just about to ask that myself, lad," Denn said. "There's a strange, purple glint in your pupils." The minute Denn looked into that purple glint his eyes widened, and then slowly closed. He crumpled to the ground. *Heehee*, Ting giggled, *I've put him into a healing sleep. He won't rouse for hours now!* As quickly as it had changed, Jack's vision returned to normal.

"Is that how you see things all the time?" Jack asked Ting.

Yes, said Ting. *That is how the world looks to an earwisp.*

"What did you do, Jack?" Harriett asked, kneeling beside Denn to check his breathing.

"I didn't do anything. I think Ting hypnotised him and made him go to sleep. She said he won't wake now until we come back to get him."

"We can't just leave him out here – what if there are more goblins around?"

"Well, we'll drag him behind those rocks there," Jack said, pointing to a group of large boulders nearby. "He'll be safe there."

"I think that is best," said a tiny female voice as a waft of purple mist took shape in the air before Jack.

"Hi, Ting!" Harriett said.

"Hello, Harriett," Ting replied, bobbing about in the air, vainly slicking her shaggy red hair behind her ears.

With considerable effort Jack and Harriett dragged Denn behind the boulders. Ting hovered overhead giving fairly useless directions, like a tiny foreman. Jack made Denn as comfortable, and inconspicuous, as possible by covering him with one of the dead goblin's cloaks.

"Right," Jack said, once Denn was secure behind the boulders, "we'd best be off then."

"I don't think we should just go marching off," Harriett said. "Without Denn we're sitting ducks."

"Well, what do you suggest?"

"I think we should use the torc to find the Keysong without getting jumped on by any more goblins."

"That's a great idea, Harriett!" Ting beamed.

"Yeah, it is," Jack agreed.

Harriett took the torc out of her pocket and, holding it firmly in one hand, offered the other side of the bracelet to Jack.

"You'd better stay here and guard Denn," Harriett said to Ting.

"Oh poo!" hissed Ting. "I want to see too!"

"But you're the only one powerful enough to protect Denn," Harriett cajoled, "and *us* – we're going to need watching while we're in the vision."

"Please, Ting," Jack said, "we can't do this without you."

"That is true," Ting said, "and I am *very* powerful."

"Very powerful and very pretty and very kind," Harriett

added.

"No need to lay it on so thick," Ting said. "I'll stay and guard the silly Pix."

"Thanks, Ting," Jack said, extending a finger and stroking her hair.

"Anything for you, my Jacky," Ting said. Jack snapped back his finger. Ting's flirty personality made him uncomfortable. Harriett stifled a snicker, holding out the torc to Jack. He grasped it and steadied himself for what was about to happen.

"Okay, get on with it then," he grunted.

Harriett looked determinedly at the torc, thought a moment, apparently working out how to phrase her question, and then spoke: "Show us a safe path to where the Keysong is kept."

Instantly Jack's vision filled with sparkling silver light. The whole valley around them turned to glittering particles. The cliff walls, the scree and the boulders looked almost beautiful and not foreboding at all. As the glittering silver particles obscured everything—the black fortress, the twilight sky, Denn's motionless body and Ting—the powerful silver light took hold of them and drew them into it. Their bodies became light, shimmering with silver auras. Jack found himself lifting off the ground, Harriett's glimmering aura beside him.

"*My* Jacky," Harriett echoed Ting as they rose into the air toward the cliff wall. "She's really stuck on you!"

"Shut up, Harrie! Try and concentrate!" Jack spat, before wondering why they were headed back in the direction of the dead goblins rather than along the base of the range toward the fortress.

They moved toward the small cave, now guarded by three dead goblins, one of them headless, and went straight inside. Just within the cave they came to a locked iron door. Their luminous bodies moved straight through the door and continued onwards. On the other side of the door a long passage headed directly into the range. A few hundred yards beyond the entrance, it split into two tunnels. One passage curved to the left as it inclined upwards. Another slid steeply downwards into the darkness beneath the ridge, swallowed a dozen or so yards down by pressing shadows. This tunnel looked to Jack like the throat of some huge beast. It emanated a sense of doom and terror. A surge of unease in the pit of Jack's stomach told him that this was the tunnel that led down to Darkgate, and Morrigan.

Thankfully, Jack and Harriett were not drawn down this passageway but along the one to the left. All along the walls of this passageway, small lamps glowed an eerie blue. As they passed by, Jack noticed that the lanterns contained winged glow worms. The tiny worms had beady eyes and miniscule mouths filled with very sharp needle-like teeth.

"Ew, they're horrible," Harriett said.

"Well don't look at them," Jack replied, as they continued gliding through the passageway. The corridor inclined upwards and curved more and more to the left, in the direction of the black tower of Pitmouth.

"Where are all the goblins?" Harriett asked, her voice echoing in the empty space.

"It's weird, isn't it? You'd think there'd be at least a few of them around."

They glided forward for some time in silence and then, as the incline of the passage became considerably steeper, heard the unmistakeable sound of gruff, goblin voices. They came to a small circular chamber with six openings leading in all different directions. Harriett gasped, for before them were the ghost-like figures of two very large, very grim-looking goblins and the bald-headed, bat-eared Dread sorceress, Hect! All three were clearly shapes of the future, transparent and not quite real. The sight of Hect sent a chill through Jack's body. Her blood-red eyes filled him with dread and the sense that, one day not too far in the future, he would have to face those eyes and fight for his and Harriett's life. Jack was very glad they couldn't be seen and hoped Hect couldn't sense their presence as Serza had.

"I don't think she can tell we're here," Harriett whispered.

"No, I think it was the Secret Gift that allowed Serza to do it," Jack replied as quietly as he could. His voice sounded strained. Nevertheless, to avoid detection, they stayed in the shadows and listened to what the Dread sorceress was saying to the goblins.

"Krungle must be told that Serza does not come in friendship. Serza's offer of alliance is not sincere. And heed this: if Krungle should waver, if he should move to surrender to the dark prince, then you must do it quickly – you must drive your daggers deep into Krungle's body and slice off his head! Then your brethren must fight the dark prince. Do this and the Pale Mother will reward you most richly."

The goblins grunted in acknowledgement, leering monstrously. Hect took two pouches from within her cloak and passed them to the goblins. They jiggled the pouches greedily and stuffed them into their jackets. Without another sound the goblins loped off, disappearing down a passageway to the far left. Hect pulled her cloak close around her and stalked off down a passageway to the right. As soon as Hect was gone, Jack and Harriett were drawn forward again, crossing the chamber and entering a passageway directly opposite. This passageway turned out to be a long flight of stairs rising steeply upwards.

"That's why the goblins aren't preparing for battle," Jack said. "Serza's tricked them into believing he's coming to make an alliance."

"That's bad," Harriett replied, making another incredible understatement.

They emerged from the stairwell into another round chamber with multiple passages leading off it. Unlike the chamber below, which had been hewn out of rock, this one had a flagstone floor and black brick walls. They were now in the fortress proper. The chamber had one small shuttered window, which was open, allowing the sound of horns and drums, answered by the tinny sound of some kind of trumpet, to drift in.

The window overlooked the shadowy valley below. Jack and Harriett were drawn to it and peered out. The sun had now completely set, leaving only a magenta smear on the distant horizon. At the foot of the valley, surmounting the low ridge, was a wall of ghostly Dark Elves and Fellwood goblins marching slowly forwards. A terrible vision of a terrible future. At the head of the army, carried on a black crystal palanquin by four trolls, was Serza. Behind Serza's litter marched a row of goblins playing drums and behind them a row of trolls blowing on long curved horns. The horn sound was deafening and was answered by a fanfare of trumpets from somewhere in the fortress above. Behind the row of marching trolls were many more rows of fully-armed Vellenor, their scimitars glinting at their sides. Their pale skin, long white hair and sharply pointed ears all added to their general air of menace.

Jack and Harriett were drawn away from the window by the force of the torc and entered another passageway. This one was also directly opposite the one containing the long stairs. A long, level corridor, it led directly ahead. After a few hundred yards, it opened onto a semicircular chamber with three large iron doors. Jack floated with Harriett to the door directly ahead of them and stopped. Beside each door there was a hook where a large rusty key hung. They hovered there by the iron door, not sure why they were not moving any further forwards.

"The Keysong must be behind this door," Jack said. He reached out to grasp the rusty key. Before his fingers connected with the key they were both dragged backwards. The chamber and the passageway turned to silver and then they were flying back in the direction they came; everything a silver, pulsing blur. In a flash they were back behind the boulder, Denn still motionless beside them. Ting sat cross-legged on Denn's chest, waiting expectantly.

OOPA

"What was it like?" Ting asked immediately.

"Interesting," Jack said. "Hect is in there. Serza has fooled the goblins into believing he wants an alliance with them."

"And we know where the Keysong is kept," Harriett said, "and how to get there and back safely."

"Did you see it?" Ting asked. "Did you see the instrument that holds the Keysong?"

Jack shook his head. "No, we just saw a door and then we came back here. I'm not sure why we didn't see it," he said, looking to Harriett.

"Maybe because I asked to see where it's kept, and not to see the Keysong itself. I'm still figuring out how the torc works."

"Either way," Jack continued, "we've got to get a move on. Serza is almost in the valley. I have another favour to ask you, Ting."

"What this time?" she asked, pouting.

"I want you to help me and Harriett disguise ourselves while we're in Pitmouth, just in case we're seen."

"What do you want me to do?" Ting's voice rang with suspicion.

"That thing you did with the dead troll, where I was in its body, could you do that with these goblins?"

"Wait a cotton-picking minute," Harriett hissed. "What do you mean *dead troll?*"

"That is a wonderful idea, Jack!" Ting clapped with glee. "The goblins in the fortress will have no idea it's you!"

"I said, wait a *cotton-picking* minute!" Harriett spluttered, aggravated at being so thoroughly ignored. "What do you mean, use the bodies of *dead goblins?*"

Ting giggled. "Don't worry, it won't hurt one bit. Your awareness will be inside the dead goblins, but your own bodies will be safe here."

Harriett's eyes boggled. "Well, what about Denn?" she said, trying desperately to find a way to avoid having to occupy the body of a dead goblin. "We can't leave him here alone."

"Don't concern yourself about him," Ting said crossly. "I will still be here. I suppose someone has to protect the silly old horseman. Besides, I will have to guard your bodies while your minds are inside those smelly goblins!" Ting laughed devilishly. "I'll have to be in your ear to do the magic, Jack. Are you ready?"

"Wait," Harriett interjected. "I … I didn't see us as goblins in the future," Harriett tried once more.

"Neither did I," Jack added. "What does that mean, Ting?"

Ting huffed. "How many times do I have to tell you, Earwisp enchantments are undetectable, even by most Faeden tricks. That silly old torc can't see the magic an earwisp makes. We are invisible, even in visions."

Before Harriett could mount another objection, Ting dissolved into purple mist and re-entered Jack's ear. No matter how often it happened, Jack couldn't quite get used to it.

"Does it hurt?" Harriett asked, noting his discomfort.

"No, it doesn't feel like anything at all. It only tingles when she leaves. It's just a weird sensation, to have someone else inside your head."

Stop whining, Jack! Ting said, giggling. The giggles echoed annoyingly in his ear.

"Stop snickering," Jack said to his ear, "and get on with it."

"What's going on?" Harriett asked, hearing only one side of the conversation.

"Quiet, Harrie, I can't listen to you both at once."

"Well, tell her if she's going to do it she better do it now because my nerves are about to snap!"

"Harriett wants you to do it now," Jack said to his ear.

I heard her — I'm not deaf, dummy!

"Sorry," Jack said.

That's okay, Jack, Ting continued. *Now, ready yourselves.*

"Get ready, Harrie." Jack's voice echoed off the boulders and took on a strange, stony quality. It reminded him of the sound of the stone lid sliding off the sarcophagus at the tomb of the Oracles. He took a deep breath, steeling himself for the very uncomfortable experience of being inside another body, and a dead goblin body at that. Without warning, his vision dimmed and went black.

Harriett gasped. "I'm blind, Jack!"

"It's okay," Jack reassured her. "This is part of it."

In the blackness before him a tiny white speck appeared. *Focus on the speck of white,* Ting said. *Tell Harriett also.*

"Focus on the little bit of white," Jack repeated to his sister. Once again, Jack didn't find focusing on the speck difficult at all, as it naturally drew his attention.

Allow the vision to grow, Ting said.

"Allow the vision to grow," Jack repeated.

Just as on the battlefield with the troll, as Jack focussed on it the speck grew so that soon all in his vision was a field of brilliant white.

Go into the vision, Ting's little voice directed.

"Go into it," Jack told Harriett as he willed himself to move into the whiteness. He had that same feeling of coming up out of deep water, and emerged to the slight sounds of the valley and the shadowy light of the evening.

He opened his eyes and, as he became accustomed to seeing with goblin vision, realised that his face was pressed into the dusty ground. He lifted his head, or rather lifted the goblin's head, and looked down at his hands. He saw not his own fingers but two mottled grey, claw-like goblin fists. Beside him another goblin sat in the dirt staring at its hands as well. He dragged himself to his feet.

"Is that you, Harriett?" he asked in a guttural, barely recognisable voice.

"Yep," the other goblin grunted back. Jack turned and saw himself and Harriett standing nearby, utterly motionless, as if in a trance. Their eyes had turned a dark shimmering purple. He staggered back a little, shocked and disoriented.

It worked! Ting crowed in Jack's ear, before rematerialising in front of them.

"Okay," Jack grunted in goblin voice, "let's go."

"Good luck!" Ting waved them off before unceremoniously landing on Denn's nose and taking a seat.

As goblins, Jack and Harriett found the small cave. Staggering a little as they got used to walking on goblin legs, they went straight inside. As the vision had shown, just within the cave there was a locked iron door.

"Key," grunted goblin Harriett, who was having just as hard a time controlling goblin vocal cords as controlling goblin legs. Jack looked around. He couldn't see a key anywhere. As he turned this way and that, looking for the key, a jingling sound made him look down. A key was hanging on his belt! He unhooked it, put the key in the door and turned it. The door unlocked immediately.

On the other side of the door was the long chamber they'd seen in the vision. Further along they came to the two passageways, one curving to the left as it inclined upwards, lit by the glass lanterns filled with the fanged blue glow worms. The other throat-like passage slid steeply downwards into the darkness. The hair on Jack's goblin hide stood up on end. He felt a strange pulsing in the air, a pulsing that induced fear and nausea. His stomach churned. Jack had felt this way before, in the dreams and visions he'd had of Morrigan. Now he knew for sure that this was the tunnel that led down to the Pale Mother's tomb: the road to Uffern, the pit of the unforgiven dead. He stood there for a moment, paralysed by a sense of foreboding, staring at the dark opening. Its walls were covered in slimy green moss and the ceiling dripped with greasy-looking water that pooled on the ground.

Jack summoned all his strength and turned away from the oozing passageway. Harriett followed, trotting along behind him into the other passage, which took them upwards toward the black fortress. Jack found that they could move much faster on goblin legs than on their own. He picked up the pace. He was pleased to find that no matter how much he exerted himself, he didn't tire.

The passage led deep under the mountain and was unnervingly quiet. The pad of their feet made an almost hypnotic sound as they trotted along. Jack felt an increasing sense of menace. His goblin skin was covered in goose bumps again, and his stomach lurched with that all too familiar nausea. The menace of the White Demoness coursed through the very air. A patch of slime and damp on the floor ahead bubbled like a fetid swamp. Was the dank of Morrigan's tomb creeping up to stop them from completing their quest? Was the pit where Morrigan was imprisoned directly below them? He turned and looked around, half expecting to see Morrigan standing behind him. But there was nothing, just the empty, eerie blue passageway. He turned back and picked up his pace again. The less time they spent in the tunnels beneath Pitmouth the better. Harriett trotted obediently behind him, nervously looking over her shoulder.

As they trotted along, they didn't expect to see any other being, excluding the glow worms of course. Just as in the vision, there wasn't a goblin in sight. They continued for some time in silence. Just as the incline became considerably steeper, they heard the unmistakeable sound of goblin voices. They slowed to a crawl, sneaking up to the juncture in the passageway. In the chamber before them were the two very large goblins and Hect. This time, however, the goblins and Hect were not merely ghost figures but fully in their flesh.

Jack and Harriett froze and lingered in the shadows as Hect outlined the plot to assassinate the goblin king if he tried to surrender to Serza and handed over the bags of coins. The goblins grunted and greedily jingled the pouches containing their reward. Just as the vision had shown, the goblins loped off and, seconds later, so too did Hect.

Jack and Harriett started off again, crossing the chamber and entering the passageway directly opposite at a full run. In their goblin bodies they were able to bound up the stairway at a rapid pace. They soon emerged from the stairwell into the second chamber with its many passageways leading in various directions. This time they did not look out the window – they heard the sound of horns and drums and knew what they meant. Serza's army had arrived. The memory of that terrible sight, in particular of Serza on his black crystal palanquin, was enough to invigorate them. They bolted across the chamber and entered the next passageway. As this passage was flat, they were able to race down it at a sprint, covering the few hundred yards to the semicircular chamber in just minutes. They crossed that chamber to the door directly ahead of them and stopped. Jack reached out and rather clumsily took the large rusty key from where it hung on its hook. He put the key in the lock and paused. There could be anything lurking beyond this door, he thought. The torc hadn't shown them behind it.

"Turn it," Harriett growled. Jack looked into her ugly goblin face and saw in its eyes just the slightest hint of something that reminded him of his sister. The way the goblin was standing, and the way its head was tilted, looking at him curiously, was very reminiscent of Harriett's body language. Somehow her personality was making itself visible on the dead goblin's body. It certainly didn't smell like Harriett though – it smelt like a wet dog that had rolled in something awful.

"You stink," Jack grunted with goblin tongue as he sniffed the air.

"Turn the key," she rumbled back.

Jack turned the key and dragged the heavy door open. On the other side was another passageway, lined on each side with prison cell doors. The torc had led them to the dungeons of Pitmouth. They loped down the passage, peering through the metal windows in the doors of each cell. They were all empty.

"Empty," Harriett grunted. Even as a goblin she couldn't help but state the obvious.

At the end of the passage there was one final door. Jack

peered in, blinking at what he saw inside. The small cell was covered with colourful drawings of flowers. Even in the darkness the drawings brought a certain light and charm to the dank room. The cell was furnished by two items: a small bed with what looked like a colourful hand-sewn bedspread and a very small chair, too small even for a halfling. Jack scanned the room and spotted a small green-skinned being hiding timidly beneath the bed. She wore a bright red dress, had long pointy ears adorning a bald head, big brown eyes and a stout little button nose.

"Girl Yoda," Harriett grunted. Jack rolled his bulbous eyes,

"Oakling," he muttered.

Jack slid the bolt to the door aside and swung it open. Before they stepped in a tiny little voice sang out.

"I might be little but I can still hex you from here to the Empty Lands, you nasty goblins!"

"We're not goblins," Jack growled in a voice all too gobliny.

"Of course you are! I can see your grey skin and your black eyes and smell you from here. You're goblins alright or my name isn't Oopa! Now stay out of my cell!"

"We're in disguise. We're not really goblins, are we Harriett?" Jack said, turning to his sister.

"Nope," Harriett said in such a dopey goblin voice that it undermined his declaration that they were not goblins at all.

"Disguise?" the Oakling asked, her voice changing from one of panic to one of curiosity. "You do seem far too smart to be goblins." She closed her eyes and stretched a timid hand in their direction, as if feeling the air with her fingers. She gasped and opened her eyes suddenly. "You are otherworlders! Are you here to rescue me?"

"No," Jack grunted a little too bluntly. "We're on a mission. Why have the goblins got you?"

"They kidnapped me," she said, crawling out from under the bed, completely abandoning her previous caution. "It was terrible. I thought they were going to eat me! They would have eaten me too, only one of them recognised me as an Oakling and brought me back to that nasty, dirty old Krungle."

"Why they bring you?" Harriett slurred, her goblin tongue heavy.

"Are you sure you're not a goblin?" the little Oakling asked suspiciously.

"Not goblin, just hard to talk," Harriett shrugged.

"Goblins are very envious of my kind," she explained. "We Oaklings are very old and we know all kinds of magic." She smiled proudly. "Goblins can't do magic, they're too stupid. So Krungle has kept me prisoner and has been forcing me to do enchantments for him, conjuring rubies. Goblins can't get enough of rubies! Blooddrops they call them, can you imagine?"

Both Jack and Harriett shook their goblin heads, indicating that they couldn't imagine.

"It's lucky that's all they wanted," Oopa continued, "because that's about all the magic I can do. I couldn't even break out of this cell. I'm more skilled at craft, me. I've been trapped here a very, very long time. That Krungle is just horrible! He smells exactly like a pigsty!"

"You come with us," Harriett grunted, indicating herself and Jack. "We get you out."

"Oh, yes please," said the Oakling, dashing about and gathering her things into a small red bag. Her belongings mainly consisted of crayons, balls of yarn and bundles of knitting. She moved with a deftness and speed that reminded Jack of Miss Butters. He wondered if in Anwynn the smaller you were the faster you could move. He told himself to ask Aelf next time he saw him. Once Oopa had all her things, she stood before Jack and Harriett, looked up at them and said cheerfully, "After you, my heroes!"

Jack and Harriett led Oopa the Oakling back down the passageway to the semi-circular chamber. As they entered the chamber, the building rocked with a sudden explosion. The familiar sizzling sound of lightning cut through the air.

Another and then another explosion shook the building, followed by the deafening roar of trolls and the shrieks of thousands of goblins.

"That's it," Jack moaned. "Serza is here."

BATTLE OF PITMOUTH

The screeching of goblins echoed everywhere around them. Somewhere beyond the chamber the clash of steel reverberated through the many tunnels, the sound of Vellenor scimitars slicing through the short broadswords of the goblins. Another huge explosion shook the fortress to its core, accompanied by the triumphant roar of trolls. Jack knew this meant that Serza's forces had breached the gates. Trolls would be swarming into the fortress to tear every last goblin limb from limb, including him and Harriett who, for all intents and purposes, looked like Pitmouth goblins.

Jack didn't know what to do. They hadn't found the Keysong. The torc had led them to the dungeon but it must have been wrong. Jack turned toward the other two dungeon doors. Maybe the Keysong was behind one of them? As he took a step toward the other doors, the nearby roar of trolls and screaming goblins stopped him in his tracks.

"No, Jack!" Harriett shouted. "Too late! Have to go!"

"But the Keysong!" Jack yelled.

"Too late!" Harriett bellowed as the blood-curdling roar of a pack of trolls carried down into the chamber from above. "Failed! Must go!"

Jack looked to his sister, her goblin head cocked in that familiar way, her eyes filled with fear. The Oakling's little brown eyes were as round as saucers from anxiety. He couldn't dawdle here any longer. He had to get them to safety. But he couldn't leave without the Keysong! He looked back to the dungeon doors and took another furtive step toward them.

"No, Jack!" Harriett begged. "They're coming!"

Another sizzling crack of lightning struck the fortress immediately above them. The building shook and the walls split. The force of it jolted Jack from his indecision. He knew that Harriett was right. They had to flee.

"Run!" he growled, sweeping up their new companion in his hands and bolting down the passageway that led out of the fortress. Harriett bolted after him. They made it to the large juncture in just moments, crossing it and descending the stairs at a headlong rush. About midway down, the roar of trolls echoed in the stairwell above them. A group of huge white beasts were leaping down the stairs after them.

"Faster!" Jack snarled. They jumped down the stairs three and four at a time. Another bolt of lightning shook the passageway so violently that Jack and Harriett tumbled forwards, flying through the air to land on the floor of the chamber below, sliding all the way into the middle of it. Jack shook his head and staggered to his feet, still holding Oopa, turning to see the trolls bounding down the stairs toward them. Harriett screamed, or rather roared. The building rocked again, struck by another explosion. The ceiling of the stairwell collapsed, crushing the trolls just before they exited into the chamber.

"That was lucky, wasn't it?" Oopa squeaked from under Jack's arm.

"Yep," Jack grunted. He and Harriett dashed into the final passageway that curved down to the entrance of the cave at the foot of the range. They ran down through the eerie blue darkness without meeting any more trolls or goblins. They descended the last quarter of the passageway in silence, with only the distant thump of explosions to accompany the plod of their feet.

As Jack jogged, the same words repeated over and over in his mind: I have failed! I have failed to find the one thing that would thwart Serza and keep Morrigan imprisoned! Harriett tried to reassure him, whispering in a guttural goblin voice that it wasn't his fault. Even still, Jack couldn't help but feel that not only had he failed Harriett, he had failed the whole world. Two worlds – Anwynn *and* his own world!

Serza could very well destroy the key and accidentally release Morrigan, who would then turn on Elvinnid and the Four Kingdoms. There was nothing to stop that now.

Neither the druids nor the elves, even with firewyrm riders like Daniselle, would stand a chance against Morrigan. Jack had never felt so awful in his life, except perhaps when he'd realised his mother wasn't ever coming home.

As the passageway straightened, Jack noticed that the explosions above had ceased. The earth was no longer shaking. An unnatural quiet had descended. When they reached the iron door in the entranceway to the cave, Jack heard outside the sound of thousands of marching feet. A vast army was moving just metres away. They lurked in the shadows of the cave and peered out. The light of thousands of torches flickered in the night – the whole valley swarmed with Serza's army. Luckily the cave was hidden from sight by large boulders. They crept out, sticking close to the cliff wall and the cover of the boulders, and retraced their steps the short way to where Ting was watching over Denn. When they found them, Ting was curled up in Denn's earlobe, as if resting in a hammock.

She squeaked when she saw them. "You made it! Did you find it?"

"No, we failed," Jack grunted as he fell to the ground. "Put us back in our bodies."

"You failed! Oh no!" Ting gasped, before spotting the Oakling and hissing, "Who's *she*?"

"I'm Oopa," the Oakling said sweetly. "Nice to meet you."

"Jack, why did you bring back an Oakling? Is it because you think she's prettier than me? Because she *isn't*!"

"Not now, Ting, change us back," Jack growled. Ting huffed and dematerialised and drifted into his ear. *I will change you back, though why I should help you I don't know, wandering off and bringing back strange girls—*

"Change us back now!" Jack growled, not wanting to entertain Ting's jealousy at all.

His vision dimmed and went black.

"Blind again," Harriett whispered, still in her goblin voice.

"It's okay," Jack reassured her and then, with a feeling of great relief, he was back in his own body and Harriett back in hers. Denn still lay safely asleep beside them.

"We have to get out of here," Jack said, "before those Vellenor stumble on us."

We can't, Ting said before she drifted out of his ear again, causing that strange ringing. She materialised before them.

"Why not?" demanded Jack.

"We're completely cut off," she replied snootily. "Serza's army is everywhere in case you hadn't noticed. I had to stay out here all alone and guard *him*!" She sneered, pointing at Denn. "I could have been killed!"

"You didn't look very worried when we arrived," Oopa said with a smile. "You looked like you were having a lovely rest in that man's ear."

"Who asked *you*?" Ting hissed.

"Nobody asked me," Oopa said warmly, completely missing Ting's hostility.

"So why are you still speaking!" Ting stamped her feet, hands on hips.

"No reason," Oopa said, smiling, before sitting daintily, ankles crossed, on a nearby stone. Jack suspected that Oopa's nature was too gentle and good to understand sarcasm.

"If we could all stop bleating over Jack," Harriett interrupted, "we might be able to think of a way out of this predicament we're in."

"Okay," Oopa said, still smiling. "But who's Jack?"

"I'm Jack."

"Oh, and who are you?" Oopa asked Harriett.

"I'm Harriett."

"Otherworld names are so peculiar," Oopa said. "Not bad, just different. I quite like them."

"Thanks," Harriett said. "I like your name too, and, you know, you speak very nicely for an Oakling."

"For an Oakling?"

"Oh, no offence, it's just that we know Wadget, and you don't sound like him at all."

"Well of course I don't," Oopa said. "I've spent most of my life with elves and civilised folk, whereas Wadget, well, he's spent most of his life in taverns with all kinds of unsavoury characters."

"Sorry to interrupt you two getting to know each other," Jack said, "but we have to get out of here somehow. We have to warn the druids that we've failed to stop Serza."

"Can you open a Way?" Harriett asked. "I mean, I know we're not in a circle, but you did banish that goblin."

"I don't think so," Jack said, thinking that he had no idea how to 'become the Way' in order to move from place to place without the aid of a magic circle. It was a pure fluke that he'd managed to banish the goblin. Opening a Way without a circle, and carrying Harriett, Denn, an earwisp and an Oakling with him was altogether different.

"You *are* the Waycaller!" Oopa gasped. "I thought you might be, but I wasn't sure."

"What do *you* know about it?" Ting demanded.

"Oh, I know *all* about it," Oopa said. "I know nearly as much as Amallayne herself. I was friends with the Great Goddess *long* before the Doom War, before *she* was imprisoned down below, and well before the making of the Veil. I was there for all of that," she said smiling, before turning to Jack and continuing. "I thought I sensed the Great Goddess' hand on you."

"*Whose* hands on you, Jack?" Ting shrieked, positively bursting with jealousy.

"Never mind, Ting! Oopa, do you know how I can 'become the Way'? I have no idea what the phrase means and it's the only chance we've got to get out of here."

"I don't understand what it means exactly, but I know that it is something like knowing, deep within yourself, that your *mind* is the Way. The light within you, rather than the sphere that you invoke when you're in a circle, acts as the means to transport you from place to place."

"The light within me?" Jack muttered, confused.

"Yes, Amallayne has granted you her blessing. That is

part of you and is more than enough power to open the Way, except for the Way between Anwynn and the otherworld. For that you must always use the Silver Bough at one of the great circles."

"So, how do I *do* it though? How can I make my mind the Way?"

"I don't know," Oopa sighed. "I think it happens naturally, either when all your will is undistractedly focussed on something, or when you are bathed in the bliss of Amallayne's grace. But I can't say for certain – only the Waycallers could possibly understand. That is, apart from Amallayne herself."

"Well, I can say categorically that I will not be bathing in anybody's bliss anytime soon," Jack said, remembering Amallayne's ambivalence and reluctance to breach the wretched Faeden covenant to help them.

"So it will have to be the other way," Harriett said. "The single-minded goal thing."

"Right now," Jack said, "I don't like our chances."

"Or," Oopa interrupted calmly, pointing into the sky, "we could just ride that firewyrm."

They all looked upwards into the night. High above them, descending in a tight spiral, was the unmistakeable shape of a dragon. Jack stared, agog, as the firewyrm came nearer. Soon, he made out two shadowy shapes astride the dragon. As a stray moonbeam struck the dragon's hide, he saw a glint of silver.

"Jossa!" Jack and Harriett gasped in unison. It was Daniselle, the Songarielle she-elf, astride her firewyrm! They couldn't believe it. They continued to gape, mouths open, as the firewyrm descended ever lower.

"But, how?" Harriett gasped, almost to herself.

"She must have left Songarielle after we spoke to her in the seeing stone," Jack guessed. "I knew Daniselle didn't want us to come here alone but this is just—"

"Fantastic!" Harriett beamed.

"Jack," Ting interrupted urgently, "I must hide! Make *her*

promise not to expose me!" She pointed at Oopa before dissolving into mist and disappearing into Jack's ear.

"You can't tell anyone about Ting," Jack explained quickly to Oopa.

"Oh no, I wouldn't." Oopa smiled knowingly. "Elves hate earwisps."

Jack smiled in thanks and looked back up into the sky. He was still shocked that a firewyrm had appeared just as they were about to give up hope of getting out of there alive. As Jossa descended, it became obvious that Serza's army had also spotted the firewyrm. A round of warning horns echoed through the valley, joined by the sound of tens of thousands of bows being strung with arrows and swiftly loosed. The arrows whirred through the air like a swarm of large, deadly insects. There were so many of them that they blackened the sky even more.

"Oh no!" Harriett gasped as the cloud of arrows sped toward their friends. Just before the arrows reached their target, there was a sudden burst of brilliant yellow light. A huge Seren Star flashed into being. The light of the golden pentagram set the arrows burning. They fell back down onto the heads of Serza's army, who howled in terror. The Seren Star hovered overhead, growing larger and larger, throwing its yellow light into every nook and cranny of the valley. Its light bathed Jack and the others with warmth but incinerated every Vellenor, goblin and troll within hundreds of yards of them. Thousands of Serza's soldiers stampeded in every direction, desperate to evade the light of Seren.

"We must hurry," Oopa said suddenly. "Serza is at Darkgate! I sense the Pale Mother's wrath rising to meet him!" Jack stared in disbelief. They had truly failed. Serza was about to destroy the key! They were all done for.

"We must hurry!" Oopa moaned to herself. "We must carry the Keysong to the Great Goddess."

"What!" Jack and Harriett said at once.

"The Keysong, the Keysong," Oopa chanted, rocking nervously to-and-fro. "We have to get the Keysong to

Amallayne!"

"But, we didn't find the Keysong," Jack said, sensing that there was more to this little Oakling than met the eye, and perhaps more in her little red bag than knitting.

"The Keysong is *with me*," Oopa said, rocking like a traumatised child as she clutched tightly to her red bag. "With me, always with me. We have to get the Keysong to Amallayne!"

"I don't believe it!" Jack shouted. "You have the instrument? Why didn't you say something?"

"It's a secret!" Oopa shouted back, losing her smiling demeanour for the first time. Her tiny green fingers clinging even tighter to her bag.

Jack didn't have time to question Oopa any further. Jossa loomed immediately overhead, beating his wings in reverse to slow his descent. As the dragon made a rough landing on the boulders nearby, the elf mounted behind Daniselle nodded to Jack and smiled. It was Ellisenn, the handsome young elf who'd carried Jack to bed on the night they'd arrived in Songarielle. His green eyes were ablaze with adrenalin and his blond hair danced on the updraft from Jossa's wings. *So*, Jack thought, it was Ellisenn who'd cast the Seren Star. He was thrilled to see the elf alive – the last time he'd seen Ellisenn he'd been falling hundreds of feet to the ground during the battle at Songarielle.

Ellisenn dismounted and rapidly traced a sign in the air with his fingers. Dozens of vivid gold pentagrams appeared, emitting blinding light. These smaller pentagrams hurtled like rockets into the goblins already fleeing from the halo of light thrown by the larger star in the sky above. At the mere sight of the dozens of bullet-like Seren Stars, most of the remaining goblins and trolls bolted in terror. The Dark Elves were a different matter. They hovered at the edge of the halo of golden light and continued to fire arrows, but soon regretted not having fled. The smaller pentagrams struck the flanks of Vellenor with a massive boom. Multiple flashes of light obliterated hundreds of them. These pentagrams may have been small but they packed a wallop. At each boom and flash the Seren Stars multiplied into ever more pentagrams, spinning off in every direction, sending golden light to strike hundreds of dark beings that instantly exploded into flames. In just moments thousands of them were vaporised. Joining in the fray, Jossa sent bursts of blue flame into the flanks of retreating goblins, turning them into running fire balls. But there were thousands more of them and the Seren Star in the sky above was fading.

"A little trick I mastered since last I saw you," Ellisenn joked, as he launched another volley of Seren Stars before jogging over to Jack. He smiled, touching Jack briefly on the shoulder before pulling his hand away and flushing. Jack didn't know how to interpret that, nor did he have time. A pack of four goblins scrambled over a nearby rock and leapt straight at him.

Ellisenn's smile turned to a grimace of alarm in seconds. He leapt forward, landing in the midst of the goblin pack, drawing his sword and cutting down a goblin that was just inches away from Jack. As it fell its blade barely missed Jack's chest. In moves too fast to follow, Ellisenn cut down a second, then another and finally beheaded the last goblin as it tried to impale Jack on a long spear. The spear missed, just, but would have found its way home if Ellisenn hadn't shoved the goblin's arm aside at the last moment. Jack stared at Ellisenn and the carnage at his feet, half awed and half horrified.

"Ah ... thanks," he stuttered, unable to force himself to say or do anything more.

"I do not need thanks, Waycaller," Ellisenn said, "it is my duty and my honour to protect—" His sentence was cut off by a blow to the jaw from a large, fat-bellied troll that leapt from behind a nearby boulder. Ellisenn staggered back, his arms windmilling to prevent himself from falling. He dropped his sword, extended his hand and cast a pulse of golden light at the troll as it lunged at him. The pulse threw the howling creature backwards, past the rock it had clambered over and far beyond. There was a heavy *thwamp* as the troll landed in the distance.

"It is not safe here," Ellisenn said, wiping a trickle of blood from the corner of his mouth.

"No kidding," Jack said, still in shock, before a sense of urgency rose in him and compelled him to say more. "We've got to get out of here," he shouted. "Serza is at Darkgate!"

Ellisenn's eyes widened. "Take your sister," he said before effortlessly throwing Denn and Oopa over each of his shoulders and carrying them to where Daniselle waited astride Jossa. The she-elf was using a longbow to pick off the Dark Elves who dared come any closer. Dozens of dead Vellenor lay nearby, all with Daniselle's arrows protruding from various parts of their bodies. Jack grabbed Harriett by the hand and rushed to where Jossa perched atop the boulder.

"Hurry, the light of Seren fades!" Daniselle reached out her hand and helped Harriett and then Jack to mount behind her.

"Thank you for coming!" Harriett beamed. "I thought we were done for!"

"After telling Ellisenn about our discussion in the mirror," the she-elf explained, "we both felt the desire to join you."

"Well, thanks again!" Jack said as he also settled onto Jossa's back.

"Take care with this one, my friend," Ellisenn said to the she-elf as he placed Denn gently in front of her and quickly tied him in place. "He has lost much vigour. I will carry the Oakling." He climbed up behind Jack with Oopa still in his arms. Oopa smiled meekly and increased her grip on her red bag.

"Whatever you do, don't drop her," Jack said, concerned just as much for the Keysong as for Oopa herself.

In the next moment Jossa lurched upwards, so fast that Jack's eyes ran with water. He could barely see anything at all. The pressure of Ellisenn's hard chest behind him reassured him that he wouldn't fall as the dragon lurched and changed direction. As they hurtled upwards and out of the valley, Ting's voice mumbled incantations in his ear. He opened his watering eyes and looked down to see hundreds of the dead goblins, trolls and Vellenor lurching to their feet and turning on their living counterparts. The dead launched themselves viciously into the midst of Serza's army, slashing, cutting and mauling those who were once their own kind. Ting had raised a troop of the dead to aid in the fight! She'd even reanimated those who were aflame, compelling them to run into the midst of their compatriots and ignite an inferno among the living. A huge burning troll ran into a cadre of Vellenor and tackled them, setting them all ablaze. Ting's power was frightening, and very effective. So much so that Jack couldn't watch anymore – it was too gruesome. Besides, the pressure on his eyes from their rapid ascent was blurring his vision and making them sting. He closed them and hung on tight to Jossa's scaly hide.

They rose higher and higher. Jack was vaguely aware of Ellisenn holding him in place and saying comforting words to Oopa. The screams of goblins coming from below slowly diminished. The whirring song of arrows lessened as well, as Jossa rose out of range. Soon they'd gone so high that the only sound was wind rushing past Jack's ears.

"We have passed beyond the borders of Pitmouth," Daniselle shouted over the wind. "Lucky we were not to have faced Serza himself."

Jack opened his eyes and looked down. Far below them was the heavy darkness of Fellwood, and in the distance behind them the murky vastness of Swampmere. Jack agreed with Daniselle – they had been lucky. The only reason they hadn't faced Serza was because he'd been down in the depths of the caves beneath the black fortress, searching for the Keysong. But Serza wouldn't find it, it was with them. The dark prince could not unwittingly release Morrigan now. Jack's body tingled with relief, even though they would have to face the prince when he turned on Pix and Elvinidd. Jack was sure he and Harriett would get to the safety of Bright and warn the druids before that happened. Luck was most definitely going their way!

"We have to get to Bright as quickly as possible!" Jack shouted to Daniselle.

"We will carry you to the nearest stone circle, just inside the border of Pix. From there you can open a Way to the great circle of Bright."

"How long until we get to the nearest circle?" Jack asked.

"Less than an hour," Ellisenn said behind him, laying a reassuring hand on his shoulder.

"That's not quick enough!" Jack yelled.

As soon as Jack's words left his mouth, Daniselle made that strange trilling sound, spurring Jossa to fly even faster. Jossa jolted forward, picking up so much speed that Harriett and Jack were pushed back by the force of it. They were now moving so fast that watching the blurred land flash past below made Jack dizzy and unsteady. He closed his eyes, the wind passing his ears as a thunderous roar. They travelled that way for some time, Jack and Harriett clutching tightly to Jossa's back, their eyes pressed closed. Then Daniselle shouted over the screaming of the wind.

"We have entered the Kingdom of Pix, in moments we will be at the circle."

Jack opened his eyes and looked down. Below them the rolling golden grassland of southern Pix flashed by, albeit blanketed in the darkness of night. Jossa slowed his pace. Ahead of them, far below, the unmistakeable shape of a stone circle came into view. This circle was very similar to the one in Bright, only much smaller. As Jack watched the circle of megaliths approaching below, the distinct sound of a small bell rang in his left ear. He shook his head, thinking it had something to do with the air rushing past his lobes. Not only did the ringing not go away but it got louder. He stuck a finger in his ear and wriggled it around.

Oh no! Jack, Ting whispered in his ear. *I can't go any further. You will have to go on to Bright without me!*

"Why?" Jack said to his ear.

Inside voice, Jack! Ting chided. *The ringing you hear is the Beckoning Bell. It is the way the empress of my kind calls us home. I cannot disobey it, Jack. The punishment would be grave.*

"You can't leave us now!" Jack shouted, ignoring Ting's admonishment about speaking to her out loud.

I must, Jack! You think I want to go? The last thing I want is to leave you alone with that floozy Oopa! But I must, Jack! I have to go before the last bell tolls!

"No! You can't!" His protests fell on deaf ears. Jack felt that strange tingling sensation that meant that Ting had exited his ear. The sound of the tolling bell ceased along with it. Out of the corner of his eye he saw a slight wisp of purple streaking away from the dragon and out of sight.

"Damn it!" Jack said.

"Quiet, Jack," Harriett whispered. "Has she gone?"

"Yes," Jack whispered back.

"It's okay," she comforted. "We'll be back at Bright soon and Serza and Hect are miles away. We'll be okay without her."

Jack wasn't so sure. Besides, he was accustomed to the idea that Ting was in his ear, listening, paying attention, ready to jump in and help him whenever he needed her. Some minutes later he was still wishing Ting hadn't left when Jossa began a spiralling descent.

As the ground rushed toward them, Jack got the same feeling he had the last time he'd rode Jossa – that the firewyrm was out of control and that they would crash into the earth and be killed. Once again, as the ground loomed vividly into view, Jossa beat his wings downwards to slow them to a stop. When the dragon's feet touched the ground there was that now familiar muffled boom and jolt. Jossa had landed just outside the stone circle. Ellisenn dismounted and deposited Oopa just inside the circle and turned to help Jack and Harriett down. The look in Ellisenn's eyes as he helped Jack dismount made Jack uneasy, but he couldn't pinpoint why. He averted his eyes from Ellisenn's and joined Oopa in the circle. The Oakling immediately threw herself around

Jack's knees and looked adoringly up into his eyes.

"You saved me!" she said. "You saved me from King stinky-pigsty Krungle!"

"It wasn't just me," Jack said, embarrassed and acutely aware of how Ting would have met this little display of affection, no doubt with a venomous round of hissing in his left ear. "It was Daniselle and Ellisenn," he continued as she squeezed his knees. "They did most of the saving stuff."

"But you and Harriett found me and brought me out of the black fortress," Oopa said, dismissing his denial.

"Well, you're welcome, Oopa," he replied awkwardly as Daniselle joined them in the circle, desperate for Oopa to detach herself from his knees. It was a bit hard to look heroic when you had an Oakling glued to your legs.

"We will wait as you open the Way and then carry your Pixish companion to Songarielle, where the horseman will be given aid," Daniselle said, glancing askance at Oopa who had now started to kiss Jack's knees.

"His name is Denn," Harriett said. "We couldn't have got through Fellwood without him. He saved us from goblins and protected us from a witch and, well, he was very brave."

"I will care for your protector," Daniselle promised. "Do not fear for him."

"Well, we'd better go," Jack said, unsure how to say goodbye in this situation.

"Travel well," Ellisenn offered. "I hope we will meet again soon."

They were innocent enough words, but Jack couldn't help feeling they held a lot more meaning. He looked at Ellisenn, whose eyes dropped to the ground as he flushed again. Something was going on here that Jack didn't understand or like.

"Farewell. May we meet again soon," Daniselle echoed.

"See ya," Harriett said.

"Oh," Jack added to Ellisenn, remembering something at the last minute, "when Denn wakes up, can you tell him that Krungle is dead? It will make him feel better."

"Of course, Waycaller. I will do whatever you ask," the young elf answered.

Again, ordinary sounding words, but there seemed so much more behind them. Jack didn't have time to ask about that now. "Great, thanks," he said instead.

Jack extended his hand for Harriett to take hold. As Oopa was still hanging onto his leg, he told her to just continue doing so and not let go. Quite self-consciously, Jack concentrated hard on visualising the circle of Bright. He had never called for a Way to open with so many spectators. Once he had the circle of Bright clearly in his mind, he put all his might into calling for a Way to open.

"Wait," Ellisenn said. "I must tell you—" He stopped mid-sentence, his eyes clearly troubled. His mouth opened to say something more, then closed. He was obviously struggling with what he wanted to say. "I am sorry, Waycaller. I ... I—"

"What?"

"I bring you the well-wishes of Anarra Settonett, the Bright One. She desires you to know that you are in her thoughts."

Jack suspected that wasn't what Ellisenn had been about to say, but he was glad to hear it nevertheless.

"Anarra is safe?"

"Yes, she is safe. She gave me leave to journey here to aid you."

That sounded a bit strange. Why would Ellisenn need Anarra's permission to do anything?

"Jack," Oopa interjected, "We must get the Keysong away from here."

"Oh, yeah." Jack nodded to Ellisenn in thanks for Anarra's message. He regathered his will and intention to open a Way, pictured Bright in his mind and called out.

"Open a Way to the great circle of Bright!"

Instantly an orb of light flashed into existence in front of them. Jack extended his free hand to the orb and touched it. That familiar sensation, of a rolling ecstatic pleasure, entered his fingers and rushed up his arm to fill his whole body. His hair stood on end. In moments, the waves of pleasure completely overwhelmed him. Dazed, he looked up to see Ellisenn staring at him, his green elvish eyes alight with … what? Fascination, awe? Or yearning? The elf looked away on being caught staring. Jack quickly closed his eyes as well and was swept away by the pleasure and the light.

THE TIDE TURNS

They were back in the open field in the Halfling Dells, in the middle of the ancient circle of standing stones. Harriett was still holding his hand, her eyes closed, and Oopa was still clinging to his leg. Harriett opened her eyes, looked into his and smiled.

"We're back!" she beamed.

Oopa let go of Jack's leg and looked around.

"This is a very *big* circle," she said, taking a few steps toward one of the stones, "and *very* old." She froze. "Oh no," she moaned.

"What's wrong?" Jack asked. Oopa didn't answer. She had gone a paler shade of green and was looking around as if waiting for something terrible to happen, her eyes filled with fear.

"Oopa," Harriett said, "are you okay?"

"Something wicked is here—" Before Oopa could say anything more, Hect stepped out from behind one of the standing stones. "So," the Dread sorceress hissed with mad delight, "here is the vessel holding the key to my mistresses' release!" She jabbed her hand towards Oopa's heart, a flash of green light causing them all to recoil. Jack was the first to open his eyes again. Oopa had snapped bolt upright as if turned to stone, her precious knitting bag dropped to the ground, her eyes rolled into the back of her head so that only the whites were showing. A strange light swirled around her tiny form. Harriett screamed and tried to press into Jack for protection, but some immense force emanating from Oopa was holding them still, holding Hect still as well. The Dread sorceress stood mere feet away from them, sneering.

The whirling light slowly lifted Oopa off her feet until she floated six feet from the ground. She opened her mouth as if trying to scream, but what came out wasn't a scream. It was the strangest, most eerie sound Jack had ever heard – like the whispering of millions of voices, each overlapping, all chanting indecipherable words that blended into each other to form an otherworldly symphony. Jack's head spun. He worried he might lose consciousness if he listened to it too closely. Harriett swayed on her feet, unable to fall, held in place by the pressing force swirling around the circle of stones.

"The Keysong," she moaned. "Oopa is the instrument!"

After everything they had been through, Jack was horrified to the point of despair. Had they failed? Had Hect forced Oopa to release the Keysong? Would Morrigan now be free? The song built to a bone-shaking howl, so filled with evident power that it forced all thought from Jack's mind. The cacophonous song reverberated through the circle, setting the megaliths to vibrate and glow with that same peculiar light. As the stones lit up, one by one, they emitted their own supernatural song. Beams of light coursed from the singing stones to Oopa's body, connecting the standing stones to her like anchors tethered to a drifting ship. With a terrible crack, a shockwave burst from Oopa's motionless body that rolled outwards like a wave, smashing into the megaliths. With a flash the great circle of Bright became one massive shining edifice. The Keysong increased in pitch, becoming a squeal so loud that the very earth shook. When it finally reached a crescendo, another pulse of light emanated from the circle of standing stones and rebounded off Oopa, knocking Jack and Harriett sideways. The beam of light extinguished, the stones went dark, and the little Oakling fell to the ground, motionless and silent. They were able to move again. Jack and Hect rose and eyed each other over Oopa's body. Before Jack could stop her, Harriett rushed to the Oakling.

"Oopa! Oopa, are you okay?" Oopa didn't respond, she just lay there, small and still. Thunder boomed over the stone circle. A rushing sound drowned out Harriett's pleading as a powerful wind whirled among the stones. Jack's skin tingled. The air was sparking with magic. With a sound like the cracking of a whip, Hect was thrown by an unseen force up against one of the standing stones and pinned there. She hissed with rage but could not move. Jack rushed to Harriett's side, glancing around for the source of the magic.

"She doesn't look so good, Jack," Harriett said when he joined her by Oopa's motionless form. "I think she's really hurt."

Jack knelt down and looked Oopa over. There was no way for him to tell what was wrong with her, or even if she was alive. He didn't know where to find an Oakling's pulse. All he knew was that the power that had coursed violently through Oopa's little body was more than enough to kill her.

"What do we do?" Harriett cried.

"You have done enough," a familiar female voice said. They turned and saw behind them the source of the magic that had captured Hect. A young dark-skinned girl of about sixteen years old approached them, her long, pitch black hair dancing on the breeze, her ebony eyes glistening with tears.

"Amallayne!" Harriett shrieked. "Please, help Oopa!"

Amallayne stretched her hand over Oopa and closed her eyes. "She will feel no more pain," she said. "She is gone, beyond my help."

Harriett broke into sobs. Jack stared at the little body, dumbstruck. Rage surged up from deep inside him. He turned to find Hect. He would tear the Dread sorceress limb from limb. Hect was pinned against one of the standing stones, her eyes fixed on Amallayne, wide with disgust and contempt.

"I heard the song and I came," Amallayne said. "I set the Dread there when I arrived – I will deal with her later." The Faeden stared down at Oopa's lifeless body.

"How did she know?" Jack asked. "How did Hect know that Oopa was the Keysong?"

Amallayne shook her head, as if irritated by the question, seemingly preoccupied with comprehending the loss of Oopa, but she turned her eyes on Hect, the intensity of their blackness seeming to bore into the Dread's mind. After a long moment, the Faeden blinked and looked away, disgust clearly showing on her face. "She captured one of Serza's generals and tortured him until he revealed that the dark prince's attack on Pitmouth was motivated by his desire to find the Keysong. When she saw the dragon carrying you and Oopa away from the black fortress, she assumed you must also have been there for the Keysong, so she followed you here, determined to gain the freedom of her mistress."

"Have we failed?" Jack asked, his voice desperate. "Will Morrigan break free?"

"How extraordinary you both are," Amallayne said, ignoring Jack's question. "To have journeyed all the way to Pitmouth, rescued Oopa from Krungle's dungeon and brought her, and the Keysong, all the way back here. I did not expect you to do it."

"But, have we failed?" Jack repeated, his throat tight.

"Can you not tell for yourself?" Amallayne queried. "Surely there is enough of mine own power in you for you to be able to feel the truth of things?" She stepped close to him. "Here, let me help a little." She touched him gently on the forehead and his body tingled with bliss. "Now, feel with your mind. Sense if the balance of the world has changed."

Jack calmed himself, opened his mind then reached out to feel if anything was different in the world. When he did so, he caught a glimpse, in his mind's eye, of Darkgate. It felt weightless to him, as though all of its potency had drained away. The power of Darkgate was broken. As quickly as the image had arisen, it vanished.

"Was that real?" Jack asked. "Or just my imagination?"

"Oh, it was real," Amallayne confirmed. "Darkgate is no more. It is just an ordinary door now."

"Why didn't you tell us the instrument was an Oakling?" Jack demanded. "It might have made a difference!"

"It would have made no difference. I did not tell you because there was a possibility you would not succeed in your task. I could not risk the knowledge of the Keysong's hiding place falling into our enemy's hands. What if you were captured by Serza or, for that matter, by Morrigan's followers?"

"But why didn't you protect her?" Harriett shrieked. "She was the Keysong! You could have put some kind of spell on her to keep her safe! But no, you didn't protect her at all! You left her alone to be kidnapped by goblins, and now she's dead!"

"Do not presume to lecture me, girl." Amallayne's dark eyes turned glassy, dangerous. "If I had placed extravagant protections around her, how long do you think it would've taken before one of Morrigan's minions guessed there was more to Oopa than there seemed? Even so, there were wards of immense power protecting her, subtle enchantments indiscernible to all. Hect, by chance, used the only curse powerful enough to break those wards, a curse only a shadowflyer could wield. There are few magical protections stronger than those I used, but all magic has its weaknesses, even Faeden magic."

"I'm sorry," Harriett mumbled. "I didn't know."

"That is the failing of humans. They do not see. They do not know." She knelt by Oopa's lifeless body. For the first time Jack thought he saw softness in her eyes. "No, no this will not do," she said as she touched Oopa's little ears. "The destruction of the Keysong means that the Pale Mother will be loosed on the world, but that is a small crime compared to the taking of my Oopa's life. She and I were old friends. I will see her avenged." Amallayne stood and pointed her finger at Hect. The sorceress writhed silently for a moment then howled and screamed. Her skin began to smoke and burst open, releasing tongues of flame – she was burning from the inside out. She wailed, thrashed and screamed until she finally erupted into a pillar of fire and was consumed, burned to nothing but ash.

Harriett screamed until she had no breath left. Even then her mouth stayed open, frozen in horror. Amallayne smiled coldly at the pile of ash that was Hect and waved her hand again. The ash disappeared. Nothing of Hect remained, nothing at all. Jack reeled at how easy it was for the Faeden to take life, how effortless it was for them to destroy someone as powerful as Hect. Hob and now Amallayne had both taken life without expending more energy than it took them to breathe. Harriett trembled, looking into Jack's eyes, her own reflecting all the terrible things she'd seen since they arrived in Anwynn. She convulsed with the weight of it all and fainted.

"Harrie," Jack cried. "Harrie!" He crumpled to his knees beside her.

Amallayne passed a cursory glance at Harriett before enfolding Jack in her arms. She ran her fingers through his hair, as if stroking a pet, like a lapdog or a kitten. He was overwhelmed by a coursing sensation of bliss, exactly the same as when he opened a Way. He couldn't move.

"Do not fret for your sister, Waycaller. She will recover." She kissed Jack gently on the cheek. Wave after wave of breathtaking ecstasy coursed through his entire body, making him weak in the knees. "How different you are in this vulnerable state," she said smirking, referring to his inability to move. "Not nearly so arrogant. Now, I want you to understand something, my Jack. When I battled Morrigan and defeated her, I needed to find a way to ensure she never rose again, and a way to keep your kin, your ancestors who were most loyal to me, safe from her and her minions. Do you understand that, Jack? I created the Veil and Darkgate to protect your family, the line of Senn. It was all for you, because your ancestors loved me and showed me great devotion. I created them in the same instant, with the same act of magic that I used to place the power of the Way in the blood of your ancestors. The power of Darkgate and the Veil and the power that courses in your veins are one and the same. Now that Darkgate is broken, its power will flow back into *you*, for you *are* the Way. There is nothing in all of Anwynn more powerful than you now – nothing, except the Faeden themselves."

Jack's mind reeled. Amallayne had created the Veil for

his family. Its power was his birthright. But could he really stand against Serza, with all his vicious sorcery?

"The ... the Gift," he stammered, remembering that Wadget had said there was nothing more powerful than Thullu's Gift.

"Did you not see the awesome power of the Keysong, Jack? That was the power of Darkgate. It has merged with the power already within you. Do not be afraid of the Secret Gift, for there is one thing we Faeden know about power – it flows to those with a purity of purpose. What can Serza do against you, even with Thullu's Gift, when you are who you are? When your very blood is magic, when your purpose is so pure?"

"Pure?"

"Yes. All you want is to protect those you love. Isn't that true, Jack?"

He didn't respond, couldn't respond. His body throbbed with bliss and his mind reeled. Morrigan would soon be free. Anwynn was facing another Doom War. And what did Amallayne mean when she'd said 'what can Serza do against you'? Did she want Jack to face Serza, to try to defeat him? Even in the midst of the bliss he felt a stab of fear. How could he face Serza and Morrigan as well? No matter what Amallayne said, he was just a kid. He wasn't a druid or a sorcerer, certainly was not powerful enough to face the Dark Prince of Fellwood *and* the White Demoness and come out of it alive.

"Do not doubt me, Jack," she said, as if she knew what he'd been thinking. "The magic I placed in your bloodline exceeds your imagining. Test it now, send out your mind and see how things fare in the world, feel for Morrigan."

"No." He closed his eyes and tried to close Amallayne out.

"Send out your mind, Jack, send out your mind now."

That piece within him that was of Amallayne obeyed. He felt his perception widen, his senses broadening to take in everything in the valley where they stood, then everything in all the Halfling Dells and beyond. His mind was like a vast eye, overlooking all of Anwynn as it slumbered. Then the night perceptibly darkened. A bitterly cold wind whipped up and raced across the fields of the dells to swirl among the stones. At the horizon far to the south, in the direction of Pitmouth, deadly, lightning-filled clouds built and swirled. A second later, a terrible gleeful groan, like a thunderclap, rolled up from the south in waves. Jack had never heard anything like it before. No, he *had* heard something like it before: the wail of Morrigan at the Battle of Bright. This was the moaning of a tongueless mouth, it vibrated in every blade of grass, in every leaf and flower, in every stone of Anwynn. It hummed in the very air. The ground trembled with it. The stars dimmed, shrinking away from it. Jack felt it surrounding him, covering him like a heavy blanket. It was as if much of the goodness of the world had suddenly been overturned, or poisoned. What did it mean? Did it mean that the Queen of Doom was free?

"I am impressed. You see far, very far," Amallayne said. "You see that Morrigan is free."

Chills of terror ran down Jack's spine. Morrigan was free. How strange, he thought, that it should have occurred with so little outer fanfare. He doubted anyone in Anwynn, apart from the Faeden and those sensitive to the ebb and flow of magic, would have noticed.

"You see, Jack, you *are* powerful." She let go of him and stepped away, clicking her fingers. In an instant the Dark Prince, Serza, was standing before them, his iridescent pink eyes wide with alarm. Jack jumped back in shock as Serza immediately raised his hand to strike Amallayne with some kind of spell. Amallayne merely twitched her finger and Serza flew through the air to be pinned against the scorched standing stone where Hect had just perished. He struggled but was unable to move, tossing his head from side to side so that his snowy hair thrashed against the stone, like white seaweed tossed against a reef in a storm. "Do you see, Jack," Amallayne snarled, "even with the Secret Gift he is *nothing* compared to me, *nothing* compared to the Faeden." She waved her hand in Serza's direction and he screamed out with pain, as if he were being crushed by some invisible pressure.

"No, you can't!" Jack shouted. "The covenant! What if he's protected by Thullu?"

"Don't quote the covenant to me!" Amallayne yelled. "Do you think I am stupid? Do you think I would risk defying Lord Thullu's will? The Prince of Fellwood will not die by *my* hands."

"What ... what do you mean?" Jack's throat constricted even more.

"Jack," she said, looking directly into his eyes, "you have the power now, all the power of Darkgate, all the power of the Veil. All you need do is defend yourself when that pathetic prince tries to kill you. Lord Thullu cannot blame me for that."

Jack felt his eyes bulge. His mind reeled in shock. Was she serious? Could Amallayne really be suggesting that he kill Serza? He couldn't do such a thing, especially not with the prince pinned motionless to a standing stone.

"Accept who you are, Jack, accept who you are or die. Now, deal with the dratted prince for me, would you?" At that Amallayne erupted into a pillar of red flame and vanished into thin air.

Jack could move again. He turned on his heels as the sound of Serza falling to the ground alerted him that the dark prince was also free. The prince leered at Jack and strode toward him. This is it, Jack thought, I'm going to die. Serza lifted his hand, making the preliminary motion of a spell. Jack lunged straight at him, knocking his hand away. If he was going to die, he was not going to die running like a coward.

Jack drew his black sword and swung it in the direction of Serza's head. Serza easily sidestepped Jack's attack, but his eyes widened in surprise. He made a sign with his hand that threw Jack bodily backwards but Jack didn't topple over. He landed on his feet and ran straight back at Serza. Serza's eyes widened even more, this time coloured with more than surprise, perhaps a hint of fear. The prince staggered then, and grabbed at his right ear, where a purple wisp of smoke was swirling. The wisp took the shape of a tiny, red-haired Tiqq. Not a flighty little female creature like Ting, a male with blazing purple eyes.

"Thullu's Gift?" Jack said out loud, finally understanding. Serza shrieked.

"No! The Gift is mine!"

"I do not belong to anyone," the Tiqq said. "I go where I choose." The little creature laughed and extended its hand. A flash of purple light sent Serza to his knees. The prince shook his head, sensing something had changed. He stared at his hands, as if searching for something.

"No, my power, *my power*—"

"*My* power, not yours," the Tiqq said. "I have taken it away. This other one, this human boy, his bravery intrigues me."

Serza screamed and pulled at his white hair, then turned his pink eyes on Jack. "You have cost me greatly, Waycaller, but you are just a boy and I can still kill you, with my bare hands if I must!" He spat on the ground before leaping to his feet and hurling a dagger.

Jack leapt aside as the dagger glanced across his shoulder. He lost his balance and fell backwards into one of the megaliths, striking his head, and glancing off to the ground with a thud. Dazed and unable to move, Jack listened helplessly, waiting for Serza to rush towards him and finish the job. But instead Serza turned his attention to Harriett, still lying defenceless on the ground. The prince knelt before her, looking over at Jack with a malicious leer, taunting him. He drew another, longer dagger from its sheath on his thigh and raised his arm to plunge it into Harriett's belly. Jack lurched up and threw himself at the prince, colliding with him and knocking him away from Harriett.

Serza thrust the dagger toward Jack's throat. Jack spun and dodged to the side so that Serza's blade scraped the skin but didn't cut deep. Denn's sword fighting lessons were holding Jack in good stead. He swung his own blade above his head and brought it down toward Serza with all his might. Serza madly blocked Jack's blow with a violent up-thrust and the two blades glanced off each other, emitting a strange metallic sound, a song of violence. The force of the blow knocked them apart, giving Serza just enough space to gain the advantage. He kicked Jack off his feet. Jack's head struck another standing stone with such force that his nose bled. He crumpled to the ground, panting, certain that the time for his death had arrived. He turned to the Tiqq, pleading for help with his eyes.

"I cannot help," the Tiqq said. "You must face this challenge alone."

Serza laughed, a laugh that spoke volumes about his cruelty and arrogance. He was certain that he'd won, that Jack was about to die. Jack struggled to move, but failed, watching with horror as Serza glanced down and saw that Harriett was within his reach again.

"Now I finish the girl," he taunted Jack, who was still struggling to lift himself up. Serza raised his dagger and lunged at Harriett.

"No!" Jack yelled, leaping unsteadily back to his feet, a steady stream of blood pouring from his nose. Consumed with a desperate desire to save Harriett, he stretched out his hand toward the dark prince and, with all his will, shouted,

"Go rot in hell!"

Serza shrieked in fury and vanished in a burst of blinding silver light. Jack slumped to the ground, spent by the effort it took to banish Serza. His head throbbed painfully, blurring his vision. He tried to stay upright, but his vision spun and the pain in his skull sent him toppling over into blackness.

He was in a dark, green-lit cavern: Uffern. Serza lay writhing on the floor, screaming. Morrigan and the halfling sorceress were standing over him. The sorceress had conjured a dark Sending, its tentacles crushing Serza to death. The prince's screams were deafening, but not as terrible as Morrigan's gurgling, tongueless laughter. His vision swirled again. He was back on the grass in the circle of Bright. The male Tiqq, 'Thullu's Gift', was sitting on the grass right in front of Jack's face.

"You won," he said solemnly.

"Won what?" Jack asked, a little delirious.

"Me. You won me, my admiration, Waycaller, and my respect."

His head throbbed. He pressed his brow to the cold grass. His vision darkened and his body succumbed to a creeping cold. The last thing he saw was his little sister, curled in a foetal position, sobbing and shaking, but alive. Alive.

PART 3: CHAOS UNMASKED

EHMAARIM

Anarra stood by the tall window looking out over Songarielle's grand square. The throne room was cold. She wrapped her arms around herself and shivered. For a moment she envied the guards, whose armour and helmets kept them warm no matter how low the temperature dropped. The large brazier to the side of the throne remained unlit, an act of mourning for the many who'd perished in Prince Serza's attack on Songarielle. Only the kitchen fires burned now, and the odd lamp. The palace and the senate were like tombs these days, dark and quiet. No one spoke above a whisper, no one smiled. War loomed over them all.

The high plateau beyond the citadel was now home to a vast encampment of elvish warriors. Their cooking fires twinkled in the dark, like fallen stars that had come to rest among the grass and wildflowers. Tessarelle and Merielle were sending their best fighters to join their Songarielle kin. They grew in number every day, ready to go to war for their new queen. Tens of thousands of them had gathered out there, the full might of Elvinidd. Would they endure? Would Elvinidd survive? Anarra couldn't answer her own questions. Too much hung in the balance. Bonemound was destroyed, Jack had sent word of that to Daniselle. A communal shudder had spread through the elvish senate when Anarra repeated the news during the morning assembly. Bonemound had endured almost as long as Songarielle. For it to fall was a mixed portent. Joyous they should be that the power of the Dread was broken, but the joy was tempered by fear. If Bonemound could fall, so could Songarielle or even Tessarelle, the oldest of the elvish domains.

Anarra glanced at the door. It frustratingly remained closed. The guards at either side looked away when her eyes met theirs, intending to preserve the illusion of her privacy but just making her feel isolated. She wished that door would open, that Ellisenn would stride through bringing news of Jack, or even bringing Jack himself. She had granted her young druid protector leave to go to Jack's aid. For hours now she'd waited anxiously in the throne room for Ellisenn to return, praying for that heavy door to open. Midnight approached and still no knock had rung out on it. She was alone, except for the dozen or so guards and the druids she knew were posted outside.

She looked back out the window, scanning the night for Jossa, Daniselle's silver dragon. The dark sky was empty bar a thin sliver of moon and a few clouds. What if Ellisenn never returned? What if Jack had already perished? What if Jack and Ellisenn had both been killed in the shadow of the black fortress of Pitmouth? Her belly filled with a cold weight. If Jack was dead all would be lost. Not only that but she would regret never having made the effort to get to know him better. She wished she'd told him how she felt, that she thought of him often. An image of Jack and Ellisenn came unbidden to her mind, their bodies bloody and lifeless, together in death as they could never be in life. She shook the image away. If they were dead, she was sure she'd know, that somehow she'd feel it as a darkening of her world. But would she? It was Ellisenn who was twined to Jack, not her. Ellisenn might feel it if Jack were killed, but she likely wouldn't not feel a thing. She wasn't twined to anyone. She readjusted the headdress of outspread wings, the crown of Elvinidd. If I am twined to anything, she thought, it is this. She was bound to Elvinidd, to the crown that sat like a terrible weight and the throne that pulled at her from the corner of the room. A knock at the door made her jump and turn. The guards opened the door and in strode Ellisenn, his blond hair shining in the dark, despite being tainted with soot. A bruise bloomed at the corner of his bottom lip, where a little blood pooled.

"What happened?" she demanded. "Is Jack safe?"

"The Waycaller is safe," he said, sounding even more relieved than she felt. He crossed the room to her in easy strides. "We found them at Pitmouth in the midst of a battle between Serza's dark host and Krungle's army."

"But Jack and Harriett are unharmed?" She could barely comprehend the news that the Prince of Fellwood had attacked Pitmouth. She needed reassurance about Jack first.

"Yes, they are both unharmed and safe in the halfling village of Bright."

"Bright?"

"We carried them to the standing stones in southern Pix. From there Jack opened a Way to Bright."

"Why?"

"I do not know. Jack did not tell me, though he made it clear it was of great importance that he go there. He was in the company of an Oakling, a female by the name of Oopa, and a Pixish horseman by the name of Denn."

"An Oakling and a horseman?"

"Yes. The horseman was badly wounded. We brought him here to Daniselle's house to be cared for by Kashashem. He is already recovering."

"And the Oakling?"

"She went with Jack and Harriett to Bright."

"Strange."

"Yes, but recent days have been full of strange things."

"And you, are you hurt badly?" She went to touch his lip. He jerked back involuntarily, then bowed his head in supplication on realising what he'd done.

"I am sorry, My Queen, I … I—"

"You did not wish to be touched by the cause of your broken heart."

"You are not the cause of my suffering, My Queen. My heart is its own enemy. It has set itself on someone who will never return its love."

"That is not your fault. The twining is not something we choose."

"True, but that truth does not make me feel less foolish, less woeful."

Anarra looked closely at Ellisenn. He masked his pain

well, but she could still see it in his eyes. "Is it terrible to be in my company, because of Jack's feelings for me?"

Ellisenn paused, glancing back into her eyes. "I am loyal to you, My Queen, to my death if need be."

"That I do not doubt. Do not think I am immune to your heartbreak, Ellisenn, to your pain. Know that I will strive not to add to it. If being in my presence causes you to suffer needlessly, I will ask Lady Kashashem to appoint another druid to protect me."

"No, Your Majesty, I wish to remain in your service, if you'll have me."

"Why, Ellisenn?"

"Jack loves you." He said this so simply and openly that Anarra nearly hugged him. It took a lot for her to hold back. She smiled at him instead and offered him her handkerchief for his lip. He took it, bowing again, and dabbed at the blood in the corner of his mouth.

"How did you get that wound?" she asked.

"A swift-fisted troll," he said ruefully. "He lies dead at the foot of Pitmouth now, so no matter."

A sharp rap at the door heralded the entry of a large group of people, all human. Anarra had summoned the ambassadors of the Four Kingdoms and their consuls while she awaited Ellisenn's return. She needed confirmation that the human kingdoms would add their armies to hers when she marched to face their mutual enemies. Anarra noted instantly the absence of a delegation from Danussan. This was not a surprise, the kings of the north had long kept to themselves, but it was disappointing. Danussan's armies were by far the largest and best trained of the Four Kingdoms. If they did not join the fight, their chance of success was slim. The diplomats were led by the ambassador from Pix: Corrus, she thought his name was. An overly thin, silver-haired man, Anarra barely knew him but already disliked him. His eyes were cold despite the rigid smile fixed permanently to his lips.

"Queen Anarra," Corrus began with a barely perceptible nod. The others bowed deeply, especially the young Pixish consul accompanying Corrus, a dark-haired, boyish woman who reminded Anarra of Harriett. Anarra made a mental note to find out the Pixish consul's name.

"Thank you for coming, ambassadors, consuls, I—"

"Is this urgent, Your Majesty?" Corrus interrupted. "It is rather late. Your messenger woke my whole household when he came to our door."

"I apologise, Lord Corrus, but in times of war none of us sleep easily or well."

"A war between elves declared by yourself, Your Majesty, not by any of the Four Kingdoms—"

"Lord Corrus will amend his tone," Ellisenn broke in levelly, "or the good lord will find himself *unable* to speak."

"Is that a threat, *boy?*" The ambassador took a step back, his eyes sharpening on Ellisenn's features.

"Ellisenn, please," Anarra said, gesturing for him to relax. "Lord Corrus, Ellisenn is no boy. He is my protector and a druid. He takes my well-being very seriously. Even so, he should not have spoken to you so. It would please me if we all treated each other with respect."

"Of course, Bright Queen," the Pixish consul said, eliciting a reproachful glance from her superior. Her shaggy black hair fell in her eyes as she bowed deeply again. She blew it out of the way and smiled as she straightened up.

The ambassador from Harshan, a stocky man by the name of Tessi Mahg, stepped forward. Though short of stature, his sinewy muscles and sun-coloured skin combined to make him look more like a street fighter than a diplomat. "Your Majesty has the utmost respect of myself and our own queen," he said, his dark almond-shaped eyes alert. "I beg you not doubt it."

"So too the nation of Anda wishes to express its love for the Elvish Sovereign," added the ambassador from Anda, his black skin and hair glistening with the fragrant oil the Andanese used to ward off illness. This handsome man's name was Mahaja, and Anarra had learned that before he became ambassador in Songarielle he had been a famous

Andanese general.

"Thank you, ambassadors, consuls," Anarra said. "I also offer the respect and affection to your nations and sovereigns that my own people have long held for them." She walked to the throne and sat down with as much dignity as she could muster, aware of Corrus' eyes on her the whole time. "I summoned you here for word of your sovereigns' response to my declaration of war. Will they send their armies to join Elvinidd's against the Dark Ones?"

"The House of Mael, overlord of all Pix," Corrus began, "does not shirk its responsibilities, no matter how onerous, nor does it shrink from war. It is the Pix who have kept the *filthy elves* of Fellwood at bay for nigh on eight thousand years."

Something about the way the Pixish ambassador said 'filthy elves' troubled Anarra. She looked him over a moment before deciding what she should do.

"Lord Corrus," she said in her sweetest voice, "might I ask your surname?"

"I am of the House of Mael," he said instantly, expanding his bony ribcage to puff his chest out as far as it would go. "My full name is Corrus Nillam Mael, Lord of the Northern Reaches."

"Ah, I see." Anarra had learnt from her father that the Maels hated elves, especially the Maels who ruled over the barren lands north of Pixett. Corrus was proof that the Maels had not learnt an ounce of wisdom or humility as they rose from bed slaves to kings. Anarra decided to act decisively. "Lord Corrus, you are dismissed."

"I beg your pardon?"

"You are dismissed, Corrus Mael. You may go."

Corrus glared at Anarra then gestured for his consul to follow him outside. As they neared the door, Anarra called out.

"Do not misunderstand me, Lord Corrus, I am not merely dismissing you from my presence. I am dismissing you from Elvinidd. You and your household will leave this place tonight. If you have not crossed out of Elvinidd into Pix two days hence, I will send dragon-riders to hurry you along."

Ellisenn's eyebrows arched but he said nothing.

"Two days!" Corrus shrieked. "That journey takes four days at least!"

"Best you make haste then, my lord, for I *will* send dragons after you if you are not out of my realm in two days' time."

Corrus Mael fled the throne room, his young consul slowly following behind, unashamedly smirking.

"Consul, please rejoin us," Anarra said. "Someone will need to represent Pix in these discussions."

Anarra was relieved when the consul bowed and rejoined the other ambassadors and consuls. She needed to know what Pix would do. "What is your name, consul?" Anarra asked.

"I am Massara Ceyr," she said.

"Ceyr?"

"Yes, Bright Queen. I see you recognise the name. It was the queens of my house who first brought Danussian slaves to Pix as bed mates. I doubt they ever expected their playmates' descendants would one day sit on the throne of Pix. I therefore offer my humblest apologies, for if it wasn't for my ancestors' libidinous urges, idiots like Corrus Mael would never have been in a position to insult you."

Anarra barely suppressed a laugh. "Apology accepted, Massara Ceyr. Every house has made its mistakes. Now, back to the issue at hand. Will the armies of Pix join mine against the Dark Ones?"

"Yes, Your Majesty," Massara said. "King Mael is no elf-friend, but he dares not refuse a direct request, especially when our own scouts tell us a dark host amasses on our southern border."

"The Warrior Queen of Harshan has already mobilised her troops, Your Majesty," the Harshanite ambassador, Tessi Mahg, added, smiling and tightening his topknot. "Our queen will lead them across the mountains herself in just days and will join you soon thereafter."

Anarra turned to the Andanese ambassador, who winked before speaking.

"I beg Your Majesty not to ask my surname, for fear it displease you as much as our friend Corrus' did. But let me reassure Your Majesty, there are no bed slaves in my lineage – some street sweeps, yes, but no bed slaves." Mahaja winked again. Massara Ceyr laughed out loud, then looked sheepish.

"Do not suppress your mirth, Massara," Anarra said. "It is much welcome in this place these days. Now, if the Andanese ambassador might give me his sovereign's answer?"

Ambassador Mahaja stepped forward, taking on a more formal demeanour. "The High Priestess of Erima, Kind Ruler of All Anda," he recited, "wishes me convey this message, Bright Queen: though deploring war, the High Priestess knows that swift and acute action must be taken to stop the spread of any pestilence. Therefore, she agrees that the armies of Anda will join those of Elvinidd, as they once did millennia ago. She hands the armies over to the personal command of the Bright Queen. Furthermore, the High Priestess has marshalled one thousand priestess healers who will travel with the Andanese army, to give comfort and care to those wounded in battle. She also offers the young queen any further aid she may require."

Anarra forced back a tear. It was better than she dared hope. Elvinidd was not alone in facing this threat. The dominion of the elves had allies, even friends. *She* had friends. She stared at the ceiling, avoiding eye contact with the ambassadors to control her emotions. Most of the ambassadors understood and looked away. Massara Ceyr coughed and looked out the window and Ambassador Mahaja had the good grace to pretend interest in the empty brazier. When Anarra was able to look at them again, she caught their attention by clearing her throat.

"Thank you, my lord ambassadors, and Consul Ceyr, for the friendship you have shown this throne today. I have no words to express my gratitude."

"All the gratitude we need," Massara said, "is for you to stay on that throne as long as your predecessor and chase every fell beast back into the dark pit it came from."

"Consul Ceyr speaks for us all," Ambassador Mahaja said. "Friendship with the elves has only ever benefitted the Four Kingdoms."

"You are all most gracious," Anarra said, meaning it sincerely, "and most likely quite tired. It is very late and there is much for us all to do once the sun rises. Let us part, for now, and meet again as need be."

The ambassadors and consuls bowed as one and departed. As soon as the door to the throne room closed Anarra turned to Ellisenn, shaking her head in wonder.

"Humans are so surprising," she said. "We should deepen our bonds of friendship with them."

"I cannot fathom them," Ellisenn said.

Anarra suspected he was thinking of Jack. "What do you mean?" she asked.

"They are confounding, both secretive and outspoken at the same time, which is made worse by their unpredictable moods. They do not have the constancy of elves."

"No, they are changeable, that is true, but it seems they are loyal once you have earned their trust."

Ellisenn merely shrugged. Anarra stood and went to the window, motioning for Ellisenn to join her. "The time is nigh," she said, her eyes fixed on the lightless sky. "Soon I must take the armies of Elvinidd into the Empty Lands, to face horrors of old." She looked into Ellisenn's eyes, glistening green even in the dark. He was focussed on a lonely cloud snagged on a distant mountain. "Are you ready to complete the task I laid on you when first you became my protector?"

"Yes, My Queen, I am ready."

"How long will it take you?"

"I can travel to Vellenhive and back by the time your army marches for Amaltor."

"So be it then. Go, Ellisenn, and may you be persuasive

when next you meet with Princess Sarritt, for if she refuses my request we are all doomed."

Without a word Ellisenn bowed and left the throne room. The guards closed the doors behind him with an echoing snap. Anarra was alone again, alone with the empty brazier and the sliver of moon barely visible through the window. She gazed out over Songarielle, dark but for the occasional lamps of watchmen. Movement at the edge of the shadowy square below caught her eye. A solitary figure cloaked in black entered the square from the street opposite. As the figure came closer, Anarra marked him as an elf, his long black hair worn in a familiar fashion – her father had always worn his hair in that style. More movement to the left of the square revealed another figure, also cloaked in black, also with the same black hair and pale, alabaster skin. Beyond him another came, a young woman armed with two swords, her eyes the same deep blue as Anarra's. A group of three followed behind her, two men and a boy. Anarra pressed her face to the glass, peering into the shadows to the left and right. Other figures were there, all dark haired, all armed with swords, all cloaked in black. They moved determinedly across the square towards the senate. In mere moments there were dozens of them, more entering the square all the time. A resonant horn blast suddenly rent the air with a solemn sound. Anarra's hand shot to her mouth to stifle a sob. After eight thousand years the night elves, the Ehmaarim, were coming out of hiding, responding to Anarra's declaration of war and honouring the ancient treaty that once united all the elves. She cautioned herself against it but couldn't help but feel a great hope. Her people had answered her call. Despite all that threatened it, Elvinidd might still endure.

BUTTERS NOB

In the darkness Jack's head throbbed, bringing him back to awareness. He could feel something soft against his face. A pillow? He was warm, covered by a blanket that smelt sweetly of vanilla. He breathed that delicious scent in. Then he thought of his little sister and alarm rose in him like a surge of bile, before he remembered: she was alive, distressed but alive. He opened his eyes. He was in a familiar room, a room with two beds and a small porthole window: Miss Butters' back bedroom. He had no idea how he'd got there. In the bed across from him was Harriett, moaning softly but otherwise still. He must have lost consciousness and been carried here. He pictured Ellisenn carrying him through the dale and putting him to bed and felt a flush of embarrassment. But no, it couldn't have been Ellisenn who brought him here. Ellisenn was with Daniselle, far off in Pix. But how long ago had that been? The night seemed no darker. He could see the moon through the window. It sat more or less in the same position in the sky as it had when they'd arrived at the circle of Bright, before Oopa had ...

He didn't want to think about Oopa. He squeezed his eyes shut, trying to squeeze the memory of her death away. It didn't work. The image of her lying still and lifeless on the ground bloomed in his mind, followed by images of the other deaths of that night playing out in his head. Hect, burnt to ash from the inside out by Amallayne. Serza, crushed to death by a dark Sending conjured by Hephaestia Hatter in the pits of Uffern. Then Morrigan's mouthless laughter filled his ears, and it was as if she were right there. He sat up and looked around, swaying a little as his eyes refocused, then sighed with relief once he was sure he and Harriett were alone.

A small lamp burned on a bedside table, while the smoky scent of an open fire elsewhere in the cottage mingled with the fragrance of vanilla. Jack eased back into the bed, knowing that the hearth ward would protect them from any dark attack. Miss Butters' low ceiling felt like a shield, protecting them from the darkness outside. The valley beyond the window was quiet – it felt wrong that it should seem so peaceful after what had happened there. Jack lay for long moments, unable to move any further. His shocked mind threw up the same images over and over again—Oopa, Hect, Serza—until he finally remembered the Tiqq. The male Tiqq with shaggy red hair and blazing purple eyes. Where was the Tiqq now? He ran his hand over his left ear and whispered, "Are you in there?" There was no reply. Had he imagined the Tiqq? He'd hit his head, hard, at least twice. No, that'd been after the Tiqq had already abandoned Serza.

"He must've been real," Jack said aloud, pulling the blanket closer around him.

"Who must've been real?"

Jack twisted around and found himself looking into the large round eyes of Wadget, who was standing in the doorway. Behind the Oakling was Aelf Ethelwulf, looking every bit as eccentric as he always did.

"The lad's a tad cross-eyed right now," Wadget said, scratching his long ear, "but he ought ter survive."

Aelf stepped around his master and came into the room. "How are you, Jack?"

Jack didn't know what to say. He certainly wasn't okay, his heart felt heavy and his gut was tight with unease. All he could think to say was probably the last thing they wanted to hear.

"Morrigan is loose." He closed his eyes, waiting for the shock on their faces to pass.

"Are yeh sure, lad?" Wadget asked, coming over to stand by the bed. Jack nodded. Wadget and Aelf passed grave looks. Jack was relieved when Miss Butters bustled in, preventing the druids from asking any more questions.

"You're awake!" she said, placing the tray she was carrying on the bedside table, nearly knocking the lamp onto the floor. The tray was piled high with food and, of course, the inevitable steaming cups of tea. "I didn't think it was possible, but you children are even thinner than when I last saw you. Well, there's nothing for it but to keep you in bed and feed you up until you're a decent weight."

"Sounds good to me," Jack said without thinking, realising on saying it that the idea of a few days, or maybe even weeks, in Miss Butters' bossy care filled him with relief and peace. He looked over to Harriett and hoped it would happen, that Harriett would be safe in Miss Butters' back bedroom and have all the time she needed to recover from their ordeal.

"Not goin' ter happen," Wadget said gruffly. "If Morrigan is loose, we must act fast. We must gather the druids an' warn the armies o' Elvinidd afore they march south. First we need ter know everythin' that happened, Jack. Every detail, no matter how small." Wadget pulled a dented hip flask out of his pocket, poured a long swig of whistleberry wine into a teacup and passed it to him.

"I'm only seventeen, I can't," he protested.

"Yeh've earned it, lad," Wadget growled. "Now drink. Whistleberry is a powerful curative."

So Jack had one cup of wine and then another, until the soothing warmth of the whistleberries massaged the pain and the fatigue out of his body. Feeling quite tipsy, he allowed Miss Butters to feed him soup and toasty bread while the druids waited for him to speak.

He slowly started relating what had happened to him and Harriett since they left Songarielle. He told them about Amallayne sending them on a quest to retrieve the Keysong, about meeting Denn in the Tomb of the Old Oracles of Senn, about being given the torc of time and about their journey through Fellwood Forest. He also divulged what the Oracle had told them: that there was a chance they may be reunited with their mother.

"Good news this is," Wadget grumbled. "The Oracles have always seen much. If the Oracle said yeh an' yer mother may see each other again, then one day it'll happen."

Miss Butters forced another piece of toasty bread into his hands as Jack told the druids about the Battle of Bonemound, about how Serza had used the Secret Gift of Thullu to decimate that awful ziggurat and kill all the Dreads, except for Hect. He couldn't tell them that Hect was dead just yet. The thought of how she'd died made his stomach churn, threatening to eject the soup he'd only just swallowed.

"Serza's power has grown too great," Aelf said in a worried voice. "To be powerful enough to destroy Bonemound—"

"He's dead," Jack said, causing Aelf, Wadget and Miss Butters to gasp. "Amallayne brought him to the circle and then I ... He tried to kill Harriett so I ... I sent him to Uffern. Then that Hatter woman, she killed him. She's with Morrigan now."

"Hephaestia Hatter!" Miss Butters hissed. "When I get my hands on her she'll regret ever being born! She must be mind-sick, it's the only explanation for a halfling becoming a disciple of the Pale Mother!"

"Until recently," Aelf said, "you would not have believed that a halfling could join the Order of Druids and be apprenticed to Master Wadget, as you have. After all, there is nothing *forcing* halflings to stay true to Eugene."

"Except for common decency, you mean," Miss Butters huffed. "Well, don't you worry, Jack, if it's the last thing I do I'll teach that indecent witch a thing or two for attacking *my* younglings!"

"*Your* younglings?" Jack said, swallowing another swig of wine and smiling.

"Oh, well ... oh just eat up, Jack!" She leapt up to get another loaf of bread from the pantry.

"Serza's death is a mixed blessin'," said Wadget. "Now he's dead it'll be harder ter discover if Thullu is involved. We might only find out once the God o' Chaos is right on our tails."

Jack was sure now that Thullu was not behind Serza's actions. If the dark prince had Thullu's blessing, surely the male Tiqq with the vivid purple eyes would not have abandoned him the way he did, not left him to be banished to Uffern by Jack and then killed. Jack's throat tightened. Serza was dead because Jack had sent him to Uffern. Even though Serza was responsible for so much death and destruction, Jack still felt a sickening guilt about the way he'd died, strangled and crushed by a dark Sending, especially as he now knew that Serza had been possessed by one of the Tiqq all along. Had the dark prince done all those terrible things against his will? If so, the male earwisp must be totally evil. Jack scratched his ear, hoping that the Tiqq hadn't possessed him while he lay unconscious in the circle of Bright. Strangely, he didn't feel all that worried about it. When he'd first suspected Ting's presence in his ear he'd been terrified. As he pondered this he realised he wasn't worried because he somehow knew he wasn't possessed. He felt sure of it. He also felt sure that Thullu was not involved.

"Serza was acting alone, not with Thullu's blessing," Jack said, surprised at how decisive he sounded. As soon as the words left his mouth a ringing, unshakeable certainty settled over him. It was a sensation like nothing he'd ever felt before, absolute clarity that cut through all doubt and confusion.

Wadget eyed him curiously. "Care ter explain how yeh know that, lad?"

"No," Jack said. "I can't explain it. But it's true." He decided not to mention the male Tiqq to Wadget and Aelf. Who knew what would happen if the knowledge that Thullu's Gift was not an object but a living, breathing being got out? He needed to speak to Ting before he told anyone about that. Especially as he didn't know where the male Tiqq had gone. That ringing certainty washed over him again. Yes, he would say nothing about Thullu's Gift to anyone but Ting.

"What of the Secret Gift?" Aelf asked, eyeing him keenly. "Did Serza surrender it to Morrigan or her followers before he perished?" Jack shook his head. The Gift had not been with Serza when he'd been banished to Uffern, he knew that for sure. Jack took a bite of bread to avoid having to say anymore. He was surprised that Aelf and Wadget didn't press him further on this, perhaps deciding that Jack was too frail to be interrogated. Jack took their hesitation as an opportunity to relate the story of how he, Harriett and Denn had journeyed to Pitmouth and how they'd snuck into the black fortress and rescued Oopa. He didn't tell them they'd done it inside the bodies of dead goblins, and he didn't mention anything about Ting. He didn't want to break his promise to Ting about keeping her involvement secret. In his tipsy state, Jack felt a twinge of sadness that Ting wasn't still in his ear. He wondered why she had been summoned by the Beckoning Bell. He didn't know if it was just the wine talking, but he kind of missed her and hoped he saw her again soon, even if she was crazy jealous. Over a third cup of whistleberry wine, Jack told the druids about being rescued from Pitmouth by Daniselle and Ellisenn, in particular about Ellisenn's devastating use of the Seren Star.

"Extraordinary druid, that one," Wadget grunted in what almost appeared to be admiration. "No other druid has ever shown such mastery so young."

As Jack continued to talk, and the story unfolded toward its culmination in the great circle of Bright, Jack felt a lot of the anxiety and shock of what occurred there return. His voice trembled as he related that Oopa herself had contained the Keysong and how it had arisen from her when Hect had cursed her. He told them how Amallayne had then appeared and what she'd done to Hect. Even Wadget flinched at that news. Jack explained how Amallayne had helped Jack to reach out with his mind and feel that the power of Darkgate was broken, that Morrigan was free. Wadget's eyes widened with either anger or worry, Jack couldn't tell which. Aelf's skin had paled and his eyes brimmed with tears. Neither druid said anything for a long time, apparently incapable of speech in the face of Morrigan's release.

"Vile, tricksy Faeden!" Miss Butters spat, making them all jump, "putting the key thingamajig inside that poor Oakling! They're all wicked, the Faeden, all of them!"

"Oopa was very old," Wadget said, his throat catching as he said her name, a ripple of sadness crossing his face. "Nearly as old as me. We knew each other long ago. She knitted me a nice cardigan. I'm grieved at her loss."

"Once Amallayne killed Hect she ... she just abandoned me there to fight Serza. Serza could have easily killed me, but she didn't care if I lived or died." Jack felt almost as bad about Amallayne abandoning him as he did about having to send Serza to Uffern. She was meant to be a goddess. She was meant to help him.

Wadget shifted in his seat, eyeing Jack knowingly. "There's a reason neither druids nor elves treat the Faeden as gods," he said. "Aelf, tell Jack what I told yeh about the Faeden when yeh were a boy even younger than him an' first got apprenticed ter me."

Aelf took a breath and began. "There are two things that will help you to understand the Faeden. The first explains why they sometimes act with a disregard for life. The Faeden have a surfeit of life – they are immortal and so do not comprehend how rare, fragile and singularly important each mortal life is. The second is the fact that power does not equal good, power is not wisdom. The Faeden are very powerful, but not all-powerful. They know much, but not everything. They are worshipped as gods, but are not ever-present. In fact, they are rarely focussed on the mortal world. They interfere in mortal affairs for their own incomprehensible reasons, often when we'd rather they didn't. Then when we really need their help, they're nowhere to be found. For most of the time they abide elsewhere, in a place we cannot sense nor comprehend, a realm of overbearing bliss. While in that place of bliss, it does not seem they are even aware of what is happening here."

"They're not gods then," Jack summarised. "They're just selfish creeps."

Wadget chuckled. "I like yer line o' thinkin'," he said. "Have some more wine, lad."

Jack gulped down the last of his whistleberry wine, his

head now light and fuzzy. "Poor Oopa," he whispered, thinking how she'd adored Amallayne and now lay lifeless on the cold grass, like a sleeping child. His chest tightened. He fought back tears.

"I'm sorry to ask this, Jack" Aelf said, "but what happened to little Oopa's body?"

"What do you mean?" Jack asked, a sick feeling rising from his gut. "Didn't you find her when you found us?"

"No," Aelf said, glancing with alarm at Wadget. "We arrived just as you collapsed and lost consciousness. We found you and Harriett in the circle, but not Oopa."

"I don't understand," Jack said. "What does that mean?"

"I don't know," Aelf answered. "It is very strange."

Wadget's ears waggled the way they did when he was pondering something difficult or unpleasant. After a while he huffed with frustration, shaking his head but saying nothing further about Oopa. "At least we found yeh alright," he said gruffly. "I thought we'd find yeh in bits an' pieces."

"We were mightily relieved to find you both alive," Aelf added. "I've never felt so relieved in all my life!"

"The same goes for me as well, Jack," Miss Butters declared. "I really was so worried about you." She popped another piece of toast in front of him and touched him gingerly on the head.

"Thanks," Jack whispered, wiping away the tears welling up in his eyes.

"We carried you both back here," Aelf added, "where Miss Butters was waiting."

"How did you know we were there?" Jack asked, the room spinning a little.

"Ellisenn sent word," Aelf answered. "We took flight as soon as we heard that you had returned here."

Ellisenn. Jack closed his eyes and nestled back into the pillows. Ellisenn had gone above and beyond to protect him. Along with Daniselle, the woodland elf had rescued them from Pitmouth, and now had acted to make sure he was safe in Bright. Jack was starting to suspect that there was more to

Ellisenn's interest in him than the handsome young elf let on. That made Jack very uncomfortable. He put that aside. He couldn't think about it now. Ellisenn had been right about one thing: Wadget and Aelf's presence in Bright did make Jack feel safe, but that safety was just an illusion. Morrigan was free. Now none of them would ever be safe again.

"It was all a waste," Jack said, opening his eyes and looking at Wadget. "We failed and now Morrigan will come after us."

"Much has been made waste o' late, but yer efforts aren't among 'em, Jack." Wadget hopped up onto the bed beside him. "It's true that Morrigan is loosed, but the Prince o' Fellwood is dead, an' our enemies have not gained the Secret Gift. That, at least, is somethin' ter be pleased about."

"But Morrigan, she will destroy everything—"

"Morrigan has not won yet, lad," Wadget grumbled. "Do not ferget that we've contended with Morrigan afore, an' at her full powers. Fer millennia we kept her at bay, right up until the Doom War."

"That's right,' Aelf added. "And this time Morrigan does not have her full powers and may take some time to regain them."

"If we hit Morrigan now," Wadget said, "an' hit her hard, we might defeat her. Without her full powers, she's just a very wicked hag!"

"So, you might win?" Jack asked, not quite allowing himself to think it possible. Until now he had felt that all was lost.

"I should ruddy well say we might," Wadget said, smirking. "'specially as Serza has already done half the work fer us by killin' all the Dread sorcerers! Now, Miss Butters, I have somethin' serious ter discuss with the lad, an' I'd rather do it with a flagon o' ale in me hand. Yeh got any ale?"

"Of course," the halfling said. She scurried off to the pantry. Jack awaited her return anxiously. What did Wadget want to discuss with him? When Miss Butters came back into the room she plonked a large glass of beer in Wadget's hand

and sat down on Harriett's bed, which creaked loudly.

"Fatty," a small, muffled voice said from under the covers. Jack sat up, peering at his sister's form beneath the blankets, her mess of black hair obscuring her face. Aelf, Wadget and Miss Butters all stared at her as well. Without opening her eyes or moving, Harriett muttered again. It was the same word: "Fatty."

"Oh, bless her heart," Miss Butters whispered, "even in her unconsciousness she's complimenting me."

"I'm not unconscious," Harriett said weakly, "and I'm not complimenting you. You're sitting on my foot."

"Oh, so sorry, dear," Miss Butters said as she scooted back, freeing Harriett's foot. Harriett pushed her hair out of her face and smiled at them all. It was a very tentative smile, but it still filled Jack with joy.

"Are you okay, Harrie?" he asked.

"No, but I will be," she said, smiling a little more strongly, making her ice-hued eyes look strangely warm.

"Of course you'll be fine," Miss Butters said, "as soon as you have something to eat you'll perk right up." The halfling crossed the room in a flash, taking a piece of bread right out of Jack's hand. "Start on that, dear," she said, giving the bread to Harriett before bustling out of the room, evidently to get more food. Harriett sat up and started nibbling on the toast.

"Now, lad," Wadget began. "Yeh have a decision ter make, an' yeh can't make it without all the facts."

"A decision about what?" Harriett asked, interrupting.

"About whether or not to cross the Veil and return to your own world," Aelf answered.

"Are you serious?" Jack said. "But, what about Morrigan, won't she come after us?"

"Morrigan was only after yeh 'cause she wanted ter use yeh ter escape her prison," Wadget explained. "She's free now, she don't need yeh no more, an' she don't have the Secret Gift an' so won't be able ter cross the Veil. If yeh go home, yeh'll be safe."

Jack's heart leapt. He looked over to Harriett. She didn't

look pleased by this news. Her brow was furrowed. Before she spoke, Jack knew what she was going to say.

"But, *you* won't be safe," she said in a small voice. "Morrigan will start another Doom War, she'll send her dark armies against the druids and the elves."

"Yes, she will," Aelf said. "The Pale Mother wants to rule over all Anwynn. She won't stop until she does."

"There's nothing we can do about that, Harrie," Jack said. As soon as he said it, his stomach tightened. He felt slightly ashamed that he was so ready to abandon his friends, but he had to get Harriett to safety and there really was nothing he could do against Morrigan and her armies.

"Yer wrong about that, lad," Wadget said.

"About what?"

"There *is* somethin' yeh can do. A lot, in fact."

Jack didn't say anything at first. He somehow knew exactly what Wadget was going to say. That feeling of certainty spread over him again – Wadget was going to bring up the prophesy.

"If you mean that prophesy," Jack started, shaking his head.

"I do mean the prophesy," Wadget said firmly. "I should've told yeh about it sooner, but so much kept happenin' ter distract me. I see somebody else has told yeh somethin' about it at least."

"Daniselle told us that it says there will be a second Doom War," Harriett said. "And that a Druid King will stop Morrigan for good."

"No, no, yeh need ter hear the exact words," Wadget grumbled. "Tell 'em how it goes, Aelf."

Aelf took on a serious demeanour and began to recite: "And not once but twice shall Anwynn be imperilled. At the time of the second darkness, a new dynasty will come to the ancient realm of Pix. Born to the House of Senn will be the Druid King, the Oracle returned. Only then will Amaltor be rebuilt as of old and Pix become great again. The fruit of the Line of Senn will be as a new dawn, turning back the night.

And the Oracle, returned from time and from death, will be as the sun against all shadows, banishing darkness forever. The Druid King, the Oracle returned, both shall face the Mother of Lies and see her destruction."

"*Both* shall face?" Jack asked, looking curiously at the druids. "

"Very few have heard that bit before," Wadget began, "except Kashashem, who heard the prophesy from the one who made it, the last Oracle o' Pix, who uttered it as she lay dyin' after bein' attacked by a swarm o' Morrigan's Dreads. Kashashem shared it with me, but no-one else."

"That can't mean me," Jack said. "It can't mean *us*." He looked to Harriett, his ears ringing. She looked back at him with those pale eyes and smiled.

"But it *does* mean us, Jack. You *are* the Druid King and I *will* be the Oracle."

Jack's mouth felt open. What was Harriett saying?

"Seriously, Jack?" she said, those cold eyes boring into him. "You can't work it out, not even now?"

"No, how could I?" He growled the words, irritated and frightened.

"Oh, I don't know, look at my *eyes* maybe!"

As soon as she said this it was obvious. Harriett's eyes had changed when he'd used the power of the Waycaller to save her life. 'Returned from time and from death' as the prophesy said. He'd seen someone else with eyes exactly the same pale, icy blue: the Oracle he and Harriett had met when they'd first used the torc.

"You're becoming an Oracle?"

"Finally! Yes!"

"So, all the Oracles have had those pale eyes?" He said this to the room at large, but it was Harriett who answered.

"Oh no, they're unique to me."

"But ... but ..." Then it dawned on him. The Oracle they'd seen in the torc vision was not their mother. She was Harriett herself, a version of Harriett from the future. He reeled with the shock of that and slumped back into the pillows. He stared at his sister, awed.

"How long have yeh known?" Wadget asked, looking at Harriett with a fresh interest.

"Only since you recited the prophecy just now, but also, always. I've kind of always known."

"Well, yeh speak riddles like an Oracle does anyways," Wadget said.

"But ... but I'm not a king," Jack stuttered.

"No, but you are a prince," Aelf said. "The son of Noble Senn of the House of Senn, and the sole heir to the throne of Pix."

"What?"

"Your father was King Mael's heir. When your father died, as his oldest child, you became the heir."

"But, I've barely even set foot in Pix!"

"No matter," Wadget said. "It's yer blood that makes yeh a prince, not yer feet."

"Why didn't you explain this to me before?" Jack's face was hot. A hurt anger was making his heart thump.

"Master Wadget didn't want to burden you with it straight away," Aelf said. "He thought it might frighten you."

"And he was right," Harriett said. "Look at him, poor Jack, he's terrified."

"You should've told us sooner," Jack said. He wanted to rage at them, to accuse them of not caring about him or Harriett, but part of him knew that wasn't true. The time had never been right for this conversation. They'd careered from crisis to crisis ever since they came to Anwynn. This moment in Miss Butters' back bedroom was probably the first chance Wadget had found to tell them. "So, what are you asking me?"

"*Us*," Harriett said. "They're asking *us* to stay and fight Morrigan, even though we could go home now and be safe."

"I will not put Harrie in that kind of danger," Jack said. He looked out the window, unwilling to meet Wadget's eyes.

"And so you shouldn't, Jack," Miss Butters said. "The very idea of taking children off to a war!"

"I won't do it," Jack repeated. "I won't."

"Well, too bad, Jack," Harriett said. "I'm staying. You can go home if you want but I'm staying. I have to. I can't explain why, but I know I have to stay and fight Morrigan. Even if she kills me, I have to stay."

That undeniable sense of certainty enveloped Jack again. Harriett was right. They had to stay. He didn't know why, but he knew that if they didn't all of Anwynn would be destroyed. And maybe not in the upcoming months or even years, but some day in the future Morrigan would find a way to breach the Veil and then conquer the human realm as well. But if they were going to stay, he had to do everything possible to make sure they survived. He turned to Aelf.

"Will you teach me how to … how to … "

"How to use the power within you?"

"Yes. I don't want to face Morrigan without knowing what I can do, how to protect Harrie and how to fight."

"Of course, I'll teach you. I'll teach you everything I know, such that it is."

Wadget chuckled. "An' so the otherworlder 'comes a prince an' a druid in one night. The prophecy moves fast now."

Jack looked into Wadget's eyes and nodded that they would stay, sealing his and his sister's fates, for good or ill.

"Great," Harriett said, "now that that's settled, I'm going back to sleep."

"You haven't eaten nearly enough," Miss Butters said. Harriett glared at her, her nearly white eyes flashing like ice refracting sunlight. Miss Butters had the good sense to back down for once.

"I'm proud o' yeh both," Wadget said, his gruff voice cracking a little. "Very proud." He looked at his green feet a while, then sighed. "I won't ever forgive meself fer this, fer layin' such a burden on ones so young, but if we're ter thwart Morrigan once an' fer all, it must be so. Now, get some rest, the both o' yeh; we have an early start in the mornin'."

Wadget and Aelf left the room as Miss Butters tucked

Jack tightly into bed. He thought he saw tears in the halfling's eyes, but his head was spinning a little from the wine so he couldn't be sure. He looked over to the bed containing Harriett. Her eyes were closed and her breathing was easier now. When Miss Butters blew out the lamp and left the room, Jack rolled onto his side so he could see her better. He decided, as he succumbed to the warm heaviness of the whistleberry wine and slipped toward sleep, that Harriett could hold his hand as much as she wanted from now on.

THE GORY

A flush of orange behind the mountains heralded the rising of the sun. The snowy summits glowed gold and sparkled. The morning half-light lasted longer in the dale, being in the shadow-cast of the high peaks that surrounded it on all sides. Jack straggled behind the others, slowed down by his full stomach. Miss Butters had insisted they all eat a hearty breakfast before getting underway. The halfling had eaten more than anyone and yet she had no trouble keeping the pace set by Wadget. Jack wished he hadn't eaten the second stack of pancakes, which had settled like a stone in his belly.

Wadget had ruled out Jack opening a Way to Amaltor, their destination, where the forces aligned with the druids were gathering, for fear it would alert Morrigan to their plans, so they were trekking out of the dale on foot. Soxy, Aelf's shaggy cow, and Miss Butters' precious Piggy-Poo had been left behind in Songarielle. Once out of the dells, they were to rendezvous with dragon-riders sent by the elves. Jack and the others all wore rucksacks stuffed to overflowing with things Miss Butters considered essential: fruit, cake, tea leaves, flour, sugar, a kettle, cooking pots and many other things. To Jack's annoyance, Miss Butters was the only one not burdened by a heavy pack. She carried a handbag, overstuffed and made lumpy by its contents, which included a dozen sweet buns, a jar of whistleberry conserve, an egg whisk and her favourite wooden spoon. Jack was sure his own pack contained the rest of the contents of Miss Butters' kitchen.

It was a dent to Jack's ego that a middle-aged druid, an obese lady halfling and Wadget, a creature whose legs were shorter than your average toddler's, were all more able to keep up the pace than him. Even Harriett, who had lain barely conscious just last night, had now recovered enough that she was almost her old self again ... almost. Her eyes still looked haunted, and though she walked hand-in-hand with

Aelf she wasn't peppering him with questions. Jack interpreted this as a sure sign her recovery still had a way to go.

Despite the heavy pack and fast pace, Jack found the lush and green countryside around Bright a pleasure to behold. He doubted he would ever grow bored of it. Grassy meadows with large oak and birch trees stretched out on either side of them, cut through by willow-banked streams where lilies grew in the shade at the water's edge. The trail they were following led straight towards the mountains and Narrownotch Pass, the only way in and out of the Halfling Dells. This more direct path would not take them past Oakholme. Even so, every time they crested one of the small heather-topped hills, Wadget looked west towards the green basin where his home lay. Jack understood how Wadget felt. Even though his life in Cairnbawn had been hard, and was neither exciting nor comfortable, at least it'd been familiar. In Anwynn they never stopped moving; each new place was stranger than the last and dangers lurked around every bend in the road. If Jack had a cosy home like Wadget's oak tree, a safe and comfortable place protected by powerful magic, he'd be pining for it as well.

At the bottom of the next rise the trail turned to the west, following the course of a rocky-bottomed brook. The brook ran, gurgling and bubbling, between two low ridges. In the permanent semi-shade of the ridges, ferns grew almost as big as people. The bank of the brook was peppered with rocks and mossy boulders that forced the path to narrow and bend in places. After a while, Jack realised they were going slowly downhill. The path grew steeper and entered a stand of birch trees, the brook becoming a series of cascades. When the trail levelled out again they emerged from the birch grove and found themselves facing a huge wall of rock - a cliff face rising so high that its upper reaches were obscured by clouds. Jack's jaw dropped. The cliff face was rent in two by a narrow crack, an opening just an arm-breadth wide. Between where they stood and the crack in the cliff face lay a deep pool, fed by a small waterfall. An ancient stone bridge was the only way across.

"Narrownotch Pass," Wadget said, pointing toward the crack on the other side of the pool. "The trail goes through 'ere an' comes out on the other side o' the mountains in the Empty Lands, where we'll meet the dragon-riders."

Wadget led the way across the bridge. Jack fell in beside Miss Butters.

"Have you ever crossed through Narrownotch Pass?" he asked the halfling as the shadows at the foot of the cliffs enveloped them.

"I come from an entirely decent family," she said, as if that were a sufficient answer.

"No then?" Wadget said from ahead.

"No."

The Oakling stopped at the entrance to the pass. "Pay attention, all o' yeh," he began. "The notch is narrow as the name suggests an' it'll take us most o' the day ter get through. I'll lead an' Aelf will go last, just in case we get attacked from ahead or behind."

"Is that likely?" Harriett asked, her voice anxious.

"Not likely, no, but not impossible."

Wadget entered the ravine first, followed by Harriett, Miss Butters, Jack and then Aelf. Jack scanned the walls of the gap all the way to the top, searching for the sky. He found the perspective disorientating, like peering up through a huge keyhole. The notch was too narrow for even two people to walk side by side. It was also dark, lit by only a small amount of muted light filtering down from the thin slice of cloudy sky visible far above. They walked in single file until the sun finally reached its zenith, sending warm sunlight deep into the pass for the first time, but only for brief moments when the clouds parted. Soon after that the ravine widened for a few hundred yards and then opened out into a circular gully. A single stunted cedar grew among a tumble of boulders there, beside an ancient fire pit, no doubt built by travellers long dead. The pass narrowed again on the opposite side of this circular space.

"This is 'bout half way," Wadget said. "We'll stop here a bit."

Miss Butters set to making lunch immediately, ordering them all to drop their rucksacks in a row beside the fire pit so she could rummage through them and find what she needed. She commandeered Jack to gather firewood from the base of the old cedar, which he did without objection due to the prospect of a warm lunch. Wadget lit the fire with a spark from his wand. Once the fire was crackling with bright orange flames, they all sat to watch Miss Butters work her magic. Jack was convinced it *was* magic too, for no ordinary cook could produce the bounty that Miss Butters could in so short a time and with such meagre supplies. Aelf sat next to Jack and started speaking quietly to him about the nature of magic.

"Magic flows from our will," he said, "but the best magic is fuelled by emotion, especially love and compassion. Magic fuelled by anger or hate is never as strong. Even when we are using magic in battle, it will be stronger if our focus is on protecting those around us rather than defeating or hurting our enemies." Aelf went quiet, looking to Jack for a sign that he understood. Jack nodded, realising with a thrill that those few words had been his first lesson in druidry.

The sun had inched a little lower in the sky by the time they'd finished their lunch and were sitting back in a post-meal daze. Jack rested against a boulder, facing the direction of the sunshine, hoping to catch a little of the light and warmth shining through with each break in the clouds. Suddenly a bone-chilling shriek rent the air, echoing in the ravine so that it sounded like a thousand voices coming from all around them.

"Goblins!" Wadget growled.

Goblin howls filled the gully, coming from ahead, the path leading towards the Empty Lands. Wadget and Aelf shepherded them all to the back of the gully, where it narrowed into a ravine again and led back to the Halfling

Dells.

"We'll make our stand here," Wadget said. "This ravine is our only means o' retreat, we have ter keep the Dark Ones out o' it, 'cause if we can't fight 'em off, we're goin' ter have ter make a run fer it."

Jack peered over Wadget's head as the Oakling drew a line in the dirt with his wand. In the shadows of the gap ahead a seething mass of screeching creatures was becoming visible, all seemingly climbing over each other to reach them, all heavily armed with swords, clubs and spears. Wadget flicked his wand and a shimmer of energy rose from the line he'd drawn on the ground and hurtled upwards to the top of the canyon. The little druid had created a huge shield wall, separating them from the oncoming goblins. He stood, wand at the ready, Aelf at his side, as the goblins poured into the gully, shrieking and screaming at the top of their lungs. There were dozens of them and the metal breast-plates over their leather doublets bore the awful emblem of a screaming white mouth, the emblem of Morrigan. Their beady black eyes gleamed with an awful hatred and their teeth dripped with froth. Jack shuddered and pushed Harriett behind him.

The goblins crossed the gully in seconds, hitting Wadget's invisible barrier at a full run. Some of them exploded the minute they reached the line in the dirt, some fell down writhing in agony, but others hurled themselves repeatedly at the thin air of the barrier and bounced back only to hurl themselves at it once more. The protective ward Wadget had placed between them and the goblins was powerful, but would it hold? More and more goblins were pouring into the gully. Wadget raised his wand and with a minute movement sent thousands of tiny green sparks to fly out amongst the advancing goblins. On contact with the shrieking beasts the sparks flashed and flared, eating away at the goblins' flesh until they were just bones. More than half of the goblins died this way, before most of the others turned and fled. Those few that remained launched another attack at the barrier, many exploding into ash on impact. Aelf stepped forward then and clapped his hands, creating a sonic boom that rolled forward as a visible force. When it collided with the remaining goblins, they were crushed where they stood and fell to the ground dead and bloodied. A tense silence fell over the gully. Jack forced himself to breathe again, his heart pounding like a drum in his ears. Surveying the carnage, Jack understood Wadget's confidence that they might win the fight against Morrigan. The goblins were no match for druids.

They stood there in silence a long time, the dead lying before them like heavy weights, a sombre mood overtaking them. Finally, Wadget flicked his wand and removed the shield wall. As soon as he did, a dozen goblins leapt out from the shadows of the ravine and pelted towards them. Jack grabbed Harriett and staggered back, readying to run. Wadget had barely raised his wand when a massive troll, the biggest troll Jack had ever seen, hurtled out of the ravine. It was easily nine feet tall, completely covered in shaggy white fur except for a black patch over its right eye. The huge troll quickly caught up with the goblins. In mere seconds it single-handedly ripped off the head of the first goblin it overtook, then did the same to another two, then another two after that. Most of the remaining goblins turned to protect themselves from the troll, but two continued on towards where Wadget, Aelf and Miss Butters had formed a line to protect Jack and Harriett. In the short time it took Wadget to flick his wand and take out one of the approaching goblins, and Aelf to clap his hands and deal with the other, the troll had pulled off the heads of all the rest. It stood panting in a pool of heads and blood. Wadget raised his wand toward it.

"No kill me, teensy green morsel, me kill them goblins good for you."

Jack shook his head. He couldn't believe it. The troll's voice was deep and each word half growled out, but it had definitely spoken.

"Who are yeh?" Wadget asked it.

"Me am Nettaxitt, teensy green morsel."

"Yeh speak well fer a troll, Nettaxitt," Wadget said.

"'Course me do. Me pappy from forest," the troll said, touching the black patch over its eye, as if the patch explained its ability to speak.

"Yer father was a forest troll?"

"Yes, me mammy from mountain, me pappy from forest. Me am but a bit from forest, but bit enough to speak your tongue."

"Why are yeh here?" Wadget asked. "Why did yeh help us with those goblins?"

"Me come find you, teensy green morsel. Me am soon to wear The Gory," the troll said, pointing to the top of its head. "Me not love Pale Mother, she bad, she gives us only sour morsels to eat." The troll pointed at the dead goblins at its feet and pulled a disgusted face, as if it'd bitten into a lemon. "Her wars no good for trolls. Many trolls die, many more than goblins or Vellenor. When me wear The Gory, me take trolls back to Trollmark. Me stay there, trolls keep to ourselves forever then. Me need your help, teensy green morsel, me need you help me make me people free. Me can help you. Me know where Pale Mother hides armies. Me show you and you kill them like me killed these goblins." The troll pointed to the carnage all around her.

"Extraordinary," Aelf said, his eyebrows raised.

"Oh, it's not so special," Miss Butters whispered, "I saw a parrot talk once and it was no smarter than this stinky thing."

"That's not what's extraordinary," Wadget growled. "This troll is the heir ter The Gory, the crown o' the troll queens, an' she's promisin' ter show us where the Pale Mother's armies are amassed in return fer our help ter free her people from Morrigan's control. That could turn the tide in our favour."

"She?" Jack said, looking at the huge beast.

"Yes, female trolls are a lot bigger than males, and a lot stronger," Aelf explained.

"I like her black patch," Harriett said. "It makes her look like a panda."

"A panda that rips heads off," Jack said.

"What be panda, little morsel?" the troll asked Harriett, her eyes curious. "You tell me what be panda?"

"It's like a bear," Harriett said, "a really lovely bear." She took a step out from behind Jack but he grabbed her so she couldn't get any closer to the troll.

"Me like bears," Nettaxitt said, her lips forming what Jack interpreted as a smile. "Me likes wrestle and pats them. Little morsel good to say me like panda, like bear."

"Why is it calling Harrie a morsel?" Jack asked, restraining his sister and casting an uneasy glance at Nettaxitt's toothy grin.

"Trolls refer to all animals as morsels," Aelf explained, "because they basically eat anything that moves."

"Including halflings?" Miss Butters asked, eyeing the big troll with suspicion.

"Oh yes, including halflings," Aelf said. "But this one seems quite civilised."

"Me standing here. Me hear you speaking 'bout me."

"Our apologies," Aelf said with a little bow. "We didn't mean to be rude."

"Morsels know no better, just morsels after all. But morsels need not worry, me not eat them, not even lovely ripe morsel." Nettaxitt pointed at Miss Butters, who shuddered with horror. "Me need all you little morsels to help trolls, 'specially teensy green morsel with sparkle magic."

"Sparkle magic!" Harriett said, beaming at the troll. "Oh, I love her!"

Cautiously, Wadget led them out into the gully to collect their packs, with one eye always on the troll. Nettaxitt watched them, her face curious, but didn't move. Miss Butters kept her distance. The halfling had just collected her handbag when a goblin lying near her feet lurched upright and lunged at her. The goblin swung its blade, which caught on the strap of Miss Butters' bag, slicing it through. The bag's contents spilled out, sweet buns rolling in all directions, the jar of conserve smashing on the goblin's foot, making him howl. With the kind of lightning fast move Jack had seen Miss Butters perform a few times before, she bent down, retrieved the wooden spoon from the gutted handbag and swung it up into the goblin's face, hard. When the spoon impacted with the goblin's nose, a loud crack and a white flash of light sent him hurtling through the air. He landed with a sickening crunch yards away, at Nettaxitt's feet. The goblin twitched a little and then moved no more. Miss Butters stared at the wooden spoon, the carnage all around her forgotten.

"Well, would you look at that," she said. "All this time I had a magical spoon and didn't even know it."

"It's not the spoon that's magical, Dorothea, it's you," Aelf said.

"Me?"

"Of course, the spoon just worked as a conduit, like Wadget's oak wand does."

"Me, magic?"

"Why do you think we invited you to join the order?" Aelf asked.

"It sure wasn't 'cause o' yeh winnin' personality, I'll tell yeh that much," Wadget grumbled.

Miss Butters stared at her spoon, then at Wadget and Aelf, then back at the spoon again. Nettaxitt laughed and stomped her feet, looking at the dead goblin on the ground in front of her.

"Lovely ripe morsel got spoon magic," the troll roared, laughing. "Me like that! Spoon magic be good!"

Nettaxitt insisted that she herself go into the ravine first, just in case any goblins lay in wait for them up ahead. Wadget followed close behind her, his wand still in his hand, in part, Jack was sure, because he didn't completely trust the troll, but also because a fair number of goblins had survived the fight in the gully. Behind Wadget trotted Miss Butters, her wooden spoon now tucked behind her ear for easy access. Jack came immediately behind her, and Harriett behind him. As before, Aelf brought up the rear, his eyes always on the narrow path behind them. They travelled this way for hours, stopping from time to time to rest and listen for any sound of goblins approaching from ahead or behind.

Nettaxitt turned out to be a good travelling companion. She was considerate of their smaller bodies and much shorter legs, and stopped often to let them catch up. She even offered to carry Harriett and Jack's packs, which Harriett was quick to agree to. Harriett would've climbed onto the troll's back herself if Jack hadn't stopped her. He was still uneasy about the troll referring to his sister as a morsel. The sun was now so low in the sky that no light penetrated deep enough into the notch to light the trail. It was so dark in the ravine it might as well have been night. They stumbled along in the gloom until Jack finally saw a faint light ahead, framing Nettaxitt as if with a halo. They reached the end of the ravine and passed out onto a rock ledge overlooking a wide-open terrain, the sky tinged with the orange of dusk.

"The Empty Lands," Aelf said, "the grassy plains that were once part of Greater Pix."

A roar and a flash of light made them all look out over the plain below. In the distance a blue dragon circled high over a group of goblins, who were scattering in every direction. A few smoking lumps on the ground told Jack what the flash had been—dragon fire—and that not all of the goblins had escaped. The dragon roared again and swept the earth with flame, catching another half a dozen goblins in its fiery arc.

A loud flapping sound and down-thrust of wind made them all look up. Jossa, mounted by Daniselle, loomed out of the half-light and landed nearby, his silver scales reflecting the orange of the sunset.

"Well met, my friends," Daniselle said as she dismounted. "When I spied that goblin troop leaving the ravine I worried for your safety. I am pleased you are not harmed." She strode over to Jack and Harriett, pushing her long black hair over her shoulder as she came. She patted them both on the shoulder, the height of mountain elf affection. "I see your company has grown since last we had word from Master Wadget," she said, looking over the troll.

"This is Nettaxitt," Wadget said, "heir to The Gory crown. She helped us fend off those goblins."

One of Daniselle's eyebrows shot up but she said nothing. Likewise, Nettaxitt remained silent, standing a little apart and looking awkward.

"Who is the other rider?" Aelf asked, straining to make out the elf on the back of the blue dragon. Jack's stomach tightened. Was it Ellisenn?

"It is Tellan," Daniselle said, and Jack's stomach relaxed. "Together Tellan and I will carry you all to Amaltor, where the armies of Elvinidd and the Four Kingdoms are encamped."

"Good, let's get on with it then," Wadget said. "There is much we must tell 'em afore they march south ter meet our ancient enemies."

REUNION

They hurtled through the darkening sky at an unbelievable speed, the clouds to the west tinted orange and red by the setting sun. Behind them, the immensely tall, snowy peaks of the Craggy Mountains shone with a halo of fading light. With every thrust of its wings, the blue dragon surged forward as below them mile after mile of grassy plain passed by. The Empty Lands that were once part of the Kingdom of Pix. The plains stretched all the way to the horizon. If Wadget was telling the truth, Jack's ancestors had once been kings of all of this. Jack shivered, from that knowledge or perhaps the cold, and squinted against the rushing wind. Harriett was holding tightly to his waist. Behind her Miss Butters clung for dear life to the dragon's scales. Jack, seated immediately behind Tellan, the blue dragon's rider, was doing much the same, using his thighs to keep him in place. In the sky ahead of them Daniselle, Wadget, Aelf and Nettaxitt rode Jossa, whose silver scales flashed orange, reflecting the sunset and the clouds.

A trilling whistle from Tellan caused his dragon to change direction to follow Daniselle and Jossa, who had veered towards the north east. Tellan could have been Daniselle's brother. One of the mountain elves, his almond-shaped eyes were dark and serious. His shoulder-length black hair only partly hid his long elvish ears. Like Daniselle, he spoke in a solemn voice, and only when necessary. He looked over his shoulder at Jack, his eyes more serious than usual. He gestured with his head at a dozen or more pillars of black smoke rising in the south and west.

"Anwynn burns," he said over the wind. "The Dark Ones hunger for the destruction of the world."

Jack stared at the billowing smoke, anger rising in him like a fire. This was why he'd decided not to return to his own realm. This was why he'd asked Aelf to train him to use his power. All of Anwynn would burn if Morrigan wasn't stopped. Jack would rather die than let that happen.

He took hold of Harriett's arms around his waist, both to hold her in place but also because he was afraid for her, for what might happen when they finally faced Morrigan. As he held his sister, his fingers sought out the silk bracelet around her wrist, the one tied there by Anarra. He caressed the soft fibre, using it to summon an image of Anarra, her long, dark hair, her shining blue eyes. It seemed like years since he'd last seen her, but it'd been mere weeks. Where was she now? Was she safe? When would he see her again? He would ask Aelf all these questions as soon as they reached Amaltor.

Three hours later, just as Jack's legs started to ache from holding on, he spotted campfires far below. The fires were all inside a large circle, visible from above only because the grass inside it was slightly greener. From the ground the circle was barely discernible, as Jack knew from the night he'd spent there with Miss Butters and Harriett after escaping the sorceress Mog. The circle was completely different now. No longer isolated and empty, it was filled with light and movement. There must be tens of thousands of warriors gathered down there. From what Jack could see there were four distinct encampments. The largest encampment, in the middle, was made up of brightly coloured circular tents with conical roofs, each roof decorated with a fluttering pennant. That looked like an elvish camp to Jack. The other camps were more military in appearance, the tents either square or round but all a dull brown. Altogether they were an impressive sight.

"Amaltor," Tellan shouted over the wind, "the place of prophesy."

Jack tightened his grip on the dragon's back with his thighs and pulled Harriett's arms more tightly around him. He knew what was coming. Sure enough, once they were directly over Amaltor the dragon pitched downwards, heading straight for the twinkling campfires. They all lurched forward as the ground rushed toward them. At the last minute, Tellan whistled and the blue dragon beat his wings downwards to slow their descent. They landed in an open area, near a cluster of tents topped with fluttering pennants.

"The Bright Queen holds council there," Tellan said, pointing to a large, elaborate marquee. Two huge pennants bearing the symbol of a flowering tree were planted at the marquee's canopied opening. Tellan dismounted and helped them do the same. Miss Butters looked very relieved to have her feet on the ground again.

"You are eagerly expected, Waycaller," Tellan said. "Your arrival will bring much relief to those gathered inside."

Before Jack could decipher what that meant, Daniselle, Wadget and Aelf joined them, with Nettaxitt trailing behind. The troll glanced nervously over her shoulder, perhaps intimidated by the huge force arrayed around her. Harriett, somehow sensing the troll's discomfort, tried to move next to her. Jack sighed and tugged her back by the collar.

"Daniselle tells us everyone's waitin' fer us in that tent," Wadget said, pointing to the marquee with the large pennants. "We best hurry up. It's not good ter keep kings an' queens waitin', they tend ter get cranky." Wadget turned to Nettaxitt and motioned for her to stay put. "Best yeh wait here with Daniselle an' Tellan," the Oakling said to the huge troll. "Yer not likely ter get the warmest welcome, some o' 'em might start swingin' swords around afore I get a chance ter explain. It'll be better if I warn 'em first."

Wadget led the way, but at the entrance to the marquee he stood aside and let Jack enter first. Jack's heart caught in his throat as soon as he got inside. The marquee was brightly lit by lamps hanging from the tent poles. Beneath one of those lamps, at the head of a long table where a group of people sat waiting, was Anarra. She was even more beautiful than Jack remembered. How could that be? Could she have grown more beautiful in the intervening weeks? Her deep blue eyes caught his from across the table. He saw in them the same yearning and relief that he knew was showing in his own. Without hesitation and without thinking he strode towards her. Many faces turned to watch him pass, their eyes either curious or surprised. He hadn't gotten far before two black-clad and heavily armed elves barred his way, their swords drawn. Jack looked from them to Anarra and back again, realising that these dark-haired, pale-skinned elves were Ehmaarim, night elves.

"No-one approaches the Bright Queen uninvited," one of the elves said, his deep blue eyes glistening and his voice icy.

"The … the Bright Queen?" Jack wasn't sure he'd heard right.

"Oh, whoops," Aelf said from behind him. "We should have told you, Jack. The crown of Elvinidd passed to Anarra on King Dhudhannan's death, as she is the last member of the High House of Sett and it is that house's turn to rule."

"Anarra is queen of the elves now?" Harriett said. "That's so cool!"

Jack stared at Anarra, his head shaking, as if that action might make this untrue. What would it mean for the future of his and Anarra's relationship if she was queen of Elvinidd? Surely it would make it difficult, if not impossible. He realised his mouth was hanging open and closed it, looking to Anarra for confirmation that she really was queen of the elves. She nodded and stood, causing all eyes to turn to her.

"May I introduce to the council," she began in a formal voice Jack had never heard her use before, "Jack Gordon, of the House of Senn, Waycaller, Prince of Pix and friend of the throne of Elvinidd."

Everyone at the table stared at him. Only now did Jack spot a couple of familiar faces. Seated on Anarra's right were Kashashem and Alva, who were both smiling kindly back at him.

"Master Wadget, Oak Lord," Anarra continued, "needs no introduction, and Aelf Ethelwulf will be known to many of you." A number of heads nodded, some smiling warmly at Aelf. Anarra gestured for Wadget and Aelf to join their druid friends at the table. "This," Anarra said, indicating Miss Butters, "is Dorothea Butters, a Brightling and apprentice druid." This caused a stir around the table, which Miss Butters took in her stride. She put her nose in the air and chose a seat close to the huge fruit bowl in the centre of the table, grabbing an apricot and some grapes before her bottom even made contact with the chair. "And finally, this is Harriett Gordon, also of the House of Senn, sister to the Waycaller, and my friend." Anarra gestured for Jack and Harriett to sit on her left, beside a stern-looking night elf. Once Jack was seated he surveyed the other people at the table. Jack doubted a more diverse group of elves and humans existed anywhere.

"Perhaps, before we begin," a stocky, olive-skinned woman with a silver topknot said, "I could introduce the rest of the members of this high council to the prince?"

Anarra nodded and took her seat. Jack couldn't take his eyes off her. It was a while before he realised that 'the prince' was him and he should pay attention to what the stocky woman was saying.

"I am Dechen Drokpa, Warrior Queen of Harshan." Jack looked more closely at the woman. She was elderly, perhaps sixty years old, with almond-shaped eyes that appraised Jack with shrewd interest. She bowed her head in formal welcome. Jack bowed in return.

"At the end of the table," Queen Dechen continued, "is General Mahaja, commander of the Andanese armies, and, in times of peace, ambassador to the Elvinidd court." The Harshanite queen gestured to a dark-skinned man with cropped hair wearing a tiny silver bell in each ear. "He sits on this council as the proxy of the High Priestess of Erima, who rules over all Anda." Mahaja smiled and bowed his head to both Jack and Harriett. Harriett beamed back at him.

"The empty chair next to the general is reserved for Varg, of Danussan, King of the North, who is yet to send word or show himself here at Amaltor." The queen's tone of voice made her disapproval clear. "Opposite you is Lord Corrus Mael, warming the seat for King Mael the Twenty-fifth, of Pix, who is late, yet again."

Corrus Mael smiled coldly at Dechen Drokpa. He was the only one who didn't bow his head to Jack, which Jack thought odd. Shouldn't a lord from Pix be friendlier to a member of the House of Senn?

"The young lady next to Lord Mael," the queen continued, "is Consul Massara Ceyr, also of Pix."

In contrast to Lord Mael, the Pixish consul bowed deeply. "Your Highness, it is a great honour to meet you," she said.

Jack flinched at being addressed as 'Your Highness' but managed a weak smile, noticing as he did so that Lord Mael was glaring at the consul with undisguised loathing.

"Last, but by no means least," Dechen said, "seated beside you there is Ansonn, representative of the returned Ehmaarim and commander of Queen Anarra's newly formed bodyguard." Ansonn, like Anarra and all night elves, had long, black hair, sapphire blue eyes and moon-white skin. He was armed with two long swords.

Jack doubted he would keep all those faces and names straight in his head for long.

"Now that all the niceties are over with," Wadget grumbled, his head barely visible above the table top, "can we get on with it? The Dark Ones aren't goin' ter wage war on 'emselves an' I have news that changes everythin'. We need ter act fast—"

"The meeting cannot begin until His Majesty, Mael the Twenty-fifth, is present," Corrus Mael said.

"And when will that be?" Anarra asked, her voice like flint.

"That would be now, young queen," a raspy voice said from the entrance to the marquee. All heads turned as King Mael of Pix strolled in. The king's pale hair was soft as silk, the colour of milk and cut to shoulder length. His eyes, a light green, were distant and cold. Jack stood, thinking it the right thing to do. This old man was King of Pix, and a distant relative. On spotting Jack, the king stopped and looked him over.

"So," King Mael said, "the rumours are true. The ill-bred spawn of my unfortunate nephew have returned to Anwynn."

Jack's mouth dropped open, along with that of Consul Massara Ceyr.

"Who's this old git then?" Harriett asked, looking at the king with distaste.

"How dare you!" Corrus Mael shrieked. "You will show the king proper respect!"

"Err, sorry, no I won't," Harriett said, glaring at Lord Mael, "not when he's calling us ill-bred and unfortunate. No way. He's a git, king or not."

Lord Mael lurched upright, knocking over his chair. He reached out, grabbed Harriett by the wrist and dragged her across the table toward him, drawing a dagger from his jacket as he did so. Jack, Wadget and Aelf were on their feet in seconds, Kashashem and Alva soon after. Before any of them could intervene, Lord Mael screamed and dropped the dagger. His eyes were saucer wide, staring into Harriett's face, whose pale eyes bore into his. He was trying to let go of Harriett's wrist, but he couldn't release his fingers, paralysed as he was by her stare. He struggled to get free, then screamed again, his face paling and beading with sweat.

"Harrie, what are you doing?" Jack asked, reaching across the table to grab her.

"No, Jack, don't interfere," Wadget growled.

Lord Mael screamed again. His eyes rolled into the back of his head and he collapsed onto the table, shaking violently. Harriett shook his fingers loose from her wrist and he fell sideways to the ground. The room was silent, everyone on their feet now. King Mael looked like he might collapse as well. He backed away from the table.

"What did she do to my nobleman, to Lord Mael?" he asked the room at large, his raspy voice a near whisper.

Harriett spun on the table and faced the King of Pix.

"I showed him all the evil that will come from his actions from now until the end of time," she said, her voice cold and terrible, especially coming from one so young. "I showed him all the horrors he has given birth to without knowing, out of his selfishness and hatred, all the death and pain that were to be his only legacy."

The whole room shivered, the very air chilled by her words. Jack staggered back. What was his sister becoming?

"That a girl," Miss Butters said proudly, plucking a banana from the fruit bowl and handing it to Harriett. "Now eat up. Showing folks horrors probably burns up a lot of energy. You don't want to get any thinner. And get off the table, dear, it's impolite."

Harriett took the banana and returned to her seat. Jack slumped into the chair beside her, wanting to hug her, to say he was sorry he had done this to her. He just looked into her eyes. She smiled up at him, as if to say she was fine and he shouldn't worry, then peeled the banana and started eating.

"Well, now," Wadget said, chuckling, "I suggest we start this meetin', unless King Mael has any objection?"

Mael shook his head. Wadget righted the overturned chair and patted the seat invitingly. King Mael hesitated, then sat down. He kept his eyes on Harriett, watching with horror as she ate her banana. Anarra's silent bodyguards whisked the unconscious Lord Corrus Mael out of the marquee, then returned to stand behind their queen's chair. Wadget took a deep breath and spoke in a grave tone. He told the council that Morrigan was loose, that the power of Darkgate was broken. There was a long, stunned silence, then many questions, which, thankfully, Wadget answered. Jack didn't think he could stand to be interrogated now. His heart was still thumping from what Harriett had done to Corrus.

A little over two hours later the high council, led by Anarra, made their first decision. As Wadget and Kashashem had advised, they would break camp at dawn and strike at Morrigan as hard and as soon as possible, in the hope of defeating her before she regained her full powers.

"This is all well and good," King Mael said, having recovered some of his arrogance, "but *where* shall we strike? We do not know where the Pale Mother's armies are."

"We've had a stroke o' luck on that score," Wadget said, hopping down from his chair and going to the entrance. He lifted the flap and called out. "Daniselle, Tellan, bring Nettaxitt."

"Nettaxitt?" the Queen of Harshan said, her eyes wide. "That is a trollish name."

"Not just any troll," Wadget said, returning to his seat. "Nettaxitt is heir ter The Gory."

Queen Dechen blinked. King Mael gasped.

"You brought a filthy troll *here*?" King Mael said, clearly appalled. "You brought a troll to sacred Amaltor, ancient capital of Pix?"

"How much do yeh know about trolls, Mael?" Wadget asked.

"Only that the only good troll is a dead one, preferably impaled at the end of a Pixish spear."

"The Gory is the crown o' the trolls," Wadget explained, ignoring Mael's comment. "Nettaxitt is set ter inherit it from her mother. She's offered an alliance. She'll reveal the place where Morrigan's armies are, in return fer help ter cast off the yoke o' the Pale Mother an' the Vellenor."

"An alliance with trolls? Are you mad, Oakling? Trolls are animals, filthy, violent beasts—"

"Don't talk about Nettaxitt like that!" Harriett yelled at the King of Pix, her eyes flaring. "She's a queen! No less important than you!"

The king's mouth snapped shut.

"Not quite, Harrie, me girl," Wadget said with a smirk. "Nettaxitt is not queen yet, but yeh make a good point. We should treat her with respect, as the future ruler o' her people."

Before King Mael could open his mouth again the tent flap was pushed aside and in walked Daniselle and Tellan leading Nettaxitt, whose shaggy head scraped the canvass ceiling. The assembled council members stared at the troll, many of them looking ready to bolt. Anarra stood, trembling a little, and bowed slightly to Nettaxitt, mustering a small smile.

"Welcome, Nettaxitt, heir to The Gory," she said in a slightly strained voice.

"You are pretty, pretty morsel," Nettaxitt replied, not helping her cause at all. Anarra's bodyguards stepped forward but she waved them back.

"Thank you, for the, um, compliment, Nettaxitt. Master Wadget tells us that you can tell us where Morrigan's forces lie?"

"Yes, me can. Me not know name in morsel-tongue, but me lead you there."

"And in return?" Kashashem asked.

"The teensy green morsel uses sparkle magic to put tent over Trollmark." Nettaxitt pointed to the canopy above her head to illustrate her point. "So nobody bad come in and no troll go out without me say so."

"You want a shield ward over the whole of Trollmark?" Queen Dechen asked, amazed.

"Yes, that's what me wants."

General Mahaja looked around the table, gauging everyone's reaction to this. Bar for King Mael, whose face looked stricken, there was no objection. "To be clear, Nettaxitt," he said, "you want this shield ward to protect you from the Vellenor, and from Morrigan?"

"Yes. Me sees how little fires keep morsels safe. Me wants for trolls."

"Is it even possible?" the general asked Kashashem.

"There are ways to do it, but none are impenetrable to Faeden magic. We could make it strong enough that the Vellenor and goblins could not pass it, but, when Morrigan's powers eventually return, she could break it."

"Then you kill Morrigan," Nettaxitt said fiercely. "Me help you kill her good."

Jack saw in the faces around the table that Nettaxitt had won their trust.

"The decision to aid Nettaxitt," Anarra said, "rests with the druids." She looked to Kashashem. "But I see no reason not to believe that she is earnest and to help her free the trolls from Vellenor oppression."

Kashashem nodded her agreement and smiled at Nettaxitt. "We will do what you ask," she said, "once you have led us to Morrigan's armies."

Nettaxitt grinned broadly but was distracted when the flap of the tent opened. One of the night elves came in, a severe-looking woman, causing Nettaxitt to shuffle away from the entrance and take up a position closer to the table, behind Harriett. The Ehmaarim watched Nettaxitt move aside dispassionately before she spoke.

"My Queen," she said to Anarra, "Ellisenn, the woodland elf, has returned. He begs entry."

"Send him in at once," Anarra said, her voice full of relief. Jack felt a pang of jealousy. Why was Anarra so pleased to see Ellisenn?

The woodland elf walked in and bowed to those assembled, his long blond hair falling forward and glistening in the lamp light. When he straightened up his eyes fell on Jack and immediately lit up. He composed himself, turned to face Anarra and bowed even more deeply, his hair falling forward again, masking his expression. Had he been blushing? Jack had seen that reaction before and knew what it meant. He shifted uncomfortably in his seat.

"Who blond morsel?" Nettaxitt whispered to Harriett.

"That's Ellisenn," she replied.

"He look tasty."

"Tell me about it."

"Me just did. Me say he look tasty."

"No, I mean—"

Jack gave his sister a quelling look, worried Ellisenn might overhear them.

"I am overjoyed and much relieved to see you returned safely from Fellwood, Ellisenn," Anarra said, causing Jack's pang of jealousy to intensify to a stab. "I am impatient for news. How fared your mission to Vellenhive?"

Jack watched as Anarra searched Ellisenn's face for some

hint of the answer. Jack wondered what Ellisenn had been asked to do in Fellwood that meant so much to her.

"Princess Sarritt of Fellwood heard the Bright Queen's request but gave no answer."

"We are doomed then," Anarra said, her face falling.

"Perhaps not, My Queen," Ellisenn said. "Sarritt is slow to make decisions and keeps her feelings close, but I know her well enough to suspect she was tempted. She may honour the treaty yet, especially as her brother was killed on the Pale Mother's command."

"This is all ludicrous!" King Mael said, unable to restrain himself any longer. "Trusting a troll and seeking a treaty with the Vellenor – are you all mad?"

At Mael's words, Nettaxitt lurched toward the table and roared at the king, her hackles raised. Jack and almost everyone else jumped and cowered back in their seats. Nettaxitt's eyes turned to pinpricks as she glared at the king, her ears craning forward.

"You no speak again!" Nettaxitt growled, her teeth bared. Something about King Mael had set her off.

"Do not give *me* orders, beast!" King Mael shrieked.

Nettaxitt roared even louder yet, stomping one foot on the ground. The hair all along her spine stood on end. She was practically frothing at the mouth. Anarra's bodyguards moved between her and the furious troll.

"You be *fouled* morsel," she spat at Mael. "He be *very* fouled!" she repeated to the room.

At that, Mael launched out of his chair and across the table. His hands were around Jack's throat before Jack knew what was happening. Mael's weight on him threw him and the chair backwards. Time slowed right down. Jack struggled to throw off Mael, but the king was too strong, unnaturally strong for an old man. Scrambling noises told him that his friends were rushing to save him. Nettaxitt's roars filled the tent, as did Harriett's screams. Suddenly Ansonn was behind Mael, trying to drag the king off Jack. The king's fingers only tightened around Jack's throat. He stared up into the old king's eyes. They gleamed with a hint of purple. Jack knew by that gleam that Mael was not acting of his own free will. He was possessed by one of the Tiqq. Then Mael screamed, his eyes rolled into the back of his head and blood gurgled out of his mouth. His grip loosened around Jack's throat and he fell sideways. Jack looked up to see Ellisenn standing over him, his green eyes grave, a bloodied dagger in his hand. Ellisenn had saved his life. The handsome woodland elf reached out, dragged Jack up and embraced him, hugging Jack tighter than he'd ever been hugged before. Jack was uncomfortably aware how strong Ellisenn was, how muscled his arms and chest were. When he'd caught his breath, he gently pulled away.

"What's with that chair?" he said shakily, smirking and indicating the chair where both Lord Corrus and King Mael had sat. "Is it cursed or something?"

Wadget and a few others chuckled. Jack chuckled with them, then took a breath and glanced at Ellisenn, who was still standing very close to him.

"Thanks," he said to the elf, aware that his face was hot. Was he the one blushing now?

Ellisenn nodded, acknowledging Jack's appreciation, then looked at Mael's body on the floor. His face paled. "I have killed a king. When I saw Mael with his hands on you I ... I—"

"You saved him," Harriett said, pushing through the crowd and throwing her arms around Jack. "You saved my brother!"

"I thought he would kill you," Anarra said, her voice full of despair. The crowd parted, allowing her through. She stood there before Jack with tears in her eyes. She seemed dazed, unsure what to do. She turned to Ellisenn. "If not for you, Ellisenn, Jack would have been lost to us."

Ellisenn looked from Jack to Anarra, then bowed his head slightly and stepped back. Anarra immediately rushed forward and took Jack in her arms. Jack thought he would die from delight. Anarra smelt like a delicious mix of vanilla and something woody and exotic. Her soft hair caressed the skin of his face. Her body pressed against his in a way that made him want to wrap her in his arms and never let go.

A sickening twisting and snapping sound made them break apart. Nettaxitt had pulled off Mael's head and deposited it on the table. Anarra recoiled into Jack, trembling, her face pale. Ellisenn stepped in to help Jack support her. Miss Butters gagged and pushed Harriett behind her so that she couldn't see what Nettaxitt had done.

"He be very fouled, earwisp be in there," Nettaxitt said, pointing at Mael's severed head.

"She's right," Jack said, "Mael was possessed. I saw a purple glint in his eye."

"You saw sign of Tiqq possession in the king?" Kashashem asked Jack, glancing meaningfully at Wadget.

"I suppose so, yes," Jack said.

"Impressive," Kashashem said.

"An' yeh can detect an earwisp by the sound o' the victim's voice?" Wadget asked Nettaxitt, sounding impressed as well. Nettaxitt grinned and nodded.

"Me know sound of one befouled," she said proudly. Jack was grimly glad that Ting hadn't accompanied him after all.

"Well, how do we get it out an' question it?" Wadget asked.

"Might I suggest," General Mahaja put in, "that we send for one of the priestesses of Erima?"

"Are the priestesses able to deal with such things?" Kashashem asked.

"There is one in our encampment who can," the general answered.

Anarra steadied herself and nodded her ascent. The general went to the entrance of the marquee and called one of his men, who bustled away after a brief whispered conversation. Not long later the tent flap opened again. General Mahaja dropped to his knees as a girl of about twelve years old walked in. Black-skinned and with her head shaved bald, she was dressed in deep burgundy robes. The girl stopped before General Mahaja and patted him gently on the head, smiling around the room.

"May I introduce," the general said to them all, his head still bowed, "Holy Saamis, the High Priestess of Erima, Virtuous Ruler of all Anda."

"Well, General Mahaja," Queen Dechen said, "haven't you been keeping secrets." The Warrior Queen of Harshan bowed deeply to the little girl.

"Do not blame sweet Mahaja," the little girl said. "I made him conceal my presence. I detest violence and did not wish to sit on a war council, even though I accept that battle is now the only way to stop the Dark Ones from destroying us all."

"Welcome, Holy One," Anarra said, stepping forward. "I wish we had met in more peaceful times. I would invite you to sit, but ..." She glanced at Mael's severed head, her face paling again.

"I am not quailed by gore or blood," the little girl said. "Besides, have you not called me to deal with what lurks behind those dead eyes?"

"Yes, Holy One," General Mahaja said. "This head once belonged to King Mael of Pix. It was removed by our troll friend there after the king rudely tried to deprive the Waycaller of his life."

The High Priestess turned her dark eyes on Jack. She smiled and he smiled back. There was a gentleness and purity within those eyes that made Jack trust Saamis immediately. Saamis faced the gathered druids and sovereigns and smiled at them too, setting them all at ease.

"No power subdues the Tiqq," the Holy One whispered, "except the power of the Lord of Chaos himself, which none who are sane dare wield. There are safe ways to make the Tiqq show themselves though, ways that have nothing to do with power, but everything to do with virtue."

Saamis crossed the room to the table and sat in the chair closest to the head. She stretched out her hand and lay it on the dead king's pale brow. She began to sing, and to stroke the brow almost lovingly with her tiny fingers. The song made Jack's heart well up so that it fluttered with an aching compassion. The soft song echoed in the tent, making the place seem like a temple, not the scene of recent horrors. Whatever Saamis was doing, it was working. A thin purple wisp coiled out of the dead king's ear. In seconds a small, hand-high Tiqq took shape on the table before the priestess. It looked a lot like Ting, her red hair scruffy, her eyes a strange green. Jack was shocked she had shown herself. Ting had told him that the Tiqq rarely showed themselves in fleshy form, because it made them vulnerable.

The Tiqq looked around the room cautiously, then focused on Saamis. She listened intently to the song, tears forming in her eyes. Suddenly she said, in that bell-like voice typical of the Tiqq: "You … you *love* me?"

"Yes, I do," Saamis said simply.

"Why?"

"Why not?"

"You do not know me. I possessed this man, I tried to kill that one." The Tiqq pointed at Jack.

"Nothing you do diminishes my love."

"Nothing?"

"No, nothing."

Jack's skin tingled with goose bumps. Harriett wiped at tears that streamed down her cheeks.

"But you love *everyone*, don't you?" That jealousy so typical of the Tiqq had reared its head. Jack hoped Saamis knew how to deal with that.

"Yes, I do. My love for all beings is perfectly equal. I love none more than any other. None more than you."

The Tiqq flopped onto her bottom, stunned.

"I'm sorry I tried to kill your friend," she said.

"You can make amends by telling us why, and if there are any more in our company who are under the control of your people."

The Tiqq thought about this for a while. Saamis started humming, the same tune as the song that had lured the Tiqq out of hiding. It had the desired effect.

"Empress Rill bid me do it. She bends her knee to Morrigan now. The Pale Mother wants the human Waycaller dead, and his sister too."

"Why?"

"The prophesy. Morrigan fears the prophesy. She fears the coming of the Druid King, and the return of the Oracle."

"And are there any others in this camp possessed by your kind?"

"No," the Tiqq said. "I was the only one."

"Thank you for telling me this," Saamis said. "You must return to your empress now."

"But ... but can't you be my host?" she asked tentatively.

"No, that would not be appropriate, but we can be friends. Now go, return home."

The Tiqq nodded and dragged herself into a standing position, her body already dissolving into wisp.

"Wait," Jack said to the Tiqq, realising something. "Tell your empress that because of her, I *am* the Druid King. Now that Mael is dead, the throne of Pix is mine. Thank her for me, and tell her that I'm coming for her, and for Morrigan."

The Tiqq dissolved into wisp and shot out of the tent in a blur of purple.

"Well, lad," Wadget said, "yeh sure know how ter put a target on yer back."

"I don't care," Jack said. "Morrigan is after us anyway, I want her to know we're not afraid."

"But we *are* afraid, Jack," Harriett said, shaking her head.

Anarra took his hand and squeezed it, letting him know that she was proud of what he'd done. Massara Ceyr seemed proud as well. The consul's eyes were glistening with tears as she walked over and bent down on one knee.

"My King," she said, "it may seem, if judged by this night's events, that the Pixish are all murderous and insane. It is not so, that is just the Maels. You will find that the rest of the Pix, your people, are loyal and courageous. They will follow you, as will I, wherever you choose to lead us."

Everyone else in the room bowed then as well, including Nettaxitt, who fixed Jack with a toothy grin. Oh no, Jack thought, I don't think I can deal with this king thing.

SECRETS IN THE NIGHT

Jack sat on the edge of the huge bed, his head in his hands. He was exhausted but too anxious to sleep. Besides, the four-poster bed had belonged to King Mael. The idea of getting under the covers creeped him out. Everything around him had belonged to Mael. Massara Ceyr had brought Jack and Harriett here, leading them through the vast Pixish encampment to the dead king's massive multi-room canvas pavilion. Kashashem and the rest of the council had decided that Jack needed to step into his new role as King of Pix straight away. Easy for them to say – whenever Jack thought of himself as King of Pix one of two things happened: his stomach roiled and he felt sick or he laughed out loud at how ridiculous the whole idea was. Who'd ever heard of a King Jack? What would the Pixish people think when they found out their new king was seventeen years old and his greatest achievement to date was failing to stop Morrigan from breaking out of Uffern? By morning Massara Ceyr would have spread the word that King Mael the Twenty-fifth was dead and that his grand-nephew, Jack Gordon, was now king. Massara had assured him that the transition would go smoothly. The troops hated Mael, she said, and everyone knew that possession by one of the Tiqq was a death sentence no matter who you were, king or peasant. Whether the transition went smoothly or not, Jack would have to front the Pixish troops in the morning.

Jack sat up straight, pushing his black hair out of his eyes. Harriett was tucked in to a makeshift bed on a divan in the next room. Aelf and Alva stood guard outside the entrance. A brazier burned in the reception room, invoking the hearth ward. Jack knew they'd be safe. The camp was quiet, it being close to midnight after all. The only movement was flickering light from the flames of the cook fires dancing on the canvas walls. He knew he should try to catch a few hours of sleep. At dawn they were breaking camp and marching south, following Nettaxitt to the place where Morrigan's dark army gathered. He lay back on the bed without getting under the covers.

He couldn't believe he was about to face Morrigan, the White Demoness, in the flesh. His mouth was bone dry at the prospect. The only times he'd seen anyone try to stand up to a Faeden, they hadn't stood a chance. Both Mog and Hect, two of the most powerful dark beings alive, hadn't even had time to put up a fight. They'd both been destroyed with a mere gesture from a Faeden – Mog by a flick of Hob's wrist and Hect by a point from Amallayne's finger. How could Jack possibly fare any better against a Faeden than them? The worst thing was that he was taking Harriett with him. He hated that he had no choice about that.

Kashashem had assured him that she would be safe. Two dozen of the Order's most powerful druids would travel with Jack and Harriett to protect them, and Harriett would be kept well back from the fighting. Even so, he couldn't help worry that something would go wrong. It was Morrigan they were facing after all. Even in her weakened state she filled Jack with dread. An image flashed through his mind: Jack standing on a desolate battlefield, a bloody sword in his hand, everyone around him dead and Harriett lying in a pool of blood at his feet. He shuddered. When they left Amaltor at dawn, were they marching toward that fate? Was every step Jack took from now on leading to that terrible event? Jack didn't want to think about that battlefield. He decided to distract himself by reading *The Way of Thullu*. Harriett had left it out before she went to bed. She must have read it a dozen times by now, but Jack knew her interest lay more in the fact that it'd belonged to their mother than in the knowledge it contained. He was more interested in the strange power it had of showing them what it wanted to show them, often what they needed to know when they were in great danger. He opened it and allowed it to select a page. It fell on a chapter about the Faeden. He read a few sections about the

Faeden, about all the religions they'd spawned despite being so unreliable and selfish, then came to another section about the powers of the Waycaller. This section was about the Power of Limitless Bright, which the book described as 'a power beyond any other'. He wished he knew how to access that power. He still doubted his ability to do anything more than jump from stone circle to stone circle. That wouldn't help him in a fight with Morrigan. He lay there a long while thinking about that impending fight, until his mind grew heavy and he slowly drifted to sleep.

He couldn't have been asleep more than half an hour when he woke with the feeling there was someone in the room with him. He sat bolt upright to see Ting standing on the end of the bed. His pleasure at seeing her again vanished instantly. She was glaring at him, her hands balled into fists on her hips. Her mouth was puckered so tight she looked like she'd eaten something very bitter.

"What have you *done*?" she hissed, without so much as a hello.

"Nothing. Nothing to make you so angry at me anyway."

"Don't lie to me, Jack," she said, stomping a foot on the mattress. "You are *changed*!"

"What do you mean?"

"As if you don't know!"

"I don't, unless you mean the king thing?"

"No, I don't mean 'the king thing', though I heard all about that. Empress Rill is furious with you, and terrified."

"Good. It's nice to know I'm not the only one who's scared."

"Stop trying to distract me! What did you do?"

"I don't know what you're talking about!"

"You've done something to keep me out!"

"Out of what?"

"Your ear of course!" she practically growled at him. "I thought we were *friends*?"

"We are friends, Ting. Calm down and tell me what you think I've done."

"How should I know *what* you've done? All I know is you've done *something*! No being can resist the Tiqq, except the Faeden. I risked a lot to come here to see you, to make sure you're alright, to help you, and what do I get in return? You've locked me out! No-one has *ever* been able to lock me out before!"

"So, you couldn't get in my ear?"

"That's what I just said, Jack. Has whatever you've done addled your brain as well?"

"No need to be mean—"

"Mean! Don't talk to *me* about mean. I'm not the one who did a terrible, loathsome, hurtful thing!" Ting's voice reached such a fever pitch that Jack worried the whole camp would hear her.

"Quiet, Ting. The druids will hear you and then we'll be in big trouble. I don't know if you know the whole story but the last King of Pix who had contact with an earwisp got his head ripped off by a troll."

"Oh, well, we wouldn't want that to happen to you," she said sarcastically.

"Ting! Do you mean that? You want me to get my head ripped off?"

The earwisp's shoulders slumped and her hands dropped from her hips to hang limply by her sides. She avoided Jack's gaze a moment before replying.

"No, I suppose I don't *really* want your head ripped off."

"I'm glad to hear it. You have to believe me, Ting, I haven't done anything to keep you out of my ear. I'm as surprised as you are." He didn't say he was also relieved. He'd never liked the sensation of having another being inside his head, possibly influencing his thoughts and actions.

"Then ... then we're still friends?" Her tiny voice sounded anxious and fragile.

"Of course we are, always."

She perked up immediately. "We have to find out who did this to us," she whispered. "Someone is trying to keep us apart. Whoever it is, I will kill them and then I will raise them up from death and kill them all over again."

Jack shook his head, shocked at how easily and fully Ting lost her temper. This was exactly why he was relieved Ting couldn't possess him anymore. The Tiqq were volatile and quite scary. Then a thought came to him.

"Ting," he started cautiously, "if you can't enter my ear, does that mean none of the Tiqq can?"

The little red-haired sprite mulled this over. "You know what, Jack, I think it does. I don't mean to brag, but there are few Tiqq more powerful than me. If I couldn't possess you, I doubt any Tiqq could."

Jack couldn't help but notice that did sound pretty boastful. He smirked, then thought of the male Tiqq, Thullu's Gift. Perhaps this was why he'd vanished, because he wasn't able to possess Jack. That feeling of deep certainty washed over Jack again. Yes, that was what had happened. So whatever made Jack immune to Tiqq possession must've occurred between Ting's departure after they'd all fled the battle of Pitmouth and the moment Jack collapsed after banishing Serza to Uffern. The only thing he could think of that was momentous enough to explain his new immunity was the breaking of the power of Darkgate. Had not Amallayne said that the magic of Darkgate would flow into him, making him much more powerful? Hadn't he felt a new, profound sense of certainty about events he hadn't directly witnessed? Was that a kind of second sight brought on by his increased power? That certainty hit him again now. The power of Darkgate was within him, making him stronger, making him impervious to the Tiqq. The phrase 'the Power of Limitless Bright' echoed in his mind.

"I know what happened," he said, looking gravely at the little sprite. "When Darkgate broke, the power came into me. That's why you can't possess me anymore."

Ting's mouth dropped open. She stared at him. "So, it's … it's permanent?" she stammered, tearing up.

Jack nodded and the earwisp started to cry. He let her grieve a while, then decided she'd felt sorry for herself long enough.

"Ting," he said firmly, "I need to talk to you about Thullu's Gift."

The Tiqq sighed then nodded her head. "I thought you might," she said. "Word came to the hive that Serza was dead and Tocsin was missing."

"Tocsin?"

"Yes, that is the male Tiqq's common name. He is known as Thullu's Gift because the Lord of Chaos gave him to the Tiqq so that we could flourish. Before Tocsin, all the Tiqq were female. He is the most powerful of all the Tiqq, except in one respect."

"What respect?"

"Tocsin does not have the power of the voice. He cannot control his host with words. He joins with the host, making them a conduit for Thullu's power."

"When Tocsin abandoned Serza," Jack mused, "he said he was intrigued by me. What might that mean?"

"Unlike all other Tiqq, Tocsin does not feed on just any thought or emotion. He feeds on singleness of purpose only. That's why Hephaestia Hatter was able to steal him from us: her mind dwelt on one thing only – Morrigan."

"And so, when Mog took him from her, that was because—"

"Mog was even more single-minded than the halfling, and Serza even more so than her," agreed Ting.

"So, that means I must be more single-minded than Serza. That's a bit scary."

"It also has to do with the form that singleness of purpose takes. Tocsin is more drawn to selflessness than self-interest. His belly is more satisfied by single-pointed love than a single-pointed desire for power. He's a bit silly like that, kind of romantic. Your single-pointed desire to protect Harrie would've been very alluring to Tocsin."

"If he prefers love over power why did he help Serza do such terrible things?"

"That is why the Empress has always kept Tocsin locked

up. Tocsin makes no distinction between bad or good. To him any use of Thullu's power makes the Lord of Chaos known in the world, and that is Tocsin's only purpose. Once, Tocsin had a host who decided to kill the Empress. Tocsin nearly did it too, but the Empress led him into a trap. All Tiqq are powerless if locked inside a lead container. The Empress tricked Tocsin into entering an ancient lead sarcophagus and then shut him in. She's kept him there ever since, until that halfling came and let him out. I hear Mog kept Tocsin in a lead jar, never letting him out to use his power. He must have jumped at the chance to make Serza his host, once the dark prince freed him from that jar."

"So Tocsin will do whatever the host wants, no matter what it is, so long as it means Thullu's power is used in the world?"

"Yes. It's like I said. He doesn't control the host. He possesses them, changes them, makes them greater, but doesn't control them."

"And this 'Secret Gift' idea, where did that come from? The druids think Thullu's Gift is a magical object."

"Oh, they've got that totally wrong. I shouldn't tell you this, but as we're friends I will. The only way to control a Tiqq, any Tiqq, even Tocsin, is if you know their secret name. Tocsin is gifted with knowledge of the secret names of every single Tiqq. Thus we call him the Secret Gift"

"So, Ting—"

"Is my common name. I have a secret name too, one I never tell anyone."

"How did you get the secret name?"

"It was gifted by Lord Thullu."

It all started to make sense. The earwisps' secret names were gifted by Thullu – Thullu's Gift, the Secret Gift. He bet the druids would love to know the truth about all of this. He wondered if he should tell them. Ting must've seen that idea on his face, for she frowned and hissed.

"You can't speak of this to anyone," she whispered. "We are much hated, we have many enemies and they could use this knowledge against us."

Jack had seen first-hand how hated the Tiqq were. He'd also seen what might happen to him if it was discovered he had been possessed by Ting. He wanted his head to stay exactly where it was. He agreed, for now, that it was best not to tell the druids or anyone else any of what Ting had revealed.

"Okay, I won't say anything. But why didn't you tell me all this sooner?" he asked.

"We Tiqq cannot speak of Thullu's Gift to any who have not already seen him. There is a powerful magic that prevents us from doing so."

"Great. I suppose there's lots of other important stuff you can't tell me right now as well?"

She nodded, smirking bashfully.

"Still won't tell me who your dear friend is, the one who sent you to bring Harrie and me to Anwynn?"

"Oh, no, I especially can't tell you that!"

"Look, Ting, haven't I shown I trust you? It's time you showed you trust me. Who sent you to get us?"

Ting's brow creased as she considered answering him. Just as she opened her mouth to speak the sound of a tent flap opening made them both jump.

"Where am I to hide, Jack? I can't go into your ear."

"You'll have to go," Jack whispered, "but come back later." Ting dissolved into wisp and darted under the canvas wall and off into the night.

Jack listened to footsteps crossing the carpet in the reception room, heading his way. He glanced at the curtain leading to where Harriett was sleeping. A shudder ran down his spine, then he remembered the burning brazier that offered warmth and invoked the hearth ward. Whoever this was, they'd been let in by Aelf and Alva and clearly had no ill intent.

"Who is it?" Jack called out, feeling relieved.

"It is Ellisenn, Your Majesty. May I enter?"

Jack's relief evaporated. He scrambled out of bed and

pulled his jacket tight around himself. He didn't want to be lying there when the woodland elf came in.

"Yes, come in," he answered, hating that his voice trembled a little.

Ellisenn entered and bowed. It annoyed Jack that Ellisenn looked so good, despite it being the middle of the night and him having only recently returned from a long and arduous journey to Fellwood. The woodland elf looked as fresh as someone who'd just risen from a long and restful sleep. His voice showed no sign of fatigue, though was a little cautious.

"I beg your forgiveness for coming to you so late, Your Majesty, but your lamp was still lit so Aelf allowed me to enter. I bring a message from the Bright Queen, Anarra Settonett."

The tightness in Jack's chest eased off. Ellisenn had been sent by Anarra, he wasn't here on his own account. Jack didn't want to dwell on any other reason Ellisenn might come to his tent in the middle of the night.

"What did she say?" he asked a little too quickly.

"Firstly, the Bright Queen wants you to know that protocol forbids her from coming to your pavilion herself. She hopes you understand."

Jack nodded that he did understand.

"Secondly, the Bright Queen sends her affection and wishes you to know that she is much relieved that you and your sister are safe." Ellisenn paused, looking into Jack's eyes. Jack was surprised to see uncertainty on Ellisenn's face, and vulnerability. What could make Ellisenn, one of the most powerful druids alive, feel so vulnerable? "The Bright Queen also asked me to tell you that, though shyness prevented her from saying anything before now, you are often on her mind. She cares for you a great deal. While you were parted she spent many nights sleepless with worry over you."

Jack couldn't stop the grin forming on his mouth. Anarra cared for him, worried about him. This was the first time she'd expressed her feelings so plainly. He felt lighter than he'd felt in weeks, lighter than he'd felt since he'd first opened the Way that brought him and Harriett to Anwynn. Jack's grin turned into an open smile.

"Thanks for bringing me the message," he said. Ellisenn nodded, though made no move to leave. "Is there something else?" Jack asked.

"Yes, Your Majesty. The Bright Queen, Anarra, has ordered me to explain something to you. I cannot refuse a direct order from my sovereign." The elf looked deeply uncomfortable.

"Okay, what has she ordered you to explain?"

"The twining."

"What's that?"

"The twining is how elves experience attraction, love. For elves, love comes just once in our long lives. We do not choose who to love. The twining strikes us and we cannot fight it. When one elf twines with another the bond is unbreakable. It is a magical bond, eternal."

Jack's throat tightened. Anarra had mentioned this to him before, just after the dark Sending had attacked them in the Druid Chambers. "Okay," he began, "why did Anarra order you to explain that to me?"

"Humans do not experience the twining." Ellisenn looked even more uncomfortable now. He could barely look Jack in the eyes.

"That I know," Jack said.

"Which means if an elf were to fall in love with a human, to twine with them, there is a risk the human might not return the elf's feelings, might not love the elf back."

"And that would be pretty bad, I'm guessing."

"For the elf, yes, it means immortal heartbreak, an eternal loneliness."

"Look, you can tell Anarra not to worry. I may not be twined, but I have feelings for her, strong ones."

"You misunderstand. The Bright Queen is only half elvish. It is not clear if the twining is in her destiny."

"So, she's not twined to me?"

"No, not at this time. The Bright Queen's feelings for you, and yours for her, are not why she ordered me to explain this to you."

"Well, why did she want you to tell me this then?"

"I believe she feels that it is always good to know when we are loved, and to know when we are causing another pain, even if we do not mean to."

"I don't get it."

"Forgive me, Jack, but I love you. I am twined to you. My love for you is beyond my control and will live eternally, or at least as long as I endure."

Jack stared at him. What could he say to that? He retreated to the bed and sat down. Ellisenn didn't move, but his eyes never left Jack's face. Finally, Jack said the only thing that came to his mind.

"I'm sorry." He was too. He said it again, trying to convey with those few words everything he meant but couldn't say out loud. He wouldn't be alive without Ellisenn. The handsome woodland elf had saved his life more than once. But his gratitude did not extend that far. He didn't, could never, return Ellisenn's feelings. He couldn't imagine what it would be like to love someone so completely with no hope of having that love returned. He felt sick just thinking about it. "I'm sorry," he said once more. When he looked up Ellisenn was gone.

Jack lay down on King Mael's huge bed, his mind jammed, unable to move past the look of total heartbreak in Ellisenn's eyes when he'd said "I love you". Jack's heart hammered in his chest. Why? Because the thought of having hurt someone that much, even though he hadn't meant to, made Jack feel worse than he'd ever felt in his life.

"Are you expecting any more visitors, Jack?" Harriett's voice said from the other room. The curtain parted and she came in. "I wouldn't ask, but I'm trying to get some sleep and it's like peak hour in here."

"What are you doing awake, Harrie?"

"I was fast asleep until Ting started screaming. She's got

some lungs for a little thing, hasn't she?"

"She sure does."

"Has Ellisenn gone then?"

Jack nodded but didn't say anything, wondering if Harriett had heard that whole conversation. The idea she had made him flush with embarrassment. A long moment passed, the only sound being a cricket off in the distance somewhere. Jack's heart was still hammering, his mind still stuck on the pain in Ellisenn's eyes.

"I think you should choose Ellisenn," Harriett said quietly. Jack sat up to face her.

"What do you mean?"

"I'm not deaf, Jack. I heard everything Ellisenn said. You, Anarra and Ellisenn have a whole love triangle thing going on. What either of them see in you I don't know, but if you're going to choose one of them, you should choose Ellisenn."

"Harrie, Ellisenn is a dude."

"I have noticed that myself. Don't be blind, Jack. He really loves you. He saved your life."

"Yeah, but Harrie, as I said, he's a dude. I'm not into dudes."

"Yeah, and that's not your only flaw." She smirked at him and patted him on the head. "Whatever, do what you want, it's your love life. Just don't pretend that you don't have a choice, that you're not choosing to break Ellisenn's heart. That's got to be why Anarra sent Ellisenn here, to make sure you knew you had a choice. You're not elvish, Jack, your feelings aren't out of your control."

"Harrie, he's a dude." Jack wished he could stop saying that, but it was all he could think to say. "I could never be attracted to Ellisenn. I like girls. I like girls *a lot*. I like Anarra."

"Okay, fair enough." She smiled and headed back towards her part of the tent. "Goodnight, Jack," she said as she parted the curtain.

"Goodnight, Harrie."

"Oh, and Jack, try to keep the noise down if any more hunky elves come visiting you tonight."

Jack moaned and flopped over on the huge bed, knowing he'd be lucky to get a wink of sleep that night.

THE DYNASTY OF SENN RENEWED

Aelf sent Alva to wake Jack as early morning light crept under the canvas walls, lifting the darkness inside the tent. She shook him gently, whispering his name. She didn't need to be so gentle – though his eyes were closed he was wide awake. He looked up at her and forced a smile.

"They are already packing up the camp," she said. "They'll do this pavilion last. Massara Ceyr has asked if she can present you to the troops before we march. What shall I tell her?"

"Sure, yes, that's fine. When?"

"In an hour or so."

"Okay, I'll be ready, or as ready as I can be."

"You'll do fine, Your Majesty." She straightened up to leave. "Oh, Harriett is with Aelf and Dorothea outside. She's already had breakfast. Dorothea brought over a hamper."

"Where did Miss Butters sleep last night?"

"In the druid encampment, which was not to her liking, as she's been telling us, repeatedly, ever since dawn."

Jack smirked. Typical Miss Butters. He wondered if there was anything left in that hamper. His stomach was gurgling in protest at being empty. After Alva went back outside, Jack got up and went to the wash basin to splash some water on his face and clean up. He grabbed his leather jacket and noticed that Harriett had left hers behind. He gathered it up, feeling for the torc, which he did automatically to make sure Harriett hadn't lost it somewhere. They'd not used it since he and Harriett had needed to find a safe path through Pitmouth. It was still there, the bracelet Anarra had given her tangled up with it. Jack untangled them and thought of Anarra, about the message she'd sent and why she'd forced Ellisenn to reveal his feelings for Jack, especially now of all times. Anarra's message said that she cared about Jack, which was great, but to care for someone can mean a lot of different things. Jack cared for Miss Butters, but he didn't want to date her. The thing with Ellisenn was not great. In fact, it was terrible – Jack hadn't slept at all because of it. He felt confused and guilty, and angry that he felt guilty about something he had no control over, that none of them had any control over. He didn't want to carry that guilt and confusion with him to the confrontation with Morrigan, which will be dangerous enough without Jack being distracted by all this. The thing that troubled him most, apart from the pain Ellisenn was in, was why it'd been so important to Anarra that Jack understand that Ellisenn was twined to him, that Jack know that Ellisenn was bound to love him for his whole, long elvish life no matter what. If he knew what Anarra was thinking, that would go a long way to helping him compose himself and face Morrigan. Were her feelings for him more friendly than romantic? Did she want Jack to choose Ellisenn? He rubbed the torc in his hand. Would it work for him? He slipped it on and tried a few questions in his mind before settling on the right wording and saying it out loud: "Show me how Anarra really feels about me." The torc glimmered silver but nothing more happened.

"It won't work for you."

Jack jumped and spun around.

"Harrie, you scared me half to death."

"Good. That's what you get for messing with things you shouldn't."

"Sorry, I know the torc is yours—"

"I didn't mean the torc. I meant you shouldn't pry into Anarra's private feelings."

"Why? They're about me, aren't they? And I can't stand not knowing. It's all I can think about. I'm about to meet Morrigan face-to-face and the only thing on my mind is Anarra, and why she sent Ellisenn to me last night. If I stay this distracted, I'm worried something terrible will happen, that I'll make some awful mistake."

Harriett's face softened. She walked over and took the torc from him.

"Alright then, seeing as the survival of the whole world

depends on it, I'll help you pry. But you don't need the torc to show you the future. I can show you."

"The way you showed Corrus Mael his future?" The memory of Lord Mael's horrified face made Jack's gut clench.

"Yes."

"I don't know—"

"It won't be like what happened to that awful Corrus. Anarra doesn't have that kind of darkness in her. I'll only show you how she really feels about you, nothing else."

Jack nodded that Harriett could go ahead. She took his hands in hers and looked deeply into his eyes. Instantly Jack felt the earth lurch beneath him. The room spun. Images swirled all around him, images of Anarra: Anarra standing alone by a tall window, an empty brazier nearby; Anarra sitting on a throne, many people around her, all speaking, but her mind not in the room; Anarra in her bedchamber, the room dark and cold, tears in her eyes; Anarra riding a horse at the head of a huge army of elves, again her mind elsewhere, dwelling on Jack. Emanating from all these images was a sense of Anarra's interest in Jack, starting first as curiosity, then a growing affection, then attraction. With each image Anarra's feelings for him deepened.

"She's falling in love with me," he said. At his words the images blurred. There was a flash of light and then a single image formed: Anarra standing on a solitary mountaintop, in the shadow of an ancient tomb. Jack staggered at the force of grief and loneliness emanating from her. He dropped his sister's hands. The image vanished. Harriett's eyes were full of tears.

"Oh, Jack, I'm sorry, I tried to stop you seeing that last image, but it was just too strong."

"Was that the future?"

"Yes."

"The tomb, whose was it?" He knew the answer but wanted his sister to confirm it.

"Jack, do you really want to know?"

"Whose tomb was it, Harrie?"

"Yours, Jack, it was your tomb."

"Was that very far in the future? Had I just died?"

"It was far in the future, long after you die. Much more than a thousand years after."

"And she still felt like *that* a thousand years later?" His knees trembled. He sat in the nearest chair.

"Jack, I know it seemed terrible—"

"I cannot do that to her."

"Jack, don't be rash—"

"Leave me alone, Harrie."

"Jack, please, just put it out of your mind—"

"I said leave me alone!"

Harriett left. Jack slumped in the chair. It took him only moments to come to terms with what he had to do. If all that pain and suffering was what loving Jack would bring Anarra, then he wouldn't let it happen. He wouldn't let Anarra get any closer to him. He'd swallow down his feelings for her and pretend that she meant no more to him than any of the other members of the war council. He got up and parted the flap to go outside. He was shocked to find that the tents that had completely surrounded the king's pavilion the night before were gone. In their place was Massara Ceyr, standing directly in front of him, and behind her, in lines hundreds deep, the whole of the Pixish army. Banners bearing the symbol of Pix, a roughly-drawn red circle on a white background, fluttered on the morning breeze. Harriett stood nearby, her eyes still damp. Aelf and Nettaxitt were with her.

"Your Majesty," Consul Ceyr said, bowing, "may I present you to the troops?"

"Yes, but how will they all see me?" Jack suddenly felt very small and inadequate.

"Perhaps, Your Majesty," said a familiar male voice, "your people will see you better if you are on horseback."

The owner of the voice held the reins of a large black horse. A tall man with unruly black hair and deep blue eyes.

"Denn!" Jack rushed over to the Pixish horseman. "Denn, how are you?"

Denn bowed before answering. "I am well, Your Majesty. The druids treated my wound masterfully. And are you well, Your Majesty?" His blue eyes were concerned.

"Irritated by everyone calling me 'Your Majesty', but otherwise fine."

Denn smirked and gestured to the horse snuffling at his shoulder.

"I bought this horse for you and another for Harriett. I doubted you would want to ride with me again."

"No, I've still got bruises from your saddle horn."

"Here then, Your Majesty," he said, handing over the reins. "Her name is Shadow. She is a brave mare." He bowed again, waiting for Jack to mount. Jack didn't know what to say. Shadow was the most beautiful horse he'd ever seen. He smiled at Denn and took hold of the saddle to haul himself up. He didn't quite make it on the first try. The horse was no bigger than Cobalt, the only other horse he'd ever ridden, but the stirrups were strung higher, a little too high for him. He flushed red, aware of the whole Pixish army watching. Just as he went to try again, Nettaxitt stepped up and lifted him into the saddle. Her touch triggered a series of images: Nettaxitt as a cub, rolling in the grass with half a dozen other cubs, her mind overflowing with uncomplicated joy; Nettaxitt being groomed by her mother, both of them emitting deep, rumbling purrs of content; Nettaxitt hunting longhorn sheep, her mind focussed, her hunger sharp; Nettaxitt standing on a grassy rise, carnage all around her, hundreds of trolls dead, their bodies scattered about the rise with those of a handful of Vellenor. As this image lingered, a troop of human cavalry rode away in the distance and rage surged through Nettaxitt, but not at the humans, at the Dark Elves. This had been a fight ordered by the Vellenor, fought to the death by trolls who were treated by Morrigan's beloved Dark Elves as slaves. Jack steadied himself in the saddle as the images dissolved.

"Thank you, Nettaxitt," he said as soon as he was sure of his balance.

"Jack morsel's legs too short for big horse. Me help."

She shrugged her shoulders as if to say helping him was no big deal. Jack was startled to notice that her eyes had changed from their usual dull brown to a shimmering silver. "Nettaxitt, what happened to your eyes?"

"Teensy green morsel put sparkle magic in me. Make me safe in sun."

She opened her eyes wide for Jack to see. For the first time, he saw the intelligence in her eyes that had been there, unnoticed, all along. Nettaxitt's difficulty with speech was not because she was stupid. Jack knew now that trolls were every bit as intelligent as humans. He smiled at her and put into that smile as much respect as he could muster. He also made a mental note to be careful of letting others touch him. The rush of images that followed was disorientating and, since he'd grown stronger after the breaking of Darkgate, much more vivid.

Massara Ceyr stepped close to Shadow's shoulder, glancing at the gathered army to make sure she wasn't overheard. "Your Majesty," she said quietly, "names and titles mean a lot to the Pix. It is custom for the kings of Pix to bear a family name and a dynastic name. In your case, the family name is Senn, your father's family name. When it comes to the dynasty name, you could use the name of your uncle's dynasty, Mael or—"

"There's no way I want to be Mael the Twenty-sixth," Jack said, balking at the idea of using the name of the man who tried to kill him. "Is there another choice?"

"You could use the dynastic name of the last king who came from the House of Senn. That might be rather poetic as he was ruler at the time of the last Doom War."

A rush of certainty compelled Jack to speak.

"Yes, I'll use that."

Massara beamed and turned to face the waiting army.

"Warriors of Pix," she called in a commanding voice, "may I present your new sovereign, Waycaller and Scion of the House of Senn, Bane of the Dark Ones, King Duan Senn, First of the Dynasty of Senn Renewed!"

THE STAGE IS SET

It took much less time than Jack expected to marshal the armies of Harshan, Anda and Pix. Even so, it took considerably longer than it had for the elvish warriors of Elvinidd to form perfect lines, cavalry at front and infantry to the rear. The elves stood motionless as statues at the head of the vast host. Denn, mounted on a large grey stallion, led Jack, riding Shadow, to the very head of the army. Massara and Harriett rode closely behind, as did Aelf, mounted on Soxy. Nettaxitt followed on foot. The troll's presence sent a ripple of alarm through the ranks, especially when they passed the Harshanites. Jack could see by their faces that they hated trolls with a passion. Soldiers stared, fingering their bows, thumbing their knives. Horses reared back and whinnied. Jack worried that one of the archers would lose his head and loose an arrow into Nettaxitt's back. Apart from being a friend, Jack needed Nettaxitt to lead them to Morrigan.

"Denn," he said quietly, "can we somehow ask Queen Dechen Drokpa to tell her troops that we need Nettaxitt, and that I don't want her harmed?"

"It will be done, Your Majesty, and I will guard the she-troll's back myself."

Kashashem waited at the head of the army, along with a handful of dragon-riders, including Daniselle with Jossa. Jack's stomach clenched when he saw Anarra there as well, and not just because she stood beside a huge black dragon. Despite being almost the same age as Jack, her regal bearing made her seem much older. Her long hair, as black as midnight, hung loosely over her shoulders. Though she dressed as she always had, in black leather jerkin and trousers beneath a hooded cloak, she had adopted the startling adornment of the night elves: her face and neck, so pale and fine, were now painted with intricate tattoo-like designs. Her shining blue eyes lit up like twinkling stars on seeing Jack, dazing him, making his heart thud in his chest. His throat tightened. He had to be strong, he had to act as though she weren't special to him, he had to treat her the same as everyone else.

"Good morning, Jack," she said, smiling, stepping forward as he and the others reined in their horses before the huge dragon. "My people have gifted me a firewyrm. Her name is Scythe. Is she not beautiful and imposing?" Jack nearly succumbed to her infectious enthusiasm, he'd never seen her so animated. Elves and their obsession with dragons, he would never understand it. He paused a moment before speaking, gathering his composure.

"Good morning, Bright Queen," he said in as formal a voice as he could muster, painfully aware that everyone was watching this exchange. "You are right, the firewyrm is imposing, though whether or not it is beautiful I would not know, not being elvish and not sharing your strange love of dragons." Jack regretted using the word strange as soon as it'd left his mouth.

Anarra blinked, an undisguised hurt on her face. Her lips parted in a confused pout. Before she could speak Ellisenn emerged from the rank of elves nearby, his green eyes looking everywhere but at Jack.

"Your Majesty," he said to his queen, "the time has come. The armies of Harshan, Anda and Pix are in position. We are ready to march."

Anarra's eyes were still on Jack. She blinked again, her face becoming strained.

"If his majesty, King of Pix, accedes," she said, using the same formal tone Jack had used, "I will give the order to advance."

Jack looked to Denn and Massara, who both nodded.

"King Duan Senn of Pix accedes," Jack said, not knowing what that word really meant but guessing it meant he agreed. Anarra's pale face flushed a little. Ellisenn stared at him, openly surprised. Without a word Anarra spun on her heels and vaulted onto her dragon's back. Ellisenn mounted Scythe behind her. The Bright Queen raised her arm in the air, signalling for the army to march. With a trilling whistle she urged the huge, black dragon to launch into the air, the flap of its vast wings creating a downwind that brought tears to Jack's eyes.

"She did that on purpose," Jack muttered to himself, wiping at his eyes.

"If she didn't," Harriett hissed behind him, "she should have." His sister glared at him with open disapproval. Massara Ceyr, normally so friendly, gave him a cold look before she and Harriett spurred their horses forward.

"Isn't it a crime or treason or something to ride ahead of your king like that?" Jack asked Denn.

"Yes," Denn said, "but even kings are not spared the requirement to treat women with respect." His voice sounded a little cool.

"Great," Jack said, "now everyone in the army is mad at me." He spurred Shadow forward, trying to at least look kingly and not merely a teenage boy following behind his little sister.

❧ ❧

A hundred dragons soared overhead, each carrying an elvish dragon-rider and one of the most powerful druids. Just as Ellisenn flew with Anarra, Aelf rode behind Daniselle and Kashashem rode the blue dragon behind Tellan. The plains stretched on endlessly, broken only rarely by rocky outcrops. The sky above them was cloudless and a brilliant blue. Nettaxitt loped out ahead of the four armies, leading them directly south. Behind Jack marched the armies of Elvinidd and Pix, to the left the army of Harshan with its queen and to the right the forces of Anda. Behind them all came one thousand magenta-robed priestesses of Erima, their bald heads reflecting the sun like black mirrors. The bells on their wrists added a comforting jangle to the sound of footfall and hooves on hard earth. True to Kashashem's word, Jack and Harriett rode surrounded by druids. Druids on horseback, druids riding shaggy cows and druids riding elk. Wadget rode on the back of the fiercest-looking longhorn sheep Jack had ever seen. They formed a moving wall around Jack and Harriett, who were accompanied by Denn and Massara. Miss Butters had started out riding Piggy-Poo, but it soon became clear that the pampered pig would never be able to keep up. As a result, Miss Butters and her pig were loaded into a supply wagon, which bumped and creaked along behind them.

In the absence of a king who knew what he was doing, command decisions for the Pixish army fell to Massara and Denn, which suited Jack fine. Denn had an artful way of making suggestions so that they seemed like Jack's idea.

"May I pre-empt his majesty and order scouts to explore that rocky outcropping to the west?" he asked just on midday.

"Yeah, sure," Jack answered, smirking, "that's exactly what I was about to do." In reality, he hadn't even noticed the rocky outcrop. On Denn's orders the scouts were sent out. They returned with news that made Jack regret agreeing to send them in the first place.

"The scouts report that a large army is marching out of the west," Denn said gravely.

"Is it Morrigan?" Jack heard the anxiety in his voice and felt ashamed.

"There was too much dust for the scouts to tell for sure who they were," Denn answered. "But look, the Bright Queen investigates." He pointed to the black shape that was Scythe veering to the west. Not long later a flash of light from the dragon's back preceded a bright shape appearing on the ground before Jack, an apparition of Ellisenn made of golden light.

"Your Majesty," Ellisenn's voice said through the shining image, "the Bright Queen sends word to the King of Pix that the army marching out of the west are Northmen from Danussan, led by King Varga. They come to join us."

"About time," Denn said.

"Varga always arrives late," Massara added. "He likes a grand entrance and to be the centre of attention."

"Consul Massara's assessment of the King of the North concurs with that of the elves," Ellisenn's golden form said with a smile before bowing and dissolving into thin air.

Jack turned to Wadget. "That new trick of his, sending a golden version of himself to talk to us, can all druids do that?"

"No," Wadget said, an inexplicable grin forming on his lips. "Only elvish druids master that bit o' magic."

"Why only elves?"

"I'd tell yeh, Jack, but the answer would only frighten yeh."

"Frighten me? Why would it? Come on, I'm a big boy, tell me."

"The Bright Sendin' can only be mastered by elves 'cause it can only be used ter speak ter one other person, the person the elf conjurin' the Bright Sendin' is twined ter—"

"Okay, enough said." Jack felt himself flush.

"...the one person they love more than any other—"

"Okay, I get it."

"...the one person who matters more ter 'em than their own lives."

Jack glared at Wadget. The Oakling said no more but chuckled to himself until his eyes watered.

On Denn's suggestion, Jack sent word to the heads of all the armies to halt and wait for Varga's troops to reach them. Soon after, Ellisenn's glowing likeness informed Jack that the Bright Queen declined to wait and would take her dragons forward to scout the way ahead. Jack was sure Anarra was avoiding him. That was probably for the best, he thought, she needs to stay away from me, for her own good. The same went for Ellisenn. Jack imagined them both on Scythe's back, cursing his name into the wind. Well, at least they had each other to commiserate with.

It took the better part of the day for the army of

Danussan to reach them. King Varga rode out front on a massive white warhorse, accompanied by two standard bearers. Jack took in the huge helmeted king and the Danussian standard, a white raven on a blue background, unsure why they made him uneasy. The Danussian troops were as organised as elves, marching in such tight formation that they appeared to float across the grass. The fair-skinned and mostly blond soldiers of Danussan wore silver helms capped with white enamel raven wings. Jack knew from the old book of his mother's, *The Word of Thullu*, that the white raven was the symbol of their god, Danuss. The warriors of Danuss wielded the axe as their weapon of choice, but many were also armed with swords. Behind the cavalry came the infantry, and huge wagons carrying machines of war, catapults, ramrods and other monstrous-looking things. It was clear to Jack that the King of Danussan was no novice at war.

King Varga ordered his army to halt and rode with his standard bearers straight for Jack, who had just been joined by the Queen of Harshan and General Mahaja of Anda.

Varga reined in his horse just feet away from them. "Dechen Drokpa and General Mahaja," he said with a nod, his voice devoid of emotion. "It is a shame that I am privileged with the company of such august personages only in times of war." Varga forced a smile as Dechen and Mahaja nodded in return. Then the King of the North's attention turned to Jack. The king's eyes went straight to the hollow of Jack's neck, to that place between his collarbones where Jack was marked by the blessing of Amallayne. "My spies tell me that this boy is none other than the self-styled Druid King of prophesy." He looked around, taking in Harriett and the large company of druids. "It must be so, for who else would travel surrounded by perverse magicians, led by a filthy troll, but a king of naught but a tattered prophecy."

Jack, stunned into silence, felt his face flush. Harriett's face went red as well, but little could still her tongue. Her mouth opened to fire back at the King of the North, but

Queen Dechen placed a hand on her arm to quiet her.

"Varga," the queen said, her voice cold, "take care how you speak to the Druid King."

Varga snorted, as though showing Jack respect was the biggest joke he'd heard in years.

"You know as well as I," Queen Dechen continued, "that the Bright Queen has invoked the ancient alliance between elves and humans. Clearly you honour that alliance by joining us in our fight against the Dark Ones."

"Long has Danussan stood against the Pale Mother and her minions," King Varga spat. "We do not need some lunatic prophesy or a tattered treaty with elves to go to war against Vellenor and goblins, and we shall not stop until every drop of Vellenor blood is spilled and that accursed breed is extinct."

"Your blood-thirst and enthusiasm for war is not in question," Dechen said. "The question of respect and to whom it is owed is what I am concerned with. Under that ancient alliance, forged at the time of the Doom War, the armies of the Four Kingdoms come under the command of—"

"Whosoever be a true king of the House of Senn. I know the wording of that alliance, Dechen Drokpa, but it means nothing since the House of Senn has seen no king for thousands of years."

Jack's sense of certainty overtook him. He knew he had to speak and he had to do it now.

"I am Duan Senn, son of Noble Senn and grand-nephew of accursed Mael, who is dead," he said. "I am Sovereign of Pix, I am the Waycaller and I am the Druid King."

Varga's mouth actually dropped open.

"Mael is dead?" Varga stuttered. "So, this boy, his ... his parentage is certain?"

"Yes, most certain," Dechen said, barely containing a gleeful smile. "Which means, as we all owe fealty to him, that he is commander of the armies of the Four Kingdoms. I assume that you will honour the full terms of the alliance?"

Varga stared at Jack, then, somewhat reluctantly, nodded. "Wonderful," Dechen said. "I am sure the Druid King will be most pleased if you convey that message to your generals immediately." She looked to Jack and Jack nodded his assent. He now understood why Denn had led him to the front of the army, why General Mahaja and Queen Dechen had deferred to him. He just wished someone had told him about this rather than it being sprung on him like that. His insides roiled. How on earth was he supposed to command this entire army?

"Your spies didn't tell you everything, did they?" Harriett said suddenly, looking over the King of the North with disgust. "Missed a pretty major bit, didn't they? I'd get new spies if I were you. They made you look really stupid."

King Varga stared at Harriett, his mouth open again and his face as red as a beetroot.

❧ ❧

The day was waning by the time Varga's troops were integrated into the rest of the army, so the decision was made to make camp for the night. Jack felt a little unsure what to do. The other sovereigns all took charge of their nation's encampment, but Denn and Massara had so competently organised the setting up of the Pixish camp that Jack was left idle. Denn had even sent riders out to inform Nettaxitt that they were stopping for the night. The troll came trotting back to the pavilion where Jack and Harriett waited while the rest of their friends finished their work. The troll sat down on the ground by the entrance to the pavilion, panting heavily. Harriett went inside and found a water skin, which she gave to the troll. Nettaxitt drank the whole thing down in one go, shaking it vigorously to drain out every last drop.

"Me thirsty," she said, as if that weren't already obvious.

"Is it much further to where Morrigan is encamped?" Jack asked.

"Another trot like just done and we be there," she said.

Jack and Harriett glanced at each other, both their eyes surprised. Just one more day's march and they would face Morrigan. The booming flap of wings drew their attention upwards. Hundreds of dragons were descending to land in the spaces allocated for them around the perimeter of the camp, except one, the huge black dragon Scythe. Anarra's dragon landed just yards away, beside the Bright Queen's marquee. Kashashem had insisted all the sovereigns be based in the very centre of the camp, their pavilions and marquees arranged around a central square guarded by druids. The square was now filled with a heaving mass of roaring firewyrm.

Anarra dismounted, followed by Ellisenn. She froze when she saw Jack, who himself felt unable to move. Already Jack's resolve to pretend he didn't care for the Bright Queen had collapsed. Curious about what had caught his queen's attention, Ellisenn's eyes travelled from Anarra across the square to Jack. Once Ellisenn understood, he froze as well, clearly pained to see Jack, but also to see his queen so unsure of herself.

"Good lord," Harriett said, breaking the spell, "you three need to get a grip. In case you hadn't noticed, we're marching into battle with Morrigan. You can feel all tortured about how unloved you all are *after* we win the war." She went inside. Nettaxitt, looking sheepish, followed her in. Ellisenn, glancing between the two sovereigns, seemed to decide he should make himself scarce. He bowed his head and backed away.

"Wait, Ellisenn, don't go," Anarra said. "You have as much reason to be here as I do."

"My Queen, my needs are—"

"Every bit as important as ours," Jack said, finding his voice. "You don't have to go."

The woodland elf stopped where he was, his head hung a little. Jack wished he could take Ellisenn's pain away, but what could he do apart from say sorry again?

"Look," he said, "I know that I've hurt you, both of

you—"

"Your petty thoughtlessness toward me this morning cannot be compared to what Ellisenn is going through," Anarra said forcefully. "The twining is all-consuming, debilitating, wrenching—"

"Okay, I get it, they're not the same, but my … my regret is. I can't put into words how bad I feel, Ellisenn, about … about breaking your heart. Believe me, I would never hurt you so much on purpose."

"I do not wish you to feel bad, Your Majesty," Ellisenn said, "nor to pity me."

"No, I know you don't, but you'll have to forgive *me* on that. I can't help but feel bad about it. What kind of monster would I be if I didn't feel bad, if I didn't care?"

Ellisenn nodded but said nothing.

"I really am sorry, Ellisenn. If I could take your pain away, if I could stop you hurting, I would, but I … I—"

"Please, do not pain yourself, Your Majesty," he said. "This twining has caused enough pain already."

"How bad is it?" Jack asked.

"My unanswered love for you has rendered my life intolerable, my future meaningless."

That hit Jack in the gut. Anarra wiped a tear from her eye.

"What a trio we are," she said. "Ellisenn loves you—"

"But I love you," Jack said, looking into Anarra's damp eyes.

"And the Bright Queen," Ellisenn began.

"Is very fond of the King of Pix, yes," she said with a small smile.

Jack chuckled. Ellisenn smirked.

"Harrie was right," Jack said, not quite believing he was saying that, "we need to focus. Who knows if we'll survive this battle against Morrigan? If we do, we can talk about all this then."

"That would be a wise course of action," Ellisenn said, his voice not as calm as his words.

"I agree," Anarra added. "We shall defeat Morrigan first, then we shall face our personal struggles."

Jack walked into the tent thinking if he had a choice, if he could either face Morrigan or deal with the mess he'd found himself in with Anarra and Ellisenn, he'd definitely choose battle with Morrigan and her dark hordes. But he didn't have a choice. None. He had to face both.

❦ ❧

Jack didn't know how he was going to cope with the day's march on no sleep. The sky outside was already lightening with the coming of dawn. He'd tossed and turned all night, Anarra's face haunting him. Ellisenn's words struck his heart every time he remembered them: My unanswered love for you has rendered my life intolerable. He sat up, wondering how long it would be until Aelf or Denn came to rouse him.

He put his head in his hands and sighed. Back in Cairnbawn all a seventeen year old had to worry about was homework and how to fight the boredom of village life. Now that he had a war with all the dark beings of Anwynn to worry about, he'd happily have that dull life back again.

"Gracious," a tinkling little female voice said. "You sure do a good job of feeling sorry for yourself."

"Ting! You're back!"

The red-haired, green-eyed sprite was settled on the end of his bed again.

"Obviously."

"Are you mad at me for something else now?"

"No, not that I know of anyway. I just like to keep you on your toes."

"Where've you been?"

"Following along. I've been hiding in the ear of one of your soldiers, a really dull man. All he thinks about is ale, lamb-knuckle stew and bosoms."

"I can see how that would be unpleasant for you."

"Yes, well, when my host went and got himself all

impervious to Tiqq magic it was the best I could do on short notice. I do have my eye on another host though, very handsome he is too. He's an archer in the Harshanite camp."

"So long as you don't get caught, or make him do anything he wouldn't normally want to do, or hurt him, or—"

"Good gracious! You could kill the fun in anything!"

"And you could get that archer killed if you're not really careful."

"Don't be cross at me, Jack. Aren't you glad I'm back?"

"I am glad, yes."

Ting beamed. "You'll be even *gladder* when I tell you what's happening."

"What?"

"Empress Rill of the Tiqq will have to break her agreement with the Pale Mother. The Tiqq won't help Morrigan in this war after all."

"Why?"

"Many of the Tiqq are still devoted to Thullu, many more than Rill thought. Many of them also blame her for the loss of Tocsin. They say she should never have locked him up like that. Led by her own daughter, they have risen up against her. To keep her throne she has to betray Morrigan. She can't afford to divide her attention."

"I wouldn't want to be her when Morrigan finds out."

"No, but Rill is more afraid of her own people than any Faeden at the moment. The Tiqq have warred against the Faeden before and survived."

"Thanks for telling me this, Ting. It's great news."

"Don't you want to know the best bit?"

"Of course I do." Jack could see that Ting was bursting to tell him something. She was practically hopping up and down on the spot.

"It was me! It was me who stirred up the Tiqq loyal to Thullu. I convinced them to rise up against the Empress! I helped the Empress' daughter to make a move for the throne. It was me who made it so that the Tiqq can't join Morrigan in the fight against you!"

"Wow, Ting, I, I don't know what to say."

"How about thank you?"

"Thank you—"

"And you could say I'm very smart and very brave."

"You are, Ting, you're very smart and very brave."

"And you could ask why I did it?"

"I don't need to ask, Ting. I know why."

"You do?"

Jack nodded. "Yes, because you love me."

Ting beamed. Her eyes welled up. "Yes, I do, Jack. But I also did it because, well, my dear friend asked me to do it."

"Your dear friend?"

"Yes. She has seen how wicked Empress Rill is and wants her deposed, so that another Tiqq, one not so enamoured with dark magic, might rule."

"She? I suppose you're still not going to tell me who your friend is?"

"Actually, I asked my friend if I could tell you and she said yes."

"Really?"

"But just not yet."

"When then?"

"When you have defeated Morrigan once and for all."

"So, probably never."

Ting's laughter pealed like a tiny bell.

"Oh, Jack," she said, "you're such a funny little king."

They marched all day, following Nettaxitt as they had the day before. Anarra and her dragon-riders held back, soaring so high above the plains that they could not be seen, so as not to alert Morrigan's army to their approach. As the sun turned golden and dipped in the sky they entered a different kind of countryside. Still grassy, but with low rolling slopes arranged in front of them like wave after grassy wave going back to the horizon. When the sun fell low enough to seemingly touch the edge of a distant slope the grass took on a golden hue, as if on fire. Shadows lengthened and the air cooled. Jack led the army to the top of one of those slopes so that they were looking down into a broad valley filled with mist. A barely visible ribbon of water sliced through it from west to east.

"The Great River," Denn said.

"That mist is not natural," Wadget said from the back of his longhorn sheep. Nettaxitt jogged back up the slope to meet them.

"Me brought you. They down there, hiding in ground clouds."

Jack stared into the mist. Soon shapes were visible, hundreds—no, thousands of shapes milling about on the bank of the river. If the sun had not been low in the sky he wouldn't have been able to see anything. Still, it was hard to make out what the shapes were. Jack thought he spotted Vellenor and goblins and large hulking creatures that could only be skinwearers.

"Do they know we're here?" he asked, his voice a barely audible whisper.

"Not yet," Denn said, "but that will change soon. We have the benefit of surprise, Your Majesty, we should hit them now."

Jack felt a spasm of terror. He couldn't give the order to attack without speaking to Anarra first, but she was hundreds of feet above them, perhaps miles away. He hadn't expected to come on the enemy so suddenly. He'd assumed there would be a chance for the war council to meet and decide how to proceed. Wadget seemed to understand what he was thinking.

"War never happens the way we think it will," he said. "Yeh need ter make a decision, lad, an' yeh need ter do it now."

A golden luminescence behind Jack made them all turn. Another golden apparition of Ellisenn stood just back from the top of the rise, out of sight of the enemy below. Jack and the others dismounted and strode over to it. Standing next to it, Jack noticed that its gentle light gave off a comforting warmth that eased his terror.

"Your Majesty," Ellisenn's voice said, "the Bright Queen sends word that the dragon-riders have sighted the Dark Ones arrayed in the valley of the Great River. Lady Kashashem has sensed the Pale Mother's presence, and that of the halfling sorceress. The Bright Queen suggests that our forces strike at once, to make the most of the remaining sun and keep the advantage of surprise."

"That is wise counsel," Denn said. "We do not want to be fighting that horde in full dark."

"What are yer orders, Yer Majesty?" Wadget asked, a wicked twinkle to his brown eyes.

Jack thought a moment. Everyone was intent on surprise. That made sense to him too. He knew nothing about battle strategy, but he knew what would surprise him if he were down in that valley under that protective mist.

"Master Wadget," he said quietly, "can your druids clear that mist?"

Wadget smirked. "I reckon they can, yes," he said.

"Can it be done quickly and with some explosions and flashes of bright light thrown in?"

"That'd be me preferred way o' doin' it," Wadget said, chuckling.

"Good," Jack said. He outlined his plan, the first stage of which involved King Varga bringing forward his catapults. Even Denn, a professional warrior, was satisfied with Jack's strategy. "Ellisenn," Jack ordered, once they'd all agreed how to proceed, "ask Anarra to wait to strike until she gets our signal, then hit them hard."

"I will relay your message, Your Majesty." Ellisenn's apparition bowed, then looked nervously at those gathered.

"Is there more?" Jack asked.

The golden form of Ellisenn hesitated then went down on one knee, looking up at Jack earnestly.

"My beloved lord—" he began.

"Oh geez," Jack said, blushing. Denn, Massara and the

others looked away, except for Harriett and Wadget who looked on shamelessly with big smirks on their faces.

"I am sorry to say this to you in front of so many others," Ellisenn said, "but if I take my last breath today I want you to know that, though you do not love me the way I love you—"

"Oh geez," Jack said again, glancing at Denn who looked very uncomfortable.

"—I do not hold you responsible for my pain. You are a good and kind person. You will be a noble and honest king. I am most pleased that my heart set itself on you. It could not have chosen a better person to love." Ellisenn's golden hand reached out for Jack's. Jack hesitated then went to take it. Before their fingers connected the apparition vanished. Ellisenn was gone, as was that golden warmth.

"Right," Jack said, flushing and desperate to move on from that scene, "let's get those catapults in place and clear that mist."

BLOOD AND ASH

The catapults were in position and primed to fire. A line of druids stood at the top of the rise, hands and wands at the ready. Miss Butters stood beside Wadget, her wooden spoon quivering in her trembling hand. Harriett had been taken back to where the priestesses of Erima had set up healing tents. Jack hoped she would be safe there, protected by two dozen Pixish warriors and fifty druids, led by Alva. If she were nowhere near the fighting, Jack's recurring vision of her death, possibly at his own hands, could not come true.

The plan of attack had been relayed to the Queen of Harshan, King Varga and the Andanese general. They were all ready to begin. Jack's heart pounded in his throat. His ears rang. All eyes were on him, waiting for the signal to launch the first strike. Each second felt like an hour. The time to face Morrigan had finally come, but he couldn't give the signal to strike, not yet. He kept thinking of Anarra, riding a dragon somewhere high in the sky above him. His determination to stay away from her had lasted less than a day. He didn't want her to be hurt over him, but he couldn't let her go into battle without some demonstration of his feelings, just in case one of them didn't survive. He glanced down at his feet. There in the grass was a tiny flower, the same deep blue of Anarra's eyes. He took it as a sign, and bent and picked it, twirling it in his fingers. It was beautiful and fragile, like life. With a sudden inspiration he gathered his will and focused his entire being on what he wanted to do. He had banished goblins outside of a stone circle before, surely he could move something as small as a flower? He whispered into the flower's petals and it glowed silver. In a flash of light the flower was gone, taking with it his words: Be careful, sweet Anarra. With his mind's eye he saw the flower appear in the air before Anarra, saw her reach out and take it as his words whispered in her ear. He smiled, then raised his hand and slashed it through the air, giving the signal for the battle to begin.

At once a hundred druids began whispering the same incantation, wands and hands directed at the mist-filled valley below. In mere seconds the mist eddied, then formed into spouts that spun like tornadoes, syphoning the mist upwards into the sky. Soon the mist was thin enough that Jack could see the full extent of Morrigan's army. There were two vast encampments, the largest by far on the bank of the river closest to them, the other on the far side.

Jack's heart pounded as he surveyed the scene. Morrigan's army was at least three times larger than his own. The goblin forces on the near side of the river were organised into three seething hordes. The centre was infantry and skinwearers, whereas the flanks were goblins mounted on bog nags. Jack couldn't have imagined a more terrifying cavalry.

"Their forces are divided by the river," Denn said. "The goblins and skinwearers are amassed on this side, the Vellenor on the other. The fools, this will make for an easy rout."

"Why would they do that?" Jack asked.

"Morrigan is not a general," Wadget answered, his wand still focussed on clearing the mist. "She wouldn't have given it a thought. She no doubt still believes she's invincible. That was always her greatest failin'. We shall see about that—"

Wadget stopped speaking abruptly, staring down into the valley. In the middle of the goblin army on the nearest bank of the river a huge white structure was becoming visible through the clearing mist. Jack had to stare at it a moment to figure out what it was – a temple mounted on an immense wheeled platform. Made out of some kind of bleached wood, Jack first thought it was splattered with mud, but as the mist swirled away he gasped.

"Blood," Wadget said.

"What is that thing?" Jack asked, his voice tight.

"The Pale Mother's tabernacle. It's how she travels. An' it seems she's resorted ter blood sacrifice ter renew her powers."

"Will she be as strong as before?"

"No, she hasn't had enough time ter regain her full strength, but the longer she stays in that bloody chapel, the stronger she'll grow. This is worryin', we won't have an easy fight o' it. To defeat her we'll have ter be brutal."

Jack immediately gave the signal for the next stage of the attack to commence. The catapults whirred into action, swinging smoking bombs down into the goblin camp. The explosions shook the ground. Goblins and skinwearers screamed and scattered, terrified. Before the smoke from the first explosions cleared, the catapults swung another volley down, shaking the ground even more than before. Then the line of druids all shouted the same word, sending balls of red fire rolling down the slope. When they hit the enemy camp they flashed and sparked, sending swirling jets of flame in every direction. The fire spread through the camp, igniting tents, burning wagons, seeking out everything substantial and turning it to ash. The tabernacle was struck multiple times but wasn't even singed. Clearly it was protected by powerful spells.

Jack made the signal to halt the bombardment. Time to draw the enemy out. The smoke slowly cleared. A bone-trumpet blew down amongst the smouldering camp and the goblins formed into lines. A splashing sound drew Jack's attention to the river and his gut turned over. Crossing the river was a vast number of trolls, being driven forward by goblins yielding whips. The trolls were moved to the front of the dark horde, where they formed long lines a dozen deep. Jack tried to do a rough count, but there were too many of them – many more trolls than Serza ever had at his command. Nettaxitt roared and stamped forward. She was staring at the centre of the mass of furry beasts where a dozen goblin warriors restrained a huge troll with heavy chains. The chained troll wore a crown made from a half-skull encrusted with jewels: The Gory. Nettaxitt's mother. Outraged that a queen should be treated so, like an animal,

Jack roared along with Nettaxitt.

"Should we let loose on the trolls with arrows?" Denn asked.

"No," Jack answered as Nettaxitt broke away and plunged down the hill towards Morrigan's horde. The goblin's whips cracked so that the sound was like a thousand thunderclaps. The trolls surged forward, heading straight for Nettaxitt.

"There are thousands of them," Massara said, awed.

"They'll tear her to pieces," Jack said, drawing his sword. Before he could mount his horse and gallop after Nettaxitt, Denn grabbed Shadow's reins to stop him.

"No, Your Majesty, do not throw your life away. Use archers, throw arrows at them instead."

"But Nettaxitt, she'll be hit too."

Nettaxitt roared again and the thousands of trolls rushing toward her roared back. The soundwave rolled up the hill, causing many of the Pixish horses to stamp and rear up. A scream jerked Jack's attention back to Nettaxitt's chained mother. She had thrown herself on her captors. Half of them were dead already, more dying each second, but the others had drawn their swords and slashed at her as dozens of other goblins rushed in to help them. The queen of the trolls collapsed under the onslaught of blades and moved no more. Nettaxitt howled. She'd seen her mother die. In seconds the mass of trolls would reach Nettaxitt and then, Jack feared, she would die too. Nettaxitt neither slowed nor flinched when she reached the oncoming mass of trolls. She just kept running, her eyes on the goblins who'd killed her mother. Jack couldn't believe his eyes when the rank of trolls split, letting her pass straight through them to the other side.

"What's happening?" he asked. The mass of trolls now turned on its heels, following Nettaxitt in a full stampede back towards the goblin army.

"Nettaxitt is queen now," Wadget said. "Her mother sacrificed herself ter save her. No troll will harm its own queen. They're followin' Nettaxitt now."

The dumbstruck goblins barely comprehended what was happening before the wall of fangs, claws and fur that was Queen Nettaxitt's army slammed into them. The screams and roars were deafening. Jack ordered the catapults to adjust their range and resume firing, so that their bombardment struck the back lines of the goblin army only, leaving the trolls to do their work on the front lines.

A tug on his sleeve made Jack spin round. A young archer stood there, smiling strangely at him. Jack had no idea who the archer was, but he was clearly from Harshan, a handsome young man with a jet-black topknot and almond-shaped eyes.

"Who are you?" Jack demanded.

"It's me, silly," the young man said, in a flirty way that made Jack blink. "It's Ting."

"Ting! What are you doing here? This isn't a good time."

"Don't you like my new host, Jack?" the archer, or rather Ting, said sulkily. "Don't you think he's handsome?" The archer did a little twirl, which would have been funny if Jack weren't in the middle of leading a battle.

"Seriously, Ting, you've come begging compliments now?"

"I've come to help, Jack, you rude boy."

"Help how?"

"Well, like this for instance." The archer walked to the edge of the rise and waved his hand over the battlefield below. A terrible chill descended over them all. With a bone-chilling communal groan thousands of dead goblins rose up off the ground, retrieved their weapons and joined the trolls in the assault on their own kind. The zombie goblins hacked and bit and tore at their living kin with such savagery that Jack had to look away.

"Well, aren't you going to thank me?" Ting demanded through the archer, hands on hips. "Now every goblin who dies on that battlefield will rise up and attack their own kind."

"Thank you, Ting, that's really helpful." Jack had to force a smile. Though what was happening below might help them win the battle, he still felt sick about it. Then he had an idea. "Ting, could you do me a huge favour?"

"Anything for you, Jacky." The archer fluttered his eyelids. Jack rolled his eyes and ignored that.

"Could you help to protect Harriett? If this battle goes badly, will you promise to make sure she survives and gets away?"

"But, Jack, I want to be here protecting you."

"Please, Ting, no-one else is strong enough to properly protect her. Only you can do it."

"Okay, Jack, I'll do it, for you."

"Your Majesty," Denn said, striding over. "It is time to launch the next stage of the attack." He looked curiously at the Harshanite archer, one eyebrow raised.

"Send word to Anarra then," Jack commanded. Denn motioned to a Pixish warrior nearby who launched a flaming arrow into the sky. Jack watched the arrow fly then whispered to Ting: "Can you go to Harrie now, Ting? Things are about to get intense."

"Okay, but promise me you won't get killed."

"I can't promise, but I'll do my best."

"Your best might not be enough. I suppose if you do die I can always raise you up again. Then I'll have you all to myself. That wouldn't be so bad, would it?"

Jack's mouth popped open. Ting smiled, looking satisfied, and strode away in the direction of the healing tents. Jack now had another very good reason not to get killed in this battle. The idea of becoming Ting's zombie toyboy made him shudder.

A thunderous sound above brought Jack's attention back to the battle. Dozens of blasts of dragon fire came out of the sky to scorch the middle ranks of the goblins. Anarra and her dragon-riders swooped down, laying waste over half the battlefield. The goblins and skinwearers were now being bombarded by catapults at the back, mauled by trolls in the front lines and incinerated in the middle. The flames scorched hundreds of the Dark Ones at once, sending the terrible smell of burning flesh and leather through the air. The sky was now so smoky it was hard to see anything, but Jack caught the outlines of Anarra's hundred winged reptiles circling above the battlefield. On the next swoop the druids mounted behind the dragon-riders used magic to further decimate the goblins and skinwearers below. Ellisenn's gold Seren Star flashed into existence so brightly that Jack flinched back. A thousand goblins screamed out their last breath as the star did its terrible work.

Denn came over and pointed to the far bank of the river.

"Look, Your Majesty," he said pointing to a line of fire being lit by Dark Elves on the opposite bank.

"What are they doing?"

"Creating a fire wall to stop the Dark Ones on this side of the river from crossing back in retreat."

"Why would they do that?"

"Look there," he replied, pointing to the back of the Vellenor camp. Jack strained through the smoke to see. By a large pavilion flying the pennants of Fellwood, that awful three-legged swastika formed out of curved swords, a group of Vellenor had raised another banner. This banner was a large white triangle of silk bearing a single green leaf.

"That is the Vellenor flag of neutrality," Denn explained.

"What does it mean?"

"It means that the Vellenor are betraying their goblin brethren."

"Seriously?"

"Yes, look who is overseeing the hoisting of that banner."

Jack peered through the smoke. Standing slightly to the side of the group raising the triangular flag was a beautiful white-haired woman, her pink eyes like pale roses. She wore a long black robe and, around her pale brow, an ornate crown made of interlocking bones. Jack had been told of Ellisenn's mission to Princess Sarritt. The princess had clearly listened to Anarra's call and had decided, at the last moment, to honour the ancient treaty that united the elves, both Bright and Dark. Anarra had delivered a crushing blow to Morrigan's forces, without even drawing her sword. Surely they could not lose this fight now? Jack whooped in delight and hugged Denn. Denn stepped away, his eyebrows arched.

"Sorry, Denn, I'm just so relieved," Jack said.

"I will be relieved when this battle is properly won," Denn said, his face a little red as he strode off to direct the catapult bombardment.

Jack spent the next moments watching the Vellenor stoke the fire wall until it was an impenetrable blaze. That done, the Dark Elves pulled down their tents and began leaving the field. Before long, Princess Sarritt was the only one left on the far bank of the river. Jack thought she looked up to him through the flames and smoke and nodded. Then she turned and was gone. The goblins, only just noticing the Vellenor betrayal, let loose a howl of indignation and horror that echoed throughout the valley.

"Now is the time," Jack muttered to himself, "now is the time to finish it once and for all." He mounted Shadow and gave the signal for a full charge. A thunderous horn sounded in response to his signal. The horn, wielded by Ansonn, captain of the Night Guard, was the ancient call to war of the Ehmaarim. Jack spurred his horse forward, hurtling down the slope. The horn sounded again and Jack heard the vast armies of the Four Kingdoms and Elvinidd surging behind him, cavalry first and behind them the countless infantry.

Jack held on for dear life as Shadow carried him at a gallop down the slope. Jack was not a horseman so it was lucky that Shadow was such a smart horse. He concentrated on staying in the saddle and let Shadow do the rest. Other riders were all around him now, humans and elves, many of them overtaking him. He heard rather than saw the first wave of cavalry strike the goblin lines, the force of the impact causing a colossal boom that echoed in the valley. Goblins shrieked awfully. The sound of swords clashing was deafening. Bog nags squealed and whinnied as they launched into the fray. The shadow of a dragon's wings passed over him and he looked up to see Anarra and Ellisenn flash by on Scythe's back. Then he was in the midst of battle. Goblins lunged at him from all directions. He struck out at them with his sword, felling a half a dozen in just moments, Shadow trampling and biting those Jack missed. Denn came out of nowhere to cut down a skinwearer that had reared up behind Jack and the horseman stayed close to Jack from then on, fighting alongside him for what seemed like hours. Nettaxitt made her way to Jack's side as well, fighting so fiercely that soon a circle of open space formed around them that few goblins dared breach. Then Wadget was there, using his wand to blast dozens of goblins at a time. The space around them grew and grew until Jack looked up from slicing the head off a particularly feral goblin and saw that the fighting was almost at an end. Only a handful of goblins were left alive.

The armies of Elvinidd and the Four Kingdoms were close to victory, but not without casualty. Many of them lay dead, elvish, Pixish, Harshanite, Northmen and Andanese, no nation was spared from grief. The sheer volume of dead took Jack's breath away. He dismounted, staggering, wanting to scream at all this terrible loss. Morrigan would pay for this. His eyes searched out the tabernacle, where the last surviving goblins had formed a protective circle. Jack roared and ran at them, swinging his sword through the air in a wide arc. A whip of silver light burst out from his sword and cut each of the goblins in two. Jack was as startled as the goblins when they slumped to the ground like felled weeds. What had his sword done? Once the last of the goblins were dead, Ting's reanimated ones dropped to the ground and moved no more.

Jack was only yards from the tabernacle when a loud crack and flash of green light threw him back. He spun in the air and hit the ground with a thud, a dozen yards away. Dazed, he dragged himself upright and found himself facing back up the slope. The armies of the Four Kingdoms and the elves were forming up again under the direction of Dechen, Mahaja and Varga. He'd just thought how glad he was they'd survived when he remembered where he was and what he was doing. He shook his head to clear it and turned around to face the tabernacle. What he saw made him stagger back. A huge dome of sizzling green energy had bloomed around the bloody chapel. Clearly this was what had thrown him backwards. A barely discernible figure lurked at the tabernacle's entrance: a short, stout figure with blond hair and gleaming red eyes – the halfling sorceress, Hephaestia Hatter. Jack heard himself growl and ran at the dome. As he clutched his sword in both hands, it flared with silver fire so bright it blinded him at first. He didn't understand what was causing the flame, was it his own power or was the sword magical? He touched the fire with his mind and knew – it was both, the sword had its own magic and when wielded by someone with great power it transformed into this flaming silver blade. With all his might he stabbed it into the dome. He wasn't thrown back this time, but the sword was barely able to penetrate the wall of energy. He pushed harder. The dome sparked and sizzled but still did not yield. The cackling laughter of Hephaestia Hatter joined the sizzling of the dome, enraging him. He tightened his grip around the hilt and pushed even harder, summoning his will to increase the energy flowing into his sword. The blade moved barely an inch deeper into the dome, but still could not pass through. He pulled it out and stepped back, wiping the sweat from his face. He needed help. He summoned his will and called out to the druids in his mind: *The dome, it has to come down. Help me!* He know it'd worked, just as he'd known Anarra had received the flower. He'd created a Way between his thoughts and theirs.

A dozen balls of energy whirred down from above, striking the green dome with loud explosions. Footfall behind him alerted Jack to the arrival of the druids, first Wadget then a dozen others, including Miss Butters. Wadget drew his wand and aimed a sustained burst of crackling energy at the shimmering dome. The other druids all did the same. Dorothea even pounded at the dome with her spoon, which flashed white with each impact and sent sparks flying in every direction. The strikes from above increased. A looming shadow and loud thud caused Jack to look behind him just as Jossa, Daniselle's silver dragon, landed nearby. Aelf dismounted and ran to join Wadget in the attack on the green shield. With all his might Jack continued to hammer at the dome with his sword. The dome shimmered, sparked and buzzed but it did not weaken. Jack stepped back, taking in the scene around him. Explosions rained down on the dome from above, fired by Kashashem, Ellisenn and the other druids on dragon-wing. The druids on the ground were throwing everything they had at it as well. Beside him Miss Butters' attack was so frenzied he doubted she could sustain it much longer. Then he realised. All their efforts were not enough. They would never bring the dome down. Like a bell being struck in his mind Jack knew what he had to do. He alone could move from one place to another at will. He didn't need to cross through the barrier to get to the tabernacle. He summoned all his will, calling for a Way to open. A shimmering silver sphere appeared before him and he reached out and took it. Bliss coursed through him and he felt himself being pulled away. He also felt tight fingers around his wrist. With a jolt he was inside the dome, the sound of the druid assault on the other side so muted he could only just hear it.

"Wonderful, Jack, you've got us in!"

The fingers clutching his wrist belonged to Miss Butters. She stood beside him, with a look of triumph on her face, her wooden spoon smoking.

"You have to stop doing that!" Jack said. "You can't just grab hold of me every time I open a Way."

Miss Butters opened her mouth to answer but was silenced by a streak of green lightning that struck near their feet. Jack flew through the air, energy coursing over his skin, sizzling and burning. He landed on his back with such force that the air was knocked out of him. He sat up, struggling to breathe. His vision was hazy, but he could see Miss Butters, moving so fast she was a blur, firing blasts of white energy at the tabernacle where Hephaestia Hatter, just a fuzzy black shape about the same size as Dorothea, fired green lightning back. The noise was deafening, adding to the pain in Jack's ringing ears. The air crackled with so much energy that his hair stood on end. He hauled himself on to his hands and knees, taking huge gulps of air, trying to get enough oxygen to his brain so that his vision cleared. A flash of green light close to his head made him duck. In the momentary light of the flash, Jack saw two eyes, glimmering purple, staring at him from under the wheeled platform of Morrigan's tabernacle. He scrambled back, realising as he did so that the eyes were getting closer. Whatever was under there was coming towards him. He searched for his sword, only just realising that he'd dropped it when he'd been hurled through the air. It was yards away, between him and the shape with the purple eyes that was now crawling swiftly towards him. Jack's heart stopped when the shape crept out from under the tabernacle, its purple eyes intent on him.

"Oopa?" he said in a hoarse whisper. Coming toward him like a ghost from that awful night at the great circle of Bright was the Oakling whose body had contained the Keysong, whose death had released Morrigan from Uffern. "Oopa, is that you?"

The Oakling reached him and smiled, her eyes not their normal brown but a glittering purple. The explosions and bursts of energy coming from the fight between Miss Butters and the halfling sorceress illuminated those eyes so that they looked bottomless.

"Jack," she said, "I'm so glad you're here."

"You're dead," he said, barely able to speak at all, dragging himself to his feet.

"I don't think I am dead, you know. I was, back in Bright. I was in such terrible agony when Hect cursed me and then there was nothing, just silent black peace. Then I was awake again, all alone in the circle, and I had this little voice in my head."

"Voice?"

"Yes, there's a little sprite in here." She tapped at her temple. "He made me come alive again. He's a funny little fellow. He has no idea what is right and good, but I've been teaching him and we've become friends." A flash of white light from Miss Butters' spoon made her jump and then giggle. She wasn't afraid at all.

"Thullu's Gift? Tocsin?" Jack asked.

"Yes, that's his name."

Jack's heart thudded. He ducked as another ball of green light exploded nearby. So Tocsin had possessed Oopa, bringing her back from the dead when he couldn't possess Jack.

"Oopa, what are you doing here?"

"Tocsin said you were very brave and that you had a single thing driving you – the wish to protect Harriett from Morrigan. Tocsin admired that very much, none of his hosts were ever so selfless. He wanted to help you. He asked me to find Morrigan so that we could follow and watch her, to learn her weaknesses. Tocsin thought that might help you when you finally faced her."

"Did you learn anything?"

Oopa's eyes flared more brightly purple. "Waycaller," she said, in a strange voice that Jack knew was Tocsin's, "the Pale Mother is almost returned to her full strength. The only way you will defeat her is by using her own power against her."

Jack didn't get a chance to ask Tocsin to explain. A shriek made them turn to where Hephaestia Hatter battled Miss Butters. The sorceress had spotted Oopa, her pale face filled with horror and hatred. She fired a bolt of green lightning straight at them. Oopa flicked her wrist. A flash of purple light flared in front of them like a shield, absorbing the lightning as though it was nothing. The sorceress shrieked again, her red eyes wide with shock. As she raised her hand to strike at them once more, Miss Butters rushed forward with that lightning fast speed of hers and belted Hephaestia Hatter square in the face with her spoon. A flash of white light and a thunderous crack sent Hephaestia flying. She slammed into one of the wheels of the tabernacle platform and slumped motionless to the ground.

"Oh dear," Miss Butters said with a grimace, "I think I've gone and killed the skinny witch." The green dome of energy flickered and vanished. Miss Butters staggered a little and then slumped to the ground herself.

Wadget, Aelf and the other druids rushed to where Jack and Oopa stood, followed by Denn, his face rigid with worry.

"Your Majesty," the horseman said, his voice stricken, "are you harmed?"

"It's okay, Denn, I'm not hurt," he said, retrieving his sword. "Miss Butters needs help though."

Aelf went straight over to the halfling and checked her pulse. "She will survive," he said, lifting Miss Butters' eyelids to check her pupils. "She has passed out from exhaustion."

"No wonder," Wadget said, "I don't reckon even Ellisenn could've fought so fiercely."

"I will have her carried to the healing tents. The priestesses of Erima will tend to her." Aelf gestured to two elderly druids to come and collect her.

Jack watched as Miss Butters was carried away. Denn however was staring at Jack's black sword. "I always found that a worthy blade," the horseman said, "but it never flared with silver fire for me."

Jack looked at the sword and shrugged. He couldn't explain what had happened.

"There's a reason fer that," Wadget said. "That is Snàthad, the Needle, given to the Night Elves by Arawn at the time of the Doom War, forged ta be used against Morrigan herself. In the hands of a magic-wielder, it has a great power of its own. How did ya come by it, Denn?"

"It has been in my family for centuries, rumoured to have been gifted to us by ..." The horseman stilled his tongue, caution overtaking him. He looked into Jack's eyes, communicating without words. Jack knew without asking who'd given the sword to Denn's family: Hob. Denn's strange connection to that deceptive Faeden troubled Jack, but there was no time to pursue it, they were on a battlefield. Morrigan's tabernacle was barely yards away.

Thunder rolled above, even though the darkening sky was clear. A tremulous moan filled the air, seemingly coming up out of the ground. It was as if a giant buried deep below the surface had woken in great despair. Jack shivered, dread crawling up his spine. He recognised that voice. He'd heard it whispering on the wind and reverberating out of the very soil when Morrigan broke free from her prison. It was Morrigan's voice returning. The thunder deepened, rolling out in waves from directly above the tabernacle. Wisps of grey smoke escaped from the seams of the wooden structure and rose into the sky. The wisps thickened as they swirled higher, forming a cloud directly above them that darkened and roiled. The cloud grew, casting its shadow first over the tabernacle, then over much of the battlefield. Thunder boomed again. They were all looking up when what Jack first thought was light snow began to fall.

"That ain't snow," Wadget growled. "It's ash."

A flake of ash landed on Denn's shoulder, puffing into a smudge of pale powder. Denn wiped it away. Jack knew straight away that something was wrong. Denn's face paled. A black substance oozed from his eyes, nose and ears. He convulsed and dropped to the ground, his eyes wide open, staring, lifeless.

"Denn!" Jack grabbed the horseman by the shoulders and shook him. "Denn! Denn!"

"'He's gone, lad," Wadget shouted. The Oakling raised his wand, casting a shield over Jack and himself. "That ash is death with the merest touch." Aelf and dozens of druids all around them cast shields as well. The two druids caring for Miss Butters cast a joint shield to protect her motionless body. They did it just in time. The ash was falling more heavily now, the roiling cloud spreading out towards where Queen Dechen had marshalled the remains of the army. A chilling scream in the sky above preceded a dragon plummeting into the river. It happened so fast Jack didn't see which dragon it was. He selfishly hoped it wasn't Scythe, praying that Anarra and Ellisenn were safe.

Wadget grunted with effort beside him. The Oakling nearly buckled under the strain of each flake of ash that broke into dust on the shimmering shield above them. It was as if the ash drained magic as much as life. Oopa, bathed in a bright purple halo, was the only one not struggling to keep the ash at bay. Aelf shouted and dropped to his knees, the shield above him vanishing. A flurry of ash struck him in the face. He convulsed and collapsed, the black fluid pouring down his cheeks like molasses tears.

"Aelf! No!" Jack reeled. Aelf had been by Jack's side most of the time since he and Harriett had arrived in Anwynn. Jack had come to think of Aelf as a kind of uncle, as family. What would he do without the old man?

"Waycaller!" Kashashem's voice rung in Jack's mind. "No magic of the druids can stop this evil cloud. I am pulling the dragon-riders back. You must order a full retreat of the ground troops. If you don't, they will all perish."

Jack spun to face the troops. The cloud had almost reached them. They had to move, but what if the cloud overtook them? They would be unprotected. With a yell, one of the druids protecting Miss Butters collapsed, his eyes lifeless, full of black liquid. He fell on top of Dorothea, completely covering her. Jack spun and sought Oopa, calling out to her. She trotted over, her face lit by the eerie purple gleam in her eyes.

"Oopa, Tocsin," he said, "I need you to tell the troops to retreat, to go as far away from this cloud as possible, and I want you to go with them to protect and shield them."

Oopa nodded and dashed off.

"Wadget," Jack said, "you have to leave too. Take all the druids with you. Together you might save the troops."

"But what o' you, lad?" His voice sounded strained, his face dripping with sweat.

"I have to stay to face Morrigan, but I have a plan." Jack

raised his hands above his head and called out in his mind for a Way to open. The silver sphere formed in seconds. Jack expanded it so that it was the shape of a shield. Wadget watched curiously, grunting to keep his own shield up as the ash fell even more heavily. "The ash will fall through the Way to another place," Jack said. "It won't touch me or weaken me."

"Where'll the ash go?"

"To Fellwood, to Mog's house. There's no-one there now."

Wadget smiled his approval. He called out for the rest of the druids to follow him and jogged away, taking his shield with him. Jack was relieved his own shield worked, no ash touched him. It was falling into the silver sphere and disappearing. He watched the druids retreat, feeling suddenly very alone. His loneliness deepened when the army withdrew, the ash cloud creeping dangerously close to their rear lines. The cloud stopped at the rise however, allowing the army to escape. The sky darkened, the cloud thickening once contained by the valley walls. That moan rolled through the valley again. Jack shivered – the air had turned bitterly cold. He looked back toward the tabernacle and froze on the spot.

Coming towards him through the falling ash, walking barefoot over the field of broken bodies, was Morrigan. Her eyes shone through the haze of the battlefield like emerald beacons. The stench of death struck Jack, accompanied by that powerful nausea. He wanted to run but couldn't, stricken by fear but also determined to face that fear. Morrigan, now just feet from him, opened her arms wide as if to embrace him. Her lips were no longer blackened, merely a little swollen and red. They broke into a terrible smile. Then she spoke, her voice returned to her.

"Look what you have done, my child, look what you have done!"

Jack swallowed down his nausea and fear and tightened his grip on his sword, turning to face Morrigan head on.

"I am not your child," he snarled.

"All who breathe will one day call me mother, including you, Waycaller." She stopped before him, her green eyes glowing, her white dreadlocks hanging down to her waist like albino snakes. She glanced at the shield Jack had cast above himself and smiled, but the smile did not reach her eyes, which remained cold, calculating. "A clever way to use your gift," she said with a nod. "The power you have within you has long thwarted my ambition. It kept the human realm out of my reach and kept me imprisoned behind Darkgate." She took a step closer. Jack nearly screamed but held his ground. "That power is stronger in you, Jack Gordon, than in any of the Waycallers before you, but it is not yet so strong that you could challenge me. I am Faeden. More than that, I am the greatest of my kind. You have no hope. None." She smiled maliciously. This time the smile did reach her eyes, turning them even colder.

"Kill me then and be done with it." He wasn't sure why he said that. Antagonising one of the Faeden, especially the Pale Mother, wasn't smart. But he was sick of being afraid.

"Oh no, no, no," she said. "It is true that the extinction of your line, of the Waycallers, will cause the Veil to fall forever, putting the human world in my grasp, but there is something much more important that I need you to help me with before I snuff out your life."

"I won't help you with anything."

"We'll see. Where's your sister, Jack? Where is the girl-child who one day will have the power of the Oracle, the power to deny me sovereignty over all?"

Jack thought of his sister in the camp of the priestesses, far away from the battlefield, and felt relieved. Morrigan could kill him if she wanted but he would never tell her where Harriett was.

"Your face is like parchment to me, Waycaller," she said quietly. "I see all your thoughts and feelings written on it, clear enough to read at a glance. You have given me all I need to know." She blinked. There was a flash of green light and Harriett appeared beside him. She screamed at the sight of

Morrigan. Jack pulled her close to him, making sure the deadly ash could not touch her. His mind raced, thinking of a way to protect her, to get her out of there. He glanced up at the silver shield, a portal to another place. Could he change where it led and send Harriett through it? Morrigan followed his eyes to the shield and waved her hand. At once the ash cloud and the portal vanished. Jack staggered back, dragging Harriett with him. He raised his sword and summoned his will.

"So brave, Waycaller, but nothing you do will be enough. You both will die now. The prophecy will be unmade and I will take what is mine – everything, everyone."

"You're wrong," Harriett said, her voice cold and clear. Her pale eyes blazed like ice reflecting sunlight. "The time of the Dark Ones is over. Be warned, Faeden, if you raise your hand against us, your own hatred will destroy you!"

Morrigan laughed mockingly. In defiance of Harriett's words she deliberately raised her hand, palm outward, which began to glow a violent green. With a snarl Morrigan pushed that hand forward, releasing a burst of green fire from her palm. Jack summoned all his strength and used his sword to meet the surge of fire with silver flames of his own. The green fire burst on his flaming sword with such force that Jack was slowly pushed backwards, his feet making a trench through the blood-drenched soil as he tried to dig in his heels and stand his ground. The heat was overwhelming. Jack's clothes stuck to him as sweat covered his whole body. His sword grew increasingly hot in his hands. The force of the green flame was sapping him of strength, making his body tremble with exertion and his mind teeter on the edge of consciousness. He put one last surge of will into pushing it away. It worked for just a second before Morrigan gathered her own will and struck back. The silver flame coursing over Jack's sword stuttered and went out. Jack and Harriett were struck by the full force of Morrigan's attack and were thrown spinning through the air. Jack landed on his stomach on top of a dead troll, cushioning his fall. Every inch of his skin felt seared, his mouth and eyes dry and stinging. He launched himself back up and ran at Morrigan. The White Demoness pointed a pale finger at Harriett, still spinning through the air, and froze her there, spread-eagled as though nailed to an invisible cross.

"No!" Jack shrieked as he raised his sword and brought it swinging down on Morrigan. A nimbus of green power flared around the Pale Mother, throwing off Jack's sword with a blaze of sparks. Jack struck again and again and again. Morrigan ignored him, her eyes intent on Harriett suspended a hundred feet above the ground. Harriett screamed, a terrible wail of pain and anguish. Jack's heart stopped a moment and resumed with a terrible ache. He launched himself at Morrigan again, chopping at the green aura around her but to no avail. Morrigan's finger remained pointed squarely at Harriett. Her screams grew louder and louder. Tears ran down Jack's face. He stabbed and stabbed and stabbed at Morrigan but could not touch her. Harriett screamed once more and then was silent. Morrigan dropped her finger and Harriett plummeted to the ground. Jack howled in terror and raced to where his sister had fallen. He sheathed his sword and dropped to his knees and turned her over. Her eyes were closed. She wasn't breathing. The terrible vision of Harriett's death on the battle field that had plagued him since his first night in Anwynn had finally come true.

"No, Harrie, Harrie, no, no!" He cradled her in his arms, sobbing, begging for her eyes to open. They stayed closed. She was already going cold in his arms. He couldn't fathom how quickly she was going cold. He thought of all that power inside him, of channelling all to save Harriett, but he couldn't summon his will. His grief blocked his power, sapped him of energy. Morrigan walked slowly towards him, grinning.

"Your turn now, Waycaller."

Jack didn't care. He wanted to die if Harriett was dead. He looked up into those green eyes and willed her to do it, willed her to kill him quickly so he didn't have to bear the pain of Harriett's loss any longer. A red flash blinded him a moment. He blinked and wiped away his tears to see Amallayne. Her black skin hummed with energy, her long, silky hair shining like a black star. She stood between Jack, who still cradled Harriett, and the Pale Mother. Morrigan screeched and struck out instantly. A wall of green power burst over Amallayne like a tsunami against a reef. A red aura of power flared into being around Amallayne, protecting her, its brilliance forcing Jack to avert his eyes. The air itself burned, making it hard for Jack to breathe. The grass around him withered and turned to ash. Jack slumped over Harriett to shield her body, the clothes on his back beginning to smoke. He looked up at a soft sound from Amallayne. The Great Goddess was buckling under the onslaught from Morrigan. Her hands were hanging limply at her sides, her shoulders were slumped. The halo around her was as thin as paper. She was losing the fight. Morrigan cackled with glee and the green wall of energy surged and brightened. Amallayne staggered back. Then her voice was in Jack's mind: "Jack, do not think you are defenceless, powerless. Did you not defeat the dark prince all on your own? You can defeat Morrigan, you are the only one who can. I give you all that I have."

She knelt down and faced Morrigan, her eyes defiant. With a flick of her hand she cast off the shield protecting herself. Instantly Amallayne burst into green flames and was consumed until nothing remained. Morrigan howled with delight and the green inferno abruptly vanished. A surge of bliss more powerful than anything Jack had ever felt coursed through his body. All of Amallayne's power was now his. He staggered to his feet, his mind shocked into detached clarity. He knew what he had to do. Tocsin had told him there was only one way to defeat Morrigan.

Morrigan had almost forgotten him, so elated was she to have destroyed her ancient enemy. On seeing him rise she raised her hand with fierce determination, summoning every bit of power she had, and cast a bolt of green lightning straight at him. Jack stood tall and faced her. Amallayne had reminded him that he was not defenceless, not just a child anymore. The image of the dark prince shrieking with fury and disappearing in a burst of silver light flashed through his mind. Jack summoned his will and called for a Way to open in front of him. The portal flashed into existence and the lightning entered it and vanished. A second later there was a flash of silver light and the green lightning streamed out of another portal just feet behind Morrigan. Morrigan spun to see what was coming. The lightning flashed across the short distance and struck the Pale Mother square in the chest. With a monstrous boom she was lifted into the air and thrown back toward the tabernacle. As she spiralled, she burst into flames before slamming into the bloodied wall of the tabernacle, which erupted into flames as well. The Pale Mother and her bloody chapel were consumed in mere seconds.

A total silence fell. The Pale Mother was gone, once and for all. Jack had used the Way to turn her power against her, literally. He had created a Way that was just a loop, a loop that funnelled the lightning away from Jack to strike Morrigan instead. Just as Harriett had said it would, the Pale Mother's own hatred had destroyed her. But Jack barely cared that Morrigan was gone. A part of him sensed the new lightness to the air, the stronger brightness of the moon, the night bird singing with joy somewhere far downriver. Though he heard the gasp run through the assembled armies as they realised that the Dark Mother was gone for good, he cared only about his sister. He knelt beside Harriett, cradling her head in his lap, and sobbed. How could he have failed to protect her? It had been the one thing keeping him going all along. What would he do without her? He didn't want to even imagine a life without his little sister.

He wasn't sure how long he stayed there, crying, hating himself, before quiet footsteps made him look up. Ellisenn stood there, his normally stoic face grief-stricken, tears flowing freely down his cheeks. Behind him was Anarra, her face pale, her blue eyes wide in shock. Then came

Kashashem, and Daniselle and Wadget. Somehow Miss Butters was there too, looking weary and ruffled but otherwise unharmed. None of them said anything. What could be said? Harriett was dead. Nothing mattered in the face of that. Denn and Aelf were dead too, and so many others. Nothing meant anything in the face of all that loss.

THE ISLAND OF TOMBS

Miss Butters dropped to her knees beside Jack. Crying softly, she put her arms around him. "Our poor little Harrie," she said quietly. "Poor little child." Jack hugged the halfling as hard as he could.

"Well, how very touching, and how very *mortal*." It was Hob who'd spoken. He had appeared on the battlefield without a sound. He surveyed the scene of carnage around him dispassionately, one eyebrow cocked, returning his gaze to Jack and Miss Butters hugging with Harriet's body propped against them with only the slightest change in demeanour. Miss Butters leapt to her feet, her wooden spoon at the ready.

"Get back from my Jack, you tricksy devil," she growled. "Your kind have done enough harm this day already!"

"My kind? It seems to me that your Jack has done more harm than any here! Why, it is because of him that two Faeden have perished on this battlefield. Until this day, none of us had ever ..." He couldn't bring himself to say the word 'died'. "How proud you must be, Jack, to have ended the lives of two who have existed since before the beginning of this world."

"What are you doing here, Hob?" Jack said fiercely, drawing his sword. "Come to gloat?"

"Gloat? Me? What an unkind suggestion to make, little boy." The Faeden glanced at Jack's black sword and smirked. "I see Denn has passed Snàthad to you, just as I wished him to. Lethal though it is, it cannot harm me. Put it away."

Jack's mind reeled. Hob had wanted this sword to come to Jack all along, had given it to Denn's ancestors hundreds of years ago, all so that one day Denn could give it to Jack and use it against Morrigan. His head ached with confusion, his heart burned with grief. He sheathed the sword and closed his eyes. He couldn't face any more pain, any more

Faeden manipulations.

"Say why yer here an' leave us ter our grief, yeh velvet ninny," Wadget said. "None o' us have time fer yer games."

"Very well, I shall do just that, Master Wadget. I come to claim payment on a debt."

"What ruddy debt?" Wadget asked.

"That shall be clear soon enough. First, I must return something to a friend." The Faeden waved his hand and a swirling blue cloud formed some yards away. Out of the cloud trotted Cobalt, Denn's blue horse, killed by Mog weeks before. Jack remembered that Hob had promised to return the horse to Denn when the time was right. His heart sank. Denn would have loved to see Cobalt again. "Where is the horseman, Denn?" Hob asked. No-one answered. Wadget gestured with his eyes to where Denn had fallen. Hob, face curious, walked over. When he saw Denn's body he actually gasped. He knelt down and tenderly rolled him over, wiping the black ooze from Denn's face onto his own velvet sleeve. He stayed there a long moment. When he stood back up his face was flushed with fury. He paced over to Anarra and roared in her face.

"One thing I asked of you! I told you how to win this war in return for one thing!"

Comprehension dawned on Anarra's face. "Denn was the one good man?" she asked. "The one you told me about, the one you—"

"Say not another word lest I end your miserable existence!" The force of Hob's voice shook them all.

"I will not be quiet!" Anarra shouted back. Jack couldn't believe her courage. To stand up to a Faeden, especially a Faeden as unpredictable as Hob, was taking your life into your hands. "You did not tell me who this one good man was," she said more quietly. "If I had known, I would have kept him away from the battle."

Hob glared at her. "Now I will have to set this right," he said. "You are lucky he has not yet passed through the gates of death. Even so, he will never be the same. He will always remember the pain of his dying. That pain is on your head, Bright Queen." He strode back to where Denn lay and placed a hand on the fallen horseman's chest. A flash of light and Denn's body changed to glittering light in a hundred shades of blue. It flickered and then vanished. Barely moments later, another blue cloud formed nearby and Denn staggered out of it, a dazed look on his face. He spotted Cobalt immediately and roared with laughter, running over to his horse and grabbing him around the neck in an ecstatic embrace. Cobalt whinnied loudly and nuzzled into his master's chest, stamping his hooves in delight. Jack gently moved Harriett's head from his lap and stood up. Hob had just brought Denn back from the dead. An urgent hope rose in him.

"Now, little queen," Hob said, "you owe me. Do as I asked you to do."

Anarra looked from Hob to Denn, confused. Hob arched an eyebrow and subtly gestured at Daniselle. If all of Jack's attention hadn't been on Hob he would've missed that gesture. No-one else noticed. Anarra nodded in understanding.

"Daniselle," she said to the mountain elf, "take Denn and his mount to the healing tents to be examined by the priestesses of Erima. The horseman has been through much. I want you to stay with him, until I ask you to do otherwise. Care for him closely, Daniselle. He is very brave and dear to the hearts of all of us." Daniselle nodded and strode over to Denn, a slightly confused look on her face. In contrast, Hob looked very pleased with himself.

Jack grabbed Hob by the arm and spun him around to face him. The pleased look on Hob's face was replaced with one of distaste.

"What about Harrie?" Jack said. "What about Aelf?"

"I cannot bring back to life everyone on this battlefield. To do so would upset the balance of things."

"I don't care about the balance of things! Bring back Harrie and Aelf!"

Hob rolled his eyes. "I consider your request only

because Denn thinks so highly of you. Why he does I cannot understand. I suppose no human is ever perfect."

"You'll do it then, you'll save them?" Jack's heart swelled with joy, his lips forming an involuntary smile.

"Aelf I can save," Hob said, "because he is not dead, only grievously injured. That old druid is tougher than he looks. Your sister, on the other hand, is beyond my help."

"What do you mean? Help her! Bring her back!"

"I cannot. I can only bring back those who have not passed through the gate into eternal death. When you dragged your sister out of the clutches of death in Amallayne's temple, she had already passed through that gate. That changed her nature and put her beyond any magic I have."

"No! No, no, no! You're lying! Please, Hob, help her—"

"I cannot."

"No ... no." Jack slumped to the ground. He could not bear his grief any longer. He covered his face with his hands. He just wanted to die, to join Harriett in that place beyond the gate. What had Oopa called it? Silent black peace? That's what he wanted, silent black peace for eternity. He sobbed, hard, so hard he struggled to breathe. He jumped then as a warm hand cradled his own. The hand pried his fingers apart and Jack found himself looking up into pale blue eyes.

"But ... but," he stuttered, thinking his grief had sent him mad. It was Harriett.

"Hob wasn't lying, Jack," she said. "He couldn't bring me back from death because ... well, because I can never die. I have gone beyond death and returned. Nothing can kill me now, not even the darkest magic. Morrigan hurt me so bad I went into the blackness for a little rest, but nothing could hold me there forever. Death can never keep me for long."

The sadness in her voice made Jack's heart constrict and ache. What he had done to Harriett in Amallayne's temple was worse than he had ever imagined. He gathered her to him, hugging her and breathing in the smell of her hair.

"Yes, yes," Hob said dryly, "this is all very astounding, but I have a task to fulfil, a task involving you, Waycaller, and the deathless brat. You must come with me."

"Where?" Harriett asked. Jack was too emotionally drained to speak.

"You'll see. I suppose first I must do *this*." Hob waved his hand and Aelf's body was enveloped in a shimmering blue halo. When the halo vanished, Aelf stirred and his violet eyes opened. Hob glanced at Jack, as if to say 'are you satisfied', and then clicked his fingers, triggering a flash of blue light and a rushing sound. The battlefield vanished. A vast chamber took shape around Jack, Harriett and Hob. Above them a domed ceiling appeared, held up by a circle of elaborately carved columns. In the centre of the chamber a circular dais of marble rose, surmounted by a huge green granite sarcophagus. A flight of marble stairs leading up onto the dais was flanked by two life-sized statues of Sovereign Guards. At the top of the stairs sat a throne made of bones, the curved backrest crowned with a row of skulls.

"*This* is where we're going," Hob said, smirking as chaos erupted around them. They had appeared in the middle of a crowd of elves and humans. By their smell and their pale, blotchy skin, Jack suspected a good number of them were dead, corpses reanimated by sorcery.

"Where are we?" Jack demanded.

"In The Lost Necropolis, the Hive of the Tiqq Empress, on the Island of Tombs."

All around them were hundreds of dead things: wolves and bears, people and elves, all milling about, their sightless eyes staring at the three strangers who had just appeared in their midst. Swirling in the air of the chamber were threads of purple mist, some of which took shape as tiny, pointy-eared beings no bigger than a hand. All of them were female, with cat-like eyes and red hair.

"Earwisps," Harriett said, sounding excited. Even dying for the second time had not instilled the slightest bit of caution in her.

Hob waved his hand. With a flash, Ting and Tocsin appeared.

"How did you do that?" Ting demanded, staring open-mouthed at Hob. "How did you tear us from our hosts and bring us here?"

"Hush, Ting," Tocsin said. "Speak not another word. This Faeden is not what he seems."

Jack was surprised that Ting did what Tocsin asked. She'd never been quiet when Jack asked her to, not ever. He made a note to ask Tocsin what his secret was, if they survived this that is, but right now had a grudge to pick with Hob, a grudge he'd been reminded of by Tocsin's arrival.

"You told Serza about the Keysong."

Hob rolled his eyes. "Why, yes, I did. You can offer me your profuse thanks another time."

"Thanks? Are you mad? It's because of you that Morrigan was freed!"

"And therefore credit is owed to me for her destruction, for you could not have vanquished her if she were still mouldering in Uffern."

Jack glared at Hob, speechless. Could the foppish Faeden really be that callous, that self-absorbed?

"I'll take your witless silence as a thank you. For more than a decade I have been working to counter Morrigan, to bring us to this moment. It's so nice to finally be shown some appreciation for my efforts."

Jack took a step forward, balling up his fists. Harriett grabbed him to hold him back. They were all interrupted when a voice drifted out of the semi-dark.

"Who are you to trespass in this sacred place?" a very handsome almond-eyed young man was staring at them from near the sarcophagus. He slowly sat on the throne of bones, watching Hob intently. Jack recognised him as being from Harshan. His black hair was tied in a perfect topknot.

"Well, that is the question, isn't it," Hob said. "Who am I? It is a question I ponder often. I am the autumn and the twilight. I am the wind on the water. I am the ember and the ash. I am the shadow by the hearth. I am dusk and I am dawn. I am life and I am death. I am Dark but no more than I am Bright. I am everything and nothing at all. Of all the Faeden, I am most like my Father."

Jack rolled his eyes. Hob *loved* talking about himself. "Just tell them who you are," he said, "and then get us the hell out of here."

"Perhaps a visual demonstration would be more efficient." Hob closed his eyes. His whole body shimmered, first with blue light, then with white. There was a bright flash and Hob transformed into a young man with wavy blond hair. He was shirtless, wearing only a short kilt, his body muscled and athletic. Jack recognised him instantly from the memory stone vision of the Battle of Bright. Hob had transformed into the young god Danuss, the Faeden who had helped Amallayne imprison Morrigan. The chamber echoed with shock and chatter. Those gathered were realising that Hob was Faeden. All Jack wanted to know was if Hob was really Danuss or Danuss really Hob. Danuss, or Hob, strode toward the throne. Everyone scattered, both the dead and the living. Harriett tugged at Jack's sleeve. She had *The Word of Thullu* in her hand.

"Good lord, Harrie! This is no time to read!"

"It's always the right time to read. Look, Jack." She allowed the book to open in her palm. It opened to a page near the back, and she pointed to a short phrase:

> *Thullu has many children, some of them Bright,*
> *some of them Dark, some of them both and some of them*
> *neither. The most like Thullu himself is Arawn, the first*
> *of the Faeden, who takes many names and many forms.*
> *Arawn is one and multitudes, and conflicted for so being.*

"So ... so Hob is this Arawn?" Jack stammered, his mind reeling.

"Yes," Harriett said, her eyes as wide as saucers. "Lord of the Battlefield, Lord of the Fallen, Lord of Power, both Dark and Bright."

Ting gasped. Tocsin's eyes nearly popped out of his

head.

"Perhaps you still do not recognise me?" Danuss asked of the man on the throne.

"I know not who you are, Faeden, nor do I care," the young man said. Jack could tell it was a lie. He cared very much who Danuss, or Hob, was, and even more so what he was doing there. Danuss closed his eyes. His whole body shimmered again, first with white light, then with an intense blue. Instead of Danuss, now a hooded and cloaked man was there, his cloak made of raven feathers. Under the cloak he wore a long leather kilt, black as night, but nothing else. His chalk-pale chest and feet were bare. Hair as dark as Hob's streamed over his shoulders, hung with black bells. His eyes – Jack had never seen eyes like them. They were a dark blue that reflected a night sky. Stars and swirls of galaxies sparkled in them. His lips, beautiful and full but drawn into a leer, were red, as if smeared with blood. Jack had read all the descriptions of the Faeden in *The Word of Thullu*, but this one he didn't recognise.

"Oh my lord," Harriett whispered, "Arawn in his true form."

"Recognise me now?" Arawn asked, his voice like a funeral drum. The room was silent in response. "No? You still don't recognise me?" With pale, muscular hands he pulled his cloak close around himself. "Well, back we go then." An intense flare of blue light transformed the hooded figure into Hob again. Recognition dawned on the man on the throne's face.

"Ah, there it is," Hob said. "Got there at last."

"You are Arawn," the man said, "the favourite of the Lord of Chaos."

"I'd like to say that no parent has a favourite, but in my case that would be a lie. I am my father's favourite, have been since the dawn of time and will be until time ends."

"What do you want of us, Faeden?"

"Just a little family meeting," he said. Hob searched for Jack among the kneeling earwisps. "Ah, there you are, Jack. I will need your help, as Waycaller."

"To do what?"

"To call my father, the Lord of Chaos. While I am in this form it will only be together that we will have enough power to do it."

"No, no way."

"I do not need your consent, boy." Hob waved a hand and Jack found that he could not move. A surge of vast power thrummed through him. His skin tingled, then shone with a bright red light. The power Amallayne had gifted him had awoken. Jack's eyes were fixed on Hob's, unable to look away. Hob closed his eyes. His whole body hummed with energy and glowed blue. He called out: "Father! Come to me!"

There was an incredible flash and boom and then a totally naked, snowy pale and completely hairless man appeared before the throne. Like Danuss, his body was muscled and athletic. Like Hob, his facial features were fine, almost feminine. Like Arawn, his eyes were swirls of galaxies. He glowed brightly white. Every creature in that chamber gasped, many howled or screamed. All but Jack and Harriett dropped to their knees. Hob staggered aside, shakily going down on one knee, clearly exhausted.

"Lord Thullu," the man on the throne said, his head bowed and his voice high and anxious, "you honour us with your sublime presence. We have mourned for an eternity over your absence."

"Only seconds have I been here," Thullu said coldly, "and already I sense a great corruption and deceit." Thullu breathed in the air of the chamber, as if reading by the scent of the stale room what had been going on during his absence from the mortal realm. His face grew serious. "Cast off your hosts," the Lord of Chaos commanded in a voice that sounded like a million whispering Tiqq. "I would see my children in their true forms." Everywhere purple wisps emerged from ears and took shape as red-haired, green-eyed sprites, all of them female except for Tocsin. The handsome man on his knees before the throne clutched at his left ear. A stream of purple wisp poured out. The wisp formed the shape of another Tiqq, who fell to her knees and bowed to Thullu. She wore a crown made of the wing bones of a tiny bird. Jack guessed she must be Rill, the Empress.

"You have disappointed me, Rill." Thullu's voice echoed throughout the chamber. "I smell your betrayal and your cruelty on the very air. I gifted sweet Tocsin to you so my children might prosper. I see everything now. For thousands of years you kept him imprisoned, like a slave, so that when a foul thief broke into this chamber he was glad to flee with her. I sense this has led to much pain and horror in Anwynn. Little Tocsin is innocent, he knows not what is good nor what is bad. His powers have been used to ill by those who care not for him nor for any of my children. Long, long ago I ordered you to always provide sweet Tocsin with a virtuous host, so that his powers might always flow to the good. I trusted you in my absence to obey me. You did not do this. You kept Tocsin host-less so that he grew weak and lay in an endless nightmare in the tomb you sealed him in."

"My Lord," Rill squealed. "He betrayed me! He conspired with a wicked host to depose me!"

"He saw you for what you were, selfish and cruel. Who can blame him for helping the host who wished to place another on that seat you call a throne. He is innocent, after all, and is easily persuaded."

"This is my throne!" Rill said. "No other shall sit here!"

Thullu clicked his fingers and Rill puffed into wisp and vanished. A startled murmur spread through the tomb. "I have returned Rill to the void," Thullu said, "where she will abide formless and nameless. Where is her daughter so that she might take the throne?" No-one spoke. Many glanced nervously at each other. "Where is Bell?" Thullu pressed. It was Tocsin who spoke.

"Father," the little male Tiqq said. "The Empress locked Bell in a lead tomb, locked her in there with her host. All because Bell tried to take the throne when Rill made the pact with Morrigan. Bell is still loyal to you. She is very nice, I think."

"It's true," Ting said. "Bell and her host have been imprisoned ever since Bell defied her mother, many days now, and without food."

"Which tomb?"

Tocsin and Ting both pointed to a lead door at the back of the chamber. Thullu waved his hand and the door flew open. Footsteps echoed from inside the dark vault, coming slowly nearer.

"Jack," Ting whispered. "Don't be upset."

"Why should I be upset?" He had a bad feeling about this.

"When you see Bell's host, you will want to know why I didn't tell you about her before now."

"What have you been hiding, Ting?"

"Bell's host is my dear friend, the one I told you about, the one who sent me to bring you to Anwynn."

"Who is it?"

"You'll see. Just don't be mad."

The woman who emerged from the tomb was pale from years underground. Despite this, she was beautiful and carried herself with great dignity. Her eyes were a deep blue, her hair a lustrous black. Jack took an involuntary step forward, staring.

"Jack, is that..." Harriett was also staring at the dark-haired woman. She looked up at her brother to see if he was seeing what she was seeing. The woman crossed the chamber toward Thullu. She hadn't seen Jack and Harriett yet. Jack, his heart thumping in his throat, took his sister's hand and led her slowly through the mass of kneeling earwisps and their hosts. They'd only made it half-way across the chamber when the woman stopped before Thullu and bowed deeply.

"Daughter Bell," Thullu said, his voice whispering around the room. "Cast off your host now that you are free of that lead prison."

A stream of purple wisp spiralled out of the beautiful

woman's ear. The Tiqq who took shape bowed gracefully to Thullu. She looked much like the other Tiqq, only her face was open and smiling. Her eyes, though still cat-like, had about them a gentle look.

"Lord Father," she said, her voice so clear and beautiful that Jack stopped in his tracks. "I prayed for this day to come, for you to return to us." She beamed when Thullu touched her tiny head, causing the crown of bird bones to appear there.

"You have suffered much, my daughter. Learn from your struggle and rule over the hive with wisdom and care."

"I will, my Lord and Father."

"Know this, my children," Thullu said to the chamber at large. "The time of corruption is over. The Dark powers are being swept away. If you do not change you will be swept away with them. From now on, you will join only with hosts who consent to share their lives with you. You will no longer possess the wicked or the cruel. You will join only with those good of heart. Those who disobey me will be returned to the void."

A murmur of shock travelled around the room. One Tiqq, perched on the back of a dead bear, spoke out. "But Father, we will starve! No being in all of Anwynn will *consent* to have us in their ear! No elf, no human, not even a goblin will willingly allow us to feed on their thoughts!"

"Do not presume to chastise your own Lord and Father," Thullu said. The outspoken Tiqq dropped her head, clearly frightened she might soon be returned to the void. "I have thought of this. Do you think your father would deprive you of sustenance? I task your new Empress, Bell, to seek treaty and alliance with the priestesses of Erima. Their love for Erima makes them immune to the power of the voice. They are virtuous and good. From among them your new hosts will come. As it once was between the Tiqq and the elves, so will it be between the Tiqq and Erima's daughters. The Tiqq and their hosts will be companions, working together to strengthen each other, to explore and to gain wisdom. This is my decree. You will all obey."

"We will obey, Lord Father, I promise we will." Bell bowed deeply, showing Thullu that she meant what she said.

"Now," Thullu said, turning to Bell's host, "there are three in this room who need to be reacquainted."

The beautiful woman looked curious. Thullu extended his arm, leading the woman's gaze to where Jack and Harriett stood. She saw them standing there and her face showed confusion, then dawning understanding.

"Jack? Harrie?"

"Mum," Jack stammered, aware that he hadn't used that word for nearly a dozen years.

"Jack! Harrie!" Eloise rushed across the chamber, enfolding Jack with one arm and Harriett with the other. "Jack, Harrie, is it really you?"

Neither Jack nor Harriett could speak. They just nodded and clung to her.

"I'm so sorry you were left alone, so sorry I wasn't there."

"What happened?" Jack asked. "Why did you disappear?"

Eloise released them, gently tidying Jack's hair. She wiped a tear away from Harriett's eyes and took a deep breath. "I didn't have a choice," she said. "A Vellenor assassin ambushed us, your father and me. Your father was killed and I ... I was struck by a powerful curse and badly injured. I was on the verge of death when one of the Faeden came and helped me. In exchange I had to agree to come here, to be Bell's host."

"You see," Hob said, making them all jump. "I wanted Bell to be strong enough to one day stand up to her mother, the Empress. I knew Rill would betray my Father. I couldn't let her get away with that. Besides, I have a special fondness for the Tiqq. They are like me in many ways—"

"Amoral, vain and selfish, you mean?" Jack said.

Hob ignored that. "As I was saying, I wanted Bell to grow strong and brave. As you saw, she is certainly that now.

That is all down to your mother. The Tiqq are very influenced by their hosts."

"It was you?" Jack said, his hate for Hob surging to new heights. "It was you who took our mother from us?"

"The Vellenor assassin did that. Your mother would have died if I did not bring her here. That curse was very powerful. Not even I could stop it, and that's saying something. I am the only Faeden whose power is akin to Lord Thullu's. I can breach the Veil Amallayne made, I can raise the dead. Even so, I could not break that curse. Only possession by one of the Tiqq was able to hold it at bay. Besides, it was only right that Eloise do something for me in return for saving her life."

"We grew up without a mother," Jack said, "as orphans. No one wanted us."

"My heart bleeds," Hob said. "Actually, it doesn't. Faeden don't have blood." He laughed at his own joke. Jack glared at him.

"Hob," Harriett said, looking at the Faeden as if for the first time. "How could you be so cruel?"

Hob faltered under her pale gaze. He opened his mouth to reply but stuttered into silence. He shrugged, unable to give an adequate answer. "I did what I thought was for the best," he finally said. "I'm not good at the niceties, feelings and things, I just don't understand them."

Harriett accepted that. She looked up at her mother. "You can leave with us now, can't you, Mum?" She took her mother's hand.

"I'm so sorry, Harrie, Jack," Eloise said gently, "but I can't." She gripped her daughter's hand. "The curse was incurable, unbreakable even by Faeden magic. I can only go a few hours without Bell before it starts to work again. If I leave here, I'll die. That's why I never came back to you. Believe me, I wanted to see you. I wanted to see you more than anything. Sometimes I convinced myself that I was prepared to die just to see you for a few hours, but I knew that would only hurt you both more. I need Bell to survive. I cannot leave this place, that's why I sent Ting to you. I sent her through the Veil to watch over you, to help you fulfil your destinies. And now you're here, and I am so proud of you both. But you cannot stay here with me. A tomb is no place for children, especially a tomb full of hungry Tiqq and dead things."

Harriett started to cry. Eloise took her in her arms. Jack wiped angrily at the tears in his eyes. Their mother was alive, but still they couldn't be with her. It was like losing her all over again. He looked into Hob's passionless face. Faeden or not, Jack was going to tell the cold-hearted fop what he thought of him.

"Don't," Harriett said, reading her brother's intentions in his eyes. She reached out and took his hand. "Let's just spend this time with Mum while we can. Hob saved her life. It's not his fault she's trapped here."

"Still, it feels good to blame him for it." Jack put his arm around Harriett and his mother. They stayed there for the longest time, embracing, crying and comforting each other. Hob moved away into a corner of the tomb, looking uncomfortable with the intensity of their grief. All around them the Tiqq watched, transfixed by the display of human emotions happening in the midst of their sacred place. Some of them were crying too.

Thullu came over and joined them, his pale skin casting its own light. He looked over Harriett with cold eyes. "You are not as you should be," he said to her. She blinked and stepped back. "You are human, yet you will never die. Like all your kind you will age, the years will mark you as they do all humans, your skin will wrinkle and your hair turn grey, but you will live on and on. For an eternity you will live, ancient and undying. I should not allow you to exist – such a being has no place in the universe I brought into being." He smiled then, illuminating the room. "But much that I made is flawed, and this change does not offend me." The father of the Faeden turned his eyes on Jack. "I am not wroth with you for doing this," he said. "I also love my family and would do anything for them, though many of them barely deserve that love." He glanced over at Hob. He reached out and touched the mark in the hollow of Jack's neck. Jack's body pulsed with an overwhelming pleasure. His skin broke out in waves of goose pimples and the roots of his hair tingled. "The blessing of my daughter Amallayne is strong in you, more so now than ever before." A look of great sadness crossed his face for a moment. He took a breath and forced himself to smile again, then faced Eloise.

"Why so sad?" he asked. "Are you not glad to be reunited with your children?"

"Yes, Lord Thullu," Eloise said, "but I dread being parted again."

"Why dread what need not be?"

Eloise frowned, confused. "Lord Thullu, I am afflicted with a Vellenor curse. It means I must stay here, and I can't allow Jack and Harrie to live in a tomb."

"Tombs are for the dead," Thullu said understandingly. He looked deep into Eloise's eyes. "Ask me, Eloise," he said.

"Lord Thullu?"

"Why be so afraid to ask me for what you want?"

"I don't understand?"

"No curse is beyond *my* power," he said simply.

"But ... what about Bell, don't you want me to stay with her?"

"I am not Hob. I am not prepared to sacrifice the happiness of one for the well-being of another, not even for sweet Bell." He placed his hand on Eloise's shoulder. I can lift the curse, but there will be a price. You will no longer be a Waycaller. The curse and that power are too interwoven, I cannot remove one without removing the other."

Eloise didn't even hesitate. She looked at her children and immediately nodded her assent. Thullu closed his eyes and a strange whispering sound filled the air. Eloise paled, then flushed, then leant into Jack for support, nearly fainting. "The curse is gone now, Eloise. You may leave this place." Thullu followed Eloise's eyes as she glanced to where Bell was patting a reanimated Lion, its dead throat rumbling in a deep purr. "Do not fret for Bell," the Lord of Chaos said, "Thanks to you she is strong and caring. Go be strong and caring for your own children now."

Eloise nodded to the Lord of Chaos and took her children by the hands, leading them towards the marble stairs that rose up out of The Lost Necropolis. Even though they passed many dead things on the way to the stairs, Jack and Harriett couldn't stop smiling.

BACK BEDROOM

Butters Nob, Bright, Halfling Dells

A perfumed breeze drifted in through the window, smelling like pine and wildflowers. Accompanying the breeze was the distant but clear song of a bird, a happy sound. Somewhere by the window-ledge a bumblebee droned its buzzing tune. Jack stretched and yawned. When he opened his eyes it was daylight, the early hours of a sunny morning. As the bumblebee departed the window-ledge, Jack looked around. He was in Miss Butters' back bedroom, tangled once more in layers of too-small, vanilla-scented blankets. A stream of warm sunlight came in the windows, warming the bed nicely. Each morning since the confrontation with Morrigan, Jack had woken half expecting to find himself back on that desolate battlefield, surrounded by the dead. Not this morning though, which was a surprise and a blessing. As it was, he'd woken twice in the night, plagued by nightmares of what had happened on the banks of the Great River. Both times he'd peered across the darkness to where his sister lay. Both times he hadn't been able to go back to sleep until he could see that she was tucked safely in her bed and breathing smoothly. This was how he'd spent his nights since they returned to Bright.

The thing that plagued him most was Amallayne's death. He'd thought she didn't care about him, didn't care about mortals, but then she'd sacrificed herself to save Jack, to save them all. It didn't make sense. Jack needed it to make sense. Until it did it would haunt him. Eloise had told Jack that it was Amallayne who'd placed *The Word of Thullu* in her hands, and that she had in turn left it with Jack and Harriett knowing it would help them understand. That book had not only helped them understand, it had helped them survive. Had that been Amallayne's intention all along? As the days passed he had dwelt more on why Amallayne had abandoned him to fight Serza on his own. The more he thought about it, the more he felt that she'd done it so that he would realise his own power, be forced to accept that he wasn't an ordinary kid anymore, and then be able to face Morrigan. The Pale Mother was gone, forever. That in itself should have been enough to comfort him, but still he dreamt of Amallayne consumed in green flames. He rolled onto his back, hoping that someday he would understand and then the nightmares would stop. Then he remembered: they were leaving today, setting out for Pix. Eloise had put off their departure as long as she could, but the Kingdom of Pix wanted their king on the throne. Jack's stomach tightened at the thought of that, but at least his mother would be there to help him through it. He chuckled, remembering the tantrum Miss Butters had thrown when she found out they were leaving.

"Impossible," the halfling had bellowed. "I won't allow it. I want my younglings to stay right here with me."

It took Jack's mother, backed up by Wadget and Aelf, to convince the halfling that the best thing for Jack and Harriett was to be with their actual, real mother, and that the best thing for the Kingdom of Pix was to have their sovereign on the throne. A lot of promises were made before Miss Butters agreed to let them go. Jack had assured the halfling that he and Harriett would see her often. He'd explained that this was inevitable given that they both had to complete their training as druids. To do that they would have to be in Songarielle regularly, and Jack promised Miss Butters it would be at the same time. Dorothea countered that Jack's duties as king would stop him from travelling, so, under Kashashem's advice, Jack appointed Massara Ceyr as Regent of Pix for those times when he would be away learning magic. Jack had first thought to appoint Denn, but the horseman's sudden engagement to Daniselle and desire to settle down and start a family had scuttled that plan.

After the battle on the banks of the Great River, Anarra had explained the deal she'd made with Hob – that in return for Hob's advice to invoke the ancient treaty and turn the Vellenor against Morrigan, the velvet-clad Faeden wanted Denn married to Daniselle, though he hadn't revealed their identities when Anarra had agreed to the deal. This was another thing that kept Jack awake at night. Hob had helped them all along. Why? Why had Hob reunited him and Harriett with their mother? Why had Hob summoned Thullu, and thus brought about a massive change to the Tiqq that would affect all of Anwynn? Jack sighed and scratched his head. More so than any of the other Faeden, Hob's behaviour was inexplicable. And yet, Denn revered him. There was much about Denn that Jack thought paradoxical. He was gruff and yet also friendly, fierce and yet compassionate, solitary and yet he was marrying Daniselle. Jack couldn't imagine Daniselle settling down at all, let alone becoming a mother, but Miss Butters said that even elves 'come good' when they get married. Despite all their planning, Dorothea wasn't convinced to let he and Harriett leave Bright until Jack swore that they, and their mother as well, would visit Bright no less that twice each year, which he'd haggled down from six visits.

"Alright then," she'd said. "I'll allow you to go, so long as you keep your promise to come back thrice a year."

"Twice," Jack said.

"Thrice or twice, or more, we'll work that out later, just so long as you do it. You won't grow up right if your only company are elves and courtiers. You need the company of good, honest and decent folk. There are no more decent folk than those right here in Bright."

"Like Hephaestia Hatter?" Jack asked, smirking.

"Don't mention that witch's name in my house, Jack. Eugene bless us, you've got a reckless tongue."

Jack bit his reckless tongue about Eugene. He didn't have the heart to argue with Dorothea about the nature of the Faeden. To her, Eugene was a god, but Jack was sure he was just like the rest of his kind, powerful but selfish. Harriett had nearly said as much a number of times, usually when Miss

Butters was regaling Harriett with endless stories of Eugene's bravery in narrow spaces. More than once Jack had had to shush Harriett before she launched into a rant. He smirked, realising that before they'd come to Anwynn his thoughts of Harriett had usually been accompanied by feelings of irritation. Not anymore however. Not since the battle with Morrigan. These days he felt nothing but pride. Harriett had to be the bravest little sister in the world – in *both* worlds.

They were being carried to Pix by dragon-riders. As always, the thought of dragons made Jack think of Anarra. He didn't know when he would see her again. As sovereigns of separate realms, neither would have the freedom to visit each other often. Another reason to look forward to journeys to the Druid Chambers in Songarielle. He felt much better about Anarra these days. On their first morning here, Harriett had sat him down in the garden and told him he was thinking about Anarra's future grief over him like a human. Anarra, she explained, thought about these things more like an elf.

"Elves live for a very, very long time," she'd said, twirling a dandelion in her fingers. "They love for a thousand years or more, and so they expect, when they lose someone they love, to grieve for just as long."

"Just because she might expect it doesn't mean it's okay."

"You're thinking about it all wrong," Harriett said. "To an elf, a thousand years is like just one of our years."

That made sense to him and eased his concern for Anarra enough that he was willing to let whatever was going to happen between them evolve naturally, without him stifling it. Ellisenn on the other hand was another matter. Harriett had no advice on that front. She still thought Jack should have chosen the woodland elf over Anarra, but Jack didn't feel that he had a choice, no matter what Harriett said. He thought about the handsome elf often. The gratitude Jack felt for him grew every day. He was especially grateful for the number of times Ellisenn had saved his life, but also for how open and vulnerable the elf had been. Jack could never be that open with his feelings. It irked him a little that Anarra had never been so open with him about *her* feelings, but Jack suspected that night elves were naturally guarded and reserved. He flushed a little, remembering when Ellisenn had got down on one knee and told him that he would love him forever and didn't hold it against him that Jack didn't feel the same way. That took real courage. He smiled, picturing Ellisenn on bended knee. A sudden warmth made him look up. He gasped, scrambling back in the bed, pulling the blankets up to cover his bare chest. A golden projection of Ellisenn was sitting on the end of the bed.

"Geez, Ellisenn, you're as bad as Ti—" He stopped himself before revealing Ting's name and changed tack. "What are you doing here?"

"I felt your mind dwelling on me, as I have many times over the last days. I have resisted until now, but I was curious why you were thinking of me, and I wanted to see you."

"So you've been reading my mind?"

"No. When your mind dwells on me I feel it, that's all. I don't know the contents of your thoughts."

"Good, I've had enough of that sort of thing with Ti—" He nearly let it slip again. "My thoughts are private."

"Of course," Ellisenn said. "I'm sorry if I have breached some human sensibility."

There it was again, the fact that Jack did not really understand the elvish way of seeing things.

"Ellisenn," he said. "If you could break the twining, you know, the bond with me, would you?"

"No." Ellisenn said this without hesitation and emphatically.

Jack found it hard to believe.

"Why?"

"It is difficult to explain to a human. We elves feel love only once and forever. Now that I have loved someone, I will never love another, even if the twining were to be broken. Though it is mixed with pain, it is wonderful to love someone."

"Even when, you know, it'll never go anywhere?"

"Where does it need to go? Humans think that the only worthwhile emotions are the ones that lead to satisfaction. We elves know better. Even the feelings that can never be satisfied are sometimes worthwhile."

"Sometimes?"

"Yes, if they better you as a being."

"Does your love for me better you?"

"It has opened my eyes to how rare a mutual love really is, which makes me value it all the more. It has showed me that elves and humans are not so different. We all want the same things."

Jack decided it was his turn to be open. "You said you wondered why I'd been thinking of you. Well, the truth is I do care about you, Ellisenn. It's not romantic love, but I respect you and am grateful that I know you and I ... well, I feel bad at the thought of not seeing you often."

Ellisenn's golden lips broke into a smile. "Thank you for telling me that, Jack. It means a great deal to me."

"You're welcome." They sat quietly a while, then Ellisenn's golden eyes looked out the window, as if listening to a distant sound.

"I must go," he said quietly. "Lady Kashashem awaits me. May I return to visit you again, Waycaller?"

"Yes, but don't just pop into my bedroom like that. Cough or something to let me know you're coming."

Ellisenn smiled. "As you wish, Your Majesty." His golden shape shimmered and vanished.

Jack disentangled himself from the sweet-smelling blankets and went to the window. He looked out into the garden and was met with a happy scene. Seated at the outdoor setting in Miss Butters' back garden were Aelf, Wadget, Harriett, Miss Butters herself and Jack's mother. In the meadow beyond the garden, Soxy grazed with Piggy-Poo, who was wearing his pink bonnet. The two barnyard oddballs had become close friends. Jack noted that Piggy-Poo had lost a bit of weight and looked fitter.

Harriett, though a little pale, finally looked well again. Miss Butters and their mother were taking turns hand-feeding her. For once, Harriett appeared to be enjoying the attention. In the bright light of morning, Jack noticed some things he hadn't before. Aelf looked quite frail. His hair was greyer and he was no longer strong enough to walk without the aid of a walking stick. Jack supposed being nearly killed twice would do that to an old man. Miss Butters was slightly thinner than usual, though no-one dared tell her so. She also had a new, more confident, bearing. Her struggle with Hephaestia Hatter had taught her that she was a lot more magically powerful than she would have ever imagined. Even Wadget had changed slightly. He looked a little tired but, perhaps because of their triumph over Morrigan, was altogether more cheerful. The Oakling chuckled as Miss Butters continued to force-feed Harriett. Not all of Wadget's attention was on his friends though. The druid master was wrestling with a dainty pink tea-cup. The cup was ill-designed for Oakling claws. After a few moments of frustration, his green ears waggling in exasperation, he waved his wand so that the cup hovered in the air before him. He twitched the wand again and the cup poured the tea directly into his mouth. Jack laughed out loud at this. Wadget and the rest of the rag-tag tea party looked over in his direction. Unfortunately, this meant that the teacup poured hot tea straight down Wadget's neck.

"Ouch!" the druid master growled. "Drat it!" He snatched the cup out of the air and dropped it back onto its saucer.

"Nuts," Jack said, smiling. "They're all absolutely nuts."

ABOUT THE AUTHOR

Family legends inspired D.J. McPhee to write *Waycaller*. The McPhee clan hail from the small island of Colonsay, off the west coast of Scotland. The name McPhee translates as 'children of faeries'. For centuries the McPhee clan has been associated with the legends of Celtic mythology and with magic. The clan symbol is an open hand – the sign of both peace and magic-making. In ancient times it was said that the eldest born of the clan were destined to be either warriors or wizards, shield-maidens or celtic priestesses. Sometimes D.J. McPhee believes these family legends to be historical fact, which is why, perhaps, he is not altogether comfortable in the modern world. D.J. lives in a small town with two bossy cats and an amazingly supportive partner.

Note from the author: If you've enjoyed this novel, I'd greatly appreciate it if you could leave an honest review on Amazon or Goodreads. Reviews are very important to authors, and it only takes a few minutes to post one. Thank you in advance.

Join me on Facebook:
https://www.facebook.com/D.J.McPhee.Author/